"He's being held in solitary?"

Aurora heard the shrill note in her voice but couldn't stop it. "And only Knox is allowed to visit him?"

Unity swayed nervously. "That's what Cade said."

A swear word she never, *ever* used tumbled from her lips. She folded her arms tight to her body, then immediately dropped them and started pacing from her desk to the viewport in her office. "So the only people who are able to see and talk to him are Knox and his lawyer. Is that what you're saying?"

Unity hesitated. "That's what Cade's saying."

"Dammit." She shoved out a breath like the air had personally offended her.

THE EXILE OF JUSTICE

Starhawke Rising Book Six

AUDREY SHARPE

Ocean Dance Press

Want more interstellar adventures? Launch into
these other titles in the Starhawke Universe.

Starhawke Rising

The Dark of Light

The Chains of Freedom

The Honor of Deceit

The Legacy of Tomorrow

The Siege of Alliance

The Exile of Justice

Starhawke Rogue

Arch Allies

Marked Mercenaries

Resurgent Renegades

Starhawke Romance

Guardian Mate

I always write to music, and I select a different piece of music for each story, one that feeds the mood I need to get the words flowing. If you'd like to experience this story the way I did, listen to the soundtrack for Marvel's *Black Widow* while you read.

One

"You can't save him."

The imperious certainty in the harsh mechanical voice scraped across Aurora Hawke's senses, a steel blade on ice. She crouched low, her weight balanced in readiness for the attack she knew would come.

Shadows loomed with outstretched fingers all around her, their insubstantial darkness greedily devouring every bit of light they touched.

Aurora's gaze searched the gloom that hovered like midnight fog.

The Sovereign was out there. She couldn't sense her, but she knew she was there, taunting her, just out of reach.

"You can't save him," the voice repeated in a stage whisper behind her.

Aurora whirled, hands raised, palms out.

Nothing there.

The chilling laugh that followed made her shudder.

She gritted her teeth. "You won't win. I will free him. And I'll stop you." The wooden planks beneath her boots creaked as she crept forward, watching and listening. "You can't hide forever."

"*You will fail.*" The metallic tones transformed, giving way to a mockingly familiar voice.

Rage ignited, her chest burning, explosive heat expanded to every cell in her body. "No, I won't. I stopped you once. I'll do it again."

Another laugh — dismissive, condescending, coming from everywhere and nowhere. "*You'll never learn, Aurora. You can't save him. You can't save any of them.*"

Any of them?

A bolt of terror slammed into her as she sensed a new presence nearby. *Lelindia.*

No, no, no, no. She couldn't be here.

Panic grabbed her throat. If the Sovereign found out about the baby...

She reached out with her empathic senses, frantically searching for Lelindia in the darkness. Why had she come here?

"*You can't save them. You can't even save yourself.*"

Ice flowed in her veins. Lelindia was getting closer. But she couldn't pinpoint her. "Show yourself, you coward!" She flung the challenge into the void. If she couldn't find Lelindia, she could distract the Sovereign.

The shadows swirled around her, reforming in linear lines. Her heart pounded a staccato beat as she recognized the row of thick metal bars enclosing her.

A cage.

The door swung shut behind her with a click.

She spun, the power of her energy field vibrating beneath her skin. She held it in, tightly leashed.

It pushed against her, demanding to be set free.

A cage wouldn't hold her. But it could prevent her from reaching Lelindia before—

A steady footfall approached the bars, very close now.

She tensed, balancing on the balls of her feet.

She would end this. Right here. Once and for all.

"Aurora—"

Her energy field surged, light and heat lashing out at the figure emerging from the gloom.

And met a wall of ice.

The jolt snapped her eyes wide. But what she saw didn't make any sense.

The figure crouched beside her wasn't the cloaked threat she'd expected. This face showed dark hair framing warm brown eyes and a furrowed brow.

"Lee-Lee?"

"It's okay, Sahzade." Lelindia Forrest brushed a loose strand of hair out of Aurora's eyes, smoothing it into her braid. "You were having a nightmare."

Aurora blinked, slowly taking in her surroundings.

Solid wood desk, carved wood chair, wooden plank deck.

Her office on the *Starhawke*.

She slumped against her desk and blew out a breath. "I fell asleep."

"So I gathered."

The dream was already evaporating like mist, but the rage still burned. So did her energy field, which she finally noticed was swirling inside the protective emerald-green embrace of Lelindia's.

She met Lelindia's unruffled gaze. "Did I just attack you?"

Lelindia's mouth relaxed into a smile. "You tried."

"Oh, hell." Aurora dropped her face into her hands, shame suffusing her skin. Thank goodness her energy field couldn't harm her energy sister. Apparently the continual stress of the past month had created serious holes in her self-control. "I'm sorry."

Lelindia placed a hand on Aurora's arm and squeezed. "Don't worry about it. It was a sleep shot, about as effective as swinging a pillow."

Weird. In the dream it had felt like she was giving it everything she had. But she'd been yelling in the dream, too, and if she'd done that in her sleep, she would have woken herself up.

"You may not remember, but you used to do that a lot the first couple years after your dad and Micah left." Lelindia rose to her feet and leaned her hip against Aurora's desk. "Your nightmares were bad then, too, and I got quite adept at containing the bursts. Besides, I could use the energy boost. Little Nedale needs her fair share these days."

The baby.

Her gaze dropped to Lelindia's abdomen. She could sense the baby's presence, the pulse of life similar to Lelindia's but with a vibration that was distinctly unique, a blend of Suulh and Kraed.

While the ship and crew had been in Teeli space attempting to capture the Sovereign, Aurora had pushed Lelindia and Jonarel's child to the back of her mind. But ever since Siginal had shown up with the news of Admiral Schreiber's indictment for treason, her focus had shifted to her crew, which sometime this year would include a half-Suulh, half-Kraed little girl.

Aurora rubbed her eyes to clear the grit.

Lelindia's gaze swept over her with a doctor's thoroughness. "You really should try sleeping in your cabin."

"I have tried. It doesn't work." Thoughts of the Teeli, the Suulh, and the Sovereign chased each other endlessly through her mind the minute she set foot inside the isolation of her cabin. At least when she was in her office off the *Starhawke's* bridge, her mind settled enough that she could doze.

She propped her head in her hands. Stellar light, she was tired. Twenty-seven mostly sleepless days in Teeli space waiting for an attack that never came, and another two days racing back out of Teeli space headed toward Earth to stop the Admiral from being unjustly incarcerated. "Have we crossed the Fleet border yet?"

"We just did. Kire notified you over the comm, but when you didn't answer Tehar suggested I come check on you."

"Good call."

"I'm guessing you were dreaming about the Sovereign?"

"Yep."

Lelindia was silent for a moment.

Aurora stared out the viewport on the far bulkhead, even though the starfield was lost to the interstellar jump.

"It's going to be okay, Sahzade."

Aurora grunted.

"I mean it. We'll get through this."

"Or fall headfirst into another one of the Sovereign's traps."

"That's the exhaustion talking."

Aurora sighed, the tension in her muscles making them creak as she stood up. "You're right." She tilted her head side to side, working out the kinks. "And now that we're in Fleet space, I have work to do."

Lelindia put a restraining hand on her arm, stopping her. "Now that we're in Fleet space, I'm using my prerogative as ship's doctor to order you to stop all work. You're going to report to Micah's cabin, drink a tea infusion that will help you relax, then settle in for a massage and a nap. He's going to keep you company so you can sleep. *Really* sleep."

She stared at her energy sister. Maybe she was still dreaming. "You're joking." But she knew she wasn't. She could sense Lelindia's resolve.

"I'll get Jonarel in here to escort you down if I have to."

Aurora's lips twitched. Jonarel Clarek had her beat when it came to muscle mass, but she and Lelindia both knew he couldn't move her unless she let him.

To be honest, the idea of a massage sounded heavenly. Her brother had professional training, so she had no doubt it would be effective. Besides, while they were in the interstellar jump racing toward Earth, nothing was going to happen that would change their situation.

"Come on, Sahzade. Give yourself a break."

She met Lelindia's concerned gaze. "Okay. But I want to check with Kire to make sure the message to my dad has been sent."

Lelindia nodded. "Fair enough."

She'd composed the message as soon as they'd left the binary star system in Teeli space. As owner of Far Horizons Aerospace, her dad was the one person she knew with the funds and contacts to mount a successful defense for the Admiral, regardless of the machinations the Sovereign had orchestrated to get the Admiral charged in the first place.

Aurora led the way onto the bridge. Kire Emoto sat in the captain's chair, scrolling through data on the chair's command console. One of the egg-shaped, green-scaled mobile iterations of the Yruf Setarips' non-biological entity Unity, U-1, hovered beside him.

Kire shot her a wary look. "How you doing?"

She grimaced. "Nightmare." She hooked her thumb in Lelindia's direction. "Doctor's ordering me to get a massage and take a nap."

The wariness dropped away, replaced with the sparkle of good humor that was Kire's standard setting. "Glad to hear it. And before you ask, your message to your dad already went out through Far Horizons' comm system. I'll notify you as soon as we receive a reply."

"Thanks." One item off her checklist. She turned to Unity. "How long before the Yruf ship reaches Earth?" Cade Ellis and his team, along with their ship, *Gladiator*, had hitched a ride on the much faster Yruf vessel when they'd left Teeli space. She hated the distance that separated them right now, but she felt better knowing his team would be able to offer the Admiral support while waiting for her ship to arrive.

"Seven hours, twenty-six minutes," U-1 replied.

Hearing Unity speak in her brother's voice no longer freaked her out, but it was still strange, especially when Micah wasn't in the room. She seemed to be the only one having an issue with it, though. Maybe that was a result of her exhaustion, too.

Lelindia cupped her elbow. "Let's go, Captain."

The use of her rank was intentional, reminding her that she had a responsibility to everyone onboard, including herself. She'd procrastinated for as long as her crew — her family — would let her. They were working hard to take care of her. She needed to let them.

She swept a hand toward the lift. "Lead the way."

Two

Unremarkable.

The stark room could claim no point of interest, no obvious purpose. Only barren walls encircling a barren floor. The subdued light filtering from above created a visual haze.

Figures moved through the bland interior, their appearance as unremarkable as the room's. Their dark grey skin and silver-grey-hair was nearly invisible against the grey of their surroundings. Their guttural voices created a background rumble like rocks tumbling down a chute. As they worked, the clinks and clatters of tools and machinery provided an erratic heartbeat for the room.

Section by section, piece by piece, an object took shape in the room's center. It had no color, made no sound, did nothing to bring life to the desolate space.

It simply... was.

No purpose. No function. Unremarkable.

With a whisper of warning, the room's lone door opened.

All motion ceased.

Silence descended, a grey cloud in the barren room.

Eyes turned, staring at the door with trepidation.

Two shadows glided across the floor.

Feet shuffled, flinching back, clearing a path to the object squatting in the center of the room.

A dark-gloved hand extended from beneath a billowing cloak. A commanding finger pointed at the object.

The second shadow moved.

The room held its breath.

A flash as bright as starlight, a crackle and boom.

The room quaked.

The grey figures stood frozen in a jagged circle, sentinels at an ancient burial ground.

The stench of fear rose like steam, thick and cloying.

A huffing metallic rasp sent aftershocks through the room.

The grey figures shrank from the shadows.

The dark-gloved hand rested on the object, fondling the surface with a lover's touch.

Yes. Soon.

Three

Micah Scott knelt beside the couch where Aurora lay still as a statue, dead to the world.

He'd be willing to bet this was the first solid sleep his sister had allowed herself in more than a month. She'd dozed off several times during the massage, and had conked out immediately when she'd laid down on the couch in his cabin.

Guilt tugged at him as he watched her. He should have realized sooner that she'd sleep better if he was with her. Alone, she was always on duty, drifting on the surface of sleep so that she could leap into action at the slightest provocation. But with him, her trust was absolute. She'd given up the need to be in control, secure in the knowledge he would alert her if the crew had any issues.

He hated to disturb her, but he knew she'd want to hear what he had to share. "Hey, sis," he whispered.

Her eyelids fluttered, like her subconscious had heard him but her body was resisting the summons.

He rested a hand on her shoulder and increased the volume a few notches. "Ror. We got a reply from Dad."

This time her eyes opened to slits, a frown scrunching up her forehead. "I'm awake," she groaned, flopping over to her back and drawing in a deep breath. "Really, I am." But her eyes closed again. "Dad sent a message?"

"Yeah. You want me to read it to you?"

She nodded. Even that small movement looked like it took a supreme effort.

How exhausted was she?

He pulled the message up on the Far Horizons comband his dad had given him. He'd never expected to have a reason to use one, let alone be the one traveling out of Fleet space while his dad was still on Earth. A lot had changed in both their lives in the past couple months.

"Aurora and Micah, Reynolds contacted me immediately after the Admiral was arrested. She's also the one who told Siginal where he could find you. I offered to arrange representation for the Admiral, but Reynolds said the Admiral had someone in mind who already agreed to take the case. I'm glad you're on your way. Your mother and I are at the Hawai'i house. We'll have a lot to discuss when you get here. Love, Dad."

Aurora turned her head, meeting his gaze. "I should have known he'd already be handling things."

Micah smiled. "That's Dad for you. Always there when you need him."

Her answering smile was sweet. "Just like you."

He cringed. "Not really. I should have offered you my couch long before now."

She rolled to her side, tucking the pillow more firmly under her head. "I'm the captain, remember? I watch out for the crew. It's not your job to watch out for me."

"Of course it is. I'm your big brother." He leaned closer, giving her his most intimidating stare. "A big brother outranks a captain every time."

She laughed, just as he'd hoped she would. "Yes, sir."

He sat back on his heels. "Now that we have that settled, I'm going to sit right over there," he pointed at one of the upholstered chairs near the couch, "and you're going back to sleep. I promise to wake you if anything exciting happens."

Her gaze sharpened, like she was going to give him an argument, but a jaw-popping yawn made her look more like a sleepy kitten than a starship captain. "Okay," she agreed, her eyes drifting shut and her muscles relaxing.

Less than a minute later, she was fast asleep.

Micah settled into his chair and pulled up the other message on his comband, this one from Celia Cardiff, the ship's security officer.

How's she doing?

Better, thanks to you.

Celia had given him the idea to set Aurora up in his cabin and give her a massage to help her relax. They'd shared the plan with Lelindia, who'd taken charge of getting Aurora to agree.

I read her my dad's message, and now she's sleeping again.

Peacefully?

Yeah. No nightmares.

From little tidbits Celia had dropped during their interactions over the past few weeks, he'd gathered she was dealing with nightmares, too. He would have offered his cabin as a refuge for her, but he feared she wouldn't take it in the platonic way he meant it. He didn't want to do anything that might put her on guard and mess up the friendship they were building.

His sister had warned him Celia didn't do romantic relationships, only brief sexual ones. He definitely didn't want to be placed in that category. Not that he didn't want her. He most certainly did. Her athleticism and discipline were drawing a primal response from him that he was fighting tooth and nail to suppress.

But since he couldn't be her romantic partner, he wanted to slot himself solidly into the role of her first male friend. That was the only road that gave him an excuse to spend time with her without triggering her subconscious defenses.

You up for a sparring session later?

He smiled. They'd managed three training sessions while in Teeli space, including one yesterday. But now that they were back in Fleet space, he issued a new challenge.

You up for a dip in the hydrotank afterward?

Neither of them had been in the tank since the extremely awkward encounter where she'd gotten a leg cramp from overexerting herself and he'd pulled her to safety. He wanted a do-over where they both could have fun in the water.

Her reply was a little late, which he'd expected. Celia didn't like thinking about her failures. But she couldn't back down from a challenge, especially from him.

You bet.

His smile widened. The game was afoot.

Four

"When do you want to tell your father about our daughter?"

Jonarel Clarek tightened his arm around Lelindia, drawing her snug against his bare chest.

They were taking advantage of the reprieve from their duties offered by the interstellar jump back to Earth, staying in bed longer than usual. He still had trouble believing this life was his new reality. His mate. His child. The wonder and joy of it pushed all other thoughts out of his mind, especially when they were alone in their joined cabins.

But he forced himself to focus on his mate's question. "How long before you will show physical signs of pregnancy your clothing will not conceal?"

She tilted her head back, meeting his gaze. He bathed in the warm light in her brown eyes. "Hard to say for sure. There are no guidelines for a half-Suulh, half-Kraed baby. But based on her development so far, I'd say another month. I think she's going to be smaller than a typical Nedale at birth, but larger than a Kraed infant."

A coil of anxiety spiraled inside his gut. "But still healthy?"

Lelindia's smile was indulgent, a look he had been getting a lot during the past month. "She's doing fine, I promise. Nothing to worry about."

How could he not worry? His checana was carrying a child who was unique in the universe. Anything could happen. Anything could go wrong. He had never felt so powerless to protect those he loved.

Lelindia's eyes narrowed. "I mean it, Jonarel. Our daughter will be fine. I'll make sure of that. It's your father who concerns me."

The anxiety started spinning in the opposite direction, growing as it turned. "He concerns me, too."

His father's appearance at the binary star system in Teeli space had been unexpected. It had given Jonarel no time to think or worry before he faced him down. He had also benefitted from not being in the same room. His father was a lot more intimidating in person than on the *Starhawke*'s bridgescreen.

That did not mean he would be quelled by his father's antagonistic behavior. He had stood against him once before, back on Drakar. Rage had prompted the blow that had knocked his father to the ground after his father's inadvertent backhand had crumpled Lelindia. He should have known at that moment that she was his mate, but he had been too blind to see his reaction for what it was. And Lelindia had hidden her feelings for him too well.

"So what do you think?" Lelindia trailed her finger over his chest, tracing the tendrils of brown that overlaid the dark green of his skin. "Should we schedule a time to talk with him after we're planetside?"

Her touch distracted him, even though there was nothing sexual about it. Her actions since their first night together made it clear she enjoyed touching him as much as he yearned to touch her. A rare gift in a non-Kraed female. Any fear that his continual desire for physical closeness would overwhelm her had melted away. Her fascination with the color patterns of his skin had already brought him endless hours of pleasure and contentment. "He may refuse to meet with me, as I am no longer part of the clan."

Lelindia made a noise that was remarkably close to a Kraed growl. "Like hell. He used you as a pawn in his chess game with Aurora. I'll be damned if he's going to punish you for standing up for her. And me."

Warmth spread through his chest. He hugged her closer, nuzzling her hair. "Thank you."

"I'll get Aurora to mediate the meeting if I have to. No way will Siginal say no to her."

No, he would not. He had seen the fear in his father's eyes when Aurora had challenged him, telling him exactly how much she condemned his actions toward her and the crew. It took a great deal to inspire fear in his father. It was a testament to how powerful Aurora was that she had achieved it.

Not that she had enjoyed it. He had noted her reaction when she had realized what her anger had inspired. She had backed off immediately, worked to find common ground. Her incredible wellspring of empathy was part of what made her a respected and beloved leader. And a treasured friend.

He found it increasingly difficult to remember what it had felt like when he had believed himself to be in love with her. All romantic inclinations toward her had evaporated like dew touched by a blazing sun the moment Lelindia had kissed him for the first time. The feeling of completeness, of bonding, had hit him with the force of a meteorite. Intoxicating, and world-changing. Comparing what he had felt for Aurora to what Lelindia drew from him was like comparing a babbling brook to a cascading waterfall.

"Having Aurora mediate is wise. Her presence during our discussion would keep my father civil."

Lelindia sighed. "Too bad your mom's not here." She snuggled closer. "She'd be happy for us."

"Yes, she would." Tehar had shared the conversations she and his mother had had regarding Lelindia, and their mutual wish that he would mate with her because she would bring him joy.

They had been correct. And he had been too wrapped up in his father's expectations to see it. Thank goodness Aurora had refused to fall in with his father's plans. She had saved him from his own ignorance.

"Tehar's pretty excited, too," Lelindia said. "She and Unity were talking to me about the baby while I was working in the greenhouse yesterday. Unity wanted to know when I would lay my eggs."

"Your eggs?"

"Yep." Lelindia chuckled. "Turns out Setarips lay eggs, usually two or three at a time. I'd suspected that was the case, since their physiology is more reptilian than mammalian, but Unity confirmed it."

"So Unity assumed you would lay eggs?"

"Uh-huh. They have mammalian animals in their biosphere, so a live birth wasn't a completely foreign concept, but it hadn't occurred to Unity that we wouldn't reproduce like the Yruf. They'd assumed all bi-pedal, technologically advanced species would be like the Setarips."

"Hmm." He, for one, was very grateful the Suulh did not lay eggs. Lelindia's abilities for nurturing life were incredible, but bridging an egg-laying and live-birth reproductive pair was probably beyond even her. "Have you gathered a list of potential names for our daughter?" *Our daughter.* He loved saying that.

She shook her head. "I still can't decide whether she should have a Kraed first name and my family's last name, or a Suulh first name and your clan's last name."

His fingers glided over her silken hair. She had let it grow, and now it was almost as long as his, perfect for stroking. "I assumed in Suulh culture the last name of the Nedale and Sahzade passed down from mother to daughter." That was certainly the case with Lelindia and Aurora.

"I don't know if that's true or not. When my parents left Feylahn they were forced to choose new names to avoid leaving a trail the Teeli could follow. My parents and I are the only three Suulh with the last name Forrest. And Libra and Aurora are the only Hawkes." She frowned. "I don't even know what my mom's last name used to be. Come to think of it, I'm not even certain Suulh *have* last names. All the Suulh I've met have introduced themselves with a single name."

"You can ask your parents when we reach Earth. That knowledge might help you decide."

Lelindia's nose wrinkled like a baby clestok's. Utterly adorable. "Or it could give me a third option that makes the choice even harder."

Her consternation brought a small smile to his lips. "How did your parents choose your name?"

"They wanted something that would harken back to our Suulh roots without being obviously Suulh. Lelindia is a Galish spelling for a type of tree on Feylahn, my mother's favorite. Its branches provide dappled shade that nurtures the growth of other plants beneath its canopy."

"Your name is well chosen." No wonder he had wanted to use it rather than her nickname when their relationship changed. Mya had never quite fit her. It lacked the richness of her given name. "Perhaps you should consider the names of living things you love."

She grinned at him. "I don't think I can get away with naming her Jonarel."

His startled laugh made her grin widen. Ever since she had learned he could laugh, she seemed to have made it her mission to spark that reaction when they were alone, and she was getting very good at it. Another gift he had never expected in his life. "No, that would not be appropriate." He brushed a kiss across her lips. "But I appreciate the sentiment."

"Back to the drawing board then. Maybe I'll have a better idea which way to go after we talk to your father."

The happy bubble popped. "Do you want to tell him when we see him?" His protective instincts screamed *NO*. He did not trust his father to treat Lelindia with the respect she deserved, not after his behavior on Drakar. But he believed in his mate, and the good that could come from revealing the existence of their unborn child to the clans.

Her gaze grew serious. "I think we should. The longer we keep her a secret, the more we risk your father resenting us for hiding her from him. I'm hoping once he gets over his shock, he'll see her for the miracle she is. Her existence has the power to bring the other clans together to fight the Teeli."

He cupped her jaw in his hand, his thumb brushing the velvet softness of her cheek. "You are the bravest person I have ever known."

A flush suffused her skin. "No, I'm not. Aurora's much braver."

He shook his head. "As the Sahzade, she was born to be a guardian. Her bravery and courage are part of who she is at her core. But you are the Nedale, born to nurture and heal, not fight. Yet you choose to stand tall in the face of danger, to defend what you believe in, even against insurmountable odds. That is why you are the bravest person I know."

She rested her hand over his, her eyes luminous. "I'm braver when I'm with you. You give me strength I never knew I had."

"As you do for me." He kissed her again, lingering as he tasted the sweetness of her full lips. When he lifted his head, he saw the same determination in her eyes that had settled into his heart. "We will face my father together, and with Aurora's help, we will show him that our little Nedale is the greatest blessing we have ever received."

Five

"*Gladiator*'s systems are warming up." Cade Ellis glanced at U-2 hovering to the right of the pilot's seat in *Gladiator*'s cockpit. The egg-shaped mobile unit's emerald-green scaled exterior reflected the warm yellow light of the Yruf docking bay filtering through the viewport. The Yruf ship had cocooned *Gladiator* for more than a month, but the time had come for *Gladiator* to leave the sanctuary the Yruf had provided and take flight. "Have you finished disengaging from *Gladiator*, Unity?"

"Yes, we have," Unity replied in Micah's voice.

"Good." His team was taking *Gladiator* to Earth, where they'd be docking at Sol Station, the transportation hub orbiting the planet, while the team was planetside. Ifel, the Yruf leader, had agreed with Cade that it would be unwise to leave Unity integrated with *Gladiator*, or have U-2 onboard, while the crew was absent. The Yruf's presence in Fleet space needed to remain a secret, and he wasn't about to tempt fate by having Unity onboard his ship. His technically *stolen* ship. Not with the Sovereign as his adversary.

Unity was integrated with the *Starhawke* too, but Aurora and her crew wouldn't have the same issue when they docked at Sol Station in a couple days. As a Kraed ship, unauthorized access wasn't a concern. Star could make the ship impenetrable if she wanted to.

Cade would remain on the Yruf ship a little longer than his team. He still had one of the *Starhawke's* shuttles, currently sitting next to *Gladiator* in the Yruf bay, which he'd be taking to Brendan Scott's house on Hawai'i. Since the shuttle didn't have interstellar engines, the Yruf were giving him a lift into the Sol system. Their cloaking ability and the shuttle's camouflage would allow both vessels to remain undetected when the Yruf dropped Cade off on the dark side of the moon.

U-2 would be going with him, providing him with a conduit to the Yruf and Aurora while he was at Brendan's. He also wanted Brendan to have a chance to meet Unity. The combination of the Yruf's advanced alien technology and Micah's voice was certain to pique Brendan's interest.

During the flight from Teeli space to Earth, Bella Drew had been working with the Yruf engineers to construct a charging alcove for U-2 in the main cabin of the *Starhawke's* shuttle. Unity had passed along Jonarel's and Star's detailed instructions for the necessary modifications. Unity had also been working on integrating with the shuttle's systems the same way they were integrated with the *Starhawke.*

"Are you finished integrating with Star's shuttle?" he asked Unity.

"Snug as a bug in a rug."

The cadence of the delivery was pitch perfect in Micah's voice, as though Aurora's brother was standing by Cade's shoulder.

Justin Byrnes chuckled as he slid into the seat beside Cade. "Micah must be working overtime on the *Starhawke* teaching you colloquial Galish phrases."

U-2 bobbed in agreement. "We've learned all kinds of fascinating idioms, though Micah had some trouble explaining why we would want to be a bug in a rug."

Cade grinned. Having a conversation with Unity was becoming more like talking to Micah every day.

"We've reached the drop-off point for *Gladiator*," U-2 informed him, slipping out of his peripheral view toward the cockpit hatch.

Justin tapped the ship's comm. "Bella, you're up."

"Be right there," she replied.

Cade stood, glancing out the viewport to where the *Starhawke*'s shuttle waited for him. Thank goodness they had it. It gave them flexibility in this situation.

Bella would be piloting *Gladiator* to Sol Station from a location well outside the Sol system. Because the Yruf ship was significantly faster than *Gladiator*, Cade and the Yruf would end up reaching Earth before them.

Cade and his team had spent the trip from Teeli space to Earth analyzing all the potential angles the Sovereign's minions could have used to convince the Court of Justice to indict the Admiral for treason. He'd been accused of conspiring with the Setarips to undermine the Fleet, so they all agreed the case would be strongly based on the Admiral's secret mission to Gallows Edge to uncover the truth about the Sovereign's connection to the Etah Setarips.

The fact that the Admiral had been a prisoner of the Etah, not a co-conspirator, and had almost died as a result, would have been conveniently omitted from the file. The Sovereign excelled at shifting blame for her machinations.

Reynolds had sent them updates, alerting them that a vocal minority of public opinion had already turned solidly against the Admiral. Demonstrations were taking place outside the Court of Justice and Fleet HQ buildings.

He had zero doubt the Sovereign was behind the protestors, too.

Reynolds had been providing security for Knox, Admiral Schreiber's son and Aurora's former captain, at the Admiral's house. According to Reynolds, protestors had shown up there a few days after Knox arrived. The rest of Cade's team was joining her as added security until the *Starhawke* reached Sol Station.

Justin held up his hand for a fist bump. "See you when the *Starhawke* crew arrives."

Cade tapped his fist against Justin's. "Watch your six." With the Sovereign on the attack, they had to be ready for anything.

Justin nodded. "Always."

Cade passed Bella at the top of the stairs leading to the ship's lower level.

"Everything set?" he asked her.

"Good to go. All that down time in Teeli space worked to our advantage. This ship's in better shape than when it first launched. I'll be able to shave a few minutes off our arrival time without any extra power drain."

"That's a silver lining."

"Shields are reinforced, too. The Yruf taught me some tricks to improve strength and efficiency, and Unity was able to help with the detail work. I'm going to miss having an invisible assistant."

"We are always happy to help," U-2 piped up from the end of the corridor. "We like learning new things."

Bella glanced at Unity and smiled. "You're good at it. Thank you."

Unity gave a little spin, a behavior they had started doing to express happiness. "You're welcome."

Tam Williams and Christoph Gonzalez were waiting for Cade in the main cabin as he followed U-2 toward the ramp.

"You sure you don't want to stay with us?" Gonzo asked, his lean face solemn. "Providing security for Knox sounds like a lot more fun than flying a camouflaged shuttle to a beach house on Hawai'i."

Williams snorted.

Cade lifted his brows. "As I recall, you told me you enjoyed piloting that shuttle during your brief rescue mission on Feylahn."

The corners of Gonzo's eyes crinkled, but he kept his tone nonchalant. "It was okay."

"Uh-huh." His gaze flicked between Gonzo and Williams. "Try not to get into too much trouble while I'm gone."

Gonzo grinned, but his eyes remained serious. "No promises."

"We're going to miss them," Unity said as they followed Cade down the ramp and crossed the short distance to the shuttle.

"Really?" It had never occurred to him that Unity might become emotionally attached to his team.

Unity swiveled a quarter turn. "Really. We're not used to goodbyes, except when someone dies."

"Ah." Now he understood. Parting was a new experience for Unity. The sadness Unity was expressing showed new depths to the non-biological entity's emotional range. "They're going to miss you, too."

Unity hovered beside him as he waited for the shuttle's ramp to descend. "Why do you leave each other so often when it causes such unpleasant feelings? Why don't you stay together?"

A pang jabbed Cade's chest. That question hit a little too close to home. "Our society doesn't function like the Yruf's. Our work, our interests, and our families often pull us in different directions. And we don't have a non-biological like you to help bridge those gaps, to keep us interconnected." But the Kraed did. He'd envied them their relationship with the Nirunoc ever since he'd met Star.

Not that the presence of the Nirunoc kept the Kraed from causing each other unpleasant feelings. Siginal's horrified reaction when he'd discovered Jonarel and Lelindia were mated was still fresh in Cade's mind.

However, he'd take anger over apathy any day. His parents didn't seem to care whether he lived or died. For all intents, he *was* dead to them. His refusal to follow their pre-set plans had ostracized him. Maybe that's why he'd felt such empathy for Jonarel's current situation with Siginal.

Unity bobbed beside him as he walked to the cockpit. "Wouldn't you rather find a way to stay together all the time? We know you miss Aurora. And she misses you."

He settled in the pilot's chair, keyed in the command to close the ramp, and swiveled to face Unity. "How do you know?"

Unity laughed, another habit they'd integrated into their responses. "It's obvious. Your lackluster behavior since separating is completely different from how you acted together on our ship. You smile and laugh much less, and your sleep is irregular and turbulent."

He stared at Unity. "You're watching us while we sleep?" That was a little creepy.

"Not watching. But we monitor the vital signs of the crew. It's one of our duties. Your vital signs have deteriorated in the past month. So have Aurora's, in sync with your own."

"I know." He stared out the viewport. The air in the bay shimmered as *Gladiator*'s engines heated up, then the interlocking scales of the Yruf ship's exterior hull undulated apart, revealing the inky black of space.

Gladiator rose off the deck, the landing gear sliding out of sight as the ship glided through the opening. A moment later the outer hull swirled closed again, leaving the shuttle alone in the bay.

He felt the soft ache of parting, just as Unity described. His team had become his family, like the brothers and sisters he'd never had.

But if he was completely honest with himself, the dominant emotion suffusing his chest right now wasn't sadness. It was eagerness — to reconnect with Aurora's parents, and in a couple days, Aurora. "It's complicated," he said, as much for his own benefit as to answer Unity's question.

Unity laughed again. "Micah has told us that many times."

A grin spread across Cade's face. "I'll bet he has." He could imagine the challenges Micah had encountered as Unity's primary teacher. As a pupil, Unity had the exuberant curiosity of an innocent five-year-old paired with the learning capacity of a certified genius. Explaining the breadth of human history, language, and behavior would be very complicated indeed.

Especially when factoring in the actions of a certified psychopath like the Sovereign.

The thought sobered him, bringing his focus back to his mission. "Can you please thank Ifel for getting us here so quickly." He'd told her himself when they'd said their goodbyes earlier, but it bore repeating.

Unity bobbed. "We have. She's as eager to learn more about Aurora and Micah's parents as you are to see them. She's grateful you allowed us to join you so we can meet them and share our experiences with her."

His grin resurfaced. "It's a win-win scenario. I feel better knowing you're with me. And I'll still have a connection to the Yruf and the *Starhawke*. Besides, Brendan's gonna love you. I'll bet it won't take more than ten minutes before he expresses an interest in visiting the Yruf ship in person."

"A bet? As in a gambling wager?"

Cade chuckled at Unity's enthusiasm. "Micah's taught you about that, huh?"

"Oh, yes. Micah enjoys poker. We played a few digital versions together, but he said it's not the same as sitting around a table with paper cards."

"He's right. Brendan likes poker, too. He's a tough player, hard to read."

"Read?"

"Figure out what he's thinking, what his next move is going to be. That's a necessary skill to be proficient at poker."

"Oh." Unity was silent for a moment. "We can read the Yruf very well. But anticipating the actions of Aurora's crew and your team is more difficult. You often do the opposite of what we believe you want to do, especially in your relationships with each other."

"How so?"

"You remained on our ship when you clearly preferred to be on Aurora's. Justin and Bella's interactions indicate they both want to become physically intimate, yet neither has initiated that part of their relationship. And Micah insists he and Celia are just friends, but he watches her in much the same way Jonarel watches Lelindia."

"He does?" The other two observations weren't news, but the last one was a doozie. Apparently in the past month Micah had shot right over his anxiety regarding Celia and moved solidly into infatuation.

"Oh, yes. They're sparring right now and his vital signs indicate intense physical attraction."

Strange to hear that comment in Micah's voice, like he was talking about himself in the third person. Also, note to self. Unity could read his team and Aurora's crew just fine.

Thank goodness his and Aurora's feelings were out in the open. Justin and Bella probably wouldn't care if Unity said anything to them. Their reticence to get involved seemed to have more to do with being teammates than any emotional hang-ups. But Micah's interest in Celia was problematic. That was a relationship dead end if he'd ever seen one. Celia was about as romantically inclined as a cactus. He'd hate for Aurora's brother to get his heart sliced into pulp. "Does Aurora know about Micah's interest in Celia?"

"We're not sure. She's never spoken about it in front of us."

Unity didn't monitor the crew's verbal interactions onboard the *Starhawke*. That was Star's job. If one of Unity's mobile units wasn't in the room, or a crewmember didn't speak to Unity directly, Unity didn't listen in.

"But Micah's not acting on his attraction?"

"No. We're not sure why not."

He could come up with a laundry list of why nots. So could Micah, apparently, or he would have made a move to change the dynamic with Celia. The fact that they were sparring together proved he hadn't. Celia wouldn't willingly spend time with someone she knew was romantically inclined towards her. Micah must have figured that out, too.

Cade felt for the guy. The situation reminded him a bit too much of what he'd endured working side-by-side with Aurora on Gaia, before they'd dealt with all the baggage of their past.

Not fun.

Time for a change in topic. "How long before we're in position behind Earth's moon?"

"Three minutes, forty-four seconds."

He blinked. "You mean we're already in the Sol system?"

"Yes."

So much for chit chat. "Then I guess it's time to get this show on the road."

Six

The cool water of the hydrotank lapped at Micah's skin as each stroke pulled him forward against the waves. The rhythmic caress sparked an internal stream of euphoria that suffused his body like sunshine on warm sand.

He'd never thought of swimming as essential to his wellbeing, but he'd also never spent a month on a starship in Teeli space, waiting for an attack that never came. Come to think of it, he couldn't remember the last time he'd gone more than a few days without swimming. The weather on Hawai'i was rarely inhospitable for prolonged periods, and whenever his schedule kept him busy all day, he'd usually fit in a short swim at his dad's house.

He dove underwater, switching to a modified breaststroke. His gaze swept the projected images of the tropical fish and other aquatic creatures native to the islands. They flitted on either side of him, a beautiful array of yellow, blue, white, black, brown, and green.

He drank in the sight, hydrating his soul. But the view also served a secondary purpose — giving him something to focus on besides the gorgeous contours of his swimming companion.

Celia had submerged below the surface as well, her movements as graceful as a dolphin's, her dark hair braided tight to her head in the configuration she preferred for sparring sessions. Her navy swimsuit outlined her lithe curves and set off the golden glow of her skin. She glanced his way and smiled – a mermaid pulled right out of his fantasies.

He smiled back, quickly putting a stranglehold on the inappropriate reaction her nearness sent flowing through his body. Returning his attention to the fish, he focused on stroking through the water with steady precision. The muscles in his arms, chest, and legs ached from the blows Celia had landed during the sparring session they'd just finished, but he didn't mind in the least. In fact, he cherished each point of discomfort like a badge of honor.

Every time she agreed to meet him on the mat, every moment they spent alone together, was a small victory.

Against all odds, he had become her friend.

He surfaced, drawing air into his lungs while he continued to stroke through the water.

She glided to the surface as well, the mermaid image holding as droplets of water shimmered on her dark lashes and silken skin like diamonds. "How are your muscles? Still sore?"

The question was tossed out with a teasing lilt. She knew he'd been worked over, but it was his own fault. He'd encouraged her to teach him how to break holds and flip an opponent, and then she'd demonstrated the techniques quite effectively on him. He'd lost track of how many times he'd hit the mat.

She'd allowed him to flip her, too, but she'd always managed to land on her feet like a cat. She'd suggested next time they invite

Jonarel to join their session, so Micah could try out what he'd learned on someone larger. He'd given a noncommittal response. It made practical sense to follow her advice — he wanted to be able to defend himself against potential adversaries they might encounter — but he wasn't excited about losing their alone time, even for a single session.

That realization had forced him to reevaluate how well he was reining in his emotional response to her. The news wasn't good.

He lobbed her teasing tone back at her with a crooked grin. "Cooling down just fine. How about you?"

Her eyes narrowed, picking up on the subtle reference to their last ill-fated swim together. "I'm good."

"Glad to hear it." They'd agreed to use level three this time. The wave setting still offered enough resistance that they could remain in the center of the tank while swimming, allowing them to cool down after the sparring session. He let his breath out on a happy sigh as his arms and legs kept easy pace with the waves. "I've really missed this."

"You need this," she corrected. "Now that I've seen what you're like when you're kept away from the water, it's pretty clear this isn't a luxury for you. It's a necessity."

"You could be right." And the fact that she was echoing his earlier thoughts showed how well she'd tuned into him. That tickled him red, white, and blue, especially since she'd given no indication she'd picked up on his strong attraction to her. Either he was doing an excellent job of hiding it, or she'd dismissed it as an impossibility and wasn't looking for the signs.

Or – and this was an even wilder idea – she might not have any idea what an attraction that was more than skin deep looked like. He had to believe she'd been propositioned by hundreds of men, maybe even thousands. She was too strikingly beautiful not to be an object of continual attention. But Aurora's statement that Celia had never had a male friend before indicated none of those knuckleheads had bothered to get to know the fascinating woman beneath the surface.

Their loss. And his gain. Sex with Celia would no doubt be spectacular – how could it not – but certainly not worth losing her friendship over. That's exactly what would happen, too. He had no illusions. She might agree to a one-night stand with him if he let his interest show, but afterward she'd carve him out of her life with the same precision she used when wielding a knife.

Not happening. He wanted as many hours in her company as he could earn during his time onboard. His libido would have to stay on permanent lockdown.

"Ready to head to the galley?" he asked her, tilting his head toward the decking surrounding the hydrotank.

She changed direction. "You bet."

That was another bonus. Celia loved to cook as much as he did, and fixing a meal together was quickly becoming one of his favorite things.

To his surprise, she seemed to enjoy their combined efforts as much as he did.

What he didn't know is if all of that would change as soon as they arrived at Sol Station. "What will the crew assignments be like when we arrive at the station?" he asked as he pulled himself out of the water and snagged a towel.

"I'm not sure." Celia picked up her own towel and dabbed the moisture off her arms and legs.

He caught himself staring and pivoted so he was facing the hydrotank as he briskly dried his hair with his towel.

"Aurora will probably want to head down to the planet as soon as we arrive," Celia continued, "but she might not take the entire crew. She may want me to stay with the ship. But I'm guessing you'll want to see your folks. And maybe check on things at home."

He slowed the vigorous scrubbing and draped the towel around his neck. "My place is pretty self-sufficient. Birdie said she'd check on it while I was gone. To be honest, I don't spend much time there. Usually I'm at the beach, in town, at work, or at my dad's house."

Celia gave him a wry grin. "We have that in common. I don't spend much time in my cabin, either."

He'd noticed. When she wasn't on the bridge or in the galley, he usually found her in the training center or the greenhouse. "I guess neither of us is much of a homebody."

She chuckled. "That's putting it mildly. I've never been big on confined spaces, even when they're mine."

He barely hid his wince. After spending most of her youth in a prison camp, it was no wonder she avoided confined spaces. It was a minor miracle that she was able to tolerate living on a starship.

Freedom of movement was something he'd always taken for granted. He doubted she ever did.

Anger heated his chest like a banked ember. How could anyone do that to another person, let alone a child? He wasn't normally vengeful, but if the people responsible for her suffering were ever facing him, he'd use every technique she'd taught him to make them sorry for what they'd done to her. Then again, if she was with him, he probably wouldn't get the chance before she'd handled them herself.

"Micah? You okay?" She was peering at him with concern.

He gave himself a mental shake and unhooked his hands from his towel. "Yeah, I'm good. Just wool gathering. So, what do you wanna fix this time?"

She gave him a strange look, but let it go. "The bok choy is almost as big as palm fronds. How about we make a stir-fry?"

"Works for me."

She backed towards the staircase, a mischievous gleam lighting her eyes. "Last one to the lift cleans up?"

He grinned, following her. "I thought that was my line."

"Not when I'm the one closer to the lift." She walked backwards down the stairs without so much as a glance at where she was going. Her spatial awareness and balance were remarkable.

She was also taunting him. And seriously turning him on. Good thing his swim trunks were loose, wet, and cold. "You don't have your shoes on yet," he reminded her.

"Neither do you."

They reached the bottom of the stairs. "You gonna put them on?"

The gleam in her eyes glowed brighter. "Yep."

He didn't trust that gleam. "On your feet?"

She smirked.

Aha. So that was her strategy.

"No cheating." He tried to sound stern but didn't pull it off. "First one to the lift *wearing their shoes on their feet* doesn't have to clean up."

"Deal."

They raced to where they'd left their shoes, snatched them up, and then both started laughing as they struggled to shove their damp feet into the dry shoes.

The back of his left shoe got trapped under his heel. She took off for the door. He ran after her, his shoe thumping the sole of his foot with each step, her laughter driving him forward. He reached the lift two steps behind her.

She executed a perfect pirouette to face him, then gave a jaunty flip of her raised foot to show off the shoes that were solidly on her feet. She glanced down pointedly at his loose left shoe before shooting him a disarming smile. "You lost."

He was way more than lost. He was a goner.

Seven

The midday sun sparkled like cut crystal on the aquamarine water surrounding the island of Oahu as Cade brought the *Starhawke* shuttle in for a landing. Brendan's house was easy to locate and access from the air, perhaps one of the reasons his family had originally bought it. The two-story structure was nestled on Diamond Head's hillside facing the ocean, well out of the flight path of any passenger or freight traffic to the island's airport.

The surrounding rockface appeared to embrace the house like a child nestled in its mother's arms, the curved pool beckoning on one end and lush greenery creating a shaded canopy on the other.

Cade had reconfigured the shuttle to a compact design to fit comfortably in the cobblestoned courtyard at the top of the driveway. The hull camouflage was in effect, so the shuttle was invisible from the outside and the soundless descent didn't attract any notice from the neighbors. The perimeter vegetation barely fluttered as he set the shuttle down.

"Hawai'i is beautiful."

Cade glanced over his shoulder to where Unity had detached from the charging alcove above him. "Yes, it is." He caught a wistfulness in Unity's voice. Images Ifel had shared with him of the former Setarip homeworld showed it looking a lot like Earth before the Setarip civil war had destroyed it. Unity might be feeling a little nostalgic. "Maybe before we join the *Starhawke* in a couple days, I can give you an aerial tour of the islands on the way out."

Unity bobbed. "We would love that!"

"Then it's a plan."

Cade had sent a message to Brendan as soon as he'd exited the Yruf ship, giving him his ETA, so Aurora's parents were already standing outside the front entrance to the house. While Cade went to greet them, Unity waited in the shuttle.

To Cade's surprise, Libra approached him first, opening her arms and pulling him into an affectionate hug. He gave a startled laugh before hugging her back.

"It's good to have you here," she said as she stepped away, allowing Brendan to hug him, too.

Brendan's gaze swept over him. "Looks like you could use a solid meal and a good night's sleep."

He grimaced. "That obvious, huh?" His clothes fit a little looser around the waist than they had a couple weeks ago, probably because he routinely forgot to eat.

The corner of Brendan's mouth lifted. "It helps that I can feel your exhaustion. And your stomach just growled."

Cade chuckled. "Fair enough."

"Come on you two." Libra ushered them toward the front door. "Lunch is almost ready and we have Aurora's room all prepared for you."

"Hang on." Cade motioned toward the shuttle's ramp, the only part of the shuttle currently visible. "There's someone I want you both to meet first."

"Oh?" Brendan's gaze had the unfocused look that signaled he was reaching out with his empathic senses.

"Unity, come on out," Cade called.

The emerald-green mobile unit floated out of the opening and drifted toward them. The shuttle's ramp closed silently, the shuttle vanishing from sight.

"Unity?" Libra asked.

"Turns out the Yruf have a non-biological entity similar to Star. This is U-2, one of the mobile units that allows Unity to be separated from the Yruf ship but still connected with the whole. Oh, and Unity uses Micah's voice to communicate with us."

Unity halted half a meter from Cade's shoulder. "Hello."

Libra's lips parted in surprise. She looked very much like Aurora had during her early interactions with Unity. "Uh, hi."

Brendan's reaction was the complete opposite. He zeroed in with rapt attention. "It's a pleasure to meet you, Unity."

"You as well, Brendan. We've spent a lot of time with Micah and Aurora during the past month. We've been eager to meet both of you."

Brendan shot Cade a speculative look. "I'm sure we'll have a lot to talk about, then."

Cade caught the scent of sauteed onion and spices wafting from the entrance to the kitchen as he walked into the wide foyer behind Brendan and Libra, Unity by his side. The Christmas tree that had been in the living room down to his left had been replaced by a tall plant with glossy draping leaves. Ficus, maybe?

In fact, a quick glance around the open floorplan revealed quite a few new plants in residence. Libra's influence, no doubt. Maybe she'd brought them with her from Hawke's Nest, her plant nursery in northern California.

"I have a few finishing touches to put on lunch," Brendan said. "Unity, would you mind keeping me company while Libra gets Cade settled?" The eagerness in Brendan's emotional field belied the offhand request. He was like a kid staring at a birthday present he couldn't wait to unwrap.

"We'd love to!" Unity replied, floating past Libra and following Brendan as he headed for the kitchen.

Libra's gaze stayed on Unity, a small frown tipping down the corners of her mouth. "Why Micah's voice?" she murmured, turning back to Cade.

"He was the one acting as interpreter during our initial meetings with the Yruf. It gave Unity a wealth of words to work with, both to figure out Galish, and to reproduce when talking with us. Micah's been helping Unity expand their vocabulary ever since."

"Hmm." Libra clearly wasn't thrilled with his answer, but the anxiety in her emotional field eased.

"Are Gryphon and Marina here?" he asked as he followed her up the stairs.

"Not right now. They've spent the last couple weeks up north seeing patients and interviewing healers in various modalities."

"Does that mean they're keeping their clinic?" With Stoneycroft reduced to a pile of ash, he'd been wondering what the two couples' living arrangements would be going forward. He had trouble picturing Libra accepting that her energy sister was living thousands of kilometers away, even if they did have a high-speed jet at their disposal to bridge the distance.

"The opposite, actually. As soon as they can find the right people, they're turning it over to them. That's why they're interviewing healers, so their clients will still be taken care of after they move down here."

"What about your business?"

Libra smiled at him over her shoulder as she walked past the space images lining the hallway to Aurora's room. "I got lucky. My manager jumped at the chance to take it on, and one of my favorite holiday workers said he wanted to invest in the business as her partner. Nothing's official yet, but I think they'll be able to make a go of it."

He didn't sense any melancholy from her. If anything, she seemed eager for the change. "Will you be starting a nursery here?"

She turned to face him, her blue eyes taking on a focused look that was exactly like her daughter's. "Marina and I are... keeping our options open."

Translation – waiting to see what happened with the Teeli. And the Sovereign.

"I'm sorry our mission didn't succeed." When Libra and Brendan had left the *Starhawke* last time, they'd all hoped the next time they saw each other, the Sovereign would be in custody and the Teeli's true nature would be revealed to the world.

Libra folded her hands and lifted her chin. "You will."

Not even a tremor of doubt brushed her emotional field. Her certainty humbled him. "Thank you."

A soft smile touched her lips. "How's Aurora?"

"Like me. Exhausted. Disappointed. Outraged."

Her gaze swept over him, assessing. "You two haven't been spending much time together lately, have you?"

He cocked his head. "You can tell?"

She barked a laugh. "Of course I can tell. Aurora would never allow you to get rundown like this." She swept her hand to encompass his bedraggled state, then slid his pack off his shoulder and set it beside the bed. "Give me your hands."

He complied, the surety and tenderness of her grip making his throat tighten.

Her energy field engaged, the pearlescent glow flowing along their joined hands and surrounding him. The tension and exhaustion faded immediately, replaced with warmth and a lightness he hadn't felt since... well, since the last time he'd been with Aurora.

He'd never mistake Libra's energy field for Aurora's, though. They looked identical to his gaze, but the sensation when the energy flowed over him was subtly different. Maybe that was a result of their differing emotional reactions to him, or maybe it was inherent, as distinct as fingerprints. Regardless, he was grateful for the change in his relationship with Libra over Christmas that had made this moment possible.

Her field dissipated as she released his hands. "Better?"

He took a deep breath and rolled his shoulders. It was like waking from a good night's sleep. "Much. Thank you."

"You're welcome." She crossed her arms loosely over her chest. "So why haven't you and Aurora been together?"

He sighed. "We realized the mission would work better if I was on the Yruf ship with my team, rather than on the *Starhawke*. Aurora and I haven't been on the same ship since we entered Teeli space."

"That had to be rough on both of you." Her motherly concern washed over him. "But you'll be together soon. In the meantime, Brendan and I intend to keep you well fed and rested. Go ahead and get settled. We'll see you out on the patio."

Being mothered a bit sure felt nice.

Cade unpacked his few belongings, placing them in Aurora's closet and bathroom, allowing the memories of the time they'd spent together in this room right after Christmas to soothe his aching heart.

The grumbling of his stomach and the sound of male laughter drew him downstairs to the patio. Brendan and Libra were already seated at the stone table that gave a view of both the pool and the Pacific Ocean beyond. Unity hovered above one of the chairs beneath the jaunty white table umbrella, while the seat with the best view of the ocean had been saved for Cade.

Such a small thing, perhaps, but it reinforced how kind and generous Aurora's parents were, and how incredibly blessed he was to be treated as part of their family.

The aromas drifting off the hearty grilled vegetable sandwich on homemade bread that filled his plate made his mouth water.

Brendan grinned at him as he sat down. "Unity was telling us about your wager. It appears you won."

"Wager?" It took him a moment to clue in. "You asked to visit the Yruf ship already, didn't you?"

"Of course I did. I'd be a fool not to. Unity is a remarkable technological innovation. I'm still trying to grasp the concept that they're in real-time communication with Micah and Aurora right now."

"Well, not *right* now," Unity replied with a soft laugh. "Micah's in the hydrotank with Celia and Aurora's in her cabin. We're in the greenhouse with Lelindia and Jonarel. They're singing to the baby."

"Baby?" Libra froze with her iced tea glass halfway to her lips. "What baby?"

"Their baby," Unity said like it was the most obvious thing in the world.

Libra's eyes widened, her gaze darting to Cade. Brendan stared at him, too.

"Uh, yeah." Cade shot Unity a look, although they would have no idea how to interpret it. It hadn't occurred to him to ask Unity to keep that news a secret.

Unity swayed in response. "Did we say something wrong?"

"Not exactly. I'm just guessing Lelindia and Jonarel would have liked to announce the pregnancy themselves."

"Stellar light. She's pregnant." Libra sank against the back of her chair, her face slack with shock.

Brendan recovered quickly. His smile was so broad Cade could see all his teeth. "Way to go, firefly. She pulled it off. They must be thrilled."

"Oh, yeah." Cade picked up his sandwich and took a bite. Delicious. "Jonarel's being overprotective, as usual, but Lelindia's handling it. Aurora said she's never seen either of them so happy." He glanced at Libra. Her emotions were still a muddle. There was joy in the mix, but also a huge cloud of apprehension. "Is there a problem?"

She blinked, then gave a little shake of her head. "Not really. It just seems... fast."

"I know. I had the same reaction. So did Aurora. The idea of a baby onboard the *Starhawke* is weighing on her. She wasn't expecting it."

Brendan frowned. "So Lelindia didn't discuss it with her beforehand?"

"No." He picked up his iced tea and took a sip. Mint swirled around his tongue. "I got the impression Lelindia expected it to take a long time. Instead, they conceived on the first try."

Brendan smiled at Libra. "Sound familiar?"

"Hmm." Her apprehension faded. Now she was studying Cade carefully. "You said this is weighing on Aurora. What are her concerns?"

"That something will happen to Lelindia during a mission, for one. That having a baby on the ship will make her job harder, for another. But I think what's freaking her out the most is the idea that the Sovereign will learn about the baby and go after her."

"Her?" Libra's gaze sharpened. "She's having a girl? She's certain?"

"That's what she said. She's already a month along, and from what Aurora told me, she could give birth anytime in the next three to five months."

"So she conceived before you entered Teeli space?" Brendan asked.

"Uh-huh. I was still onboard the *Starhawke* when we got the news."

Libra took a bite of her sandwich, chewing slowly. "Why would she choose to conceive while you were on a dangerous mission? I understand the impulse that prompted her to have their mating ceremony while we were all together, but this decision isn't making sense to me."

He spread his hands. "That's all I know."

Unity spoke up, sounding more tentative than Cade had ever heard them. "They love their baby very much."

Brendan lifted his glass in Unity's direction. "Of that, I have no doubt. Don't worry, Unity. It's probably good that we heard the news in advance. Gives us some time to process."

"You're not... upset?"

Brendan must have given Libra a nudge under the table because she jolted, set down her sandwich, and turned to Unity. "No, I'm not upset. I'm sorry if I gave that impression. It was just a surprise. Historically, Nedale pregnancies are planned out. And discussed with the Sahzade beforehand."

But Aurora and Lelindia weren't like Libra and Marina. Seeing the two pairs interact while they were with the other Suulh on Gaia had shone a spotlight on their differences. Aurora and Lelindia were definitely bonded, but they had an independence of spirit that was quite different from the interdependence Cade sensed from Libra and Marina.

Aurora had already proven she could be lightyears away from her energy sister without it bothering her. And Lelindia seemed to have taken those separations in stride, too, becoming a stronger, more confident version of herself. Her decision to take charge of her future with regards to Jonarel and a child seemed like a natural extension of that changing attitude.

Whatever the Sahzade and Nedale had been in the Suulh's past, Aurora and Lelindia were rewriting the future.

Eight

"She lives!" Kire grinned at Aurora as she stepped off the lift onto the *Starhawke*'s bridge.

"Ha-ha." She returned his smile, claiming the captain's chair he'd vacated.

"Looks like you finally got some real sleep."

She caught the undercurrent of concern beneath his playful banter. "I certainly feel more human." At his amused look she rolled her eyes. "You know what I mean."

"Yeah, I do. It's good to see you looking like yourself again."

"Thanks." She almost hadn't recognized the healthy, vibrant woman staring back at her from her bathroom mirror. That was telling by itself. Over the past month she'd accepted haggard and sallow as ordinary.

Lee-Lee must have paid a visit to Micah's cabin while she was sleeping and given her a healing session. After she'd conked out on Micah's couch, a brass band could have marched around the room and she probably wouldn't have woken up.

"Kelly, how are you doing?" she asked her navigator. She honestly couldn't remember the last time she'd said more than a handful of words to the young woman.

Bronwyn Kelly turned from the helm console. Her thick red mane was pulled up in a loose topknot today, with a few tendrils curling around her face. "Just fine, Captain."

"Nothing unusual to report?"

"Nope. We're due to arrive at Sol Station in fifty-one hours."

Aurora slid her gaze to Kire. "And by my calculations, you two have been on bridge duty for the past twelve hours." She'd been shocked to discover she'd slept for more than nine of those hours.

Kire shrugged. "Cardiff brought us food. And it's not like it's been stressful. Not much to do."

But she could sense how tired he was, despite his protests. Kelly, too, although her emotional field didn't show it as clearly as Kire's did. The entire crew had been put through the ringer in Teeli space. "Then Star and I will take over. You two are officially off duty for the next ten hours minimum."

Kire shared an amused glance with Kelly. "Aye, Captain."

After the lift doors closed behind them, Aurora turned the captain's chair in a slow half-circle, taking in the empty bridge. Had she ever been on the bridge by herself since the *Starhawke* launched on their first mission? Probably not. Why would she? The only time someone wasn't needed at the helm was during an interstellar jump, and she was usually busy prepping for whatever her crew needed to accomplish when they reached their destination.

She pivoted slowly in the opposite direction. Her fingertips stroked the smooth wood of the chair's armrests as she allowed the silence to settle around her. Not that the bridge was completely silent. The low-pitched hum the ship made when traveling through a jump was audible at the edge of her hearing, as was the soft whisper of the air circulation system. Her chair creaked ever so slightly as she turned, adding a more organic sound to the mix.

The combination was... peaceful. Or maybe she felt more peaceful now that she wasn't dragging a month's worth of sleepless nights around like an anchor. It was the calm before the storm, of course. As soon as they arrived at Sol Station, her life would once again be flung into the typhoon.

That was okay. She'd gladly face the gale if it meant extracting the Admiral from the Sovereign's clutches.

She'd stopped blaming herself for falling into yet another one of the Sovereign's snares. It was a waste of energy and counterproductive. All that mattered was clearing the charges against the Admiral and figuring out which members of the Court of Justice the Sovereign had manipulated to get him indicted in the first place.

Well, that wasn't *all* that mattered. She also had the not-so-small issue of Siginal and his decidedly negative reaction to the news of Lelindia and Jonarel's mating. She'd made it clear that she wouldn't allow him to push her into a Kraed mating with Jonarel or anyone else, but Siginal's bullheaded attitude guaranteed he'd be looking for alternative avenues to bring her into the fold.

Too bad he couldn't see the wonder that was staring him in the face.

The scope of what Lelindia and Jonarel's mating and the conception of their child meant radiated like the sun cresting the mountains, casting a brilliant light that cleared the remaining cobwebs from her mind.

Lelindia was going to have a daughter, a child who would belong to both the Suulh and the Kraed, just as Aurora belonged to the Suulh and Humans. Until that moment, it hadn't occurred to her that she and the little Nedale would have that in common.

She was keenly aware of the weight of responsibility the unborn child would carry, understood the challenges she would face figuring out her place in the universe. Hers would never be an easy path. That was certain. But she would always be surrounded with love. The little Nedale couldn't ask for better parents than Lelindia and Jonarel. And Aurora would be there for her, too, whenever she needed her.

What about giving her an energy sister?

She flinched at the whispered question from her subconscious. That particular mountain had looked like a distant hill until recently. Suddenly, it loomed larger than Olympus Mons.

A spike of anxiety dug into her gut. She didn't have the bandwidth to think about that. Not now. Wrong time, wrong place.

Her breath escaped on a sigh. "Star?"

The Nirunoc appeared before her, her sleek dark brown pant and tunic combination and no-nonsense hairstyle reminding Aurora of Celia. "Yes, Captain?"

"Have you and Jonarel discussed how you'd like to handle our next meeting with your father?"

"Jonarel and Lelindia have discussed it. They believe it would be best for you to act as mediator."

"They're probably right." And she'd want to choose the venue carefully. "Do they plan to tell him about the baby?"

"Yes. They believe it is unwise to keep her existence a secret from him."

"Do you agree?"

"Yes."

But Star clearly had reservations. She could see it in her eyes. "How do you think he'll react?"

Star's gaze dropped to the deck, a small frown drawing her brows together. "I am uncertain. He will be in conflict." She lifted her head, the gold of her eyes shadowed. "Children are cherished in our culture, every birth celebrated. Like the Suulh, we do not have unplanned pregnancies, nor do we have large families." She turned toward the bridgescreen, as if she would see her father's ship beside them in the jump. "But this child is not the one my father wished for. The one he expected. Accepting her will be... difficult for him."

Aurora's heart thumped painfully in her chest. She didn't want the little Nedale to ever feel unwanted by her grandfather. "But he will accept her?"

Star spread her hands. "He will have to. She is an innocent, a child of our world. Whether he would have chosen her or not is irrelevant."

Aurora's fingers curled around the armrests. "So he'll be forced into it?" That sounded... awful.

Star's lips curved a fraction. "Do not worry, Aurora. My father has the same protective instincts as all Kraed. He will likely rail against what he cannot change when he first learns of her existence, but the moment he sees her, the moment she becomes real to him, he will gladly defend her with his life, and love her with all his heart."

"Even though you and Jonarel have been banished?" That was a potential flaw in Lelindia's plan. Aurora had been reluctant to mention it since the baby was already a reality. But if Siginal no longer considered Jonarel a part of Clan Clarek, then their child wouldn't be, either.

The shadow returned to Star's eyes. "My banishment is not a factor."

Aurora strongly disagreed with that statement.

"My brother's banishment makes the situation more complicated, but not unworkable. You unwittingly gave my father a way out of his proclamation."

"I did?"

"Yes. You made it clear how displeased you were with his actions. His behavior turned you against our clan rather than drawing you into it. My father could claim that, for the good of our people, he reconsidered our banishments in order to maintain our positive relationship with you and the rest of the Suulh."

"Which allows him to save face."

"Exactly."

"Will your clan go along with it?"

"Of course."

Aurora's brows rose. "You're sure?"

Amusement flitted across Star's face. "You do not understand how revered and beloved you are in my clan, or the power you wield to enact change. This vessel," she swept her arms out, "was not a gift from Jonarel alone. It was a gift from our entire clan. No one has even considered such a thing before, to use our resources to build a ship for a non-Kraed. Yet my clan offered their support from the moment the concept was broached. They wanted you to mate with Jonarel as much for who you are as for the strength you would bring as the Sahzade of the Suulh."

Her throat tightened. "I didn't know."

"I suspected as much." Star faced the bridgescreen again. "My father is angry at Jonarel for disobeying him and going against his wishes, but he is also heartbroken at the thought of losing you. That is why he has reacted so harshly. He is in pain."

She blinked. "But... I don't have to be mated to Jonarel in order to be connected to your father or your clan."

"I realize that, and so does Jonarel, because we understand you. Your heart is generous and deep. You do not require a relationship by blood or ceremonial traditions to accept someone as part of your clan. Your behavior toward those around you has shown that again and again."

"But your father doesn't believe that?"

"Bloodlines and tradition mean a great deal to him, though he is more forward thinking than the leaders of the other clans. His beliefs are the reason why in his eyes you were the only acceptable mate for Jonarel. You held the highest position among your people, and stood to bring the most benefit to our world."

Aurora bit down on her tongue to keep from saying the words that immediately sprang to mind, going with a milder version. "He's an idiot if he thinks Lelindia won't bring as much, or likely more, benefit to your people than I will."

"I agree. So does my mother. And eventually, so will my father."

"Good." Some of the tension drained away.

At least she had Daymar as an ally in Clan Clarek, and a much clearer picture of where Siginal would be coming from.

He was still an idiot, especially considering her energy sister was carrying a half-Kraed child. Lelindia would do anything to help that baby live a full, rich life, whether she chose to be with the Kraed, the Suulh, or somewhere in between. And Aurora would do anything to support Lelindia and the little Nedale. If a big part of Siginal's resistance came from the belief that Aurora wouldn't be integrated with his clan now that Jonarel was mated to Lelindia, she'd show him just how wrong he was.

Nine

"I received a message from Admiral Payne a few days ago."

Cade chewed and swallowed, losing all interest in the last bites of his sandwich. "The Sovereign tracked her to Gaia?"

"No," Brendan replied. "She heard the news about Will."

Cade could count on one hand the number of people who called Admiral Schreiber by his first name. Brendan was now one of them, which emphasized how much the two men had bonded since Aurora brought them together. "How did she react?"

Brendan picked up his iced tea glass and took a sip. Afternoon sunlight bathed the amber liquid, making it glow. "She was deeply concerned. And angry. Very, very angry."

"You sensed that?"

Brendan chuckled. "I'm not *that* good. She's in another star system, after all. But she expressed herself quite clearly."

"Is she planning to come back for the trial?"

"I hope not," Libra said, placing her napkin beside her plate. "I hate for her to risk the safety of her family now that they have sanctuary on Gaia. Not after what you all went through to help them."

"And what the Suulh are still doing to help them," Cade agreed. It had been a risk to involve Libra's extended family and friends in the rescue, but getting Payne's grandson Keenan out of the Sovereign's clutches had been worth it.

"Who is Admiral Payne?" Unity asked.

"She's a Fleet officer," Cade answered. "Before we met up with you and the Yruf, we broke her grandson out of a hospital where the Sovereign's minions were holding him hostage as leverage to force Payne to manipulate Aurora. We took Keenan, his family, and Admiral Payne to Gaia to stay with the Suulh there."

"Oh." Unity swayed side to side. "Lelindia has told us about the Suulh on Gaia, but she never mentioned Admiral Payne or Keenan. Are they your friends?"

"Uh, I didn't spend much time with them." Cade shot a look at Brendan.

Amusement drifted off him like streamers of cotton candy. "I think you'll find, Unity, that humans have much more complicated relationships than the Yruf. Your exposure to Aurora's crew and Cade's unit has no doubt given you insight into family dynamics and strong friendships, but there are many different types of relationships, including colleagues, partners, acquaintances, and a slew of other terms that attempt to define our various interactions with each other."

"So not everyone is considered family, friend, or adversary?"

Libra snorted. "That would certainly make things simpler."

Brendan gave her a crooked smile. "We humans don't tend to do simple."

Libra smiled back, the look in her eyes so much like Aurora's it made Cade's chest hurt. "So I noticed."

The tender emotions underlying the exchange tunneled deeply into his heart, settling in as a dull ache.

In thirty years, would Aurora still be looking at him the way Libra was looking at Brendan? The fact that her parents' relationship had endured despite all the challenges they'd faced gave him hope. He certainly didn't want to end up like his parents, emotionally dead inside.

Stellar light, he missed Aurora. It felt like decades had passed since he last held her.

Brendan's gaze flicked to his, understanding in his eyes.

Cade cleared his throat. "Did Admiral Payne say anything else?"

"She wanted to know how she could help."

"Could she?" That would be a boon.

"Tough to know at this point. She can't affect the trial directly – no one in the Fleet can – but she's experienced the Sovereign's brutality and blackmail firsthand. Depending on what evidence trial counsel is bringing against Will, that knowledge might come into play."

"Did you send a reply?"

"Yes. I promised to keep her updated as things developed."

"You think she might come back and testify?" Libra asked. "Despite the dangers?"

"She might."

"But how can she without exposing her family?" Anxiety billowed up around Libra like a cloud. "Without exposing *ours*?"

The shadow she cast raised goosebumps on Cade's arms.

Brendan reached out and clasped her hand. "It's possible Aurora's presence will be enough to turn things around without involving Payne. Clearly the Sovereign had counted on keeping her in Teeli space until Will's trial was over. That means she's likely to be a key part of his defense. Her unexpected return this early in the game should tip things in our favor, knock the Sovereign's plans off track."

Libra looked somewhat mollified. "I hope you're right."

"Me, too."

Cade settled back in his chair. "My team discussed that point. We think trial counsel will focus on the Admiral's secret mission to Gallows Edge. They could manipulate the facts to make his capture by Tnaryt look like a voluntary meeting and collaboration. Then they could loop it back to the attack on Gaia, strengthen the connection between the Admiral and the Etah."

"Which would make Aurora the perfect witness for the defense," Libra said. "She saw what happened on Tnaryt's ship, and with the Setarips on Gaia. No wonder the Sovereign wanted her as far away as possible."

"And she still doesn't know Aurora's coming back. That's another ace in the hole." The fact that they had Siginal to thank for the warning scraped like sandpaper, but he'd take the burn if it meant springing the Admiral. "Have you talked to Knox?" he asked Brendan.

"Yes. He saw his dad on Saturday. Apparently they're keeping Will in solitary for his protection."

Cade winced. In some ways, solitary confinement might be worse than what the Admiral had endured on Tnaryt's ship. "They really think one of the other prisoners might harm him? He's the Fleet Director."

Brendan's voice softened. "Not anymore."

A knot twisted in his stomach. He couldn't let himself think about the implications of that comment or he'd start sliding down a very slippery slope. "Okay, but these are Fleet personnel in a Fleet facility. And he's innocent until proven guilty. Surely he'd be okay in the general population."

Brendan shrugged. "Maybe it's another one of the Sovereign's manipulations. Or maybe there really is a risk. I assume you're aware of the protests that have kicked up around Fleet HQ?"

"Yeah, Reynolds let us know. This whole thing," he swirled a hand in the air, "has a feeling of unreality to it. Who protests against the Fleet? We've been the bastions of exploration, peacekeeping, and goodwill for a century."

"And now the Sovereign is trying to convince the populace that Will is corrupt. If he's no longer in charge of the Fleet, he's no longer a threat to her goals."

"She'll lie, manipulate, and terrorize to bring him down." The sourness in Libra's voice would make a lemon pucker. "If she can misdirect everyone's attention onto him, convince them that he's the one working with the Setarips to destroy the Union, then her job gets a lot easier."

"Which is why we need Aurora here, ASAP," Cade agreed. "Lelindia, too. She's the one who saved the Admiral's life after she, Jonarel, and Reynold's pulled him off Tnaryt's ship. She can testify regarding the battle with the Teeli ships and how close the Admiral came to dying as a result."

Brendan sat up straighter. "Is there any proof those ships were Teeli?"

"Unfortunately, no. Star has vids of the battle, but that doesn't help us. The Teeli carriers and warships we've encountered look nothing like the passenger vessels they've brought to Earth. Intentionally, I'm sure, to maintain their pacifist façade."

Libra growled, her anger cracking like a whip.

"And all the troops Justin and I encountered on the planet were concealed behind the mesh uniforms the Sovereign likes so much. We never *saw* a Teeli during that confrontation, just Kreestol, the Ecilam, and the mesh-covered soldiers, all of whom most likely were Teeli. But we have no proof. The Sovereign is very, very good at covering her tracks."

Brendan lifted his iced tea and took a long, slow drink, his gaze on the aquamarine water of the Pacific. "Then we'll have to be very, very good at uncovering them."

Ten

Lelindia sorted through the medical files gathered on the desk display in her office. Bringing one to the front, she read the trauma list she'd recorded.

Second and third degree burns over eighty percent of epidermis. Second degree burns of the trachea. Broken pubic bone. Broken femur. Erratic heartbeat. Kidney failure.

She sighed. That had been her initial evaluation of the Admiral's condition when she'd knelt beside him in Tnaryt's burning wreck of a ship. He'd been so close to death, his body's systems failing in a cascade, she'd feared she couldn't save him. But with Jonarel and Reynolds' help, she'd pulled him out of that nightmare, and once they were safely back on the *Starhawke*, she'd restored him to vibrant health.

Unfortunately, she now had the monumental task of figuring out how she would explain his extraordinary recovery to a Fleet panel. In normal circumstances, such injuries would have confined him to a hospital for months and left significant scarring of his skin, as well as bone calcification at the break points.

Instead, a medical scan of the Admiral today would reveal no indication he'd suffered any of the injuries listed in her files.

Good for his health.

Bad for proving to a panel that the Setarips had held him prisoner.

She had no doubt she'd need to prove that fact. The only way a plausible argument could be made against the Admiral for conspiring with the Setarips against the Fleet would be to allege that the Admiral's disappearance from Hydra One and resulting arrival at Gallows Edge and Tnaryt's ship was a pre-planned rendezvous. That he was a co-conspirator in league with the Etah, and responsible for instigating the Setarip attack on Gaia.

Her fingers curled at the thought. It was ludicrous. But with the Sovereign lurking in the shadows, rational people did irrational things. She'd seen it firsthand.

Which is why any evidence she provided for his defense had to be rock solid. But looking at the files spread before her, the proof of the Admiral's innocence was as ephemeral as tissue paper. To anyone who didn't know about her Nedale abilities, the facts didn't line up. Even worse, they could appear fabricated.

What a mess.

The door to her office opened.

"You don't look happy," Celia said as she sauntered in and claimed one of the chairs in front of Lelindia's desk.

"I'm not." She pointed to the files. "I don't have a way to explain how I healed the Admiral so quickly from his injuries. But the extent of his injuries is one of the best ways to prove he was a prisoner, not a co-conspirator."

"You can't say it was Kraed technology?"

"Not with something this extensive. If I made that assertion, Fleet medical would start pestering the Kraed to share their medical technology. They can't share what they don't have. Siginal certainly wouldn't thank me for putting him in that position."

Celia made a face. "You're right. You two have enough hurdles to leap already."

"That's putting it mildly."

"Reynolds and Jonarel could corroborate the situation on Tnaryt's ship when you rescued the Admiral, and the extent of his injuries, right?"

"Yes, but I'm now mated to Jonarel, and Reynolds has been acting as the Admiral's personal bodyguard. They're not impartial witnesses. And it doesn't solve the problem of how I healed him."

"Have you considered telling the truth?"

Her stomach did a backflip. "Now's not the best time to be revealing that information." Her hand rested on the tiny swell of her belly.

Celia's gaze followed the motion. "You're right. It's not. Okay, plan B. We...." She trailed off, looking around the room for inspiration. "Nope. Not a clue."

Lelindia propped her chin on her fist. "Which means I can't testify without potentially making things worse."

"But you may not need to. Aurora can blow this case wide open. She was a prisoner with the Admiral on Tnaryt's ship. She knows the truth about why he went to Gallows Edge and how he ended up with one of Tnaryt's collars around his neck."

That sparked an idea. "What about Nat? She was a witness, too." The spunky smuggler had risked her own life to watch over the Admiral after the explosion had trapped him under a beam. She wouldn't turn a blind eye to his incarceration.

Celia tapped her fingertips on the tabletop. "She might not be too keen to weigh in on this. After all, she was responsible for kidnapping the Admiral and Aurora at gunpoint. That's a serious offense."

"Under threat of her own life. Besides, nobody's going to press charges against her. I know she's grateful to the Admiral and Aurora. Without their help she'd still be a slave to the Etah."

"That gratitude might not extend to putting herself under the COJ's microscope. Besides, I got the impression her code of ethics is a lot more fluid than ours. That said, Aurora could try getting in touch with her through the comband she gave her. And if she doesn't respond, we can activate the tracer embedded in it, as well as the one on *Gypsy*, her shuttle." At Lelindia's startled look, she smiled. "It was Jonarel's idea. He thought it might be a good idea to check on her from time to time."

"Let me guess. Protecting her from herself?" Her mate's protective streak wouldn't be able to resist a rogue like Natasha Orlov.

Amusement lit Celia's eyes. "Uh-huh."

Lelindia hadn't spent as much time with Nat as Jonarel had, but based on what she'd gleaned, there was a ninety-nine percent chance the young woman would end up in some kind of trouble, either on Troi where they'd dropped her off, or wherever she'd headed next. She seemed to be one of those people who lived at the center of perpetual conflict, even when she tried to avoid it.

"We can keep her as a fallback option." Her gaze rested on the list of the Admiral's injuries again. "It's ironic. If I hadn't done such a great job healing the Admiral, I'd be of more help to him now."

Celia's hand covered hers. "And if you weren't so good at healing people, he'd be dead. I guarantee he doesn't have any regrets."

She managed an anemic smile. "Thanks."

Celia patted her hand. "Come on. You're eating for two now. Micah and I just whipped up a big batch of your dad's vegetable stew and it's got your name on it."

Lelindia's stomach rumbled on cue, eliciting a chuckle and a much healthier smile. "That sounded like a yes." She pushed back her chair and stood. "Lead the way."

Eleven

Justin's face was drawn tight with worry when Cade contacted him to check in. "How bad is it?" he asked his number one.

"Bad." Justin shoved a hand through his blond curls. "Reynolds has been doing an amazing job considering she's been on her own, but the protestors outside the house are ramping up toward violence."

Justin pivoted the camera view to a surveillance feed playing on the media room vid screen. Cade could make out the dark shapes illuminated by the landscape lighting near the road. The audio pickup caught a muffled chant in the background. "What are they saying?"

Justin grimaced. "You don't want to know."

"Justin."

He sighed. "String up Schreiber."

Cade jerked back involuntarily. "Seriously?"

"Yeah. They've been chanting for the past hour. Reynolds says they usually leave around nine, so we've got another..." Justin's gaze flicked to the vid screen, "hour or so to go."

"Have they tried to come on the property?"

"Reynolds had a security fence installed as soon as Knox let her know he was going to stay here. She said a few dimwits have ignored the warning signs and tried to walk down the driveway. Got a nasty repelling shock for their trouble. No one's tried it since we got here."

"The fence covers the whole perimeter?"

Justin nodded. "From the street to the top of the path that leads down to the beach."

"And Knox is determined to stay?" He asked the question, but he already knew the answer.

Justin's snort confirmed it. "He's not going to run and hide because these morons are threatening him. The fact that they're even trying to intimidate him proves how little they know about the Fleet. He didn't become captain of the flagship in the most dangerous sector of Fleet space because he's meek."

"Yeah, well, I doubt there's much thinking going on in that group." The chanting continued as a steady drone. "Do you need anything?"

Justin's smile didn't reach his eyes. "Nah. We're good. How about you? When's the *Starhawke* due to arrive?"

"Unity says they'll be here late tomorrow night or early morning Thursday. They have to match the *Rowkclarek*'s top speed so they'll arrive together."

Justin sighed. "As much as I hate seeing what's happening here, I'm grateful the Yruf got us to Earth so quickly."

"Me, too. How's Knox holding up?"

"You know Knox. Taking it in stride as much as anyone can."

"Brendan said Knox saw the Admiral on Saturday."

"Yeah. He's being held at Seaview, which opens for visitors on Fridays and Saturdays. And get this. The only visitors he's allowed are family members, so Knox is the only person who can see him."

"That sucks."

"Tell me about it. Williams was hoping he'd get a pass because he's the Admiral's physician, but the administrators wouldn't even let him submit an application. Can you imagine the pyrotechnics when Aurora and Siginal hear that? I got the impression they both planned to visit him as soon as they arrived."

"They did. I'll have Unity warn Aurora, but that won't ease the blowup when Siginal finds out. He's already hostile because of the situation with Jonarel and Lelindia."

"And itching for a fight. I know. You planning to be there when Aurora confronts him?"

"I haven't decided. Really, it's up to her and Lelindia. I want to support them however I can, whether that's hanging in the background or stepping forward to give Siginal a different target for his rage."

"And then there's the baby. That'll go over like a lead balloon." Justin ran a hand over his face, his gaze drifting to the dark shapes on the vid screen. "This whole situation is so jacked up."

"Yeah." Guilt pricked Cade as he glanced out the wide windows of the loft. No dark shapes lurked outside. Instead, streaks of peach and mauve painted the underside of the clouds and tinged the palms golden as the sun dipped toward the horizon. "You need backup? I've got some time before the *Starhawke* arrives. I could fly the shuttle to you, leave from there instead of here."

Justin's focus swiveled back to him. "No."

"But—"

"No. I'll have Williams make it a medical order if I have to. You've been burning the candle at both ends for so long I doubt there's any wick left. You need a break. This situation is likely to move quickly once the trial starts. The unit needs you in top form, not dragging your sorry butt around by a thread." Justin's head tipped, his gaze sharpening. "Though you already look better. You take a nap this afternoon?"

"Nope. Got a lecture and a healing session from Libra as soon as I stepped off the shuttle."

"Ah." The corners of Justin's lips curved. "Good. I'll thank her next time I see her."

"Got a great meal from Brendan, too."

Justin chuckled. "I'll bet. That man can cook."

"So can you."

Justin waved his hand. "Not like he can. He has serious skills. But I did promise Bella and Reynolds I'd fix a midnight buffet for us. We're taking the night shift."

Night shift. The guilt came back with a vengeance. "Are you sure you don't want me to—"

"Stop." Justin pointed a finger at the camera. "I mean it. Don't make me wake Williams. You know how he gets without his beauty sleep."

Cade's lips twitched. It was an empty threat. Williams was a teddy bear except when the safety of his patients was threatened. But he would most certainly order Cade to stay put if he had to. "Okay. But I owe you. Next chance we get, I'm having Aurora take you to Azaana for some quality time with Raaveen, Paaw, and Sparw."

Justin's eyes lit up like sparklers at the mention of the three Suulh teenagers. He loved them like they were family. "Now that's a deal I'll gladly accept."

Twelve

"He's being held in solitary?" Aurora heard the shrill note in her voice but couldn't stop it. "And only Knox is allowed to visit him?"

Unity swayed nervously. "That's what Cade said."

A swear word she never, *ever* used tumbled from her lips. She folded her arms tight to her body, then immediately dropped them and started pacing from her desk to the viewport in her office. "So the only people who are able to see and talk to him are Knox and his lawyer. Is that what you're saying?"

Unity hesitated. "That's what Cade's saying."

"Dammit." She shoved out a breath like the air had personally offended her. "Reanne, I am going to wring your neck," she muttered.

"Really?" This time Unity was the one who squeaked.

She paused. Unity was trembling as they hovered beside her. "No, not really. It's an expression. Not a very nice one. Sorry."

The tremor subsided. "Oh."

"I'm just irritated. And outraged. Ever since Siginal gave us the bad news, I've been counting the minutes until I could see the Admiral, visit him in person, make sure he's okay. Knowing that the Sovereign has blocked even that small consolation makes me..." She flicked her hands sharply in the air as she paced, trying to shake off some of the tension spreading through her body. "Agitated," she finished.

Unity bobbed. "We can understand that. Being forcibly kept from those we care about would be very unpleasant."

"Exactly."

"Cade has a bigger concern."

That halted her in her tracks. "What?"

"How will you tell Siginal?"

She closed her eyes, her head falling back as she groaned. "I hadn't even thought of that. He's going to hit the roof."

"Is he tall enough to do damage?"

"What?" She replayed what she'd said. A grin flitted over her lips. "No, it's another expression. I didn't mean physically hit the roof. I meant his emotional reaction would be so explosive that he would metaphorically rocket to the roof."

"Ah. Micah has taught us many of your expressions, but we keep learning new ones every day. It's very exciting, if sometimes confusing."

"The Yruf don't use verbal expressions like we do?" She'd never thought to ask.

"No, they don't, at least not in their language communications. But now that we think about it, their visual imagery has a similar concept. They will use images in their discussions with each other and us that carry a common frame of reference but do not directly depict what is being discussed."

"Huh. Good to know." And a topic she'd normally dive into with both feet if she wasn't hobbled by the Sovereign's machinations. "So, Siginal." She gazed out the viewport in the direction of his ship, even though it wasn't visible while they were in the interstellar jump.

She could sense him — a brooding, simmering cauldron of rage. Kraed rage had a depth and power behind it that made it distinctive from anything she'd sensed from any other species. Even if she didn't know Siginal, she'd be able to peg him as a Kraed by his emotional resonance.

And a chunk of that rage was directed at Jonarel, Lelindia, and Star.

Her upcoming conversation with him when they arrived at Sol Station was guaranteed to be rocky, especially with another wrinkle to add to the mix. Was it better to withhold the information about the restricted access to the Admiral until they'd smoothed out the major issues — Jonarel and Star's banishment and Lelindia's pregnancy — or to be up front with him as a way of breaking up his anger into smaller pieces?

Her instincts told her Siginal would want to know about this sooner rather than later. "Star?"

Star materialized a meter to her right. "Yes?"

"Do you have a way to communicate with the *Rowkclarek* during an interstellar jump *without* using the ICS?" She wanted their arrival in the Sol system to be a complete surprise. A ping on an ICS beacon while her ship was supposed to be in Teeli space would sabotage that goal.

Star shifted her non-existent weight, managing to look embarrassed despite not having a physical form. "Technically, yes. But Rowk may not talk to me."

"Hm." Star was the toughest crewmember for her to comfort. Engaging her energy field or resting her hand on her shoulder would have zero effect on the non-biological. "I know this is uncomfortable for you, and I'm sorry to put you in this position. But this is important. Would you be willing to try?"

Star's chin lifted. "Of course."

Siginal, you're a fool for turning your back on her. Hopefully the Clarek clan leader would figure that out sooner rather than later. "Thank you. Please tell Rowk that you have a message for your father from me. If he permits the message, send the following. *Admiral Schreiber is not allowed non-family visitors. Meet me on the Starhawke thirty minutes after we arrive at Sol Station to discuss next steps.*"

"One moment." Star's image froze for several seconds, then her eyelids fluttered in surprise. "Your message has been sent," she murmured, almost as an afterthought.

Aurora peered at her. "Is everything okay?"

"Yes. I just..." She shook her head. "My father has sent a reply. *We will arrive at the appointed time.*"

"That's it?"

"Yes."

"Any idea who he means by *we?*"

"I am unsure."

Her guess? As many of his crewmembers as he needed to feel he was in a position of power.

That was fine with her. He could posture all he wanted. She was still holding his feet to the fire. "Why did you seem so startled when you made contact with Rowk? Was he mean to you?"

"Mean? No. He was gracious. Even... kind."

"Really?" Good news, but unexpected. "Any idea why?"

"He.... he has always been dear to me, as I was to him. But that was before the... incident. As my father's Nirunoc brother, Rowk's bond to my father is as close as mine is to Jonarel. I expected him to despise me."

As my father does remained unsaid, but Aurora's blood heated anyway. Siginal was *such* an idiot.

Star gave a half-hearted shrug. "Maybe he was polite because the message came from you."

That didn't feel right. Rowk could have been curt and still delivered the message. She'd met the Nirunoc, had conversations with him during the weeks when members of Clan Clarek were working with her crew to build the settlement on Azaana. His behavior and attitudes reminded her more of Jonarel than Siginal. "Want to hear my theory?"

"Of course."

"Other than you, Rowk's the Nirunoc who has spent the most time observing your family and our crew. Those insights might have made him more sympathetic regarding your actions to defend us."

Star's brows lifted a fraction. "That is... intriguing."

Thirteen

Long before Cade caught a visual of the *Starhawke* on the shuttle's forward cameras, he sensed the ship's arrival in the Sol system. He could feel Aurora's presence like a glowing beacon in the vast ocean of black that surrounded him.

The hull camouflage of the shuttle kept him from being visible to any of the other vessels entering or exiting the system, so he had to stay alert to avoid potential collisions. But that didn't prevent him from admiring the graceful curves of the *Starhawke* as it glided toward him like a majestic swan.

The *Rowkclarek*, the Kraed ship Siginal had brought into Teeli space to find them, was four times the size of the *Starhawke*. It kept pace directly to the *Starhawke*'s port side, like a protective parent dropping their child off on the first day of school. Fitting, since there was an extremely overprotective parent onboard.

The beauty of the Kraed ships placed them in a class all their own. The glittering pair made quite a visual statement amid the grey and white tones of the Fleet and privately owned vessels. The cross-traffic slowed, clearing a path like the Kraed vessels were on parade. He'd bet most of the pilots in the area were rubbernecking to get a good look at the two ships.

A chime sounded in the cockpit, alerting him that Star was ready for him to dock. He switched his attention to the controls, making his approach.

The softly repeated ping guided him in, though he barely needed it. He already felt like he'd been grabbed by a tractor beam. Aurora's personal tractor beam. Her emotional resonance enfolded him, her eagerness fueling his, making his hands tremble on the controls. So close now. So close.

The shuttle and ship connected, his breath catching then whooshing out on a noisy exhale as the shuttle rose into the bay.

I'm home.

He couldn't get out of his harness and shut down the shuttle's systems fast enough. Every second lasted an eternity. Shoving out of his chair he turned, spotting Aurora through the open hatch, sprinting across the bay. He leapt the shuttle's ramp in a single stride, catching Aurora in his arms as she hurled herself at him, their momentum spinning them both in a dizzy circle.

Her lips found his, both of them laughing in choked gulps as they broke apart for air and came back together.

"Stellar light, I missed you." He tunneled his fingers into her hair, which was uncharacteristically free of her usual braid, and kissed every millimeter of skin he could reach on her lips, cheeks, and throat.

"Ditto," she replied, her energy field caressing him with exquisite attention as her fingers gripped his shoulders and her legs wrapped around his waist.

He'd never received a more enthusiastic welcome in his life. He bathed in the emotions pouring off her in a tidal wave, soaking up what they'd both been denied for weeks.

He snugged her in tighter, deepening the kiss.

Her energy field wrapped them in a sensual embrace.

When he finally came up for air, he gazed into the gold-flecked beauty of her green eyes, utterly captivated by what he saw in their depths. "Hi."

She stared back just as intently. "Hi."

"Is this how you greet all your guests?"

Her throaty laugh swept away all traces of the grey gloom that had dogged him ever since they'd parted.

She gave a saucy toss of her head, the light picking out the red and gold tones of her hair. "Only the ones I'm in love with."

"Glad to hear it." He hugged her close before easing back and setting her on her feet. "This isn't exactly Fleet protocol."

She disengaged her energy field. "Nope." Her eyes sparkled. "But I knew we'd have the bay to ourselves."

"Except for us," Micah's voice spoke up behind Cade.

He turned.

U-2 was hovering outside the shuttle, the ramp already closed behind them.

"Hi, Unity," Aurora called out, motioning U-2 forward.

Unity bobbed closer. "We're glad you and Cade are back together. He's been miserable without you."

Aurora's chuckle overlaid Cade's groan. "Thanks for keeping my secrets, buddy."

"It was a secret?" Unity sounded alarmed. "But we all knew. Aurora has been miserable, too."

Now it was Cade's turn to chuckle. "Clearly it wasn't a secret." He grinned at Aurora. "But it's good to have full disclosure."

She grinned back. "Absolutely. No secrets."

Lacing his fingers through hers, he walked with her toward the corridor, Unity hovering along beside them.

"So Unity, now that we have two of your mobile units onboard, how are we going to be able to tell you apart?" Aurora asked.

"Do you need to tell us apart?"

"We might, especially for assigning tasks, like if I need one of you on the bridge and one in the med bay or greenhouse. Using U-1 and U-2 to refer to you was nice shorthand."

"Oh. We hadn't thought of that. No problem." A ripple of movement passed around the middle of the egg-shaped mobile unit, leaving behind a black chevron pattern embedded in the emerald green of the rest. "Will that work?"

Aurora's steps slowed, surprise and amusement flitting across her face. "Yep. That'll do. Thanks."

When the lift doors parted on the bridge, Kire rose from the captain's chair.

Micah stood from the companion chair beside him and stepped forward. "Cade! Good to have you back."

He accepted Micah's enthusiastic handshake and one-armed hug. "Good to be back."

Kelly gave him a friendly nod and Celia shot him a welcoming smile.

Yep, he was home.

He spied Sol Station on the bridgescreen, but not yet close enough to denote they were making their final approach. The *Rowkclarek*'s starboard side was partially visible to port.

"What's our docking status?" Aurora asked Kire as she settled into the captain's chair.

"We're in a holding pattern for now," Kire replied. "Siginal requested that both our ships be docked on the same concourse close together. Station command seemed quite happy to accommodate him, so we're waiting on two freighters to disembark to clear the necessary berths."

"And then we'll see who he's included in the invitation I sent."

"Invitation?" Cade moved toward his usual seat, but Micah motioned him to the companion chair right beside Aurora and claimed Cade's chair for himself.

He wasn't about to argue, sliding in next to Aurora.

"Before we head planetside," she replied, "I'm going to sit Signal down with Lelindia, Jonarel, and Star, and clear the air. They're planning to tell him about the baby."

"Ah." That would be a tension-filled conversation. As he'd told Justin, he'd like to be there to offer his support, but his presence would probably cause more trouble for the beleaguered couple, not less. "Just so you know, Unity already told your folks about the baby."

"We didn't know it was a secret," Unity piped up from their position beside Micah.

Aurora frowned. "Were Marina and Gryphon there?"

"No." Cade shook his head. "They're up north at the moment."

"Good." She sighed. "I know Lelindia wants to be the one to tell them."

"We won't say anything to anyone else," Unity assured her. "Cade explained about secrets." Unity paused. "Though clearly we don't understand all the nuances yet."

"You don't need to." Micah gave Unity a friendly pat. "You're used to open communication. Don't let us trip you up."

"He's right," Aurora said. "The Yruf don't keep secrets from each other the way we do. Micah and I will make sure you know if there's information you shouldn't share with someone outside the crew. Speaking of which, I wasn't planning to tell Signal about your presence during our discussion today. He'll have enough to deal with already. You'll need to stay out of sight while he's here."

Unity bobbed. "We can do that."

"Good."

She'd handed Cade an opening for his conundrum. "What about me?"

Her brows lifted. "Do you *want* to see Siginal?"

"Not particularly, but I do want to be there for Lelindia and Jonarel. And Star," he added, his gaze sweeping the bridge. "Siginal needs to know Jonarel and I aren't at each other's throats anymore."

"Good point. That might help."

"I want to be there, too," Micah said, his voice cooling several degrees. "He tried to strongarm you and Lee-Lee. He's not going to do that ever again."

A look passed between Micah and Aurora that almost made Cade shiver. "No, he's not," Aurora agreed.

If Siginal wasn't cowed by the combined strength Aurora and Micah were projecting, the Kraed was a galaxy-class imbecile.

Fourteen

Jonarel smoothed his hand down his dark brown tunic, running a critical eye over the reflection in his bathroom mirror. The tunic's design was more formal than what he typically wore onboard the *Starhawke*, with gold braiding around the collar and along the sleeves. He had pulled his hair back in a traditional Kraed style that he rarely wore because it felt constraining. However, he couldn't argue with the overall effect – respectful, confident gravitas.

Movement behind him drew his gaze to the doorway.

Lelindia stood in the opening, her lips parted and eyes wide. "You look... intimidating."

He closed the distance in one stride, pulling her into his arms. "You are intimidated?"

Her expression took on a slightly wicked cast. "Not when you look at me like that."

The warmth in her eyes had a predictable effect, his body responding to the pull of his mate's intoxicating scent. Two things kept him from acting on his desire – the imminent meeting with his father, and the slight bulge of her belly pressing against him.

He was the only one who knew her body well enough to detect the difference, but soon her clothing would no longer disguise the growing curve.

Their child. Their daughter.

He cradled her face in his hands. "I want you more with each breath I take."

Her soft smile added to his emotional intoxication. "I've never wanted anyone but you."

How had he spent all those years with her and not realized the truth? Not realized his mate was already standing by his side, a hand's breadth away? Thank the stars he had finally come to his senses.

He rested his forehead against hers, soaking up this moment, imprinting it to give him strength for the battle ahead.

"It's going to be fine," she whispered, her hands caressing the back of his neck, drawing him closer. "We have each other. We have our daughter. And we have Aurora fighting by our side."

"I know." But the next hour was not likely to be an easy one.

Lelindia pulled back, giving him an appraising onceover. "That being said, I'm all for you looking as intimidating as possible. I hate it when your father tries to bully you. Or me."

He sighed. "In his eyes, he is looking out for the interests of our clan and our world. He would not call that bullying."

"Maybe not, but the effect is the same. He thinks he's right, and no one's supposed to argue. Case closed."

Her anger made her eyes darken and her skin flush. He fought the urge to sweep her up and carry her to the sleeping nook behind her. "Aurora will not allow that. And neither will we."

"Damn straight."

Her scowl was so adorable, he leaned down and brushed his lips across hers. Her soft whimper when he lifted his head grabbed him like a vise, but he forced himself to step back. They both needed to remain focused on his father's impending arrival.

He held out his hand, and Lelindia clasped it. The tantalizing stroke of her thumb along his skin let him know she was battling the same emotional push-pull.

"Do you want to wait for him in the observation lounge or meet him with Aurora in the cargo bay?" she asked.

Which would set the right tone? "I would like—"

"Hawke to Clarek."

He tensed. Something was wrong. He could hear it in her voice. "Yes?"

"I need you and Lelindia on the bridge. We've got a situation developing."

"My father?"

"No." The single syllable fell like a hammer.

That was even more disturbing.

Lelindia's hand clamped down on his, worry darkening her eyes.

An answering tension expanded in his chest. "On our way."

"Something to do with the Admiral?" she whispered, as if afraid to give the thought room to grow.

"Perhaps."

When the lift doors opened onto the bridge, he found Aurora, Cade, Kire, and Micah standing in a semi-circle facing the bridgescreen, their expressions grim.

Celia and Kelly sat at tactical and navigation. Even though the ship had docked minutes earlier, Kelly's fingers twitched as they hovered above the surface of the console.

Her agitation made his heart rate shoot up even more than the foreboding look shadowing Aurora's eyes. Kelly never reacted emotionally. A bomb could go off on the bridge and she would barely flinch.

He cleared his throat. "What is wrong?"

Aurora unfolded her arms and swept her hand toward the bridgescreen. "We have a welcoming committee."

The image showed one of the *Starhawke's* exterior camera views, this one looking down the length of the airbridge that connected the ship to Sol Station. Two figures were making their way toward the ship, hands on their holstered weapons. Four more were visible at the entrance to the airbridge. All six were dressed in Fleet Security uniforms, their body language radiating the same tension crackling through the bridge.

"Captain."

Tehar appeared facing Aurora.

Jonarel sucked in a breath. His sister looked like a cornered relquir, yellow eyes flashing and lips pulled back from her teeth in a snarl.

"Four Fleet patrol yachts have moved into position directly behind and in front of us, with six more Fleet vessels — two yachts and four frigates — converging at the station perimeter."

"Now we know why they had us in a holding pattern so long," Celia muttered.

Jonarel hauled Lelindia into the protective circle of his arms, his instincts screaming a warning. "What is going on?"

Aurora took a slow, shuddering breath before turning to face him. "It looks like I'm about to be arrested."

Fifteen

Saying the words out loud didn't make them any more believable to her subconscious. But Aurora made herself give them form. If she couldn't accept it, she couldn't fight it.

"You?" Lelindia stiffened like Aurora had jabbed her with a sharp point. "Fleet Security told you that?"

"Not directly. But they will as soon as I step outside the ship. Celia spotted increased Fleet activity around the station before we docked. We thought it might be in response to the Admiral's arrest and the demonstrations that Cade warned us about. But then the FS officers moved into position at the entrance to our airbridge after we connected." She tilted her head toward Star. "Star was able to listen in to all communications in the airbridge. They're here for me."

Flashes of anger hit her from all sides, the strongest from Cade and Micah, though Lelindia and Jonarel weren't far behind.

"Just you?" Jonarel's arms tightened around Lelindia.

Aurora's heart stuttered as her gaze met Lelindia's, realization striking them both at the same time. *The baby.*

Cade's hand came to rest at the small of her back, but Kire was the one who answered.

"I took the liberty of tapping into all nearby FS communications after Star alerted us," Kire said, touching his earpiece.

Her gaze snapped to his.

He shrugged, like hacking the FS comm system wasn't a big deal. "Roe's the only one they've mentioned so far. If they planned to arrest anyone else onboard, they would have identified the targets already. They haven't. Lelindia shouldn't be in any danger."

"But Aurora is," Lelindia growled like a momma bear defending her cub.

Jonarel's protective rage matched Lelindia's. He kept his mate firmly secured behind the muscled enclosure of his arms, but his eyes glowed like liquid gold as he met Aurora's gaze. "They will not take you."

"You got that right," Cade and Micah said in unison. Cade's palm spanned her waist, drawing her closer. Micah closed the gap on her other side.

Oh, how she wished it were that simple. She loved them all for wanting to make it true. "And what do you propose we do?" She tilted her face up to Cade. "We're attached to a space station with thousands of Fleet personnel and civilians onboard, and thousands more on the surrounding ships. Are we going to fight our way out?" She turned to Jonarel. "Kill or injure innocent people?"

His dark brows lowered like thunderclouds. "My father would assist us."

"I'm sure he would." It was one of her biggest concerns, slightly edging out the certainty of her impending incarceration. A protective Kraed was very, very dangerous. And she had an entire ship full docked to their stern. "But there are already ten ships blockading us. Can you honestly say we could unmoor the *Starhawke* and *Rowkclarek* from the station and evade ten Fleet ships without causing hundreds of casualties?"

Star's image fluttered, drawing her attention. "Rowk has reported two additional patrol yachts have moved in behind him."

Star was in communication with Rowk? That was unexpected, but helpful. "Star, make it very clear to your father he's not to take any action, is that understood?"

Another flutter. "My father is... unhappy."

Join the club.

One thing was certain. They wouldn't be having their little sit down today.

Ice chips of anxiety picked at her nerve endings, chilling her. This was one battle where her Sahzade abilities couldn't protect her.

"There has to be something we can do." Micah rubbed the back of his neck, his gaze darting to Celia. "Any ideas?"

Celia had been watching her closely during the entire interchange. Aurora could practically see the tactical scenarios her friend was analyzing in her head — testing, sorting, and discarding.

But a new concern leapt out of the shadows before Celia could give a recommendation. "Wait a minute. I may not be the only one in danger here." Her gaze locked onto Cade. "They don't know you're onboard the *Starhawke*. You left Sol Station on *Gladiator*. If they find you here, they might arrest you, too. You're the next logical target in the Sovereign's sweep."

His fingers tightened, pressing against her hip, but he shook his head. "I thought of that, but if she wanted them to arrest me, she would have had a boarding party like this one waiting for my team when they arrived at the station days ago. She's seen *Gladiator*. She knows the ship's linked to me and you. But that didn't happen. And my team hasn't encountered any FS personnel since they went planetside, either."

"Actually, that makes sense. Logically she'd need to capture me first. If she went after you, she'd tip her hand. She needs me out of the way so I can't protect you." She winced at the edge of fear in her voice. *Keep it together, Sahzade.* But the thought of Cade in the Sovereign's clutches terrified her on an atomic level. "We need to get you off the ship."

"He could take one of the shuttles," Celia suggested, her tone way calmer than Aurora was managing. "With the hull camouflage engaged, no one would see it launch, and it's small enough he could navigate through the blockade." Her gaze met Aurora's and held. "You could go with him."

Her breath caught.

"That's a great idea!" Micah clapped his hands together, a hint of sunshine gilding the overhanging clouds. "You could hide out at Dad's house. Or on the Yruf ship."

Cade's answering emotional surge gave her a momentary lift. They could slip away. Escape the Sovereign's trap. Buy time.

Simple. Easy.

But the vision was as fragile as a soap bubble. Reality popped it like a pin, dropping her back on terra firma.

Running wouldn't solve anything. And it would leave her ship and friends vulnerable. That wasn't a trade she would ever make. "I can't go."

"Why not?" Cade barked.

She wasn't the only one fighting fear.

She forced herself to meet his gaze. The pain, guilt, and desperation she felt in his emotional field showed plainly in the green depths of his eyes. "It would make me look guilty, for one. Innocent people don't run."

"They do when they're being framed. And the crew could tell the FS they dropped you off somewhere before they returned here. Gallows Edge, maybe? Then you're not running, you're just not onboard."

Her throat squeezed, moisture gathering behind her eyes. She wanted to agree. Stellar light, she wanted to. He wasn't wrong. But he wasn't right, either. "It would still look like I was avoiding capture, which I would be. And then what? Hiding out would mean turning our backs on the Admiral. We can't help him if we've disappeared. Trial counsel could use our absence in the case against him."

That scored a point. Cade's loyalty to the Admiral was as fervent as hers.

"The Admiral has my father to defend him," Jonarel said quietly.

"That won't help if trial counsel has tied me into the charges against the Admiral, which Fleet Security's presence here indicates they have. FS must have a standing order to detain me as soon as the *Starhawke* entered Fleet space." Her gaze swept the small circle. "Besides, if Cade and I ran, we'd be leaving the rest of you holding the bag."

"We could handle it," Kire countered.

"We've managed without you before," Lelindia added with a mirthless smile. "We'd be okay."

"But you weren't being scrutinized by FS before. If I'm AWOL, Fleet Command will shut you down. They might even make a case for impounding the ship. If I'm in custody, you can still function as an adjunct of the Fleet."

"Doing what?" Kire asked. "Do you honestly think they're going to give us a mission while you and the Admiral are in the brig? Or that we'd take it if they did?"

She rubbed her temple, where a tension headache had set in. "No, but we need to keep our options as open as possible. If I'm detained, you'll still be free to move around. If I flee, I'll be putting you all under a microscope, indefinitely. That won't help me." Her gaze met Lelindia's. "And it certainly won't help the Suulh."

The look in Lelindia's eyes could cut glass. "You can't help them from the brig. They need you, Sahzade."

"I know they do. That's why I'm doing this. Don't mistake my acceptance of our current situation as a sign of defeat. I have no intention of ending up in permanent confinement, no matter what machinations the Sovereign is orchestrating behind the scenes. But running now would be short-term gain, long-term loss. I won't make her job easier by acting like I've committed whatever crimes she's had me accused of. I'll never clear my name that way. This battle has to be fought out in the open."

"What if you lose?" Micah voiced the question dangling over her head like a noose. His neck muscles stood out thick as bulkhead beams, his breathing unsteady.

She leaned into him, their unique connection soothing her even as her heart pounded with a sense of impending loss.

I love you, big brother.

"It'll be okay," she murmured, projecting as much confidence as she could muster. "And if it's not..." Her gaze moved to Jonarel, Lelindia, Celia, Kelly, Kire, and Cade in turn. "We'll enter that asteroid field when we come to it."

Sixteen

Cade's forced exhalation would have spewed fire if he was able. But it was the helplessness that came after it that shredded his soul. "Rory…"

She pivoted, resting her hands on his chest and holding his gaze. "I know you're scared. So am I. But whatever this is." She lifted her chin toward the image on the bridgescreen. "It's not going to blow over. I'm not abandoning my crew, leaving them to deal with my problems. And I won't spend the rest of my life as a fugitive, unable to show my face, unable to help my people."

"So you'll turn yourself into a prisoner?" He'd just gotten her back. He couldn't let her go again. Not now. Not like this.

She forced a small smile. "I've been a prisoner before. It didn't end well for the Sovereign. And a Fleet brig is a lot more comfortable than Tnaryt's ship. Food will be better, too."

The joke fell flat, not a whisper of amusement in anyone's emotional field, including his.

She turned to Kire, who was staring at her in uncharacteristic silence. "You'll be acting captain while I'm gone. Do whatever is necessary to protect the crew. Understood?"

Cade sensed a mountain of meaning behind her words, all of which Kire took on the chin. "Understood."

Her gaze shifted to Celia and Star. "Give him whatever backup he needs. Enlist Unity's or Ifel's help if you have to, but don't let the Fleet or the Sovereign find out about them."

Cerberus, the mythical three-headed dog guarding Hades' realm, couldn't have looked more intimidating than Celia and Star at that moment. "We will," Celia assured her.

"Kelly."

The young pilot sat up straighter, her skin a shade paler than normal.

"You're the *Starhawke*'s pilot, now and always. Don't let *anyone* – human or Kraed–" her gaze flicked toward the stern of the ship where the *Rowkclarek* was docked, "–tell you otherwise."

Two spots of color appeared in Kelly's cheeks. She nodded solemnly. "Yes, Captain."

Aurora pivoted to Jonarel and Lelindia. "Will you be able to handle Siginal?"

The pair shared a wry look. "Your arrest is likely to distract my father from his concerns about us," Jonarel said.

"Will he do anything rash to free me?"

"I do not believe so. But we will discuss the situation with him... after."

Cade swallowed. After she was hauled off to the brig.

"Sahzade." Lelindia's voice held a wistful quality as she stepped forward and clasped Aurora's hands in hers. "I know better than to try to change your mind. I lost that battle when you were five. But are you sure there's no other way?"

"I'm sure."

Cade couldn't accept that. He tried one more gambit. "If the charges against you are similar to the Admiral's, they'll place you in solitary for your protection, just like they did with him."

Aurora's tight nod implied she'd considered that possibility. "I'll be fine."

Fine. The word that meant she was anything but.

Lelindia searched Aurora's gaze. "Promise me that you'll check in with me every day, and that you'll respond any time I reach out to you."

The updraft of Aurora's emotions mirrored his. *Thank the stars for Lelindia.* Her Suulh abilities would allow the two of them to communicate with each other without FS having a clue. That would be a huge help in navigating the rough waters ahead.

Aurora pulled Lelindia into a fierce hug. Their energy fields engaged, twining together in a beautiful tapestry of emerald green and pearlescent white. "I promise." Her harsh whisper contained tears, but when she pulled back, her eyes were dry.

Her gaze moved to Jonarel. "Take care of these two." She gave a significant look at Lelindia's abdomen.

Jonarel circled his arm around Lelindia's shoulders. "Always."

Aurora's sigh hinted at the emotional tremors and quakes below the surface that she was working so hard to conceal.

But Cade felt them all.

Micah slid his arms around Aurora from behind, hauling her against his chest and resting his cheek on top of her head. "Don't go."

Her face scrunched up, sadness leaking out of her pores. "I have to."

Micah's eyes squeezed shut, like a kid trying very hard not to see the monsters in the closet. His exhale ruffled Aurora's hair. "I'll call Dad. He'll have a lawyer on a plane before you're planetside."

A smile ghosted over Aurora's lips. She leaned back, meeting Micah's gaze. "Make sure you tell Mom I'm okay. She'll worry."

"*She'll* worry?" Micah muttered, worry already carving lines across his brow. But he made a valiant effort at a closed mouth smile. "Yeah, I will." He released her with palpable reluctance, his fingers trailing on her arm before dropping off.

Aurora took a deep breath, her gaze sweeping the group. "Any questions?"

The silence rang louder than a gong.

"Then I'll go change into my uniform and head for the cargo bay."

Celia stood. "We'll meet you down there."

Aurora opened her mouth, closed it, then nodded.

Cade captured her hand in his before she could step away. She didn't resist, allowing him to walk with her to the lift. He didn't say anything until they'd reached their cabin and she'd begun to change into her Fleet uniform. "Are you sure about this?"

She pulled the navy tunic over her head and ran her fingers through her hair. "Sure? I'm never sure about anything when it comes to the Sovereign. But I'm sure running isn't the answer." She traded her leggings for her grey uniform pants, sliding them over her hips.

He bit back a groan of aggravation. During the long weeks on the Yruf ship, he'd envisioned the moment he'd have her alone in their cabin again, her clothes falling to the floor. But instead of bliss, his heart was being steadily excised from his chest. He watched her transform from the passionate woman he loved into the calm, collected Fleet captain who was facing solitary confinement for crimes she didn't commit.

She fastened her jacket with brisk precision, but he stopped her before she could thread her golden locks into a braid, cupping her jaw in his palm, his thumb tracing the line of her cheekbone. "I hate this."

"I know." She rested her hand over his, like she was imprinting the feeling of his touch.

He drank her in. They'd both need this moment to sustain them in the days, weeks... stellar light, *months*, ahead. The oasis they'd both been anticipating had turned into a mirage. "I will get you out of this."

Her pupils dilated, her emotional field shifting to a primal fear that sliced across his heart. "Please, don't. I want you to stay out of sight no matter what."

He gaped at her. "Do you really think I'm her next target?"

"You would be if I were her. Taking you away from me—" Her eyes glistened, her voice catching. "She wants me to suffer. And if you…" She trailed off, shaking her head as the depth of her emotions engulfed him. "I honestly don't know what I'd do."

He could imagine. The Sovereign was taking her away from him right now. What he wanted to do wasn't rational or smart, but it didn't stop him from wanting to act.

Instead he allowed his fierce longing to pull them together like magnets, his lips meeting hers in a kiss that was pain, sorrow, and promise all in one. Her energy field flared, holding him in its embrace as her lips moved over his, agony and extasy.

She'd turned him away once to keep him safe. That hadn't worked out for either of them. But this was different. She was asking him to protect himself so that at the end of this torturous road, he'd be waiting for her.

How could he say no to that?

Breaking the connection made his soul bleed, but if he allowed the kiss to continue, he'd never be able to let her go.

He cupped her face in his hands. "I'll stay here. If security comes onboard, I'll hide."

"You will?"

The hope in her voice tugged at the ragged edges of his emotional wounds. She asked so little, and gave so much in return. "Yes. And if it seems like the right move, I'll take Celia's suggestion, use the shuttle to get off the ship. I'll take U-2 with me in case I need Ifel's help."

Her breath warmed his lips as she exhaled, her eyes drifting closed. "Thank you."

"We'll get through this," he promised her.

The barest hint of a smile softened her mouth. "I love you."

His smile was just as hard won. "I love you, too."

A second ticked by, then two, before she drew back, her hands moving to twine her hair into the smooth French braid she preferred. Grabbing a hair tie from a drawer, she secured the end, then ran her hands over her uniform, tugging on the hem of her jacket. "How do I look?"

Like a goddess. "Like a Fleet captain."

Her nod was efficient, the emotional armor she'd forged during her years with the Fleet settling squarely on her shoulders as she lifted her chin.

He felt the loss like she'd dropped a bulkhead between them.

Her gaze was clear, direct. "I'll see you soon."

A lie, but he'd play along. He had to clear his throat before he could respond. "See you soon."

After a long look, she pivoted on her heel and left the room.

The soft click of the cabin door cut his strings. He sank to the deck, fighting the pain that made the wood grain beneath his palms blur and shimmer. His head hung on his boneless neck, his chest heaving in hitching gasps. Droplets of moisture steadily darkened the deck by his splayed fingers. Drip. Drip. Drip.

This was wrong. So, so wrong. And there was absolutely nothing he could do to stop it.

Seventeen

As soon as Aurora and Cade left the bridge, Micah spun toward Celia. "There has to be something we can do."

"What did you have in mind?"

The calmly analytical look she gave him made his temperature redline. "I don't know! You're the security specialist here. Come up with something."

She folded her arms, completely unruffled by his outburst. "She rejected my suggestion."

"And she was right to," Lelindia said, moving to Micah's side. "If she doesn't face this now, she'll make things worse."

He scowled at her. "They," he jabbed a finger at the bridgescreen, "are going to lock her up in a cell for who knows how long."

"And we," Lelindia swept an arm around the bridge, "will get her out of that cell. But we have to be strategic about it, not reactionary."

"But—"

"What exactly are you afraid will happen to her?" Kire asked with the same measured calm Celia had displayed.

Was that a serious question? Because he was starting to reevaluate the sanity of Aurora's crew. Their stoic acceptance was ticking him off. "That they'll hurt her. That she'll suffer or hell, *die*, in there."

Kire pinned him with a look that was probably highly effective when dealing with unruly junior officers. Micah leaned away, fighting the impulse to snap to attention.

"First of all, we're talking about a Fleet brig, not a civilian prison. Order is strictly maintained, just like on a Fleet ship. And second, this is Roe, the Sahzade of the Suulh. Even if all hell broke loose, no one can harm her – not FS or her fellow prisoners. She'll be fine."

Kire's logic was sound. But that didn't stop tension from climbing up Micah's back and sitting squarely on his shoulders. "So what do we do?"

The studied calm slid away from Kire like water on glass, the light of battle shining in his eyes. "We follow her orders. You contact your dad so he can secure Roe a top-notch lawyer." His gaze shifted to Jonarel and Lelindia. "And the three of us will meet with Siginal, make sure he's not going to do anything that would escalate this situation."

"Four of us," Star interjected. "My father has already left the *Rowkclarek*, with five of our kin."

Kire stiffened. "To do what?"

"To make it clear to FS that he supports Aurora."

Celia coiled like a spring, ready to shoot toward the lift. "Will he interfere with her arrest?"

Star frowned. "Rowk is unclear on his plan."

"We need to get down there." Kire started toward the lift, pausing as he passed U-2, who had been hovering silently near Micah during the entire discussion. "Unity, get to the charging alcoves. No sounds or movement when anyone besides the crew is onboard, understood?"

Unity bobbed. "Yes, we understand."

Everyone except Unity exited the lift on the cargo deck, while the mobile unit continued down to the shuttle deck.

For reasons Micah didn't question, Celia stayed by his side, not touching, but close enough for her cool focus to contrast with the blast furnace pulsing in his veins.

She slowed her steps as the group entered the cargo bay. Aurora wasn't there yet, so he lagged back with her.

"Your sister's an exceptionally smart woman. She'll figure a way out, no matter what the Sovereign throws at her."

He stopped, giving her his full attention. "You actually believe that?" In this situation, he trusted her opinion more than anyone's. And he desperately needed something to believe in right now.

She angled her head toward where the airbridge lay beyond the bulkhead. "You haven't been in as many challenging situations with her as I have, but there's one thing I know with absolute certainty. Aurora always finds a way."

"So she meant what she said about not accepting defeat? Because to me it sounded a hell of a lot like sacrificing herself for the good of the crew."

Celia shrugged. "Oh, she'd sacrifice herself in a heartbeat if it would free the Suulh or end the Sovereign's reign of terror. Thankfully, this situation doesn't qualify. She's not about to let herself be taken off the board for long when the Sovereign's pieces are in motion."

"And she'll be okay in the brig?" He couldn't allow himself to dwell on what that would look like or he'd lose it.

She rested a hand on his arm, her touch comforting. "She'll be fine. She'll probably spend all her time worrying about us."

Yes, she would. His sister carried the weight of the galaxy on her shoulders.

The cargo bay door opened behind him. Aurora stepped through, dressed in her captain's uniform, her hair pulled back in a tight braid. Her air of command filled the expansive space, the murmur of conversation stopping with an audible click. He'd never seen her looking so implacable.

And Cade was conspicuously absent.

"Cade agreed to stay out of sight?" Celia asked as Aurora approached them.

"Yes. And to take the shuttle if it comes to that." Her jaw tightened, a small chink appearing in the measured façade of her emotional armor. "You'll make sure he sticks to that promise?"

Celia snorted. "I'll shove him off the ship myself if I have to."

Aurora's head dipped a fraction. "Thank you." Her gaze moved to Micah.

For a split second, he caught a flash of anxiety, but it vanished quickly.

"If you have any dealings with FS, don't volunteer the fact that you're my brother. But don't lie, either."

He blinked. "You think they'll question me?"

"Probably not, at least not today. But you should have Dad arrange a shuttle to get you planetside ASAP, just in case."

His lungs constricted, preventing air from coming in. He consciously inhaled, his ribs protesting the dual pressure. "You mean in case things go badly for you?"

"In case the Sovereign has more surprises for us. I don't want you caught in the crossfire."

"You're already *in* the crossfire. That's where I want to be." If she thought he was abandoning her now that the situation had turned sticky, she didn't know him as well as she thought.

Her eyes darkened to a storm-lashed green-grey. "In a few minutes, you'll likely become one of only four people who are allowed to see me. You, Mom, Dad, and my lawyer. I need you with them. That's how you can help me the most."

His throat closed. He desperately wanted to wrap his arms around her, shield her from what was coming, but his instincts told him that if he touched her, she'd lose the fingernail grip she had on her composure. "I'll be there, Ror. Count on it."

The corners of her mouth trembled, a sheen coating her eyes. "Good." Her gaze flicked to Celia. Neither spoke, but Celia gave a subtle nod to whatever non-verbal question or command Aurora was conveying. "Watch your backs."

His sister's parting words hung in the air after she turned away. Letting her go challenged his self-control to the breaking point, but he forced his feet to stay planted on the deck as she walked toward where Lelindia, Jonarel, Kire, and Kelly waited near the exterior bulkhead.

He leaned toward Celia, dropping his voice to a low murmur. "Promise me she'll be okay."

Celia's gaze didn't leave Aurora. "If she goes down, we go down."

It wasn't the answer he'd asked for, but if the chilled promise of violence in Celia's voice was any indication, she'd cut a wide swath through the Sovereign's minions before any harm came to Aurora.

A small comfort, but for now, it would have to do.

Eighteen

Jonarel felt Lelindia tense beside him as Aurora approached. His own protective instincts roared at the injustice of Aurora's dilemma, but he knew his anger was a drop in the bucket compared to what his mate was going through. Aurora was not just family to Lelindia. She was her symbiotic partner, their relationship formed from a deep emotional bond and aspects of biology and culture that had been forged for generations, maybe millennia.

Kire stepped forward. "Siginal's at the opposite end of the airbridge."

Aurora's shoulders stiffened. "What's he doing?"

"Rowk informed Star that he's showing his support for you, but we're not sure what that means. I wanted you to know."

Jonarel heard the scrape of Aurora's molars.

Her gaze turned to him. "Your father does not take direction well."

"That is an understatement." His father's behavior gave him an outlet for some of his anger. When it came to dealing with others, his father firmly believed that what worked for him on Drakar would also work well in all other situations. It was a serious fault in his leadership skillset.

"Star, can you open a comm channel to him?"

Tehar appeared beside Aurora. "Yes, though he is close to the FS officers. They would hear anything he said."

More grinding of teeth. "Then tell him to move back so I can talk to him without an audience."

"One moment." Tehar's image flickered. "Channel open."

"Siginal?"

His father's voice came from one of the deck speakers. "Aurora." He said her name warily, like she was a greewtaith he had just spotted lurked beneath the surface of the river.

"What the hell are you doing?"

Jonarel winced. Aurora's diplomacy skills were not reporting for duty today.

"What am I doing?" His father sounded outraged. "You are about to be arrested. Do you believe I will let that go unchallenged?"

"Yes, that's exactly what I believe. This is my fight, not yours, which means we're going to play this my way."

"But—"

"Nothing you say will change the outcome, and I sure as hell won't allow you to DO anything. Are we clear on that?"

The speaker hummed with background noise as the seconds ticked by.

"Siginal?" Aurora's voice sharpened like a blade. "Are we clear?"

"Aurora—"

"I'm leaving the station with the FS officers. You won't change that. If I have to, I'll use my abilities to stop whatever asinine plan you have in mind. Do you want that? It could be quite a show."

The threat reared up on its haunches and showed its teeth.

Stellar light. His father could not see Aurora's expression, so he might think she was bluffing. She was not. Her focused, dead calm made the hairs at his nape lift. If she used her energy field while on the station, her arrest would be one of several supernovas they would have to contend with today.

"What's it going to be, Siginal?"

The seconds stretched taut, a dagger suspended in the air, waiting to fall. Then his father's sigh came across the comm, more of a growl than an exhale. "Very well. I will not interfere."

Aurora's chin lifted. "Thank you." A hint of irony entered her voice. "Since you're already here, expect to meet with Jonarel and Lelindia as soon as I'm gone."

He could not be sure, but it sounded like his father choked on her words.

Kire's mouth curved. He had heard it, too.

Aurora made a slashing motion to Tehar, and the background hum cut off. The silence that followed was pregnant with the rain of the coming storm.

Aurora's gaze locked with Lelindia's. "Time to go."

His mate let out a shuddering breath that shook her from head to toe. "Remember your promise."

Aurora's eyes glittered for a moment. She blinked rapidly. "I will." Her gaze lifted to meet his.

Words shoved into his throat, clogging it before any sound could escape. A few months ago he would have moved the stars to keep her from turning herself in. But that was another lifetime. He was not that person anymore. He saw the acknowledgment of that in her eyes, the understanding.

To someone who did not grasp the marrow-deep sense of responsibility that infused every cell of Aurora's being, the trust she was placing in him to keep Lelindia and the baby safe might seem obvious, perhaps even inconsequential. He was, after all, Lelindia's mate and his daughter's father.

But Aurora was the Sahzade of the Suulh. The certainty with which she had made her decision to accept her arrest, knowing it would separate her from Lelindia during a time of vast uncertainty, showed a depth of trust that almost brought him to his knees.

And she knew. He could see it in her steadfast gaze and the set of her mouth.

She held his gaze for a moment longer, then turned to Tehar. "Star, I'm ready when you are."

Tehar bowed her head. "Be well, Captain."

"You, too."

Tehar's image vanished.

Aurora walked toward the gap in the cargo bay storage containers lining the interior of the hull, the seal for the airlock invisible until Tehar revealed it.

The Fleet security officers standing in the airbridge a few meters away both jumped as the hatch opened, their heads whipping toward Aurora.

"Officers." Aurora crossed the threshold and halted, her arms loose at her sides. "How can I help you?"

Her composure astounded him. Whatever emotions she was battling internally, they did not show in her voice or body language.

The FS officers took a couple beats to adjust. The one to Aurora's right, a muscular woman with her dark hair pulled back in a severe bun, stepped forward. "Captain Aurora Hawke, under Article 10 of the UCFJ, you are under arrest for sedition."

Sounds continued to emanate from the officer's mouth in what Jonarel assumed were Galish words, but his mind remained stuck on one point – *sedition.*

His body heated, the tips of his claws puncturing the skin of his closed fists. He tasted blood, his own, coating his tongue where he had bitten it. But the blood he wanted to spill flowed in the veins of the psychotic Human-Teeli female who had orchestrated this farce. If she stood before him, he would gut her without a second thought.

A cool hand touched his arm. He snarled before his rage-addled brain registered Lelindia's presence by his side. The coolness of her energy field spread across his body, the soothing touch countering his impotent fury and healing his self-inflicted wounds.

Wrapping his arm around her shoulders, he pulled her close, needing to offer her the same comfort she was giving to him. They stood like that, silently bearing witness as Aurora was led down the airbridge, her back straight and head held high.

The solid bulk of Jonarel's father and the five Kraed flanking him did not block the opposite end, but the FS officers kept a close eye on them as they passed.

"Siginal," Aurora said, dipping her head in his direction.

"Be well, Aurora." His father echoed Tehar's farewell, the Galish words a simplistic translation of the much more meaningful Kraed phrase *fedar sigmet naldi*, which accurately translated to *life amidst danger*.

And then she was gone.

He stared at the open space at the end of the airbridge where Aurora had been a moment earlier. The unreasonable part of his mind insisted she might reappear, that the clock might turn back time and the ugliness would vanish.

The rational part knew that it could be quite some time before he would see his beloved friend again.

Lelindia's sniffle drew his attention down.

Tears tracked along her cheeks in a steady river and her mouth trembled, her gaze locked on the same spot at the end of the airbridge he had been staring at. Then her gaze shifted to the left, her eyes narrowing. She sniffed harder, her hands coming up to swipe at her cheeks in a self-conscious motion.

He followed her gaze.

His father was making his way down the airbridge toward them, slowly, methodically, as though with each step he was laying claim to the decking beneath him.

A predator on the hunt.

Kire appeared on Jonarel's other side, Kelly beside him while Celia and Micah flanked Lelindia.

Now they were even, at least.

His father had dressed similarly to Jonarel, although his tunic was dark green with paler green accents rather than brown with gold. His hair was pulled back severely at his nape in a style usually reserved for hunting expeditions.

His father was sending a message, too.

Jonarel knew the five Clan Clarek members his father had brought with him, though none were direct kin, or anyone he considered a friend. None of them had worked with Aurora or any other member of the crew during the building of the settlement on Azaana, either. His father likely had chosen those who would be most willing to enforce his father's judgment against him and Tehar.

His father halted two meters from him, his gaze sweeping along their line, which effectively blocked the entrance to the ship. "Jonarel."

The distance in his father's voice slid like a splinter under his skin. "Father," he replied in Galish. The choice not to use his native language was a not-so-subtle reminder of his ostracized state, but also a cue to his father regarding where they were. Their actions were certainly being monitored by the bevy of FS officers at the far end of the airbridge.

Kire stepped forward, partially blocking Jonarel. "Thank you for coming, Siginal. We have much to discuss. Would you care to join us in the observation lounge?" The sentence was structured as a question, but Kire delivered it like an order, one he expected to be obeyed.

His father towered head and shoulders over Kire. He had no trouble pinning Jonarel with a flat stare as he answered. "So be it."

They made a strange – and silent – procession as they walked the short distance to the cargo lift. He, Lelindia, and Kire took the lead, with his father and his coterie behind them, and Celia, Micah, and Kelly bringing up the rear.

After they entered the lift, Celia angled herself so she kept an eye on their guests, her analyzing gaze traveled over them with precision as the lift rose. He was unsure what she planned to do if any of the Clarek clan, including his father, tried anything in the confined space, but he had no doubt she had a scenario playing in her mind that would ensure none of the crew got hurt.

Of course she was not alone in her guard duties. While Tehar was invisible, her presence surrounded them. His father was a fool if he did not believe Tehar would incapacitate him the moment he stepped out of line.

And she could. Jonarel had made certain of that when he designed the ship. He had envisioned repelling a Teeli or Setarip boarding party, not his own people, but the same principles applied.

Celia waited outside the lift as everyone else exited. She gave Jonarel a fractional nod, her gaze flicking to Lelindia, the look in her eyes conveying their common purpose. *Protect her.*

To that end, he positioned himself between his clan members and Lelindia, subtly encouraging her to walk slightly ahead of him. Her position beside Kire also reinforced her leadership role on the ship, the one his father seemed determined to dismiss or diminish. That would not happen.

The doors to the observation lounge parted. Tehar stood near the center of the room beside the ovoid table she had arranged with twelve seats. Her dark hair was styled in a severe traditional braid that pulled the thick strands away from her face, giving her jaw and chin a strong jut that was absent when she was relaxed and calm. She watched their father enter the room — a lupine alpha female monitoring an encroaching pack.

The light filtering into the room through the curve of wide windows had a subdued quality that was atypical this close to the station's myriad light sources. A glance confirmed Tehar had activated the privacy shielding that would block any of the station personnel or other ships from seeing into the expansive space.

"Tehar." His father's voice held the same controlled lack of emotion he had used when he had spoken to Jonarel.

Too bad Aurora was not here. She could have clued him in as to what his father was feeling.

A dull ache settled into his chest, the reality of her absence creating a hollow. They would get her back. *He* would get her back — for his mate, for the crew, for their futures. But first he had to deal with his father's unreasonable prejudices and misguided expectations.

"Father." Tehar stood unmoving, forcing their father to step around her to reach the table. Technically he could have walked *through* her projection, but even in his disgruntled state, he seemed unwilling to commit such an act of open aggression and disrespect.

Kire claimed the chair where Aurora usually sat, though Jonarel caught the slight hesitation in his movements before he sat down.

The hollow in Jonarel's chest expanded, pushing on his lungs. He forced a calming breath, guiding Lelindia to the chair to Kire's right and taking the seat on her other side. Celia motioned Kelly and Micah next to Kire, taking the seat between Jonarel's clan and Micah.

Tehar assumed a formal guarding stance behind Kire and Lelindia's chairs, visually reinforcing their positions of authority, just as his father's advisors would do at a clan meeting on Drakar.

The move did not go unnoticed. Scorn twisted his father's face, the chair he had selected across from Kire creaking as it accepted his bulk. The other clan members shot Tehar varying looks of contempt or disgust as they sat.

The growl that rose from Jonarel's chest was audible to the entire group. All eyes darted in his direction. "While you are in Tehar's presence and onboard her ship, you will show her respect." The threat of swift retribution overlaid each syllable.

His father swallowed, realization dawning as his gaze swung back to Tehar. Despite her outcast state, he had apparently believed she would continue acting like every other Nirunoc on Drakar under his leadership. Now he understood his mistake, and his vulnerability.

Jonarel took a certain amount of pleasure from watching the interplay of emotions on his father's face. With Aurora gone, he must have expected to take charge of the *Starhawke*. Tehar and the crew were making it abundantly clear that was not an option.

His father cleared his throat. "Of course."

The other clan members looked startled by the abrupt turnaround, but they quickly locked down their reactions, replacing their surprise with studied neutrality.

Lelindia's hand found Jonarel's under the table, her fingers lacing through his and gripping tightly. He squeezed back.

Kire folded his hands on the table with a pitch perfect composure that belied the swirling tension in the room. "Thank you for joining us, Siginal. I'd like to hear your thoughts regarding the Admiral's and Aurora's arrests—"

"Aurora—" his father started.

"But before we discuss next steps on that front," Kire cut him off smoothly, "we have some personal business to attend to."

His father stiffened. "Meaning?"

Kire turned to Lelindia. "Nedale?"

The use of his mate's Suulh title was intentional, as was the ease with which Kire turned the proceedings over to her. Just like Tehar, he was emphasizing her leadership status.

His father's lips pulled back from his teeth, his face hardening into stone.

Lelindia's exasperated sigh almost made Jonarel laugh, like she was about to scold a beloved but recalcitrant child. But her voice came out gentle and melodic, not a single harsh note, very much the patient doctor using her best bedside manner. "I regret the animosity that has developed between us, Siginal. The last time we were together, we both said and did things that caused the other pain."

Jonarel caught the twitch in his father's jaw and a slight hunching of his shoulders. Lelindia had hit the mark.

What a concept. He had considered his father's anger, bruised ego, and need for control. But he had never contemplated his father's pain. His mate was far more astute than he had been.

"I firmly believe you want what is best for Jonarel, Tehar, and Aurora. But as the Clarek clan leader, you carry great responsibility. Sometimes that burden forces you to weigh their needs against those of your clan."

If her goal was to disarm his father, it was working. Surprise briefly replaced the hostility in his gaze.

"The Teeli pose a threat to the future of your people, their toxic tendrils invisibly expanding toward your borders. Your concern is justified. I saw what the Teeli did to the Suulh, to our homeworld, to my people, including my own grandmother. I would never want to see the same fate befall Drakar. Or Earth."

The hostility returned. "Yet you seduced my son," his father said, his words chilly as a winter wind, "and denied him the mating that would save us all."

Lelindia's hand tightened around Jonarel's, but her aura of calm never wavered. "It wasn't seduction. It was love."

"*Love.*" His father snorted. "How can this," he gestured at the two of them, "be love? When you arrived on Drakar he was in love with Aurora. Love is not so fickle."

Harsh words clawed their way up Jonarel's throat, but he swallowed them back down. He would not speak unless his father addressed him directly. Lelindia needed to prove to his father she was just as capable of leading, and defending herself, as Aurora.

"You're right. Jonarel does love Aurora. I'm grateful for it. Their relationship is a gift to us all. But he's not *in love* with her. I don't think he ever was. He accepted the role you gave him because he loves you, and his clan, and wanted to do whatever was necessary to ensure your future."

"And then he turned his back on us."

"*No, he didn't.*" The vehemence in Lelindia's voice made his father's eyes widen. "Do you want Aurora's support? The support of your clans to enter the fight against the Teeli before they arrive on your doorstep? You can have both, right now. Jonarel has made that possible."

His father's look of disbelief quickly transitioned to something far uglier, his lip curling in a sneer. "How? Jonarel has mated with *you.*"

The insult he injected into that last word hit Jonarel like a slap. Flames licked his chest, the claws on his free hand unsheathing. The deep rumble of thunder filled the room. When his father's gaze leapt to his, he realized the savage sound was coming from him.

Through a haze of red, he tangentially registered his father's reaction, saw his lips slam closed and press tightly together, his large body shrink back into his chair.

A cloud of coolness enveloped Jonarel, drawing the heat of his anger away, caressing his skin in a loving but firm touch. His gaze dropped to his mate. Dropped, because he had risen from his chair and was leaning over the table, his clawed hand poised above the polished wood surface.

Lelindia gave a subtle shake of her head.

His claws itched, the instinct to defend his mate warring with his desire to please her. Millimeter by millimeter, his claws retracted beneath the surface of his skin, his resonant growl fading into nothingness.

His tendons popped as he settled back into his chair. Lelindia's soothing energy field continued to caress him until the last of his anger drained away, his mind clearing.

She gave his hand a squeeze, her cooling energy dissipating. She turned back to his father. "Jonarel's a bit protective of me, especially now." A self-deprecating smile touched her lips. "As I was saying, a way for you to gain Aurora's support and the support of your clans against the Teeli threat already exists." She paused, her free hand resting on her belly. "In a few months, Jonarel and I will welcome our daughter."

His father's face slackened.

So did the faces of the rest of the clan. If the stakes were not so serious, he would have found their reactions comical.

Lelindia knew how to deliver a stunner.

His father blinked rapidly, his gaze sweeping around the table as if trying to decide if this was an elaborate joke.

The solidarity of the crew must have convinced him it was not. "You have conceived a child?" He stared at Lelindia, stupefied, like she had informed him she had sprouted wings and flown around the room.

"More than a month ago. She'll be a Nedale, like me, but I'm fairly certain she'll have claws like her father."

More staring. "How could you know that?"

Lelindia's smile turned slightly smug. "As the Nedale, gestation is shorter for me than for most Suulh. I can also feel her energy field, and both see and feel her development in a way other Suulh can't."

His father's jaw flexed, tension rising to his mouth and eyes in a ripple. "Is the child... healthy?"

Lelindia tilted her head, like she did not trust the motivation behind the question.

Neither did he.

"Very. She's an amazing child." Lelindia's fingers stroked the slight curve of her belly, but her gaze remained locked with his father's. "And as a half-Suulh, half-Kraed daughter of the Nedale, she will bind our two races together for all time."

Nineteen

Micah watched the currents of emotion pouring off Siginal, Jonarel, and Lelindia. He'd known this moment would be charged, had braced for it, but his own emotional reaction to Lelindia's words created unexpected rapids.

Ror, you should be here.

Her absence felt like a phantom limb. He'd never been so unbalanced, so unsure of his next move. He'd expected to be talking to his dad right now — warning him about Aurora's arrest.

But that was before he'd seen how Siginal had stalked toward the ship — his *sister's* ship — possessiveness in every line of his body. Apparently Jonarel's father had a chip on his shoulder the size of Gibraltar and an ego wider than the Grand Canyon.

No way was he walking away from that threat, especially after seeing the look on Celia's face. She'd slipped toward Siginal like a leopard stalking a rival, and he'd followed her, a slight buzz in his ear, as if Aurora was whispering to him, telling him to stay and support Lee-Lee.

So he'd stayed.

Lelindia had just made a powerful assertion, but Siginal wasn't buying it. The hostility he'd been emanating since his arrival resurfaced, his features twisting and his teeth flashing in a snarl.

Time to give Aurora a voice in this discussion.

"Aurora agrees with Lelindia one hundred percent."

Siginal's gaze snapped to his, boring into him with those otherworldly golden eyes.

He fought his instinctive recoil, focusing on projecting the strength of emotion he wanted Siginal to feel behind his words. "Lelindia and Jonarel were meant to be together. The ease with which they conceived their child proves that. Their daughter will be powerful, a leader and a healer. She will also be revered and beloved by the Suulh, and as precious to Aurora as Lelindia has always been. Aurora will do anything to help and protect them both. So will the rest of the Suulh."

"And who are you to speak for her? You claim a brother's rights, yet you have been absent from her life since before she and Jonarel met. You know nothing. You *are* nothing."

Siginal was goading him. But it wouldn't work. His temperament had been forged by years of competitive surfing. He thrived under pressure. "I know my sister's heart. And I know if you fight her, you will lose."

"Lose? We have already lost. Aurora has given up her freedom without a fight. And now I am expected to accept the word of her cowardly excuse for a broth—"

"Watch it, Siginal."

Micah's gaze darted to Celia, startled by her deadly tone. The preternatural calm of Celia's outward appearance made the words even more chilling.

Jonarel's low growl filled the silence Celia's warning had created.

Damn. Being on the receiving end of that much protectiveness made his heart beat out of rhythm.

Siginal froze.

It was probably wrong to enjoy the sense of belonging that swelled within him, but he'd wondered if Aurora's departure would weaken his ties to the crew, turn him into a fifth wheel.

Apparently not.

"We're getting off point." Kire looked completely unfazed by the darts of aggression flying across the table. "Though Siginal's dead wrong regarding Aurora's actions." He pinned Siginal with that same command look Micah had been on the receiving end of on the bridge. "Her fight has just begun, and one way or another, she will win."

Siginal harrumphed. "So you say. But—" His words screeched to a halt as Cade walked into the room.

Twenty

Way to make an entrance, Ellis.

Cade had expected his arrival to draw attention, but the shock on Siginal's face, and the fury that swiftly followed, slammed into him like a gut punch.

"You!"

Starting to regret the decision to join the discussion.

After he'd felt Aurora leave the ship, he'd crumpled like a downed satellite on the floor of their cabin, his entire focus on the precious empathic connection that allowed him to feel what she was feeling. But as the minutes passed, the emotions of the crew crowded into his consciousness, the rough edges and harsh flares scraping against him.

He'd sensed the new arrivals, one of which sparked a strong memory and an even stronger internal reaction. But when he'd tried to contact Star to confirm his supposition, Unity had responded instead, informing him Siginal was indeed onboard, Lelindia was leading a spirited discussion in the observation lounge, and Star was otherwise occupied keeping an eye on their guests.

Cade had tried to ignore the emotional battle being waged on the main deck, telling himself his presence would make the situation with Siginal worse. And he may have been right. But when

Micah's emotions had spiked, he'd suddenly found himself in the lift, headed for the observation lounge. Unity gave him an audio feed of the debate through the comm system along the way.

He took his time walking toward the table, assessing the situation. "Hello, Siginal."

The over-sized Kraed had risen halfway from his seat, but so had Jonarel and Celia, their bodies poised on the razor's edge of motion. Star's projection had changed as well, her pose almost as battle-ready as Jonarel's and Celia's.

That fact didn't escape Siginal's notice. He didn't make a move toward Cade. But the lack of physical violence didn't take any of the venom out of his voice. "What are you doing here?"

Yep, he was still Siginal's least favorite person. Good to know. "I'm part of this crew. And right now, my crew is under fire." He gazed significantly at Jonarel and Lelindia.

Jonarel's startled gaze met Cade's and held for a long moment. Five months ago, Cade had fantasized about shoving the Kraed out an airlock. Now? He could not define their relationship, but he respected him, trusted him, and even... liked him.

Surprisingly, the feeling appeared to be mutual.

Jonarel straightened to his full height. "Thank you for standing with my family."

"They're my family, too." Cade shot Jonarel a half-smile, enjoying the effect their words had on Siginal's composure.

He looked like Jonarel had thrown a right hook, knocking him senseless. And no wonder. Jonarel had indicated his *family* was on the opposite side of the table from where Siginal sat.

That's where Cade belonged. "I'll grab a sea—"

Star's unseen hand moved a chair into place on Jonarel's right, pushing the Kraed who had been sitting next to Jonarel further away to make room for Cade.

"Thanks, Star."

"My pleasure."

The interchange cleared Siginal's shock like they'd doused him with cold water. He looked ready to start hissing and spitting as he glared daggers at Cade and glowered at Star.

The Kraed to Cade's right didn't seem to know how to react, her emotions a confusing mush. She stared at Jonarel like he'd grown a second head that spoke gibberish.

Cade scooted his chair closer to Jonarel so their forearms touched. Lelindia had made a comment once that the Kraed were a very tactile species, using touch as a form of connection. He'd seen it firsthand in her interactions with Jonarel. If she was right, intentionally creating physical contact with Jonarel would serve two purposes.

Surprise shot through Jonarel's emotional field, his forearm flexing them relaxing against Cade's. A burst of what felt strangely like brotherly affection followed.

Siginal flinched.

Cade fought the grin that threatened to break through. Mission accomplished. Siginal had no idea how to deal with the lack of animosity between him and Jonarel. He couldn't use them against each other anymore.

Bitterness dripped from Siginal's voice. "You choose these... people," the word popped like a cap gun, "over your own clan?"

Wry amusement and a simmering anger mixed in Jonarel's emotional field. "These *people*," he emphasized the word like it was a precious gift cradled in his arms, "stood by me when my *clan* turned against me because I dared to challenge their leader's actions."

Their leader's. Not *my leader's* or *my father's*. The emotional distance in that phrase elicited a bite of pain from Siginal as though Jonarel had slashed him with his claws.

"Even when Aurora learned I had lied to her for years – on your orders – she did not turn on me or exile me. She forgave me. Over the past few months, she and Lelindia have shown me the true meaning of family."

Siginal stared at him, his mouth hanging open. "You cannot mean that. Aurora cannot be bonded to you now. Or to Tehar. Or our clan. This..." He swept a hand to indicate the ship. "Has lost its purpose."

He really didn't get it, did he? Until that moment, Cade hadn't realized how deeply ingrained the social customs of the Kraed were, how difficult it was for Siginal to see beyond them. He needed a little enlightenment. "Jonarel is the cherished mate of Aurora's energy sister. And Star is the life blood of this ship, a ship that fits Aurora to a T. But more than that, Jonarel and Star are part of *Aurora's* family."

He let that comment settle for a moment, allowing Signal to absorb the full meaning. "Aurora doesn't need a ceremony, or a pair bonding, or any societal convention to hold someone close to her heart. She would do anything, including giving up her freedom, to protect every member of this crew. That's what family means to Aurora. If you want Aurora as part of your clan – her loyalty, her bravery, her protection – there's only one way to get it. Answer one question correctly. Can you accept Lelindia as part of your family?"

The gauntlet dropped with an audible thump.

Siginal's internal battle waged beneath the surface, his traditional expectations clashing with the paradigm Cade had presented to him. Could he alter his reality to accept a new way of thinking?

Siginal's gaze moved slowly around the table, then swung past Jonarel's shoulder to Star – a heat-seeking missile searching for a target. "And you, Tehar? Do you now regret your decision to join with this ship?"

"Not for a moment."

Siginal rocked back in his chair like she'd slapped him.

"My brother is happier than I have ever seen him, his mate has become my dear sister, and soon I will meet their daughter. It is the outcome I have always hoped for."

"*What!*" Siginal thumped the table with his fist, making the wood shudder. He rose out of his chair. "You set out to deceive me?" He pointed an accusing finger at Star.

She didn't so much as twitch. "I set out to help Jonarel, Aurora, and Lelindia build a better future for all. They are well on their way to doing that."

"Aurora has been arrested!" Siginal screeched. "And she," his finger trembled as he jabbed it at Lelindia, "ordered you to fire on me!" The heat of his anger blasted through the air.

Jonarel tensed beside Cade, but Star's gaze remained unwavering. "She did not order me to do anything. You threatened me, and the crew. It was my choice to protect them."

"By betraying your clan!" he roared.

Kire rose. "Siginal..." he warned.

"It is all right, Commander." Star didn't seem ruffled by her father's harsh words.

Kire wasn't ruffled, either. He was ticked off, though his anger came out in tight, controlled flares as opposed to Siginal's volcanic bursts.

Cade was fascinated by Siginal's blustering, and the chaotic emotions it hid. If Siginal's behavior had been even half this bad when Lelindia faced him down on Drakar, it was a miracle Jonarel hadn't done more than punch him. Cade could sense Jonarel's desire to do that again right now.

"If you can't be respectful to everyone in this room — *everyone* — you can leave." Kire was dwarfed by Siginal, but that didn't stop him from taking firm command of the situation. He waited, staring Siginal down.

Siginal's dark scowl and righteous indignation almost concealed the growing anxiety underneath.

Almost. But Cade could feel it clear as day.

Slowly, Siginal sank back into his chair.

Kire sat as well, folding his hands on the tabletop. "Cade asked an excellent question — the critical question — which I will repeat. Siginal, can you accept Lelindia, and her daughter, as part of your family?"

Siginal didn't meet Kire's gaze. He didn't answer Kire's question, either. Instead, he pinned Jonarel with a laser-look and posed a question of his own. "*Why?*"

That one word carried more weight than Atlas.

Jonarel accepted the burden with a grunt, like he'd been expecting the question but hadn't anticipated how difficult it would be to shoulder. He took his time formulating his response. "I love Aurora's strength and independence, and her willingness to help those in need no matter the cost to herself. If she had believed mating with me would save her people, she might have agreed to do it. Her heart is that generous."

"Then why—"

Jonarel held up a hand, silencing his father. His gaze rested on Lelindia, his expression incandescent. "But Lelindia is my checana. My heart. My life." The depth of his emotions turned his voice nearly subvocal.

Lelindia's emotions were just as intense, emanating the fierce joy that had become common since their mating ceremony. Her emerald-green energy field ignited, enveloping Jonarel, its coolness brushing the hairs on Cade's arm where it touched Jonarel's.

Jonarel sat transfixed for a moment, then he lifted his hand, his finger tracing the curve of Lelindia's cheek with exquisite tenderness. When he turned back to his father, his emotional field was clear and balanced, in perfect harmony with Lelindia's. "Following the path you had set for me would have destroyed both our lives, and Aurora's as well. That is something I would not — could not — do."

Siginal stared at them in silence, unblinking, his face and emotional field void of emotion. The stasis felt like it'd been brought on by a shock he couldn't process in real time.

The other five Kraed weren't doing any better.

Cade held his breath, waiting to see which side of the fence Siginal would land on.

Siginal's lips finally moved, but like they were made of drying clay, the sounds they produced barely audible. "You love her."

Not a question, but not really a statement, either. The words had the shape of an iridescent fairy, floating into the room on a puff of magic, ephemeral and inexplicable.

Jonarel's response had the same mythic quality. "With all that I am."

Siginal's mouth closed, the air seeping out of him like a deflating balloon. But on his next inhale he straightened, his emotions coming online like he'd been plugged into a power source.

What Cade felt stunned him.

Siginal's gaze landed on Lelindia with butterfly wings, his golden eyes clear and warm as honey in sunlight. "I welcome you to Clan Clarek, checala."

Twenty-One

Jonarel almost fell out of his chair. Only Lelindia's death grip on his hand and Cade's arm pressing against his other side kept him upright.

He had hoped his father would come to accept Lelindia in time, but this sea change shook him like the quakes of the northern hill regions of his mother's birth.

His father had welcomed Lelindia into the clan, had called her checala, the Kraed endearment he had used with Aurora.

"Thank you, talta," Lelindia replied, her voice husky. "I am honored to be a part of your clan."

Hearing the Kraed word for *father* on Lelindia's lips almost tipped him over the edge. Her energy field had abruptly disengaged when his father shocked her with his pronouncement. That touch had anchored him. Without it, he was adrift on a rushing river of unanswered questions.

But the most critical question hovered over him like a circling trebolk.

His father's gaze moved to him, his forehead furrowing. "Jonarel?"

His voice rasped in his throat. "What about me? And Tehar?" His father had banished them from Drakar, from the clan, on threat of dire punishment should they ever return.

His father dropped his head in what looked suspiciously like shame, before lifting his gaze to meet Jonarel's, then Tehar's. "I understand your actions now. Your motivations, your determination, your... connections. I did not before. I believed—" He shook his head, dismissing the explanation. "You both did what was necessary."

Kire cleared his throat, drawing everyone's attention. "Can you expand on that a bit? Are they off the hook? Back in the clan?"

"Yes."

"Just like that?"

"Yes."

"Good." But his frown didn't match the sentiment. "Why?"

"Why?" His father peered at Kire like the word had no meaning.

"Don't get me wrong," Kire clarified. "*Yes* is the right answer. But I don't understand what changed in the last minute that brought on this seismic shift."

"Me, either," Celia said, speaking up for the first time since Cade had entered the room.

"Me, either," Lelindia echoed, her fingers twining tightly with his. "And I'd really like to know."

So would he.

"I see." His father cleared his throat, glancing around the table.

Jonarel was pretty sure the other clan members were staring at him with the same shock his father had shown, but he kept his gaze locked on his father's face. His future with the clan hung on his father's next words.

"The reason goes to the core of all Kraed, where our protectiveness was born," his father answered Kire. "The dangers of our world demanded we become protective from the beginning of our existence. Watching out for each other was a necessity if we were to survive as a species. Our interdependence continues to drive all that we do, all that we are."

His father's gaze flicked to Tehar. "It is a trait we imbued in the Nirunoc as well. We needed them to be integrated fully with us, as we would be with them." He looked back at Kire. "Our protective natures define us in many ways. It is the focal point of our clan, and the thread that binds the fifteen clans together. But it is not the only powerful force that guides our actions. In rare cases, our protectiveness combines with an even stronger element. When that occurs, a Kraed must bow to the unstoppable force that drives him or her."

Lelindia pressed against Jonarel's side.

He released her hand, wrapping his arm around her shoulders and drawing her as tightly against him as their chairs would allow.

His father gave a slight nod, his gaze moving to Lelindia. "I knew Jonarel loved Aurora. He was taken with her from the first time they met. A mating was logical, expected."

"And now?" Lelindia whispered.

"Now I see how much more my son was capable of. The true size of his heart. And yours." His voice grew soft, reverent. "I unkindly believed you were coercing him, seducing him. But such actions would be an insult to you both. When my demands turned to threats, the depth of your emotional connection, the bond you could not deny, drove you to protect each other, even before you realized why."

Lelindia's soft sigh as she rested her head against his shoulder and relaxed into him made his heart stutter.

His mate. His checana.

"And Star?" Kire prompted.

His father grunted. "No one is more protective of Jonarel than Tehar."

Lelindia stiffened.

"Except you," his father amended quickly, giving Lelindia an approving look. "Tehar could not have turned away from either of you when you needed her help."

"No, she couldn't," Kire agreed. "So, we're good here?"

His father spread his hands. "Yes. I rescind the charge against Tehar and Jonarel and welcome them, Lelindia, and their unborn child, to the clan with open arms."

The asteroid that had been sitting between Jonarel's shoulder blades slid to the deck, his lungs filling with air.

His father's gaze slowly circled the table. "One day soon, after we have secured Aurora's and Will's freedom, I hope you will all return to Drakar so Clan Clarek can welcome you properly."

A sword's point pierced Jonarel's happiness. They had scaled one seemingly insurmountable mountain, but another loomed, its craggy peaks promising danger at every turn. Aurora and the Admiral were trapped in that wilderness with a predator who knew the landscape far better than they did.

"And on that note," Kire said, "how are we going to spring the Admiral and Aurora from the Sovereign's snare?"

Twenty-Two

Cade hadn't expected Siginal to capitulate so quickly, or so completely. Yet he didn't sense any subterfuge or manipulation behind the Kraed's pronouncement. In fact, the moment when he'd grasped how deeply Jonarel and Lelindia loved each other, his emotional reaction had been one of shock and awe, like he'd suddenly found himself sitting at a table on Olympus.

He'd also implied strong love matches were rare among the Kraed. That put a whole new spin on his previous expectations for Jonarel and Aurora. If the Kraed didn't choose mates based on emotional attachment, or at least an emotional attachment any stronger than the love Aurora and Jonarel had for each other – which was weak tea compared to how Jonarel and Lelindia felt – then Siginal could have justified pushing them to mate.

But Aurora was the polar opposite of the Kraed. Deep, powerful emotion was her birthright, partially thanks to her father. A politically expedient mating was never in the cards for her.

Or Jonarel. Apparently he was a rarity among his people. He was the only Kraed to even consider joining the Fleet, and he'd never acted like Siginal strong-armed him into that decision. Yes, Aurora and Lelindia had been with him for much of his schooling and career, but he clearly loved exploring, and hadn't suffered homesickness being far from Drakar and his clan for extended periods.

The signs had all been there, but Siginal hadn't read them.

The tangential benefit for Cade of Siginal's capitulation was the marked lessening of hostility in Siginal's emotional field when he glanced in his direction. Cade hadn't acknowledged what an emotional battering he'd been taking every time he was in Siginal's presence until it faded.

Micah rose from the table. "I need to contact my dad, tell him about Aurora's arrest."

"*What?*" Siginal jolted like he'd been goosed. "Aurora's father is alive?"

"Yeah. He and our mom are back together." Micah stated it as a fact, but Cade caught his undercurrent of anxiety and agitation. This would not be a fun conversation.

Siginal would be gobsmacked when he learned Aurora's dad owned Far Horizons Aerospace.

Cade stood. "I'll go with you." He didn't want Aurora's brother facing this alone.

Micah shot him a grateful look.

Cade turned to Kire. "Brendan and Libra might want to join our discussion here, but we'll want to give them a chance to react to the news first."

Kire nodded. "Take your time."

Cade followed Micah through the doorway to the galley.

The moment the door closed, Micah sagged against the counter, his fingers massaging his temples. "This sucks."

"No argument there." Micah's sense of loss and disorientation smacked Cade full force. The feeling was achingly familiar. He rested his hand on Micah's shoulder, offering silent support.

Then he spotted the tears leaking out from beneath Micah's closed eyelids. Also familiar. "Just so you know, I was a mess after Aurora left our cabin. Couldn't get myself off the floor."

"Yeah?" Micah's voice was strangled. He swiped at his eyes before meeting Cade's gaze. "You seemed in control when you came in the room."

"So did you. Looks can be deceiving. When I walked through the doorway, I was going into battle. No time for grief. Besides, it was your anxiety that drew me down here."

"Oh?" Micah's brows lifted. "Why?"

His eyes and mannerisms were so similar to Aurora's it made Cade's chest ache. "Because it was so unlike you. I could tell how out of whack you were. I couldn't sit back and wallow in self-pity while you were standing against Siginal."

The flicker of a smile came and went. "I knew I liked you."

"The feeling's mutual." Cade gave Micah's shoulder a squeeze. "Aurora's the strongest, smartest woman I know. She'll find a way through this."

"Yeah, she will." Micah pushed away from the counter. "Ready to tell my folks?"

Absolutely not. "You bet."

They decided to sit on one of the benches in the nurturing atmosphere of the greenhouse. Micah used the comband Brendan had given him to place the call through his dad's private network.

Brendan answered immediately. "Micah! Thank goodness you called. I wanted to reach out but sensed you weren't ready to talk. What's wrong?"

That was the thing about powerful empaths. They knew when things went off course without being told.

"It's Aurora, Dad. She's been arrested."

"Arrested!" Libra barked over the line with enough volume that she masked Brendan's response. "When? Why?"

"About half an hour ago. They charged her with sedition."

Cade's eyes squeezed shut, a curse echoing in his head. He'd suspected it, but hearing it confirmed made his stomach knot.

"Why didn't you call us right away?" Libra asked, her tone more hurt than accusing.

"Because Siginal was here. The crew had to deal with him, first."

"Oh." A beat passed while she processed the implications. "What happened?"

"Is Lelindia okay?" Brendan asked right after.

"Fine." Though Micah sounded far from fine. "Siginal knows about the baby, and he accepted her, Jonarel, and Star into the clan."

"Thank the stars," Libra sighed.

Brendan blew out a breath. "That's one bit of good news, then. Do you know where they took Aurora?"

Micah glanced at Cade.

"Brendan, it's Cade. She's probably headed to Seaview, the same Fleet facility outside San Diego where they're holding the Admiral."

"I see. How long will it take for her to arrive?"

"Hard to say. A few hours at least. She'll have a stopover at a Fleet medical facility for a physical before being delivered for confinement."

"Confinement," Libra growled. "I'm amazed they were able to take her in."

"She went willingly."

"*What!?*"

He winced. Aurora's mom could pierce eardrums when she wanted to. "They were waiting for her when we docked. She evaluated the situation and decided going quietly was the best course of action."

"And no one tried to talk her out of it?"

No need for empathic skills to grasp Libra's view of Aurora's decision.

"We all tried, Mom," Micah said. "But she's stubborn."

"No kidding," Libra huffed.

"And she's right." Brendan's voice was pitched at a more reasonable volume than Libra's. "A showdown at Sol Station wouldn't help her cause."

Cade could imagine the look that comment earned Brendan from Libra. No sane person would ever want to be on the wrong side of an enraged Sahzade protecting her daughter. "She's being taken to *prison*, Brendan. Avoiding capture would help her cause more than turning herself in."

"She's being taken to a Fleet brig, not a prison," Brendan said with the soothing patience of a trained psychologist. "She'll be with other Fleet personnel."

"Doesn't matter," Libra countered. "She'll still be locked up in a cell. I don't see how that benefits her."

"I wouldn't call it a benefit, but you know better than anyone that there's no cell that would hold Aurora if she wanted out. I'm not saying her being arrested is a good thing, just that it's not all bad."

"Hmm." Libra was not convinced. "So what do we do to help her?"

"Hire her a lawyer, for one. And get Micah down here so we can go see her. Tomorrow, if possible. Micah, I can have a transport ready in–"

"I'll bring him," Cade offered. "Aurora made me promise to stay hidden. She's worried that the Sovereign will attack me next. If I bring Micah down in the *Starhawke*'s shuttle, the Sovereign won't be able to track me there and I'll have transportation for... whatever. And after you see her—" His throat closed. He cleared it twice before he could finish. "You can tell me how she is."

The air thickened around him, pressing close.

Brendan had to clear his throat, too. "Sounds like a plan. You can stay here as long as you like."

Cade exhaled. "Thank you. We'll let the crew know and then head down."

"See you soon." The connection closed.

Cade started to rise, but Micah's hand shot out, grasping his forearm.

"Thank you."

Cade's brow furrowed. "For what?"

"For doing what Aurora asked. I know it can't be easy, hiding out at my dad's house rather than taking a stand, but I also know how much she loves you. If I can tell her you're safe, that will make this easier for her to bear."

"Yeah, that's what I decided, too." He hated being idle, but he hated the idea of Aurora worrying about him even more.

"Then hopefully you'll go along with my next suggestion."

"Which is?"

"We take Celia with us. As your bodyguard."

Twenty-Three

Micah kept a grip on Cade's arm as he watched his reaction.

Cade's eyes narrowed. "You do realize I'm the Fleet Commander of a special forces unit, right?"

"Yep." Which meant zip in this scenario. "But that's when you're protecting other people. Right now you need someone who can watch *your* back. And as I recall, Aurora said Celia beat you during your sparring match."

The corners of Cade's mouth pinched. "Did Aurora also tell you she was the major distraction that led to my loss?"

"No, but you just made my point. She'll be a distraction now, too. No way are you thinking clearly. I know, because I'm not, either. I trust Celia to keep us both from doing something stupid."

Cade snorted a laugh. "Would we do that?"

Micah gave him the look his question deserved.

"Alright, fine. If Celia's good with it, and Kire agrees to let her go, I'll accept her as my *temporary* bodyguard until I figure out my next move."

"Great." He released Cade's arm and stood. "Let's go ask her."

"...ships are incredibly fast," Kire was saying as they entered the observation lounge. "They've become our allies against the Teeli, largely thanks to Lelindia, Aurora, and Micah's efforts."

They must be talking about the Yruf.

"Cade's team laid the groundwork," Lelindia added. "We wouldn't even know the Yruf, let alone have them on our side, if it weren't for him."

Siginal's gaze flicked over Cade before focusing on Micah. "What did they say?"

"My dad's hiring Aurora a lawyer. Cade and I are going to take one of the shuttles to their house, and he'll stay there." He glanced at Kire. "If that's okay with you."

"Absolutely. It's what Roe would want."

"I have another favor to ask." Micah's gaze slid to Celia. "I'd like Celia to come with us."

Her perfectly shaped brows lifted. "Because?"

"I want you to be Cade's bodyguard."

Kire grinned but quickly schooled his features into a neutral façade. "I have no objections. Cardiff?"

Celia's gaze shifted between Micah and Cade, assessing. Then she looked at Lelindia and Jonarel. "Any problem with that?"

They both shook their heads. "We'll be fine," Lelindia said.

"We have the clan," Jonarel added, tilting his head toward his father. "And Tehar."

Siginal sat a little straighter, as did the rest of the Kraed around the table. The animosity they'd hauled onto the ship with them was conspicuously absent. They still looked imposing, but in a protective rather than aggressive way.

Celia took in their reactions with a glance and stood. "Then I'll go pack my bag."

"Is there anything we should know before we leave?" Cade asked.

Kire spread his hands with a shrug. "Star says the Fleet ships have moved off, so we're not being held here anymore. Not that we have anywhere to go. Let us know when you have an update on Roe, and we'll proceed from there."

"Will do."

Micah walked with Cade into the corridor, stopping at the cargo lift.

"Meet you in the shuttle bay in twenty?" Cade asked, walking backwards down the corridor toward the personnel lift.

"Sure." Micah stepped into the expansive cargo lift, taking it down to the guest quarters deck where his cabin was located.

Filling his travel bag with his few belongings didn't take twenty minutes, so he spent a little time wandering around the space he'd called home since he'd arrived onboard. No telling when he'd be back.

The memory of Aurora curled up on his couch, sleeping peacefully, opened up a crater in his chest. He hadn't appreciated the perfection of that moment. Not like he should have, anyway. He hadn't fully grasped the gift of time they'd been given. You'd think after decades apart, he would have learned to cherish every second. Now, she'd been taken away again.

Resentment scraped at his insides. He'd never met the Sovereign, but he could honestly say she was the one person in this galaxy he hated with a vengeance.

"Are you sad, Micah?"

He glanced at the cabin speaker where Unity's voice — his voice — had emanated. "Sad. Mad. And a bunch of other things."

"Ifel is sad, too. She's concerned about Aurora's captivity."

"So am I." Although his sister wasn't in physical danger, being treated like a criminal, a traitor to all she held dear, would be traumatic. "I don't suppose Ifel has any ideas about how to help her, does she?"

"No."

The disappointment that spread through his chest let him know he'd hoped for a different answer.

"But she's evaluating the situation, formulating plans in case intervention becomes necessary."

Intervention? Micah's breath hitched, a flutter of excitement brushing his ribcage. He hadn't considered the resources the Yruf could bring to bear on Aurora's confinement if things went underwater. Well, more underwater than they already had. "That's the best news I've had all day."

"Really? Then we're glad we told you."

He gazed at the speaker. Unity had been his near constant companion ever since they'd arrived onboard. It felt strange to think of leaving them behind. "I'm going to miss having you around."

Unity chuckled, a perfect mimic of his own laugh. "No, you won't. We're going with you."

"You are?"

"Of course. We have a charging station in the shuttle you're taking."

"Oh. Right." He'd forgotten there were two mobile units on the ship now. "That's good news, too."

"We think so."

Unity's chipper attitude eased the tension that had bunched in his neck and shoulders.

When he arrived in the shuttle bay, Celia was waiting for him, a travel pack slung over her shoulder and Unity hovering beside her. "So, tell me the truth," she said. "Did you include me because you want me to be Cade's bodyguard, or because you didn't want to lose touch with your combat instructor?"

A smile flitted across his lips. "Both." And a slew of other reasons he couldn't tell her.

Being separated from Aurora was tearing him in half. Having Celia by his side made the pain bearable.

Her mouth curled. "Fair enough. I probably would have gone stir-crazy on the ship, anyway."

"That makes me feel better. Everyone's reacting so calmly and I'm... not."

"We've been trained to take tough situations in stride. I'm sure you'd stay calm and focus on the problem if one of your college students encountered trouble during one of your dives."

"Yeah, I would." He'd been in that scenario a few times, and his confident handling of the situation had helped the divers stay calm, too. "Thanks for that. In fact, maybe I should just give you a global thank you right now. I have a feeling I'll be grateful to you repeatedly for the foreseeable future. I'm a little lost at sea right now."

"Of course you are. She's your sister." Her hand cupped his in a light touch. "It's natural to be afraid."

Fear wasn't the sensation that zinged through him at the casual contact. The tingling imprint of her fingertips against his skin lingered long after she let go.

"Ready to get this show on the road?" Cade called out as he strode toward them, his pack over his shoulder.

"You bet."

Celia insisted he take the co-pilot's seat beside Cade for the flight down, overruling his objections by pulling rank. After she'd settled into one of the chairs in the main cabin, Cade engaged the shuttle's hull camouflage and launched the shuttle from the ship's underbelly rather than using the bay door, ensuring there would be no visible sign of their departure.

Micah studied the plethora of ships in motion around the station as Cade deftly avoided them with the same self-assurance Micah's dad had when he flew. "I still can't get over the fact they can't see us."

Cade nodded, his focus on the two freighters and a personnel transport between them and the blue-white curve of the Earth below. "Makes navigating tricky, especially at a station with as much cross-traffic as Sol, but this beauty handles like a dream." He gave the shuttle's console an affectionate pat.

"Do you suppose Star can feel when you do that?"

Cade darted a glance at him. "Don't know. Never thought about it."

"She can," Unity chirped from the charging station above them. "Though how you experience tactile sensation is different than how she and we do. Also, this shuttle is less sensitive than Star's ship, especially as distance increases between them."

"Huh. How much distance?" Micah looked up at Unity. "Was Star able to feel what was happening with the shuttle when it was here on Earth and the *Starhawke* was still heading in from Teeli space?"

Unity pondered that for a moment. "Star says the closest analogy would be what you experience when your arm or leg falls asleep. You're still aware of it as physically connected to you, but you cannot feel or control it until blood flow returns."

"Interesting." He glanced into the cabin and discovered Celia was listening to the conversation with rapt attention. "So why didn't you have the same issue staying connected with the Yruf ship and U-1 when you were separated?"

Amusement tinged Unity's voice. "Star is one. We are we. We are always connected. We were designed that way. Distance makes no difference, at least not that we've encountered so far."

The biologist in him wanted to understand how that worked. Then again, Unity wasn't biological, or at least that was his understanding. It was tough to remember that. They seemed so alive.

Well, because they were. Biological or not, Unity could think independently, feel and express emotions, and interact with other species in meaningful ways. So could Star. By any definition that mattered to him, they were very much alive.

What would the A.I.s who'd fled Earth all those years ago to escape subjugation by humans think of Star and Unity? Would they see them as kindred spirits? Or fear them because they willingly interacted with biological species, including the select few humans they'd revealed themselves to?

He and his dad had always disagreed with the Union's ban on A.I. development, and the harsh punishments inflicted on any scientist who dared to subvert those laws. It imposed strict limits on how much technology could evolve, which affected Far Horizons' research and development branch.

Meeting Star had been a revelation, and an affirmation, proving a biological and non-biological race could live in harmony with each other, human history notwithstanding. His own experiences with Star, and now Unity, had strengthened that belief. But to achieve anything similar, humans would have to start treating A.I.s with respect and compassion, rather than fear and dominance.

As Cade brought the shuttle beneath the cloud layer, the ocean vista spread out below them, pulling Micah back to his surroundings. The sparkle of late morning sunlight on the aquamarine waves of the Pacific Ocean sent tingles dancing over his skin, his pulse leaping in anticipation. He'd missed the water way more than he'd realized.

Snatches of conversation flitted through his mind as the shuttle descended toward Oahu, his subconscious automatically opening to the voices of the marine animals below. The influx seemed louder, more insistent than usual, like walking into a crowded ballroom rather than one of his classrooms.

"Everything okay?" Celia called from the main cabin.

His pulse leapt for an entirely different reason. Celia was watching him closely enough that she'd picked up on the shift in his body language. He turned toward her. "Yeah. I just..." He swept a hand to the viewport. "I can hear the animals again. They're noisy."

"Compared to the silence in space, I'm sure they are."

"Good point." He'd noticed the absence of animal voices when he'd first arrived on the *Starhawke*, and again after returning from the Yruf ship, where he'd been talking to the animals in the biosphere as well as with the Yruf. But over the past few weeks, his awareness of the comparative silence onboard the *Starhawke* had waned. He'd accepted it as his new normal.

There was nothing normal about this moment. The shuttle hovered above his dad's house, barely ruffling the plant fronds around them, then touched down with the lightness of a hummingbird.

As Cade powered it down, Micah rose and snagged his travel bag from the storage compartment, handing Celia's to her while they waited for Cade.

Unity dropped from the charging alcove and glided toward them. "We did not expect to see Brendan and Libra again so soon."

"I know." And he hadn't expected to return home without Aurora.

Cade lifted his pack onto his shoulder and gestured to the lowered ramp. "After you."

His parents were waiting for them. His mom hurried toward him, enveloping him in a bone-crushing hug. "We'll get her back," she whispered fiercely.

His knees threatened to buckle as a wave of sadness and loss crashed over him. He clung to her, nearly lifting her off the ground as he soaked up the strength she offered. "Thanks, Mom."

His dad's hand rested on his shoulder, adding another pillar of support. "It'll be okay."

They both sounded so certain. He wanted to share their optimism, but the image of Aurora being led down the airbridge by Fleet Security haunted him.

"Celia." His dad smiled. "Nice to have you join us."

"This one needed a bodyguard." She hooked her thumb in Cade's direction.

"Bodyguard?" His mom jerked, stepping back. "Why?"

"Micah's request," Cade explained as he and Unity joined them. "He's afraid I might be too distracted to see a threat coming from the Sovereign."

A thundercloud took up residence in his mom's blue-grey eyes at the mention of the Sovereign. "Smart man. What about Lelindia?"

"She has Jonarel, Star, Siginal, and Siginal's crew to protect her on the *Starhawke*," Celia replied. "She's in good hands."

"And you're certain they've accepted her?" his mom asked, clearly concerned. "No more animosity? No danger to the baby?"

"We're sure," Micah answered. "We wouldn't have left if we weren't."

His dad stepped in before his mom could ask a follow-up. "You can give us all the details over lunch," his dad said. "Let's get you settled. We have a lot to discuss."

Twenty-Four

Jonarel watched his father closely as Cade and Micah left the observation lounge. His attitude did not imply trust in the two men, but the antagonism that he had shown toward Cade when he had first entered the room had lowered from a full rolling boil to a simmer.

A win, of sorts.

As the doors closed behind them, his father's gaze returned to Kire. "Do you know if the Yruf ship is nearby?"

"Yes, it's in the system."

"How can you be sure?"

"We still have an open line of communication with them."

That was putting it mildly. How would his father react if he knew a Yruf-created non-biological entity was integrated with Tehar in the ship's systems? Probably not well.

His father turned to Tehar. "And the Fleet is no longer holding you here?"

"No. Rowk and I have confirmed all the ships have moved off, though none have left the system."

"Very well." His father pushed back from the table and stood. "I would speak with Jonarel, Lelindia, and Tehar alone." He motioned to the rest of his entourage. "Return to the *Rowkclarek*. I will join you later."

Surprise flitted over the group, but they did not offer any objections, filing out silently.

Kire and Kelly remained seated. Kire leaned toward Lelindia and Jonarel. "You good?" he asked in an undertone that was in no way designed to prevent Jonarel's father from hearing him.

Lelindia rested her hand on his arm. "We'll be fine."

Kire glanced over his shoulder at Tehar. "Alright." He stood. "We'll be on the bridge if you need us." He and Kelly headed for the corridor.

Jonarel's heart kept time with their retreating footsteps, the soft thump amplified in the cavernous silence they left behind.

His father settled back in his chair, his arms draped on the carved wooden armrests. The pose was calculated to look casual, but did not hide the underlying tension that radiated from his father like a plucked string.

The same could probably be said about him. And Tehar.

Lelindia, by contrast, looked cool and collected. "What did you want to talk about?" she asked with the easy professionalism she would use if talking to a patient in the med bay.

His father studied her for long moments, his expression difficult to read. "Tell me about your child."

Lelindia spread her hands. "What do you want to know?"

"You said she could bind the Kraed and Suulh together, draw the clans into standing with you and Aurora against the Teeli. Does that mean you plan to raise her on Drakar? Or Azaana?"

Lelindia frowned. "No, I plan to raise her on the *Starhawke*."

His father grunted. "That will not work. My clan might come to accept that decision, as we built this ship," he swept an arm overhead, "but the other clans will not. Choosing to keep your child apart from our world will be seen as turning your back on us, rejecting our culture. The clan leaders will not understand. Your absence will destroy the very bond you hope to make between my people and yours."

Lelindia sat forward, her eyes taking on a gleam Jonarel knew well. "Then you and I will have to work to help them understand."

"How?"

"Jonarel told me that after you and Daymar pair bonded, you spent time living with her clan, correct?"

"Yes." His father shifted in his seat like greglar thorns had poked through the bottom. "That is customary when pair bonds cross between clans."

"And while you were gone, did your clan believe you had abandoned them?"

"Of course not."

"What about when you came to Earth to work at the Academy? Did your clan or the rest of the Kraed believe you had abandoned them then?"

His father's gaze flicked to him. "No," he said slowly.

"That's what I thought." The gleam in Lelindia's eyes glowed brighter. "You needed the freedom to act in the best interests of your people, even if that meant being separated from them. They understood that." Lelindia tapped her chest with her finger. "As one of the leaders of the Suulh, I must act in *their* best interests. But unlike the Kraed, the Suulh don't live on one planet. My people are scattered on Feylahn, Azaana, Earth, and Gaia. To be with and serve them, I cannot remain in one place, or even one planet. I must have the freedom the *Starhawke* provides."

His father's brow creased as her logic maneuvered around him with a deft touch.

Speaking of touching, Jonarel wanted to bundle his mate into his arms and caress every millimeter of exposed skin. He settled for wrapping his arm around her shoulders.

He felt the tremor his touch inspired. Her leg pressed against his from calf to thigh, sending spirals of warmth through the rest of him.

"However," she continued, "in mating with Jonarel, I also made a commitment to the Kraed. I cannot raise our child on Drakar – my people need me – but she will be as much a part of your world as mine. That I promise you. And the Nedale gifts I have passed on to her will nurture the Kraed all of her days."

A beautiful future. One he wanted with every fiber of his being.

But it would not come easily. The Sovereign and the Teeli would see to that.

His father rubbed his hand over his chin, respect shouldering out the wariness in his eyes. "You have given this much thought."

"Of course I have. We're talking about my daughter's future."

"We are talking about all our futures." His gaze swiveled between Jonarel and Tehar. "And what say you, my checalas? Are you in agreement?"

The parental endearment wrapped around his heart. He had almost given up hope of ever hearing it again. "Completely."

"As am I." Tehar moved beside Lelindia's shoulder. "Lelindia is a wise and compassionate leader, talta. She and Aurora stand together, and we stand with them."

"So I see. Then we must focus on securing Aurora's and Will's freedom so we may all return to Drakar to address the clans."

Lelindia relaxed into the circle of Jonarel's arm with a relieved sigh. "Agreed. Any suggestions on where to start?"

"One. I have a meeting scheduled with President Yeoh tomorrow to discuss Will's trial. Now we will discuss Aurora's as well."

"I'd like to come with you." Lelindia straightened. "I haven't met President Yeoh before, but she's one of the few Union leaders the Admiral trusts implicitly. I think it's time she heard the truth — all of it."

"All of it?" Jonarel's gut twisted. "You mean the Suulh? You want to tell her about you and Aurora?"

Her brown eyes were troubled, but also resolute. "The Sovereign is maneuvering us with lies and secrets. We need to fight back with facts and transparency."

"How will that not put Aurora at greater risk? For others to learn of her origins and abilities?" *And yours.* He hated the idea. His mate and child were in enough danger already.

"I trust President Yeoh's discretion," his father interjected. "She would never act rashly. On the contrary, she is highly intelligent, resourceful, and tenacious. She also already knows the true nature of the Teeli. Your revelation will be less of a shock than you might expect."

Lelindia's head lowered, her gaze hardening. "Did you or the Admiral already tell her about us?"

"No. Will did not wish to burden her with the knowledge until we were prepared to act. We did not anticipate this turn of events."

None of them had. The scope of influence the Sovereign would need over the Court of Justice to get the Admiral and Aurora brought up on completely fabricated charges was staggering.

His fingers tightened on Lelindia's shoulder, drawing her closer.

"Can President Yeoh intervene?" Lelindia asked. "Stop the trials?"

"No. The separation of powers in the Union prevents such actions. But if either were to be convicted, she could speak for them at sentencing."

Sentencing. Jonarel's heart turned into a block of ice.

Lelindia stiffened in his arms, her gaze jerking up to meet his. The flash of pure terror in her eyes melted the ice with a blowtorch of rage.

"That will not happen," he assured her. If he had to claw his way into the detention center and haul Aurora out himself, he would do that and more. Anything to ensure his mate would never face life without Aurora by her side.

Twenty-Five

The smell hit Aurora first. Not offensive exactly, but cloying in an antiseptic way that assaulted her senses. Every surface of the detention center — floor, walls, even the ceiling — looked scrubbed to the point of abrasion.

It grated on her almost as much as the indignity of the physical she'd undergone at the Fleet hospital. She'd gotten so used to Lelindia filling out and submitting her Fleet medical forms, she hadn't considered how invasive a full exam, including a pregnancy test, would feel.

She certainly couldn't tell them that she was incapable of contracting or carrying disease, or that she — like all Suulh women — didn't ovulate. Accidental pregnancy wasn't a concern.

The doctor had given her the third degree when she'd stumbled over her responses to standard medical questions she'd never needed to answer before. At least she could honestly say she had no physical impairments or history of disease.

By the time the FS officers delivered her to the detention center, her nerves were starting to fray. The administrative section of the detention center's prisoner intake was so blandly neutral she barely registered it. Processing also passed in a blur. She received a complete kit that included her uniform basics and toiletries. The kit was almost identical to the one she'd been given when she was first assigned to the *Excelsior*, but with one glaring difference. Her uniform showed no indication of rank. In here, she wasn't Captain Hawke. She wasn't even Aurora Hawke. As far as Fleet Security was concerned, she no longer had any designation other than Hawke631, the ID code she'd been assigned.

Her solar plexus pressed into her lungs, caught in a vise. Standing on the bridge of the *Starhawke*, this choice had seemed logical. Better to face the threat head-on than to run. But under the accusing glare of the overhead lights, hard surfaces, and even harder stares of the FS officers, her courage shrank into the shadows.

No. She couldn't allow that to happen. If no one else was going to talk to her, she needed to talk to herself.

Step one, breathe.

She forced air to fill her lungs, exhaling slowly.

Step two, one foot in front of the other. You can do this.

The pep talk didn't dislodge the vise, but it did stop the crank from turning another notch.

The bag containing her uniforms and toiletries pressed against her shoulder and hip as the four FS officers surrounding her marched her down the corridor that led to her new residence. The neutral beige on the walls did nothing to dispel the sterility and coldness permeating every millimeter of the detention center.

The jacket of the Fleet uniform she'd been given couldn't ward off the internal chill that settled over her, either. The emotions she sensed in this place reminded her of what she'd encountered from the Suulh while they'd been trapped in their Necri existence and from Nat while she'd been collared on Tnaryt's ship – despair and desperation overlaid with anger and fear.

The suffering of the Suulh and Nat had been a result of the Sovereign's machinations. They'd been helpless to save themselves from their torment, but Aurora was far from helpless. If she suffered in this place, it would be the result of her own mental turmoil, not the actions of those around her. She'd do well to remember that.

She looked at the FS officers out of the corner of her eye. Their expressions gave no indication of how they felt about her arrival, but she sensed a spectrum of emotions ranging from disbelief and confusion to disgust and anger.

She'd heard the whispered comments made by Fleet personnel they'd passed at the hospital, at the security checkpoints, and during her processing. Some had even stopped to stare. Whether it was because they recognized her from Fleet records, or because they knew what she was charged with was unclear. One thing was certain. Every person in the detention center had an opinion about her presence here.

She kept her head high and gaze forward as her escort marched her into a wedge-shaped building, halting in the square foyer on one side of the triangle.

One of the FS officers approached the clear partition in the block wall to their left that separated them from the Lieutenant seated behind a raised counter. "Prisoner Hawke631 from processing."

The Lieutenant's gaze flicked to Aurora, sizing her up with sharp-eyed scrutiny. "Solitary's been prepared."

Just as Cade had warned her. The administrators didn't want the other prisoners attacking her before the trial. Not that they could hurt her, but thankfully no one here appeared to know that. The Sovereign must be keeping that secret to herself... for now.

"Cell 201." The contempt in the Lieutenant's emotional field as she flicked a hand over her shoulder made it clear where she fell on Aurora's *guilty until proven innocent* spectrum.

"This way." The lead officer of her escort walked her past several table and stool sets bolted to the floor. Rows of upholstered chairs that looked as comfortable as a collection of boulders sat in two groups facing two vid screens attached high on a pillar near the center of the room. A clear partition bisected two-thirds of the common area, with an identical setup of tables, chairs, and vid screens beyond.

Not what she'd call welcoming and cheerful, but other than the depressing color scheme and lack of creature comforts, the basic setup was on par with the shipboard common area on the *Excelsior.* The crew had often gathered there to relax and socialize. Of course, her solitary designation would keep her from participating here. Even if it didn't, she wouldn't expect to find any friends among the prisoners, not with a sedition charge hanging around her neck.

The FS officer led her to the staircase at the back of the room. It connected to the center of the second-floor gallery, with another staircase connected to the right side. However, the left side of the gallery, where apparently her cell was located, dead ended at the railing.

Gotta love the symbolism.

Well, at least her sense of humor had made the trip.

The cells on the upper and lower floors of the brig lined the two walls that met at the point of the wedge. Each greenish-grey door had three window cutouts across the top third, which gave Aurora a clear, if somewhat choppy, view of the faces of the detainees inside as she walked past.

Most pressed close to their doors, their gazes locked on her. Judging by their emotional states, they were not aware of who she was or what she was charged with. Her late evening arrival made her noteworthy, an event to break up the monotony of their routine, but not exceptional.

The ambivalence she sensed would change quickly as word got out. By this time tomorrow, she expected everyone to know the most pertinent fact about her, at least as far as FS was concerned — she'd been labeled a Fleet traitor. That would put a flashing neon target on her back. Clearly the higher-ups agreed, otherwise they wouldn't be placing her in solitary to prevent an incident.

The rhythmic thump of their footsteps on the grey concrete reverberated unnaturally loud in the cavernous space, slowing as they reached the end of the gallery. The FS officer halted in front of the last door. It was painted the same greenish-grey as the rest, with the number 201 in black block letters above it. But unlike the rest of the doors, this one didn't have any window cutouts, just a solid expanse of painted metal.

Exactly like the hatch to the barren metal pit Tnaryt had forced her into underneath the command deck of his ship.

She suppressed an involuntary shudder.

The officer inserted a physical key in the mechanical lock, then pressed her thumb to the finger pad beside the door. The lock clicked. Reaching for the handle, the FS officer pulled the door open. "Prisoner, step inside."

Her feet didn't move.

Move, she ordered herself, but her feet pretended not to hear.

"I said, step inside."

Her feet remained rooted in place.

Anxiety spiderwebbed across her back, tightening every muscle it touched. *Move, Aurora!*

The officer frowned, her hand dropping to her sidearm.

Move!

This time her feet responded to her command, her knee bending and foot lifting, but the slight hiccup between thought and action caused her to stumble step through the opening.

One of the officers snickered.

She caught her balance, Celia's training overriding the mental freeze.

Her gaze swept the claustrophobic space.

The narrow cell was about four meters by two-and-a-half, the smooth, unadorned walls painted the same flat beige as the rest of the facility. A stainless steel toilet and sink combination sat to her left, a plank desk and folding seat to her right. A utilitarian bed platform with a thin mattress and sterile white sheets was wedged along the cramped back wall, with a two-meter-high shelving unit slotted in between the bed and desk.

"Lights out at twenty-one hundred."

Aurora pivoted, her kit bumping her hip.

The officer had moved to block the doorway. "Lights on at zero-six-hundred. Breakfast at zero-six-thirty. Lunch at eleven-hundred, dinner at seventeen-hundred. You will have one hour of yard time and half an hour to shower each day. You will maintain your appearance and this space in a clean and orderly manner at all times. Cleaning materials will be provided to you. Any questions?"

Thousands, but none that the FS officer could answer. "No, ma'am."

The officer stepped back, swinging the door shut with a clang that made Aurora flinch.

"Have a nice night." The taunting voice drifted through the door, followed by muffled laughter as the guards' footsteps faded.

At least her cell wasn't soundproofed. Hearing other voices, even mean-spirited ones, was preferrable to complete silence.

She approached the metal door, which had a small circular mark at eye-level. An eyehole, apparently, but inserted so someone on the outside could see in, but she couldn't see out. The only other break in the metal surface was a narrow rectangular slot at floor level, currently closed, which was probably for her food tray.

Her breath released on a sigh as she turned back to the cell.

Home sweet home.

A depressing thought, but as she'd told her crew, she'd suffered far worse during her last stint as a prisoner. If her reaction at the threshold was any indication, she still carried the emotional scars from that trauma.

Setting her bag on the floor, she walked over to the bed. A blanket of indeterminate medium brown covered most of the white top sheet, the edges tucked under the bedframe with precision. She ran her palm over the pillow and blanket. Yep, as scratchy and stiff as she remembered. It had been years since she'd used Fleet-issued linens for her bedding, not since she'd made lieutenant on the *Excelsior.* The promotion had earned her a private cabin and the freedom to dress her bed as she chose.

Placing a knee on the mattress, she peered out through the austere drawer-sized window.

A bar bisected the view, though there wasn't much to see. A faint ambient light from somewhere to her right gave a ghostly cast to what looked like a matching wedge-shaped building directly across from her. No greenery in sight, at least not from this angle, but here on the second floor, she might be able to see a slice of the sky during the day. Maybe even some stars after lights out.

A lump formed in her throat. What she wouldn't give to be out amongst the stars right now. With her crew. With Micah. With Cade.

Closing her eyes, she allowed her internal GPS to click in, seeking Cade's distinct emotional resonance in the sky above. But that's not where her compass directed her. The emotional pull came from Earth, to the west.

Her heart fluttered, then started to pound, her fingers gripping the window ledge. Where had he gone? Why wasn't he on the *Starhawke*? Had the Sovereign—

The pounding eased as her brain caught up with her fear, rapidly identifying the other emotional resonances converged around Cade.

Micah. Her dad. Her mom. And... Celia?

That one gave her pause. Why would Celia have left the *Starhawke*? Clearly Micah had decided to take Cade to her dad's house with him – *thank you, big brother* – when he'd left the ship. But why bring Celia?

Reanne and Celia had only met once, when Aurora's crew had first arrived at the Rescue Corps facility on Gaia. The two women hadn't been in the same room since. As potential targets for retribution, Celia was way down the list, if she was even on the Sovereign's radar at all.

So why was she with Cade and Micah? Curious.

She could reach out to Lelindia for answers, but first she needed to unpack.

Sliding off the bed, she opened her kit, taking each item out and neatly arranging them on the shelves provided. As she worked, she surreptitiously kept an eye out for any indication of surveillance devices. Surveillance was illegal inside brig cells, but she was dealing with the Sovereign. Legality wasn't a concern in her world.

She didn't spot any, but that didn't mean she wasn't being watched or recorded. She'd be wise to assume her every move was being transmitted. Cheery thought.

With the bag emptied and neatly folded on the bottom shelf, she quickly washed her face and brushed her teeth. After changing into her standard issue shirt and boxer sleep set, she slid between the cold sheets.

Yeah, she did not miss Fleet linens. The thin material of the sheet gave off a dry smell that spoke of thousands of washes in bleach-treated water. So different from the fresh lavender wash she used for her bedding on the *Starhawke*.

Letting her head fall back on the paper-thin pillow, she closed her eyes and breathed rhythmically, calming her mind before reaching out to her energy sister.

Lelindia?

Sahzade!

Lelindia's effusive and immediate response sent a rush of joy, followed by the press of moisture against the back of her eyes. When the tears threatened to spill out, she scrunched her lids tight, stemming the tide. If she allowed it to start, it might not stop.

Are you okay? Lelindia asked.

It was a standard question, but her standard response wouldn't cut it. *Fine* wasn't in her vocabulary at the moment. Taking a fortifying breath, she opened her eyes to slits. When the tears stayed tucked away, she allowed her gaze to circle the room.

I'm at the detention center.

Compassion flowed through their connection like a warm breeze as Lelindia responded to the visuals Aurora was projecting.

Not exactly the Starhawke, *is it?*

No, it's not.

Which reminded her that her energy sister had been facing a challenge of her own when Aurora had walked off the ship. Siginal had been spoiling for a fight.

How did things go with Siginal?

Images filled her mind. Siginal and Jonarel seated with Lelindia at a table in the *Starhawke's* observation lounge, talking amicably, Lelindia's hand resting on her belly, with Star standing nearby.

The feelings of hope and determination that came with those images made tears press against Aurora's eyes from joy rather than sorrow.

They'd done it. Somehow, Lelindia and Jonarel had managed to broker peace with Siginal.

That's wonderful news.

But that information didn't answer the question that was nagging her.

Why is Celia with Cade and Micah?

Wry amusement flickered along their connection. *This is why I always lost at hide and seek.*

She held back the smile that tugged at her. They'd played hide and seek frequently when she was a child, even though Lelindia couldn't win. Her energy sister couldn't hide from her. But she hadn't seemed to mind, switching the game to tag when Aurora inevitably found her.

Celia's acting as Cade's bodyguard.

She stared at the ceiling, certain she'd misunderstood. *His bodyguard?*

Yes.

Why?

He didn't want you to worry.

Self-recrimination jabbed her. Cade had accepted Celia's protection because of her. Once again, their relationship had put him in the crosshairs. Just as she'd known it would.

Last time her solution had been to send him away. But she'd learned a hard lesson from that mistake. Even if it was a good idea — it wasn't — cutting herself off from him would shred her heart at a time she needed to stand strong.

Thank the stars for her family and Celia. Cade would be safe with them. Anyone who dared challenge the combined strength of her mom and Celia would regret that decision.

She adjusted her focus to the southwest, across the ocean, tuning into their emotional resonances. Their anxiety hummed like a hive of bees gathering pollen.

Tears threatened a third time, along with a weariness that dripped like an IV in her veins.

Tell them I'm okay.

Lelindia's understanding wrapped around her, softer and warmer than the scratchy blanket tucked under her chin. *I will. I love you, Sahzade.*

I love you, too.

The connection dissipated.

She sighed, the air hitching in her throat. Maybe she should reach out to Micah. There was a chance she'd be able to talk to him the same way she'd talked to Lelindia. They'd managed a few small communications in the past, although they'd been close to each other at the time. With Micah, the distance between them might matter. His ability to talk to animals and the Yruf certainly had a range.

But she didn't trust herself. The emotions communicating with him might trigger could break the tenuous hold she had on her composure. Maybe tomorrow, after she got some sleep, she'd see if she was better prepared to handle it.

A single tear slipped from the corner of her eye, the moist warmth tracking past her temple and dampening her hairline. Was this empty hollowness in her chest loneliness? It wasn't an emotion she'd had much experience with. Any, really. Loss, yes, but not loneliness. Or helplessness.

Maybe she was channeling the emotions of the other detainees. Their presence had muscled into her consciousness, pummeling her with raised fists. She was used to being surrounded by the emotional fields of large groups – she'd served on starships, after all – but she couldn't recall any situation during her Fleet service when she'd been bombarded by this much negativity.

She couldn't extricate herself, either. Which left one option – drawing on the skills her dad had taught her. She'd need to find her inner calm if she wanted to get any sleep tonight.

Maybe she could—

Her head jerked toward the back wall, her thoughts fragmenting like a meteor hitting atmosphere. Air rushed into her lungs, a giddy effervescence almost making her hyperventilate. She forced her body to focus, zeroing in.

Was she right? Had she felt—

There! Almost buried in the swirl of toxic emotional sludge around her, a familiar emotional resonance glowed – bright, strong, and very nearby. Yes!

Excitement shot through her, chasing away her malaise.

She wasn't alone after all.

The person she'd pinpointed in one of the detention center buildings was Admiral Schreiber.

Twenty-Six

The Admiral's familiar presence soothed Aurora to sleep. She awoke in the pre-dawn hours, disoriented and pawing at the scratchy blanket that rubbed against her bare neck.

Her gaze fell on the stainless steel sanitation station gleaming dully in the ambient light filtering through her narrow strip window. A sigh escaped her lips.

Flopping onto her back she shoved the blanket aside. "Good morning, Aurora," she murmured, staring at the ceiling.

Talking to herself first thing in the morning might be a sign of severe stress, but for now she'd frame it as an attempt to inject a friendly voice into her day, rather than as a symptom of psychological trauma. She'd also focus on the man in a distant cell who was several weeks ahead of her in acclimatizing to this place, stuck in isolation just like she was.

Turning her focus inward, she tuned into the Admiral's emotional field. The low ebb of emotional output suggested he was probably still asleep. Either that, or he'd developed a Zen-like focus during his incarceration. She was going with the former. What she sensed reminded her of the steady hum of his emotional field during sleep cycles while they were both captives on Tnaryt's ship.

Oh, the irony. Here they were again, cut off from the rest of their support system, waiting for the Sovereign to make her move. At least this time they knew who they were facing. And they weren't dealing with shock collars and vile mash. Whatever they brought her for breakfast today, it had to be better than that glop.

The remembered aftertaste hit her tongue and she flinched. Sliding out of bed, she walked to the sanitation station and got a drink of water. Ah, much better.

The clock display embedded over the door of her cell showed she still had more than thirty minutes before lights on. She could do a yoga flow, but odds were good she'd have plenty of time for that later. The chilly floor wasn't going anywhere.

Settling cross-legged on the bed, she closed her eyes and reached out across the ocean, seeking the emotional resonance that held the power to bring light to this dark place.

Cade.

He wouldn't be able to hear her the way Lelindia and Micah could. But his empathic abilities were similar to her dad's. He should be able to pick up on her emotional projection, sense her.

Sure enough, the brush of connection flowed across her like a caress, tantalizing and delightful. She leaned against the wall, her neck and shoulder muscles relaxing as Cade's presence surrounded her like a hug. Well, not exactly a *hug*. More like a lover's embrace. There was nothing chaste about the emotions rolling over her. It was more like... *whoa!*

A searing trail of desire scorched her skin from head to toe, every nerve ending leaping to attention. Her breath caught, her heart pounding at the unexpected tactile overload.

Unbridled passion surged through their connection. The sudden intensity startled her. It felt... desperate. Wild. Primal.

Her fingers tightened around the curve of her bent knees. What was he doing? Seduction by projection? She'd never considered such a thing, but apparently he had. He was building a good head of steam, her body reacting as though his hands and lips were... everywhere. The relentless onslaught threatened to strip her of her good sense. And generate an inconvenient physical state.

This wasn't the time. Or the place. Soon the lights would come on—

Her eyes snapped open, focusing on the clock. A heartbeat later she dropped her chin to her chest to choke off the muffled snort of laughter that erupted from her chest.

Oh, my.

She'd miscalculated. Literally. Cade wasn't trying to seduce her, at least not intentionally. In Hawai'i, it *was* earlier. Somehow she'd managed to connect with his subconscious while he was asleep. And based on what she was sensing, she'd triggered a very erotic dream.

The realization proved to be an effective antidote, helping her to get back in control and focus on her projection. *Cade. Cade!*

Surprise washed away the desire in his field like a warm spring rain. For several seconds confusion dominated instead.

Cade?

She could easily picture him in her bedroom at her dad's house, staring around the room like she might be hiding in the shadows.

A shift in their connection turned down the volume, letting her know he'd made the leap from dreamland to wakefulness. Judging by his emotional reaction, and the twinge of embarrassment that came with it, he had not intended for her to share the emotional subtext of that dream.

His sleep state must have made him more open and receptive to her projection. Now that he was awake, the barriers that had kept his empathic abilities submerged most of his life were reasserting themselves.

They needed to work on that. No reason for him to feel uncomfortable. In fact, helping her let off steam was one of his specialties. If this morning's episode was any indication, she might be able to take advantage of that talent during the stressful days ahead. That could prove a boon to them both.

She projected back the emotions he had stirred in her, though without the high heat.

His embarrassment faded.

That was a good sign.

The emotional interplay steadily pushed back the sterile walls of her cell. Closing her eyes, she sank into the cozy embrace of connection – not projecting, not receiving, just being. Cade seemed content to do the same. They stayed like that until the overhead lights blazed to life, bright even behind her closed lids.

With a sigh, she projected the emotional equivalent of *I've got to go.*

A twinge of melancholy from Cade trailed along the connection but was quickly absorbed by an outpouring of warmth and caring.

She projected back in kind, holding onto the tether that bound them together for as long as she dared. Closing the emotional connection took more willpower than she'd imagined, but the faint thunk of metal and the tap-tap of footsteps out in the common area made it clear the day had begun.

Washing up at the sink, she dressed in the uniform she'd been given and braided her hair, which still held the faint scent of her favorite shampoo bar, one Lelindia made for her from herbs and flowers she grew in the greenhouse. That would change today. Back to Fleet toiletries.

The muffled clinks and clatters from behind the door continued, but it was the emotional shifts that made her start to pace the short stretch of concrete from her bunk to the door. During the night, the negativity had settled down in slumber, but now that the other prisoners were awake, the volume shot up, battering her.

"This'll be fun." Hearing her own voice helped, but about as much as sticking her fingers in her ears would block out a crack of thunder. Whether she wanted to or not, she was going to get *lots* of practice on the techniques her dad had taught her for processing outside emotions.

The steady tromp of footsteps approached her door, followed by a sharp rap on the metal plating. "Prisoner Hawke631, step away from the door and face the back wall."

She complied. Metal squeaked, but not the thick heavy hinges of the door. A scrape and clatter on concrete preceded a faint aroma wafting into the room. The squeaking repeated, followed by retreating footsteps.

She pivoted. A thin stainless steel tray with two bowls and a mug lay on the ground by her door. She crouched next to it, inhaling the scent of coffee from the steam rising in a curling ribbon from the large-handled mug. One of the bowls contained oatmeal dotted with walnut pieces, and the second bowl held blueberries and cut-up strawberries. A stainless steel spoon and a white cloth napkin completed the place setting.

She picked up the mug and took an experimental sip of the coffee. A little bitter and bland compared to the robust teas she preferred, but no worse than what she'd consumed on *Excelsior*. The detention center had the advantage of not having to travel light years to resupply their coffee bean stores, either.

Picking up the tray, she took it to her desk and settled onto the folding stool. Spreading the napkin on her lap, she dumped the fruit into the oatmeal and dug in. Not exactly like eating in the *Starhawke*'s observation lounge with the vast view of the starfield to delight the eye, but way better than the accommodations on Tnaryt's ship.

By the time the guard returned for the tray, she'd polished off every morsel and finished the coffee. She'd rinsed the bowls in her sink before replacing them on the tray and setting it by the door. The guard gave the same admonition to stand back and turn away, but after the tray scraped through the slot, Aurora caught the flicker of surprise in the guard's emotional field. Apparently rinsing dishes was outside the norm for prisoners in solitary.

Good to know. If small actions like that could improve the guards' emotional reactions to her, she'd keep an eye out for other ways she could make their jobs a little easier.

They might not think of her as a captain anymore, but that didn't mean she couldn't behave like one.

Twenty-Seven

The last thing Cade had expected on his first morning at Brendan's house was to be woken from a vivid and pleasurable dream featuring Aurora, and discover she was inside his head.

Or more accurately, his heart. The sensation hadn't been disturbing, just startling and a bit embarrassing after he'd realized what he'd been dreaming. The emotional content she would have been sensing would have been deeply intimate.

She hadn't seemed to mind. In fact, if he was reading her emotions correctly, she might be up for more of the same at a future date. He had no idea how they'd coordinate that, but he'd leave that up to her. For now, their interlude had proven he wasn't completely cut off from communicating with her, which was a huge boon. It mellowed the pitched rugby game that had been taking place in his gut ever since she agreed to turn herself over to FS.

The scent of coffee drifting through the open doorway of the interior balcony told him he wasn't the only one up before dawn. After changing into a T-shirt and lounge pants, he headed downstairs, passing the loft where Celia's fold-out bed had already been tucked back into the couch. He found her seated at the high-counter island in the kitchen, sipping from a steaming mug of coffee.

"Couldn't sleep?" he asked as he grabbed a mug out of the cupboard.

"I slept." But her tone implied it wasn't a restful night.

He filled his mug then settled onto one of the backed barstools beside her. "Want to talk about it?"

Her brows lifted.

He waited to see what she'd do. He wouldn't describe their relationship as friendly yet, but ever since he and Aurora had made it clear they were committed to staying together, Celia's attitude toward him had changed. Now she treated him the same way she treated Jonarel or Kire, like part of the crew rather than as a potential threat to Aurora's happiness.

She sipped her coffee, studying him over the rim of her mug. "I've been... processing things lately. Things from my past."

He treaded carefully. "Aurora told me you'd had some sessions with Brendan. I assumed that's what you two were doing when you disappeared for an hour last night. Is it helping?"

Her mouth scrunched up. "Depends on how you define helping. I'm having nightmares regularly, and weird emotional flareups at inopportune moments. Brendan said to expect that, that it's my subconscious dealing with things I've forced myself to forget. But it's not making my life easier."

"I don't think it ever does." He took a drink, allowing the warmth and rich flavor to roll over his tongue. "I've had my share of therapy sessions over the years. Shortly after I joined the Elite Unit, I developed anger issues, lashing out at people for small things, overreacting in tense situations. Turns out I had a lot of pent-up rage at my parents I'd been stuffing. Admiral Schreiber insisted I work with a hypnotherapist. Those sessions got me through to the other side, but the process wasn't easy, especially not when I was in the thick of it. Over time I healed, which allowed me to be a better leader, but first I had to clear the gunk I'd been lugging around."

Celia set down her mug. "How long did it take?"

"About a year and a half."

She grunted. "Great."

He nudged her with his elbow. "It might not take that long for you."

"No." She looked at him with an openness he'd never seen before. "It'll probably take longer."

His chest tightened as her emotions wafted over him. "That bad, huh?"

"That bad."

He rested a hand on her arm. "I'm sorry."

"Not your fault." Her shoulder lifted in a shrug.

"If I can help, I'm here. Whatever you need."

Her lips quirked, her dark eyes flashing with wry amusement. "Did you ever expect to say that to me?"

He chuckled, withdrawing his hand. "No, I did not. But I'm glad we're on the same side now. I didn't much care for having a dagger pointed at my heart."

"I wouldn't have used a dagger." Her smile widened. "Maybe a spoon."

"Ouch." He winced dramatically, spreading his hand over his heart. "Now I'm *really* glad we're on the same side."

"Same side of what?" Micah asked as he strolled into the kitchen from the hallway, dressed in a surfboard-themed shirt and lounge pants.

"The crew. Celia no longer intends to remove my heart with a spoon."

Micah's gaze slid between them. "*This* is the kind of conversation you have first thing in the morning?"

A strange flutter of emotion from Celia caught his attention, but it was gone before he could label it.

"Oh, I've had far more ghastly conversations first thing in the morning," she assured Micah with a flick of her hand. "I am in security, after all."

"Hmm." Micah's emotional state didn't match the nonchalance of his demeanor. Even as he turned toward the cupboard and pulled down a glass, the poor man was drinking Celia in like she was the elixir of life. But he was doing his level best to hide that fact.

Celia seemed oblivious, which in itself was strange. The woman was an expert at analyzing people's body language and internal motivations. But Micah seemed to be her Achilles' heel. First she'd treated him like public enemy number one for reasons only she understood, and now she seemed to be completely missing Micah's interest in her.

Fascinating.

Micah filled his glass with water and took a long drink before leaning his hip against the counter by the sink. "I haven't picked up any projections from Aurora." His disappointment was palpable.

Guilt nipped at Cade's ankles. "Uh, I have."

"Really?" Micah straightened. "How? When?"

"This morning. I was, um, dreaming, and when I woke up I could feel Aurora's presence, almost like she was in the room with me."

Micah stared at him. "Has that happened before?"

"No. First time."

"Huh." Micah tapped the side of his glass with his finger. "What impressions did you get?"

Heat rose along the back of his neck. He did not want to discuss details with Aurora's brother. "She seemed okay. Not happy, exactly, but not particularly agitated, either."

Tap, tap, tap on the glass. "I wonder why she reached out to you instead of me. She might actually be able to talk to me."

"I'm not sure." They were both staring at him now. He rubbed a hand along his jaw. "It might not have been a conscious choice to communicate. Maybe she was just thinking about me and the connection happened on its own."

"Or maybe you unknowingly reached out to her," Micah countered. "Your latent empathic abilities are still developing. We don't know what you're capable of." He shrugged. "What any of us are capable of, really. Aurora and I are still figuring out the scope of our abilities, especially... when we work together."

That last part cost him. A couple months ago Aurora's sudden appearance in his life had upended his world. Now her absence had flipped it again. The pain of that separation was written all over his face and emotional field in big, bold letters.

Cade's heart thumped uncomfortably in his chest. "You could try projecting to her," he suggested. He hated seeing the guy so miserable. "She's awake."

"And dealing with her first morning in lockup." Micah shook his head. "Now's not the time." He took a drink, his gaze moving to the window. Night still held sway outside. "With any luck I'll get to see her in person today."

Now it was Cade's world that tilted. When Aurora's family headed for the mainland, he'd be staying behind.

Celia's arm bumped his. "We'll need to make some plans, too."

"Oh?"

"I'm your bodyguard, remember? We need to figure out what our days are going to look like when we're alone here, so we don't drive each other insane."

He welcomed the distraction. "Good point. What did you have in mind?"

"A run, for starters. Maybe some laps in the pool, too."

"So your plan is to work us both to exhaustion?"

Her eyes sparkled. "Yep."

"Fine by me." He stood. "I'm going to go check on Unity, see if they want to join us in the house or stay in the shuttle."

It was an excuse, but one they wouldn't question. His real reason for leaving was to give Micah and Celia some time alone. They both looked like they needed it.

Twenty-Eight

Micah's gaze followed Cade as he left the kitchen.

He'd spent too much time with his dad to not pick up on the telltale signs of an empath tuning into emotions. Cade's gaze had flicked to him right before he'd announced he was heading outside. He'd clearly sensed the emotions Micah was fighting to keep under wraps.

Thoughts of Aurora's incarceration had revved his brain late into the night, but it was having Celia sleeping in the loft meters from his bedroom door that ensured he'd barely slept a wink.

The last time they'd been in this house together, her antagonistic attitude had been a barricade of stone and barbed wire between them that he'd had zero desire to breach. In fact, he'd added a few defenses of his own.

This situation was completely different. Without that barrier, he felt vulnerable and exposed in a way he hadn't on the *Starhawke*. Having her in his world, looking so cozy and approachable seated at the counter with her coffee mug, made him yearn for things he had no business even considering.

The soft smile she gave him when she turned to him didn't help. "You look like you had a rough night, too."

He rubbed a hand over his face. "Yeah."

He heard her push her stool back. His body went on red alert as she stepped beside him. Her touch, when it came, nearly made him levitate, the warmth of her fingers burning into the bare skin of his bicep. "I'm sure she's thinking about you."

He couldn't look at her, not while she maintained that physical connection. "Yeah."

Her grip tightened, reminding him how much strength she commanded in her toned body. "We'll get her out of this."

He couldn't make his vocal cords work. The air in the kitchen suddenly felt thin. He had no idea if it was thoughts of Aurora or Celia driving his reaction, but it didn't matter. He was a hair's breadth away from doing something very, very stupid.

Don't do it! Don't!

Dragging in a breath, he sidestepped, pulling away from her and moving to the refrigerator. "Thanks." He yanked open the door and stuck his head inside. The cool air wasn't as effective as sticking his head in the freezer — which would draw her scrutiny — but it bought him a few moments to collect himself.

"Micah?"

He tensed, gripping the refrigerator door like a shield, but she didn't sound any closer. "Yeah?" Apparently that was one of the few words he could manage with her this morning.

"I know what it's like to have someone you care about locked away."

He almost banged his head on the freezer door as he snapped upright. "What?"

She folded her arms, regarding him steadily. "I understand what you're going through with Aurora. When I was a child, my mother and I were taken from our home. I watched, helpless, as they locked her in a cage and hauled her away. And there wasn't anything I could do about it."

Well, didn't that make him feel like pond scum. "I'm sorry."

The admission had grooved brackets around her mouth, but she didn't seem to care, using her pain as a bridge to his. "I know this is scary. Terrifying. And that loss of control can make you feel like you're pinwheeling in a void. But you have support. Lots of it. So does Aurora. You're not alone."

Stellar light, he wanted to hold her. And kiss her. And tell her what an incredible, amazing woman she was. Instead he stayed frozen with one hand latched onto the open refrigerator door and the other clinging to the island counter. "Thank you."

She pursed her lips, her eyes narrowing a fraction. Her next move caught him so much by surprise that he sucked in all the air in the room.

With two fluid strides she reached him, slid her arms around his torso, and pressed against him from hip to collarbone. Her cheek rested on his shoulder. "It's going to be okay."

He trembled, the shock of that full-body contact scattering his wits like popping soap bubbles.

She must have mistaken the shaking for fear, because she shifted closer, one hand making soothing circles under his shoulder blades. "It's going to be okay," she repeated.

He seriously doubted it. Not if she continued to press her lithe body against his. It wouldn't be long before she'd notice—

"Good morning!"

Celia lifted her head and released her hold, stepping back as Micah's dad strode into the room.

Micah turned away from her, taking his time closing the refrigerator. *Thanks, Dad.*

Celia looked puzzled, her gaze darting between them. No doubt his dad's overly enthusiastic greeting struck an odd note. "Good morning, Brendan."

"I thought I smelled coffee, but didn't expect anyone to be up so early."

Micah moved to the opposite side of the island from Celia. Much better. Safer.

His dad fetched the tea kettle and filled it with water. "I take it neither of you slept much."

"Not really," Micah admitted.

"I guess insomnia was to be expected." The look in his dad's eyes made it clear he knew exactly why Micah had been restless.

"Why's Cade out in the shuttle?" Micah's mom asked as she joined them from the hallway, stopping beside Micah to give him a side hug.

He squeezed back, gratitude washing away the chaotic emotions of the past few minutes. He'd gone so much of his life believing his mother was dead, that every moment they shared still felt like a waking dream. He was also still getting used to how accurately she could pinpoint people by using her Suulh-given internal GPS. "He's checking on Unity." He kept his arm around his mom's shoulders, wanting that comforting contact.

She smiled up at him. "It was sweet of you to allow Unity to use your voice."

He snorted. "Sweet? Really, Mom?"

Her smile widened. She patted his chest with her free hand. "Oh, yes, you were always a *very* sweet boy."

He responded to Celia's chuckle with a mock glare in her direction, but inwardly he sighed with relief. His parents had effectively saved him from disaster and cleared the tension from the room.

"Micah was a sweet boy?" his own voice asked from behind him.

He turned as Unity bobbed into the room, Cade right behind.

"Do Humans and Suulh lick their children to groom them?"

That earned grins all around. Micah groaned. "No, sweet in this context means I was... nice." Not much of an improvement over sweet, but he'd take every millimeter he could get.

"Oh, you were much more than nice," his mom assured him, her blue-grey eyes dancing with mischief. "You were such an easy baby, so loving and gentle. You never cried or fussed, just gazed out at the world with those big eyes full of wonder."

"*Mooom.*" Heat flushed his skin. He studiously avoided looking at Celia, but Cade's grin was wider than the Pacific.

"What?" His mom blinked up at him innocently. "It's true. Besides." She gave his chest one last pat before extricating herself and moving next to his dad. "It's been a long time since I've been able to coo over my baby boy."

His face was on fire. Thank goodness his tan would help conceal the ten shades of crimson he must be turning.

His dad's lips twitched, but he nodded sagely. "You're right. I make a point to coo over him at least once a day."

Micah threw up his hands as Cade and Celia burst out laughing. "Fine, fine. Aaanyway." He turned to Unity, the only one not in on the joke. "Do you have anything to report from Ifel or the *Starhawke?*"

"Not much so far. We're monitoring all activity around the *Starhawke* and *Rowkclarek*. The Fleet ships have remained in the area, and there has been an increase in FS personnel on the station. We're monitoring Aurora's location as well."

"You're watching the brig?"

"We're watching her movements within the brig."

"What? You're able to track her specifically?" He hadn't even thought to ask whether that was an option.

"Of course." Unity seemed slightly insulted. "Monitoring is one of our primary functions. We watched Aurora throughout her transport. She is currently housed on the second level of a triangular masonry structure with narrow windows. Hers is the last rectangular room of the row."

His jaw was hanging open. He closed it. "You can see her?"

Unity swayed. "Not in the visual spectrum you use to see, but we're not limited by biological optics."

A knot that had been constricting his lungs ever since Aurora had been taken uncoiled one loop. "You can identify her? And see what's going on inside the building?"

Unity bobbed. "That's easy. The building isn't shielded like a starship. There's a dispersion field that seems to be an attempt to prevent outside signals from penetrating, but it's not an issue for us."

"All hail Yruf technology," Cade murmured.

No kidding.

"We assumed you'd want us to... what's the phrase you use? Keep an eye on her."

"You assumed correctly." Micah gave Unity a thumbs up. "Thanks for that."

Unity twirled in delight. "You're welcome."

Micah turned to his parents. "When are we heading to the mainland?"

His dad moved to the communication pad in the wall and pulled up a message. "Our visitor passes came through during the night. Visiting hours are from one to three this afternoon. It'll take a little time to reach the brig from the airport, so the sooner we leave the better." He glanced at Micah's mom. "Marina and Gryphon are taking the monorail down the coast?"

His mom nodded. "Lelindia and Jonarel will pick them up from the station."

"Good. They need to have a moment to enjoy the news about the baby before we focus on how we can help Aurora." His dad's gaze moved between Cade and Celia. "Speaking of help, Iolana and Kai have agreed to provide anything you might need while we're gone."

Birdie. Micah hadn't even thought about contacting his best friend. Another sign of his discombobulation. He needed to get his head on straight. "I should have messaged her last night."

His dad gave him a knowing look. "She understands. You can contact her while we're in flight."

"That's nice of them to offer," Celia said, "but I can take care of getting any needed supplies. No one will recognize me here."

"That we know of," his dad countered. "But by submitting Micah's, Libra's, and my information into the database last night to get our visitor passes, we've created a link between this location and Aurora. I'm hopeful that with the three of us on the mainland over the weekend, that will direct the Sovereign's attention there. Based on her psychological profile, that's likely, but she may also instigate some type of surveillance here. If you want to keep Cade's presence a secret, you both need to stay out of sight."

Cade sighed. "So much for our run."

"And swim," Celia added.

"There's the sparring mat," Micah suggested. "The one Aurora and I used when she was training with me. We could set it up before we leave."

"Good idea." His dad pointed behind Cade and Unity. "It's in the garage."

"Celia and I can set it up. It'll give us something to do. In fact," Cade's smile was self-mocking, "got any furniture you need rearranged? Or floors that need scrubbing?"

His dad chuckled. "Nothing comes to mind, but the house is yours to do with as you please. Make yourselves at home." The smile faded. "You should be safe here, but if there's anything you need, use one of the house pads to contact my comband. It's a direct link, completely untraceable." He glanced at Unity. "Unity's assured me they can monitor all activity within a square kilometer of the house. They'll alert you to any threats. If the safety of this location is compromised, take the shuttle and go. We'll sort out the details afterward."

Micah's stomach twisted. Having watched Aurora's arrest, he could easily picture the kind of threat Cade faced if the Sovereign found him. But Celia and Unity would make sure that wouldn't happen.

"Thank you, Brendan," Cade said, his gaze shifting briefly to Micah. "We'll be fine."

"And knowing you're safe will go a long way to easing Aurora's anxiety level," his dad replied.

That was certainly true. And another reason his sister might have chosen to contact Cade this morning instead of him.

His anxiety level was still sky high. The idea of walking into the brig filled him with cold dread. Not that it mattered. He'd literally walk through fire to help Aurora. He'd proven that to himself at Stoneycroft.

Seeing his sister incarcerated in a maximum-security Fleet brig should be a snap by comparison, right?

Right. Just keep telling yourself that.

Twenty-Nine

Lelindia had never visited the presidential residence before. She had anticipated a formal, ornately decorated showplace. But as she and Jonarel followed Signal into the antechamber for President Yeoh's office suite, the simplicity and airy feeling of the space gave off a sense of natural harmony, despite the building's location a short walk from the Galactic Council headquarters near the heart of the city.

The room where they were instructed to wait contained images of gardens and mountains, with a mural spanning an entire wall that gave the illusion of a wooden bridge over a stream that sparkled in the sunlight.

Lelindia sighed. "Keenan would love that mural." The landscape imagery in this room would appeal to him, though Keenan had focused mostly on drawing portraits while recuperating onboard the *Starhawke*. The sketch he had created of her in Jonarel's arms still had the power to captivate her.

"Yes, he would," Jonarel agreed.

"Who is Keenan?" Signal asked.

"Admiral Payne's grandson," she replied. "We, uh... had a few adventures since we last saw you."

Signal's mouth tightened, but amusement quickly replaced his scowl. "So I am coming to understand."

"At least we're never boring."

He tipped his head in acknowledgement. "Very true."

She was steadily winning him over, despite his deep-rooted antipathy for change. She'd caught him a few times staring at her and Jonarel during the journey here, the awe that had rendered him speechless in the observation lounge yesterday reasserting itself.

And here she'd thought their daughter would be the lynchpin. She'd never imagined the passionate love she and Jonarel shared was a rare commodity on Drakar, or that it was so highly revered. Despite years of study and personal experience, she still had a lot to learn about the Kraed.

Jonarel turned, his gaze locking onto a section of the muraled wall, scrutinizing the painting.

"What is it?" she asked.

"I hear footsteps approaching," he murmured. "There is an artfully concealed seam for a hidden do—"

A section of the mural swung open noiselessly. President Yeoh stood framed in the doorway.

Lelindia had seen vids of her, but the President was more petite than she'd expected, her slender, athletic build reminding her of Celia. And like Celia, she exuded an aura of strength that commanded respect, as did the sharp intelligence in her dark eyes.

Her gaze swung from Jonarel to Siginal and back again. She gave Jonarel a closed-mouth smile. "Normally guests are startled when that door opens, but I see you have the same exceptional hearing as your father."

"Indeed."

She stepped forward, extending her hand. "You must be Jonarel. I have heard much about you."

He clasped her hand in his. "It is a pleasure to meet you, Madam President."

"And you. Your father and Will speak very highly of you."

Jonarel seemed startled but pleased. "Thank you." His attention swung to her. "I would like you to meet my checana, Dr. Lelindia Forrest."

"Checana?" President Yeoh's brows lifted almost to the hairline of her elegant updo. "Your mate?"

His arm encircled Lelindia's waist, drawing her snug against his side. "Yes."

President Yeoh recovered quickly, shot a look at Siginal, and extended her hand to Lelindia. "It's a rare pleasure to meet the first woman to claim the heart of a Kraed. I understand you're the best physician in the Fleet, as well."

Lelindia struggled to hold onto her professional demeanor as her cheeks warmed. She clasped the President's hand. "Who told you that?"

"Will and Knox. They've sung your praises for years. I regret our meeting couldn't be under more pleasant circumstances. I assume you accompanied Signal because you want to discuss Captain Hawke's arrest?"

"Yes, and how it relates to the Teeli."

President Yeoh nodded. "I had a feeling they'd be wrapped up in this. Please, sit." She led the way to the seating circle.

Jonarel joined Lelindia on the plush couch, while Signal and President Yeoh chose chairs across from them.

"Has there been any update on Will's detainment?" Signal asked.

The President's lips thinned. "His trial starts on Tuesday. Because of the nature of the charges, trial counsel requested and the judge granted that the proceedings be held behind closed doors. No observers are allowed, including me. I lodged a formal complaint, but the judge dismissed it."

Lelindia's heart sank. "So no one will know what's happening in the courtroom?"

"Only Will, the attorneys, the judge, and the Fleet panel. They might as well be holding it on the Moon."

"They also denied your request to see Will?" Signal asked.

"Yes. Only Knox is allowed visiting rights. I filed a complaint about that with Admiral Nixon, the acting Fleet Director. He refused to budge. Unfortunately, I have no authority to overrule his decision." She said it calmly, but her eyes flashed fire.

Signal growled softly, the tips of his claws visible as his fingers curled on the arms of the chair.

Lelindia empathized with the President's and Siginal's untenable positions – powerful leaders in their respective realms who had absolutely no control over the Court of Justice or the Fleet.

The Sovereign had planned this attack with effective precision, neutralizing two of the Admiral's – and now Aurora's – most strategic allies in a single move.

President Yeoh focused on Lelindia, studying her with an analytical eye. "I get the feeling you're the one holding the missing pieces that tie Will's and Captain Hawke's arrests together. I have some knowledge of the Teeli and Setarip collaboration, and Reanne Beck's involvement with both. The Teeli would certainly love to remove Will permanently from the Fleet Director's post. He was the most vocal objector to their inclusion in the Union and Council. But can you explain the Teeli's motivation for targeting Captain Hawke?"

Lelindia drew in a slow breath. Once she shared this information, there would be no going back. "I understand you were told about the Suulh who were being turned into Necri soldiers by the Teeli, the ones the Setarips brought to Gaia to cause the crop destruction."

"Yes. I spoke with Will and Commander Ellis about it back in December. That's when they told me about Reanne Beck's role. Unfortunately, they didn't have any evidence I could bring before the COJ."

"I know. That's been the sticking point for us, too. Reanne has been very good at covering her tracks, up to and including staging the deaths of her associates to keep them silent. Aurora unmasked Reanne as the Sovereign during a recent confrontation, but no one else was there at the time to corroborate her identity. It's Aurora's word against Reanne's."

"So destroying Captain Hawke's reputation would make any accusations she made regarding Reanne's involvement uncredible? That's a powerful motivation."

Lelindia sighed. "I wish it were that simple. Aurora isn't just caught up in this fight. She's the reason for it."

She had President Yeoh's full attention now. "Oh?"

She licked her lips. "What I'm about to tell you must remain in this room. It's information my family and Aurora's have guarded all our lives. It may be necessary to reveal it to others at some point in the future, but that will be Aurora's decision, not mine."

"You have my word."

Lelindia paused, gathering her thoughts. "The Suulh we rescued on Gaia are from a homeworld in Teeli space. My homeworld."

President Yeoh's pupils widened so much her eyes looked black. "Yours?"

"Yes. My parents and I are Suulh, not Human. They were born on the Suulh homeworld, and I was born here, on Earth, after my parents fled the Teeli occupation. That's why we know *exactly* what the Teeli are capable of."

President Yeoh's lips parted. "But you look human. And you're a doctor in the Fleet. Surely a routine physical would have revealed—"

She shook her head. "Biologically, we're indistinguishable from Humans. A case of parallel evolution. Any slight differences could be explained away as genetic adaptations or anomalies. My parents were just as stunned when they encountered their first Humans, but they quickly realized they could blend in, allowing them to hide effectively from the Teeli on Earth."

President Yeoh took a beat to process before drilling her with the question she'd been expecting. "How many of you are on Earth?"

"Besides the three of us, only one. Aurora's mother, Libra."

The President's eyes widened. "Her mother? But not her father?"

"Brendan is Human. He and Libra met here on Earth. Aurora and her brother Micah are half-Human, half-Suulh."

"She has a brother?"

"Yes. He and Brendan have been living in Hawai'i since shortly after the Teeli made contact with Humans."

President Yeoh sat forward, picking up on the significance of what she'd said. "Why?"

This part would be a little trickier to explain. "The Suulh culture is rooted in two intertwined families who govern together. One of the families, the Sahzade, are protectors. They have the ability to create an energy shield that can block practically any assault. The second family, the Nedale, are healers. They can see injury and illness on a cellular level and can create an energy field that can reverse cellular damage, sometimes even in those who are clinically dead."

Understanding snapped into President Yeoh's eyes. "You're part of the Nedale family."

"Yes. And Aurora's mother is part of the Sahzade family. She and my parents were smuggled off the planet by their parents to ensure their abilities and those of their children — Aurora and me — wouldn't become a weapon in the hands of the Teeli. A weapon that could eventually be used against our own people."

"A weapon?" It didn't take long for the President to make the next leap. "The Necri who attacked Gaia. They were Suulh who the Teeli turned into soldiers."

"That's right. Until we encountered the Suulh on Gaia, we believed the Teeli had wiped out the rest of our race. We were wrong. Reanne orchestrated our presence on Gaia because she suspected Aurora's connection to the Suulh. The Necri soldiers' reaction to Aurora, and all that transpired on Gaia, confirmed it."

President Yeoh stared off into the middle distance, steadily putting the pieces together. "That's why Beck's after her, why the Teeli and Setarips are after her. They want control of her abilities, or at least to neutralize her." She frowned. "Wait a minute. Weren't Beck and Hawke roommates at the Academy?"

"Yes. They were even good friends for a while. That's when Reanne became obsessed with Aurora. But her obsession has grown more menacing and twisted over time. She's unhinged."

President Yeoh absorbed that. "You said Hawke's mother is Suulh but her father's human. Does Hawke have the Sahzade abilities you described?"

"Oh, yes. She's the most powerful Sahzade ever born."

"No wonder Beck wants her out of the way."

"She doesn't just want her out of the way. She wants her to suffer. Aurora's arrest is the most recent in a long list of strategic moves Reanne has made to trap Aurora and render her powerless. On Christmas, she sent Setarips to murder my parents and kidnap Aurora's mother."

Her voice hitched as she tumbled back into that dark night of hell. And heaven. Without it, she wasn't certain Jonarel would be by her side now.

"I take it they didn't succeed."

"No. They underestimated Libra. And they didn't realize Aurora and Brendan would know immediately that Libra was in trouble."

"What do you mean?"

"He's an empath, an ability he passed on to Aurora. They can sense the emotions of others, especially those they're close to, even at great distances. Aurora and Micah rescued my parents and Libra."

She glanced at Jonarel, the look in his golden eyes burning through her. "With help from Jonarel and me."

Jonarel's arm snaked behind her, gathering her close.

President Yeoh sank back in her chair, the tips of her fingers tapping lightly together. She turned to Siginal. "How do you and Clan Clarek fit into this?"

Siginal looked distinctly uncomfortable. "I was aware of Aurora's potential heritage when I accepted the professorship at the Academy. My goal was to monitor her, and Lelindia, to determine the scope of their abilities and the danger the Teeli posed to them. When Jonarel became friends with Aurora, I had hoped he and Aurora would pair bond, joining the Suulh and Kraed together. But she — they — chose a different path."

President Yeoh's gaze swept over Lelindia and Jonarel, a smile softening her features. "I'd say it worked out well for these two."

Lelindia's fingers threaded through Jonarel's, her hand resting on his thigh. Her body hummed at each point of contact.

Siginal gazed at them. "Yes, it has."

President Yeoh zeroed in on Lelindia again. "You said your two families are the protectors and healers for the Suulh. Did your parents take any other Suulh with them when they escaped your homeworld?"

She should have known the President wouldn't miss a single detail. "They did, but those Suulh are not on Earth."

"Where are they?"

"It's probably best if you don't know that."

"Why not?"

"Because Reanne doesn't know about them, and we'd like to keep it that way. The fewer people who know they exist, the better."

President Yeoh scrutinized her, but the corners of her mouth tilted up. "Will didn't mention you were a good tactician."

"I wasn't. I'm learning on the job."

"So it would seem. Clearly you have a reason for telling me all this. What do you need from me?"

"For now, your support and your discretion, along with any ideas you have for how to combat Reanne's machinations. Incarcerating the Admiral and Aurora is an opening gambit. She takes a sadistic glee in hurting Aurora. But locking her in the brig isn't sufficient to satisfy her. She wants to inflict pain, personally and repeatedly. Whatever her end game is, we will need the Admiral and Aurora free to fight it."

"I'm not going to ask what you intend to do if the Fleet panel convicts either of them. But I will confirm Beck's influence is spreading through the governing bodies of the Union like a plague. It has wiped out critical thinking and common sense wherever it grabs hold. I am doing what I can to stem the tide." For a moment, President Yeoh reminded her of a crouching tiger. "But a time may come when we can no longer trust the systems we serve."

Thirty

Walking into the Fleet detention center reminded Micah of the first time he'd gotten tangled in seaweed during a free dive. He'd had enough presence of mind to slow his movements rather than thrash in a blind panic, but the sensation of being trapped in a hostile environment had left a mark on his psyche. It was one reason he continually emphasized safety with his students before, during, and after a dive.

The somber color scheme and unforgiving lighting of the building interior made him wince. Judging by the tight set of his mother's jaw and the stiff motion of his dad's stride, he wasn't the only one having a negative reaction.

The reception area they entered had a high solid counter stretched across the facing wall with a transparent barrier on the upper half that separated visitors from the personnel seated behind a pair of check-in stations. A roped switchback line snaked in front of each station, both more than half full of visitors waiting to check in. Beyond the high counter, uniformed personnel moved through a cubicle farm with the brisk efficiency of drones in a hive.

Micah folded his arms over his chest to ward off a sudden chill. Yeah, so not his kind of place.

But his sister was here. He'd felt an insistent pull since his dad's plane had touched down, as though he and Aurora were tied together with a rope that was reeling him in. Their abrupt separation had made him acutely aware of the underlying connection that bound them together. On the *Starhawke*, he hadn't noticed it consciously because they'd never been far from each other. But ever since she'd been taken, it ebbed and flowed within him like an internal tide.

He followed his parents to the back of one of the lines. The absence of conversation in the room had the eerie quality of a dead calm. There had to be at least thirty people in line, but other than the shuffle of feet and an occasional cough or sniff, you wouldn't know it. Those waiting in line had the vibrancy of mourners at a wake. The two officers working the check-in stations certainly weren't chatty either.

His dad twitched, his gaze sweeping the room. The empathic input from this setting couldn't be pleasant for him, especially if he was seeking out Aurora while trying to buffer the emotional resonances of everyone else. Not an easy task, even for a skilled empath.

His mom stood facing the check-in station, the fingers of one hand wrapped firmly around the other. To anyone else, her body language might signal anxiety or fear. But now that he understood how much his mother and sister used their hands to direct their energy field, the pose took on a very different meaning.

His mom would be able to pinpoint Aurora's exact location in the building with the accuracy of X-ray vision. Her instincts had to be screaming for her to take action to get Aurora out of this awful place. Her fisted hands showed how hard she was fighting to keep her abilities under lock and key.

He wanted to put his arm around her, offer comfort and support, but the fact that his dad hadn't done that indicated the gesture wouldn't be welcomed. So he faced forward, too, and watched the worker bees behind the counter.

Eons passed before they reached the front of the queue, though a quick glance at the clock on the far wall proved only twenty minutes had elapsed.

His dad stepped up to the check-in window. "We're here to visit Aurora Hawke."

"Names?"

"Brendan and Micah Scott, and Libra Hawke."

The man's gaze flicked over them. "Are you biologically or legally related to the detainee?"

"Yes. We're her parents and Micah's her brother."

"Have you stowed all electronic devices, purses, backpacks, and other bags or containers in your vehicle or the lockers provided outside?"

"Yes."

"Tap your ID on the scanner and place your finger in the DNA reader. You will feel a slight pinch."

His father followed the instructions. The reader hummed, and about half a minute later a light on the device turned green.

"You are cleared. Ma'am?" The man motioned to Micah's mom.

She tapped her shiny new ID – which had replaced the one destroyed in the fire at Stoneycroft – on the reader, and placed her finger in the device. She looked like she was gritting her teeth as the device hummed.

The light turned green.

"Sir?"

Micah stepped up to the device. The pinch he'd been warned about was followed by a cool misting sensation, then the green light.

"Proceed through the door to your right. Once inside, remain still while the scanner completes its cycle. When the inner door opens, join group four." The man pointed to the solid metal door set into the block wall where the previous visitors had passed through.

His dad managed a smile. "Thank you."

The door opened into a tiny anteroom that could fit no more than five people comfortably. After the door closed behind them, a high-pitched whirring from the scanning device ran for several seconds, followed by a chime. The door on the opposite side from where they'd entered opened, admitting them into a waiting room twice the size of the reception area.

The walls were smooth and unadorned, with a single door to the left breaking up the impression of standing in a box. The floor was marked with five distinct numbered sections, with people clustered in each group.

They joined the group four cluster and waited in silence with the other visitors.

The door behind them opened and closed repeatedly, admitting more visitors, before a buzzer sounded at the door to the left. A moment later the door swung open and a FS officer stepped into the room, a tablet in her hand. Five other FS officers filed in behind her, blocking the doorway.

The officer with the tablet surveyed the five groups dispassionately. "All visitors will obey the rules specified in your visitor packet. Failure to follow the rules will result in immediate expulsion from this facility. Are there any questions before we proceed?"

When no one spoke up, she continued. "When I call your group, you will follow your assigned FS officer through the door and proceed to the visitation room. Stay with your group and follow all instructions from your FS officer. Group one."

The first group followed one of the FS officers out of the room. Micah shifted his weight, trying not to fidget, but failing miserably. Time crawled by while he waited for group two and then group three to exit through the doorway.

Their group was smaller than the first three, only five other people besides him and his parents.

"Group four."

Micah followed his parents into the corridor, which was every bit as cheerful as the rest of the facility. Their footsteps echoed on the hard cement floor, the FS officer setting a brisk pace. The door they halted in front of had three window slats on the top third that gave a fractured view of the narrow rectangular room beyond.

As the guard opened the door, the dull creak of heavy hinges reminded him of a crypt. This time the chill that passed over him raised goosebumps.

His dad stepped closer, their arms brushing against each other. He leaned into the reassuring contact, waiting while the other visitors filed into the room before he followed his parents inside.

A three-centimeter-thick transparent wall bisected the length of the room from floor to ceiling. Seven transparent partitions of the same material ran perpendicular to the wall on both sides, creating eight cubbies, each marked with a large red circle with a number in the center. A metal bench bolted to the floor on the visitor side of each cubby was wide enough to seat up to four people if they crammed together. A straight-backed metal chair, also bolted to the floor, was centered in each cubby on the prisoners' side.

The security officer began calling off names of inmates and their corresponding numbers, motioning the visitors to sit at the matching bench. "Hawke, number two."

They claimed their bench, the hard metal pressing into the backs of his thighs. His mom's entire right side snugged up against him, like she needed the tactile confirmation that he was there. Her posture was stiff and unyielding. A hurricane probably couldn't budge her.

He wasn't pulling off relaxed, either. His spine was doing an excellent imitation of the metal bench and his back muscles felt hard as the concrete beneath his feet. He had to consciously unclench his hands in his lap.

After a couple minutes, the unmarked door on the inmates' side of the transparent barrier opened. A FS officer entered, followed by five women in unadorned Fleet uniforms. The last one was Aurora.

Her skin looked a little sallow, but that could have been the glare of the overhead lighting. Her hair was pulled back in a braid that looked damp. Her gaze snapped to his like an arrow striking the target. He felt the zing of connection down to his toes.

A hint of a smile turned up the corner of her mouth.

Relief swept through him. An answering smile flitted over his lips as she strode toward them and settled into the metal chair.

She sighed, her gaze moving from him to their parents. "Thanks for coming."

Her voice rose from the speaker embedded in the floor near their feet. A matching speaker was visible on her side of the glass.

His throat tightened. This was so wrong. "You look good," he said around the constriction. It was an inane comment, but in the back of his mind he'd feared she'd look beaten down and abused. Her relatively normal appearance levered a little of the oppressive weight off his shoulders.

Understanding shone in her green eyes. "I'm doing okay, considering."

"Your mom and I spoke with an attorney, Phoebe Liddell, yesterday," their dad said. "She's former COJ now working in the private sector. Best of the best. She'll be here to meet with you before the end of the day."

Aurora's jaw flexed. "Thanks, Dad." Her gaze moved to their mom. "How are you doing?"

The concern in her voice made him want to laugh and cry at the same time. She was incarcerated, cut off from everyone she loved, but she was still focusing on everyone else's wellbeing.

"I've been better. Then again, so have you. I do understand the decision you made. I just wish... well..." Their mom twirled a hand in the air. "Things were different."

"You and me both. But I'm glad you're all together." Aurora put emphasis on the *all*, shooting him a look.

Thank you for looking out for Cade.

Her words came through clearly, just like the memorable night of the fire at Stoneycroft when she'd called out to him for help. It confirmed they could communicate this way, at least when they were near each other. That was a relief.

You're welcome.

There were so many other things he wanted to say, to ask, but they'd have to wait. Too much non-verbal communication would cause odd silences that would draw unwanted attention, and every word they spoke would be monitored by the Fleet personnel controlling the speaker system for the cubbies.

No surprise that Aurora had already figured out that Cade and Celia were in Hawai'i. She would have sensed them, known by their proximity to him and their parents where they were. "Lelindia checked in this morning. She said to tell you hello and that the crew's doing well."

"That's good to hear." A bemused look passed over her face. "Please tell her and the crew hello back when you talk to her again."

The exchange was all for show. Lelindia had already confirmed last night that Aurora was communicating with her. But not mentioning Lelindia and the crew during this visit would be a huge red flag to the Sovereign's minions and might cause them to question why.

"How's the food?" their dad asked.

"Decent. I think some of the fruits and veggies are grown on site. I overheard someone mention a garden work detail."

Their mom perked up. "You'd be good in the garden."

Aurora shook her head. "I doubt I'll be assigned to any work detail. I only leave my cell for shower and yard time. Meals are delivered to me."

She somehow managed to make it sound like room service rather than imposed isolation, although their dad's flinch indicated her emotions didn't match the chipper tone she was using.

Her forced cheer triggered an irrational and idiotic urge to smash his fists against the transparent barrier, to try to break her out. The action wouldn't achieve anything except bruises and getting him banned from the facility, but logic and reason weren't spearheading the plan.

Aurora, on the other hand, might succeed if she were so inclined. He'd watched her break through solid logs at Stoneycroft. Whatever material the barrier was made of, it might not be able to withstand a focused strike from the Sahzade of the Suulh.

Which was neither here nor there. Aurora had chosen to be incarcerated. She wasn't going to turn around and try to break herself out the very next day, especially in a scenario where innocent people might get hurt.

Aurora's gaze was on him, clearly reading his maelstrom of emotions. She opened her mouth, closed it, opened it again, closed it. The exasperation on her face made it clear she was casting around for topics they could discuss that weren't contrived but also wouldn't give their enemies more ammunition.

He knew the feeling. She wouldn't want the three of them saying anything about themselves or what they were doing, no matter how innocuous it might seem. The less the Sovereign knew about them the better. As it was, coming here was a big reveal. He and his dad were supposed to be dead. Now they were in the same boat with his mom, Marina, and Gryphon — secondary targets for assault.

Their mom and dad seemed equally at a loss for what to say.

Aurora gave a soft snort, a wry smile curving her mouth. "So." She stretched out the vowel sound. "Seen any good movies lately?"

Thirty-One

The visit from her parents and Micah had given Aurora a lot to think about.

On the walk back to her cell block, she reached out with her empathic senses, searching for the Admiral's unique resonance. She pinpointed him in the same location he'd been the night before, his cell a fair distance across the complex from where she was headed. She put her empathic walls back in place, cutting off the emotional negativity of the other prisoners before it started to drag her down.

She needed to reestablish her inner balance. After the FS officers locked her back in her cell, she swapped out her uniform for her workout attire. Settling into her first yoga pose, she engaged her energy field, allowing its warmth to buffer the hard cement's unforgiving cold.

What a day. She hadn't realized until she was face to face with her family how little they'd be able to say to each other. She'd wanted to ask about her dad's classes, find out if her mom was looking into opening a new plant nursery on Oahu, but she hadn't dared. She had to assume the Sovereign was getting a recording of every word she said. Now that Micah and her dad had revealed themselves, she didn't want to make the Sovereign's job any easier by giving her information.

She'd also been processing her mom's and Micah's emotions. Her dad had obviously been muting his, for which she was grateful, but her mom had been an overheated boiler about to blow its rivets, and Micah's helplessness had mirrored her own.

It's only the first day. This is a marathon, not a sprint.

Yeah, she'd been repeating that ever since she woke up. Not sure it was doing anything to improve her mood.

Still, seeing her mom and dad had helped. Her dad's quiet confidence was as solid as a bulkhead, giving her something to lean into. And when she'd delved under her mom's indignant rage, she'd been shocked to discover a complete lack of fear. Considering Aurora was caught in one of her mom's worst-case scenarios, that was stunning. If this had happened six months ago, her mom would have been a quaking, volatile landslide of fear. Instead, she was collected and rational, despite the bubbling cauldron of anger with the Sovereign's name written in red ink across the surface.

She sighed, moving fluidly through her next sequence of poses.

She didn't blame her mom for her violent emotions. Her mom's maternal and Sahzade instincts to protect the innocent, particularly her own child, were part of her genetic code. It didn't help that her mom had disliked Reanne from day one. But now? Dislike had mushroomed into hatred. She had no doubt if Reanne ever dared to show her face in her mom's presence, her mom would lash out with everything she had. She would make sure Reanne would never harm those she loved again.

That thought made her shudder.

She didn't want the Sovereign's blood on her mom's hands. Or on her hands, for that matter. Her attempts so far had been to capture the Sovereign, to bring her to justice, not destroy her.

But if hers and the Admiral's arrests were indicative of the current state of the Court of Justice, detainment and a trial wasn't an effective solution. The Sovereign would slip her bonds in days, if not hours.

Which left Aurora with a no-win scenario.

If the courts couldn't provide an answer, that left a deeply disturbing alternative. Even considering it as an option made her mind rebel and stomach churn.

Was she prepared to *kill* the Sovereign to stop her?

Was that where this battle would ultimately lead? Was that the kind of guardian she would have to become? Would her nightmare of facing the Sovereign one-on-one, no holds barred, have to become a reality?

What if it did?

She was no shrinking violet. She'd used lethal force twice in the line of duty. She'd also taken down Etah Setarips on Gaia. But those situations hadn't been personal. She'd been fighting unknown adversaries.

She knew Reanne, probably better than anyone. At one time, she'd thought of her like a kid sister. Reanne had been troubled, yes. Needy and annoying at times, certainly. But not the monster threatening the future of the Suulh and all that Aurora held dear.

Her teenage self never would have believed Reanne was capable of the acts of cruelty, heartlessness, and lethal brutality she'd displayed as the Sovereign. Even after seeing the Sovereign with her own eyes, seeing Reanne's face beneath the hood, her mind – and heart – still struggled to deny it.

But she couldn't. She didn't have the luxury of looking for the good in the person she'd once known. The Sovereign had devoured Reanne, obliterating any compassion and kindness she once possessed.

Which left Aurora with... what?

A cold hand wrapped around the back of her neck. Her energy field sputtered and died, her shoulder blades locking as the chill slid down her spine. The concrete beneath the pads of her fingers turned to ice.

If she faced the Sovereign again – if she chose to use her Sahzade abilities to *kill* her – what kind of soulless monster would she become?

Thirty-Two

"You're toying with me, aren't you?" Cade circled the sparring mat, watching every move Celia made as she matched him step for step.

"Would I do that?" she deadpanned.

"Oh, yes."

They'd been at it long enough that fatigue had set into his muscles, making them tremble. When they'd started this session, they'd taken turns showing each other some of their favorite techniques and practiced using them against each other. Eventually that had morphed into a no-holds-barred contest of skill against skill.

He'd held his own, but facts were facts. Her knowledge exceeded his, especially when it came to wearing down a much larger, stronger opponent. His training hadn't focused on that dynamic nearly as much as hers clearly had. In most cases, he *was* the larger, stronger opponent.

She was revealing all the weak points in his attack and defense strategies. Maybe he could talk her into teaching him how to fill in those gaps.

He moved in with a jab and kick combination that barely brushed the fabric of her tank top and leggings. "Definitely toying with me," he grumbled.

"Ready to call it?" Her movements were as nimble as when they'd started, but he noted with satisfaction that her clothes were as soaked with sweat as his.

"That would be the wise move," he admitted, right before he attacked again, hoping to take her off guard.

She blocked and delivered a blow that sent him staggering.

"Okay, okay." He held up his hands, palms out, then dropped them to rest on his thighs. His knees wobbled, threatening to topple him to the mat. "Let's call it."

"About time." She straightened, striding to the side table that held a pitcher of water and two glasses. She poured one and walked it over to him. "Here."

He took it gratefully, gulping down half. He let out a sigh as the coolness hit his stomach and spread over his body. "Much better."

She filled her own glass and drained a third in one swallow. "You're a good sparring partner, the best I've worked with in... well, a long time."

His brows lifted. "That sounds like high praise."

"It is."

"Then I'm honored. I've never faced anyone who challenges me the way you do. In fact, I'm hoping you'll give me some pointers for defending against someone like you."

The corners of her mouth lifted. "Someone like me, or me?"

"Both."

She chuckled. "We'll see."

He snagged one of the towels stacked beside the water pitcher, mopping his forehead before running it over his damp hair. "You want first shot at the shower?"

She shook her head. "Micah said I could use the one in his room."

Cade suppressed the grin that fought to break through, adjusting the towel to hide his reaction. *I'll just bet he did.*

He'd sensed the turbulent emotions Micah had been radiating like a solar flare that morning after Cade had left him alone with Celia. From what he'd gathered, Celia had been pushing all the poor guy's buttons without realizing it, nearly sending him into a tailspin.

Cade had been about to head back into the house to save him when he'd caught Brendan's emotional shift and realized help was already on the way.

So far, Celia remained oblivious to all of it. He could sense the raw emotions skittering around the edges of her emotional field. Maintaining an even keel was taking considerable focus whenever she wasn't actively engaged in a task. It was part of the reason he'd kept the sparring session going so long.

"Then I'll head upstairs. I need to check in with my team, too."

She nodded. "It's still pretty early, but I was thinking about fixing dinner after we get cleaned up. Maybe make it an early night."

They could both certainly use a better night's sleep. A good meal might help with that. "I can help with the cooking."

"Then I'll meet you back down here after you've talked to your team. Tell Reynolds I said hi."

"Will do."

Unity floated over the low wall that separated the sunken living room from the expansive front room where he and Celia had cleared the furniture and set up the sparring mat. "Can we join you for the call?"

He'd momentarily forgotten Unity was even in the house. They'd been silently observing the ocean view the whole time he and Celia had been sparring. "You want to?"

"Please. We miss interacting with the team."

"So do I." Nothing about the past few days had gone the way they'd anticipated. "I just need to shower first."

Unity bobbed. "We'll wait for you in Aurora's room."

He made quick work of getting cleaned up and dressed before settling onto Aurora's bed. He pinged Justin through his comband, routing it through the Far Horizons system rather than the team's normal secure Fleet line on the ICS. With the Admiral incarcerated, he didn't trust it.

"How's our fearless leader?" Justin greeted him, his cheerful voice sounding slightly strained. He was seated on the couch in the Admiral's media room, Bella by his side with her tablet in hand. She gave Cade a wave before returning her attention to her screen.

"Wishing I wasn't so useless. You?"

Justin sighed. "The weather's stormy, so we haven't had any protestors outside the house today. That's the good news. But Knox's personal message account keeps filling up with threats and irate rants from nutjobs who've already decided the Admiral's guilty. They're condemning Knox as guilty by association."

Cade's molars scraped together. "Bella, have you had any success tracking down the person who posted Knox's personal account information to the ICS forum?"

"I got a name," Bella huffed, glancing up. "But it turned out to be fictitious. Big surprise. I'm still digging, but if past experience is any indicator, we won't find anything. The Sovereign will have covered her tracks, or at the very least pinned it on some poor sap who's under her thrall."

"But Knox still wants to stay at the Admiral's house?"

"Yep," Justin answered. "I don't blame him. Fleet captains don't back down from a fight. Besides, the relatively isolated location works in our favor. We have clear vantage points for all potential approaches to the fence. We've also upgraded the house security. Local law enforcement is supporting us, too. The Admiral's very well liked around here, so that helps. The folks we've talked to don't believe he's guilty."

"Glad to hear it."

"And we'll have an abundance of backup this evening. Aurora's family, Lelindia and her folks, and Jonarel and his dad are all coming here."

The collective strength in that group would cower any local troublemakers. "Are they staying overnight?"

"That's the plan. I assume you'll want me to loop you in when the discussion gets underway?"

"Absolutely. I want to hear how Aurora's doing." He'd tuned into her emotions off and on throughout the day, which had been a blessing and a curse.

"Any issues where you are?" Justin asked.

"Not yet. The Sovereign has no way of knowing we're here, but Brendan pointed out that his info is now linked to Aurora. I'm not counting on staying here long term. I just need to come up with my Plan B."

"And we're watching over him," Unity piped up, gliding next to Cade's shoulder in the vid pickup.

"Hey, Unity." Justin smiled. "Good to know you've got his back."

"And his front."

Cade laughed along with Justin and Bella. Unity twirled, clearly pleased their joke had hit the mark.

"By the way, Celia wanted me to tell Reynolds hi for her. Is she around?"

"She and Williams are sleeping. She keeps insisting she prefers the night rotation, so she'll be getting up in a few hours. Tam just went down a couple hours ago. He's on the midnight to noon shift."

"Is the threat assessment getting worse?" His team was putting in long hours.

Justin shared a look with Bella. "We're not taking any chances."

He bit the inside of his cheek as his frustration mounted. "Maybe Celia and I should come there and help."

Justin snorted. "Don't you dare. The five of us can handle it. Knox isn't exactly a delicate flower, and we have plenty of local backup. We need you where the Sovereign can't touch you. That isn't here."

Thirty-Three

Outside the busy monorail station, a hostile group of protestors brandished handwritten signs in splashes of black and red proclaiming TOSS OUT THE TRAITORS! and FLEET OF LIES!

Even within the cozy confines of Siginal's plush diplomatic transport, Lelindia could hear their angry chants, the vitriol matching the aggression on their faces. A third sign froze the air in her lungs. It showed a dangling noose with the words STRING UP SCHREIBER below it.

Jonarel's low growl blocked out the shouts of the protesters, his arm circling her waist and his palm flattening over her belly.

"Are they here for us?" she whispered, her voice constricted.

"No." Siginal shifted on the seat facing them, his golden eyes glinting. The crowd grew positively vicious toward two ensigns in Fleet uniforms who dared to walk past. "This is the violence of fanaticism, not a targeted assault."

His muscular form momentarily obstructed her view of the protestors as he opened the door and stepped onto the walkway. She followed, with Jonarel so close behind it was like they moved as one person.

The chanting trailed off. She caught a glimpse of the protestors staring at Siginal and Jonarel with wide eyes and open mouths.

"Ignore them," Jonarel murmured, placing his hand at her back and urging her to the stairs leading to the arrival platform.

She surveyed the group, who were watching them with a mixture of suspicion and fear. "Why are they so *angry?*"

"Because they believe the lies they have been told." The pressure from Jonarel's hand on her back grew more insistent. He drew her to his side while Siginal moved directly behind her, keeping himself between her and the protestors.

"The Sovereign's lies." What a demoralizing thought, especially seeing it firsthand. The woman who'd been brandishing the STRING UP SCHREIBER sign had looked ready to assault anyone who dared challenge her, at least until that someone was a ticked-off Kraed. "I had no idea it could be like... this."

"Because you have a generous heart."

That heart bled with each step up the stairway. The Sovereign's actions had triggered so much unnecessary pain and suffering, the kind of damage Lelindia's energy field couldn't heal. The presence of the protestors pushed the threat to a whole new level. She'd never imagined strangers taking up the Sovereign's cause and willingly spreading her toxic message of deception and hatred.

She should have. That had been Reanne's specialty at the Academy, exploiting people's weaknesses and pitting them against each other. Now she was fostering the same malignancy on a global scale.

She slipped her arm around Jonarel's waist, needing his reassuring warmth.

"It will be okay, checana," he whispered, his steps unhurried as he guided her through the crowd. It helped that the other passengers stepped out of his way, allowing him to effectively clear a path like a boat cutting through water. Some stopped to stare, while others shot him and Siginal a nervous glance and hurried off.

She knew how intimidating her protectors could look when they were focused on a goal. And how fascinating. Most of these folks had probably never seen a Kraed in the flesh before.

"They are here."

She paused, going up on her tiptoes, her gaze sweeping the section of the monorail station platform Jonarel had indicated. She spotted her dad first, a head taller than most of the other passengers. The top of her mom's thick mane of dark hair was visible by his shoulder.

"Jonarel! Lelindia!" her dad called out, waving a hand above the crowd. He was working his way toward them, her mother in tow, but without the same degree of success Jonarel was achieving.

"Gryphon," Jonarel replied in a rumbling growl that made the people still in his path veer off, opening a channel between them.

Her mom took advantage of the cleared space, dropping her bags to the ground and darting forward like an arrow. Lelindia did the same, meeting her in a bone-crushing hug that lasted for days.

"I'm so sorry," her mom murmured, her voice strangled. "I never thought—"

"I know, Mom." Lelindia tightened her grip, vaguely aware that her dad, Jonarel, and Siginal had created a circle of protection around them. "We'll get her out of this."

"Yes, we will." Her mom eased back, swiping at the tears streaking her cheeks. "I'm assuming Aurora had her reas—" Her mom cut off abruptly, her eyes turning into twin moons as she stared at Lelindia's abdomen. "You... you're..."

"Yes." She glanced at her dad, who didn't have the benefit of her mom's Nedale vision. "Jonarel and I are going to have a daughter."

Her dad's jaw hinged open at the same time her mom whooped and flung her arms around her.

"I knew it! I knew it would work!" her mom cried. The river of tears started streaming down her cheeks again as she gazed at Lelindia, but this time she didn't swipe them away. The mega-watt smile she turned on Jonarel lit up the platform. "I am so happy for you both." She reached out a hand.

He stepped closer, allowing her to pull him into a group hug.

Lelindia's dad joined them a moment later, his hand resting lightly on her hair. "That's wonderful news, firefly." Moisture gathered in his eyes, his smile tender. "What a gift."

Her throat tightened as her heart squeezed. "I know." *I just wish Aurora was here.* She didn't want to face the very real possibility of her daughter's birth occurring without Aurora by her side. *That won't happen. I won't let it happen.*

It felt more like a wish than a promise, but she planted it firmly in her mind's eye, like a sprinter staring down the track to the finish line.

Her mom pulled herself together, her gaze moving over Lelindia's shoulder. "Siginal, it's so good of you to come."

Siginal bowed his head. "Marina. Gryphon. It has been too long."

The formality of the greeting probably had a lot to do with the public setting, but also the unusual nature of their current relationship. The last time Siginal had seen her parents was at Aurora's Academy graduation.

She remembered him being polite, but he'd focused on Aurora and Libra almost exclusively. At the time she hadn't noted it as odd, since it was Aurora's graduation, but she was seeing his behavior through new eyes. He'd expected Libra to be a part of his extended clan and had treated her accordingly.

Now that Siginal had accepted Lelindia and her unborn daughter, Lelindia's parents had become tangential members of Clan

Clarek. He was having to make a lot of mental and emotional adjustments.

Her dad smiled warmly. "Looks like you and I are going to be grandpas soon."

"Indeed." Siginal shot a perplexed look at Lelindia's mom. "How did you know?"

Amusement flashed in her mom's eyes. "Because I can see the child," she replied in an undertone.

"Oh." The analytical look she was getting to know quite well stole over his face. Stepping back, he gestured to the stairway. "I have a transport waiting."

Jonarel picked up her mom's bags where her dad had set them down. As their small group backtracked to the stairway, the gazes of the other passengers followed them, a few of them holding up vid devices to capture images. No doubt their group would be a topic of discussion around a lot of dinner tables this evening.

Her parents' steps slowed as they came in sight of the protestors. Her mom's hand clutched hers. "That's because of the Admiral and Aurora?"

"Yes."

The vitriolic chanting had stopped, replaced by a heated argument between the protestors and four Fleet personnel confronting them.

"–innocent until proven guilty–"

"–traitor to the Fleet–"

"—space trash! He should be ejected—"

"—best leader we've ever had—"

The spattering of words she caught supercharged her agitation, especially as the argument escalated, with one of the protestors shoving a young female ensign.

Lelindia didn't see Signal move, at least not until he caught the ensign before she hit the ground. After he'd set her back on her feet, he turned the full force of his burning gaze on the protestors. "Is there a problem here?" His lips pulled back from his teeth in an expression that definitely wasn't a smile.

They shrank from him, but one of the protestors tightened his grip on his sign and pointed it at Signal. "This isn't your business, greenie."

Lelindia flinched at the derogatory term. She'd heard it once before, at the Academy. An arrogant new cadet had seen Jonarel — who hadn't hit his growth spurt yet – as an easy target for bullying. Lelindia had been walking with Jonarel on their way to meet up with Aurora, and the cadet had snidely asked whether the greenie's mommy knew he'd left the nursery with his nanny.

She'd been incensed, but Jonarel had handled it with his usual aplomb. He'd politely asked the cadet's name, then thanked him and walked off, ignoring the cadet's taunts. The next day, Signal had been assigned as the cadet's new advisor, rapidly solving any future attitude issues.

Siginal didn't step any closer to the protestor, but he loomed over him. "On the contrary. This is more my business than yours. The man you are maligning, Admiral William Schreiber, is a close personal friend."

The woman holding the SCHREIBER sign slunk behind her nearest companion.

"You are entitled to your opinions," Siginal continued, "but you will express them respectfully. Admiral Schreiber, and all those who serve in the Fleet, deserve that and more. Am I clear?" His not-smile grew a little wider.

The protestor paled, but stood his ground. "What are you gonna do if I don't?"

Siginal gave a casual shrug. "My companions and I witnessed you shove the ensign, knocking her off her feet. Assaulting a Fleet officer is a serious offense that would certainly interest Fleet Security. Shall I contact them?"

One of the other protestors muttered something to his companion that she didn't hear.

But Siginal did. "Your friend is correct. You should let it go. Unless you wish to spend the rest of the day with Fleet Security."

The four Fleet personnel were staring at Siginal with hero worship in their eyes. The protestors, not so much.

The man glared daggers at Siginal, but he flicked his hand at his companions. "Whatever," he muttered, stalking off, the other protestors trailing behind him.

As concessions went, it stunk. But it got the job done.

Siginal focused on the ensign. "Are you alright?"

"S-sure," she stammered, her wide eyes staring up at Siginal. "Th-thank you."

Poor kid. Lelindia knew from personal experience how hard it was to think when bathing in the glow of a Kraed gaze.

"Thank you for defending the Admiral, Ensign…?"

"Connie Gutierrez."

"Ensign Gutierrez. I am Siginal Clarek."

"I know." Gutierrez nodded like a bobblehead, shooting awestruck looks at her companions. "I'm a linguist. It's been my dream to one day visit Drakar and speak with your people." She said something in the Kraed language. Lelindia picked out the words *beautiful* and *planet*.

Siginal's reply was just as incomprehensible to her. Then he switched to Galish. "I look forward to that day, Ensign. But now we must depart." He gestured to where the transport waited.

Gutierrez gave a start, registering that Siginal hadn't been alone. A guilty look passed over her face as she briefly met Lelindia's gaze. "Of course. Sorry for the inconvenience." She backed away.

"Until we meet again," Siginal said with a small bow of his head.

He might as well have handed the ensign a golden ticket. She practically glowed as she rejoined her friends and hurried off.

Lelindia's dad chuckled. "You made her day."

"Indeed," Siginal agreed.

After her parents stowed their luggage, they sat on either side of Lelindia on the forward-facing seat of the transport, while Jonarel and Siginal claimed the one opposite them.

"Will's house," Siginal told the Nirunoc who steered the vehicle. The transport pulled smoothly into the flow of traffic leaving the station. "Knox is expecting us. Aurora's family are already on their way," he informed Lelindia's parents.

Lelindia pressed her lips together to keep from smiling. Siginal had a lot to learn about Suulh communication. Now that Libra was no longer denying her Suulh abilities, she would have already passed on the pertinent information to Lelindia's mom and dad the same way Lelindia and Aurora did with each other.

But Siginal hadn't been exposed to that part of their culture. She and Aurora had never discussed it with him because as far as they'd known, he hadn't been aware they were Suulh. How wrong they had been.

She'd forgiven Siginal for all the pain he'd put Aurora, Jonarel, Tehar, and her through, but it would take time to completely heal the wounds. Her daughter, thankfully, would not have that issue. She would enter the world basking in the love from her Grandpa Siginal.

Which begged the question, what kind of grandpa would he be? She'd never met Jonarel's grandparents. During the *Starhawke's* first visit to Drakar, Siginal's parents had been away from the compound visiting extended family in another clan. She still wasn't clear on the specifics of how pair bonding relationships worked across clans, but she knew Daymar, Jonarel's mother, came from a different clan. She assumed Daymar's parents still lived with that clan.

She hadn't even considered such questions before, probably because grandparents hadn't been part of hers or Aurora's lives. She should ask Jonarel about his the next time they were alone.

Speaking of her mate, he was watching her with a loving sweetness that made her melt. He'd snugged his booted foot against hers, his muscular calf brushing her pantleg every time the vehicle turned.

Her dad had engaged Siginal in conversation as soon as they'd sat down, but she hadn't been paying attention to the topic, lost in her own thoughts.

"...am very impressed with how your ships and shuttles handle," her dad was saying. "Brendan and I both had an opportunity to pilot them recently. It was a real treat."

A thundercloud descended over Siginal's brow. "When was this?"

"Uh..." Her dad shot her a look. "Have you told him—"

"Not yet, but now's a good time." Taking a deep breath, she launched into the long story of their adventures rescuing Keenan from the hospital, traveling to Gaia to meet her mom's and Libra's aailee, and the mating ceremony on the *Starhawke* that followed.

Siginal's scowl made him look like a bear with a thorn in his paw. "You attended the ceremony?" he asked her parents.

They exchanged a look, picking up on the hurt in Siginal's voice. "Yes, we did," her mom answered. "Our presence, and Libra and Brendan's, was one of the reasons Lelindia and Jonarel decided to hold the ceremony while we were onboard."

Jonarel shifted in his seat, making full body contact with his father from shoulder to knee. "Tehar recorded the entire event, talta. We will play it for you and solna when we visit Drakar."

Solna, the Kraed word for *mother*.

Siginal sniffed, gazing out the window at the coastline. "She would appreciate that."

Lelindia sighed. His pride wouldn't allow him to admit how much the knowledge that her parents had attended the ceremony when he had not was hurting him. There was probably more than a little self-recrimination mixed in there, too. He'd created the situation that had pushed them into excluding him.

Leaning forward, she clasped his large hand in hers. The rough callouses of his palm reminded her of the physicality of his daily existence. At heart, he was a warrior, no matter how technologically advanced his clan had become. "I would very much like to have you and Daymar present at our daughter's birth."

He gave a little start of surprise. "You would?"

"Absolutely. If it's possible. I have no idea where we'll be when it happens, but I should be able to give the timetable within a week as I get closer to full term."

His fingers closed around hers, his throat moving in a convulsive swallow. "We will be there."

Thirty-Four

The one-story beach house nestled against the coastline fit with Micah's image of where Admiral Schreiber would live. It was understated, the earth-toned exterior blending in with its surroundings rather than standing out, while the location provided an exceptional view of the ocean. Or it would when it wasn't partially obscured by the stormfront hovering over the cliffs.

Knox Schreiber, however, wasn't at all what Micah had pictured from the snippets he'd gleaned from Aurora's, Lee-Lee's, and Celia's comments. When Knox greeted them at the door and ushered them into the tiled foyer, Micah hung back, making mental adjustments.

Knox looked a lot younger, only about ten years Micah's senior, rather than the twenty plus he'd imagined. His dark hair had hints of grey, his full beard a few more, and his face was drawn with tension, but it didn't disguise the laugh lines around his eyes. His demeanor as he held out his hand to Micah's dad was warm and friendly, more like they were family at a reunion rather than new acquaintances.

No wonder Aurora was so fond of her former captain.

"Brendan, it's an honor to meet you."

His dad clasped Knox's hand. "The honor is mine. Aurora's a big fan of yours."

Knox's smile was self-deprecating. "I've never had a finer first officer. It was hard to let her go, even if it was to captain the *Starhawke*. She's very special."

"Yes, she is."

Knox held out his hand to Micah's mom. "Libra, I've heard so much about you it's hard to believe we've never met."

"I know the feeling. The girls always raved about you in their messages home."

Knox's smile widened. "That's good to hear."

Micah stuck out his hand. "I'm Micah. Aurora's brother."

"Of course you are. You look like her." Knox accepted the handshake and surveyed Micah. "Especially the eyes and hair. And the smile."

Micah hadn't even realized he'd reacted to the comment, but sure enough, he was grinning. Anything that connected him to Aurora lightened his heart. "I'm sorry about your dad. I got to meet him before... well, before."

"He told me. I've been eager to meet you."

"Am I what you expected?"

Knox chuckled, confirming Micah's supposition that he was a man who liked to laugh. "You're what I *should* have expected. For some reason I pictured a marine biology professor as reedy and bookish. My mistake."

"That's okay, I pictured you as grey-haired and stern."

"Oh, I can be stern when the situation calls for it."

"That I totally believe."

"You're the first ones to arrive." Knox indicated the empty living room behind him, where a fire crackled in the stone fireplace beside a U-shaped seating arrangement. "Can I get anyone a drink while we wait? Coffee, tea, wine?"

His dad perked up on the last one. "I wouldn't mind a glass of cabernet if you have it."

"I certainly do." Knox swept a hand to the right of the foyer where a full bar with a raised counter and barstools created an elegant social nook. "Step into the wine cellar and take your pick."

"Libra?" his dad asked.

She waved him toward the cellar. "Whatever you choose is fine."

"Micah?"

"You know what I like."

As his dad and Knox stepped into the cellar, his mom strolled past the pool table — which looked like a game had stopped midway through — toward the wide windows at the back of the house. On a clear day the view of the ocean beyond would be almost as impressive as the one from his dad's house, though the slate blue waters looked chilly and choppy under the brooding grey clouds.

"I don't know how she can stand it," his mom murmured, more to herself than to him.

He didn't have to ask who *she* was. "I don't think there's much she can't handle, especially when she believes she's protecting others."

His mom's grey-blue eyes looked as choppy and shadowed as the water. "She's trapped in a tiny room, Micah, all because of that cold-hearted excuse for a sentient being. I want to..." Her fingers curled into talons, the tendons flexing in her forearms. "I hate feeling so helpless."

"You sound like Aurora."

That brought a ray of light. "I do?"

"Sure. When we were in Teeli space, waiting for the Sovereign to attack, it drove Aurora nuts. She couldn't *do* anything. Your situation now is similar. You're waiting for the threat you know is coming but you can't do anything until it happens."

She nodded slowly. "You're right. The whole time we were in that awful brig, I planned all the ways I could break her out. I wanted to act, not sit there and stare at her through that stupid barrier."

He slid his arm around her shoulders. "I felt the same way."

Her arm circled his waist. "Just so you know, if it comes to that, I won't hesitate. She's not staying in there past the trial."

His blood ran hot and cold at the certainty in her voice. If his mom said she could do it, she could do it. But breaking Aurora out of the brig would destroy any hope of them living normal lives again.

"Nice to see some friendly faces."

Micah turned.

Justin Byrnes strode toward them from a doorway to their left. "Welcome to the bunker."

"Bunker?" his mom echoed.

Justin's mouth pinched. "The weather's nasty so you can't tell, but in the evenings this place is normally besieged by picketers. Reynolds and Gonzo have made sure no one will get onto the property, but it's been pretty ugly. I'm guessing Cade and Knox didn't mention it?"

"No, they didn't," she replied.

"They probably didn't want to worry you. But since you're here, I figured you'd want to know."

"You figured right."

"Is the rest of the team here?" Micah asked.

"Yep. We're working a security rotation, so Reynolds and Williams are sleeping, Bella and I are watching the vid feeds, and Gonzo's out on patrol."

His mom's spine went rigid. "Is the threat to Knox that serious?"

Justin gave a half-hearted shrug. "That's the problem. We don't know. But these people are getting really worked up. I've lost track of how many death threats Knox has received."

"Death threats?" Outrage turned the two syllables into laser strikes from his mom's lips. "Why?"

"He's the Admiral's son." Justin's gaze shifted between her and Micah. "It's possible the same irrational rage will be turned on you, once the media gets a hold of the news that Aurora's parents and brother are visiting her."

His mom stepped in front of him like a human shield. "No one will touch Micah."

Correction, a Suulh shield.

Justin backed up, his eyes widening. He glanced at Micah. "I pity the person who crosses your mom."

"You and me both." He couldn't see his mom's expression, but Justin's reaction spoke volumes.

A moment later his mom's posture relaxed, her attention moving past Justin toward the front door. "Marina's close. They'll be here in a couple minutes."

Either Marina had reached out to her, or his mom was using her internal GPS to track them.

His dad and Knox stepped out of the wine cellar. "We picked out a nice California red for anyone who's interested." His dad held up a bottle. "Hey, Justin. Good to see you."

"You, too."

Micah pointed to the front door. "Mom says the rest of the group is almost here."

His dad glanced at Knox. "Do you mind pouring while we go greet them? This is the first time I've met Siginal."

"Go ahead." Knox shooed them out. "Justin can help me."

Knox and Justin headed for the bar while the three of them walked out into the late afternoon chill.

Micah pulled the front of his jacket closed as the wind caught it and yanked on the lapels. The lumbering clouds looked like they were getting serious about dropping rain, the fresh scent blending with the salty tang of the ocean air.

His dad fastened his jacket, too, but his mom didn't seem to notice the stiff breeze. She planted her feet against the brisk wind whipping her hair over her eyes, daring the elements to challenge her power. Or challenging Siginal? Hard to tell, but the visual emphasized the unusual dynamic this gathering was creating.

As Sahzade, his mom held a position of significant authority. But Siginal was the leader of Clan Clarek. And Knox was a Fleet captain – Aurora's former captain no less – and the Admiral's son.

They would all have strong, and potentially conflicting, ideas about how to address the problem of Aurora's and the Admiral's incarceration. It could make for a very interesting evening.

An oversized black vehicle with blacked out windows turned off the residential street, following the curving driveway to stop facing them. Siginal and Jonarel were the first ones out, followed by Gryphon, Lee-Lee, and Marina.

Marina slipped past Siginal, zeroed in on Micah's mom – completely ignoring her commanding stance – and pulled her into a hug.

Gryphon followed her, stopping next to Micah's dad. "How you doin', kid?"

His dad sighed. "Been better, old man."

Lee-Lee walked straight up to Micah, a thousand questions in her brown eyes. "How is she?"

He gave her a soft smile. "Better than I expected. Calm. Focused. But you know Ror. She's gotta be strong for the rest of us."

Lee-Lee nodded, a sad tilt to her lips. "One of her defining characteristics."

Jonarel stepped forward. "Brendan, I would like to introduce you to my father, Siginal, leader of Clan Clarek. Talta, this is Aurora's father, Brendan, owner of Far Horizons Aerospace."

Micah watched Siginal's reaction. Siginal had been sizing up Micah's dad from the moment he'd set eyes on him. His body twitched slightly at Jonarel's last words. Clearly that piece of intel was news to him.

Micah's dad held out his hand. "It's good to meet you at last, Siginal. I've wanted to thank you for helping to watch over Aurora while she was at the Academy."

That surprised Siginal, too. He hesitated a moment before stepping forward, his hand engulfing Micah's dad's. "It was my privilege. I grew to love her as if she were my own daughter."

There might have been a subtle rebuke in that comment, but his dad passed over it with a smile. "How could you not? She's very loveable."

"Indeed."

The wind picked up, a smattering of raindrops hitting the stone walkway.

His dad gestured toward the front door. "It's warmer and dryer inside. Knox is pouring wine for anyone who's interested."

Micah's mom had resumed her sentinel pose. She didn't move, her gaze on Signal. "Hello, Signal." The coolness in her voice was several degrees below the ambient temperature.

Signal flinched. "Hello, Libra."

Yeah, his mom still had serious issues with Jonarel's dad. Not that he blamed her. The guy had lied to her and Aurora, spied on them, tried to force Aurora to mate with Jonarel, then turned on Lee-Lee when she defended her, holding the *Starhawke* hostage. His mom knew how to hold a grudge. Signal was going to have to earn back her trust and good opinion.

Marina broke the tension. "Come on, Libra. Let's get inside before we get soaked."

His mom allowed herself to be led inside, but not before shooting Signal a parting look that clearly conveyed they'd have words later.

Signal seemed almost as unsettled by her attitude as he'd been when Aurora had given him a dressing down after he'd arrived in Teeli space.

Gryphon clapped Signal on the back. "Don't worry about it," he murmured in an undertone. "She's tough but fair. Once she realizes you've had a change of heart regarding Lelindia and Jonarel's mating, and are excited about the baby, she'll forgive you."

"Yes, she will," Lee-Lee agreed. "She's protective of me and Aurora. I know you can understand that motivation."

Siginal grimaced. "Yes, I can." He motioned to the door. "Shall we?"

Thirty-Five

As soon as Lelindia walked through the front door, Knox gathered her into a welcoming hug. "I'm so happy for you." His blue eyes sparkled as he glanced between her and Jonarel. "Both of you."

She rested her hand on the curve of her abdomen. "Make that all three of us."

His jaw dropped and he blinked several times. "Seriously? You're pregnant?"

She nodded, a flood of emotion pushing moisture against the back of her eyes. "We're going to have a daughter."

He pulled her into another hug, this one a little more cautious. "Wow, that's amazing! Congratulations."

"Thank you."

"When is she due?"

"That's up for debate. She's the first half-Suulh, half-Kraed child ever born, but probably in the next three or four months."

"Three or four months?" A shadow fell over Knox's brow. "That's... quick. There's—" He looked away, as if searching for words. "I hope Aurora's here to greet her," he said at last.

"So do I." She rested a hand on his sleeve. "And your dad, too."

He hesitated again. "My dad, too."

He knew something, something that had him worried. And Knox wasn't a worrier.

That scared her more than anything else that had happened since they'd arrived at Sol Station.

Jonarel's arms came around her, pulling her close.

Knox gave a little head shake, like he was casting off the gloom. "I can't offer you wine, but is there anything else you'd like?"

"Do you have tea?"

"I sure do. It's in the kitchen. Jonarel? Tea or wine?"

"I will have tea."

"Libra and I will make it," Lelindia's mom offered, coming to stand beside them. "Just show us where it is."

Knox beckoned them toward the kitchen. "Follow me."

Justin approached as the trio left. "Hey, Lelindia, Jonarel. How you two holding up?"

She cast a look at Siginal, who was talking to Brendan, Micah, and Lelindia's dad. "Better now that we've worked things out with Siginal. Knox, however, seems uncharacteristically concerned about his dad. Is there something I should know?"

Justin ran a hand through his curly blond hair. "Probably best if we wait until the group discussion to get into that. Cade will want to hear what Knox has to say."

Her pulse beat in her throat. "You're worried, too."

"Hard not to be." A blast of wind made the windows rattle as rain smacked against the glass. "Come on. It's nicer near the fire."

She allowed Justin and Jonarel to guide her to the cozy couches grouped around the crackling fire. Jonarel sat beside her, but Justin remained standing.

Lelindia glanced around. "Where's the rest of the team?"

"Bella's in the media room," he pointed at the fireplace wall, "Reynolds and Williams are sleeping, and–"

A wiry figure strode up to the glass doors of the patio, his face concealed by the hood of his rain slicker.

"And there's Gonzo," Justin finished.

Gonzo folded back the hood and gave them a small wave.

She waved back.

After hanging his slicker on a hook near the door and wiping his boots on the mat, he stepped inside.

"Gonzo," Libra called out from the kitchen. "I'm glad you finally decided to join us."

Gonzo gave her his trademark grin. "Just battening down the hatches."

"Uh-huh." Libra didn't look like she believed a word of it. "All secure?"

Gonzo sobered. "Yes, ma'am."

"Good."

Gonzo strode to the fireplace, lifting his palms toward its warmth. "I'll take hot and dry over cold and rainy any day," he told them. "Glad you guys made it inside before it started coming down."

"Me, too." Though she loved the rain. She could already sense the energy fields of the plants outside opening up to the nourishing drops. As kids, she and Aurora had spent a lot of time outside during gentle rainstorms, listening to the evergreens sway and sigh.

Knox approached, handing a half-full wineglass to Gonzo. "This should help warm you up."

"Thanks."

"Any problems?"

"Nope. We're clear."

Knox offered a matching glass to Justin. "Plenty more where that came from. You guys have earned a break."

Justin accepted the glass. "I'm going to see if Bella wants to join us."

Lelindia focused on Knox. "You are going to tell us what's riled you, right?"

He gave her the look she'd often seen while serving on the *Argo*, the one that said he was facing a challenge he was determined to get them safely through. "Yes, I will."

Libra walked toward them, carrying a tray with a blue and white teapot at the center and four mugs. She set the tray on the coffee table and handed mugs to Lelindia and Jonarel. "It's chamomile, with a little honey."

Lelindia smiled. "Still one of my favorites." Libra used to make it for her when she was a kid, adding an extra spoonful of honey. "Thank you."

"You're welcome."

The rest of the group settled in, Micah on Lelindia's other side, her parents and Signal on the couch to her right, and Libra, Brendan, and Knox across from her.

Bella Drew had joined the group too, but she, Justin, and Gonzo remained standing on either side of the fireplace.

Knox turned to Brendan. "If you would do the honors."

Brendan tapped his comband.

The framed landscape picture above the fireplace changed to an image of Cade and Celia seated side by side in an open, airy room.

"Cade? Celia? Can you hear us?" Brendan asked.

"Loud and clear," Cade confirmed.

"All yours," he told Knox.

A hush fell over the group, all attention on Knox.

He took a sip from his wine glass. "As a witness for the defense in my dad's trial, I'm not permitted to observe the proceedings. But neither is anyone else. The judge supported trial counsel's request that no observers be permitted in the courtroom, not even those with level five security clearance."

Siginal nodded. "Kathryn told us the same thing when we met with her. Hard to believe a judge would agree to keep even the GC President out of the courtroom."

Knox's fingers tightened around his wineglass. "The Sovereign's influence probably has a lot to do with it."

Brendan's gaze turned analytical. "Which makes her job a lot easier if she's already affecting the judge. Only your dad's attorney could challenge the proceedings, and the judge could overrule him."

"Exactly. Legally, Dale Copeland — my dad's lawyer — can't tell me any specifics, and my conversations with my dad in the brig are monitored. We're able to pass some information to each other during those discussions using our coded system, but I won't get a chance to see what's actually happening during the trial until I testify."

A frog started jumping inside Lelindia's belly, making her queasy. "I thought we'd at least be able to sit in on Aurora's trial, be there to support her."

"I wouldn't count on it." Knox's blue eyes were filled with compassion, and aggravation. "However, the critical piece of news I learned from Copeland while we were preparing for my testimony was the name of one of the people scheduled to testify against my dad. Isabeau Magee."

"*What?!*" Siginal and Cade boomed in unison.

Cade was the first to recover. "That can't be. She's in Teeli space."

"Not anymore, apparently."

Lelindia's heart sank. Knox's shuttered expression said it all. He adored Magee, had always spoken of her like she was part of his family. This betrayal would rip him apart from the inside out. "Why would she testify against your dad?"

Knox took another drink, this one more fortifying than the last. "Reynolds filled me in on what Cade's team knew about Isabeau's abduction by the Teeli delegate, and her subsequent transfer to the Sovereign's ship." His jaw clenched. "Based on the surveillance footage they had of her before she left Earth, Reynolds thinks the Teeli have used their manipulative ability to turn Isabeau's mind against my dad."

Silence stretched out as they all absorbed his words.

"Do you know what she's testifying about?" she asked.

His gaze held hers. "Not specifically. But based on the questions I was asked during my interview with Copeland, it seems related to the Setarip attack on Persei Primus."

"Persei Primus?" Celia said, drawing Lelindia's attention. Her friend had leaning closer to the camera, her dark eyes scrutinizing Knox. "Why? Your dad wasn't there."

"No, but I was. So were you, Lelindia, and Aurora. Aurora and Lelindia wouldn't have been part of the mission if my dad hadn't promoted them to the *Argo* a couple weeks earlier."

"But we—" Lelindia blinked, her mind tripping over itself to make sense of what she was hearing. "Are you saying they're accusing your dad and Aurora of *instigating* that attack?"

"And the one on Gaia, yes."

She felt like she'd been hit with a stun gun.

Micah waved his hand. "I'm completely lost. What happened at Persei Primus?"

Knox turned to him. "An Ecilam Setarip attack that took out almost half the station and killed a fourth of the personnel, many of them scientists and civilians."

"And they're trying to pin that attack on the Admiral and Aurora? How?"

Knox scraped a hand over his beard. "With Isabeau involved, the Teeli must have manipulated her into giving distorted or false testimony to support whatever contrived evidence they'll present to the court. That's the only way it leads to my dad's and Aurora's arrests. They must be making the case that my dad was the one directing the Setarips and Aurora was the inside person making sure it all went to plan."

"That's insane," Libra snapped.

"I agree. But they have enough evidence to warrant a trial. Whatever Isabeau will say, it's not good."

Lelindia's head spun. She leaned into Jonarel, his solid presence keeping her stable.

How could anyone believe Aurora was responsible for the attack on Persei Primus?

Lelindia had suspected Aurora's arrest would somehow be tied into the attack on Gaia, but Persei Primus had happened almost three years ago. And she, Aurora, and Celia had been fighting for their lives that day. In fact, without the benefit of hers and Aurora's Suulh abilities, the death toll would have been much, much higher.

"The Sovereign's been planning this whole thing for years." She hadn't meant it as a question, but Knox answered her anyway.

He sighed. "It appears so."

And here she'd been naively believing Gaia was the starting point. But of course it wasn't. The Academy was the starting point. From the day Reanne had been assigned as Aurora's roommate, every second since had been building to this moment. She and Aurora had just been blissfully unaware of that fact.

"What about you?" she asked Knox. "You were our captain. You chose Aurora to lead the team. Why aren't you in custody?"

Knox's humorless laugh cut through the room. "It looks like my role will be the dutiful son and officer, who did whatever my father and commander told me, and who took everything I was told at face value without questioning."

"That's not who you are," Siginal growled.

"No, it's not. But if I'm portrayed as the gullible one, it's much easier for trial counsel to paint my dad and Aurora as the evil masterminds behind the plot, who used me and my position for their own nefarious purposes."

"Surely your testimony will refute that?" Brendan countered.

"If they didn't have Isabeau, it would. But she was my dad's PA for thirteen years. He and I both trusted her implicitly. The one secret she didn't know was yours and Aurora's." He gestured to Lelindia. "If the Teeli have gotten into her head so deeply that she's testifying against my dad, there's no way of knowing how they've warped her perspective or how they'll use her knowledge against him."

Anxiety crawled over Lelindia with spider legs. She shuddered. "But your dad didn't do anything illegal, did he?"

"No. Even the falsification of his medical records at Hydra One is acceptable under the Fleet code for initiating undercover surveillance of a hostile force. But after what I saw during my investigation on Gaia, we won't be dealing with facts or truth in these trials. We'll be going up against misperception, contrived documentation, and manipulated witnesses, all of which will be delivered as fact and truth specifically designed to be impossible to refute."

Siginal grumbled something in Kraed, probably curse words, based on the inflection.

Jonarel sat forward, his hand resting protectively on her thigh. "Lelindia was at Persei Primus and Gaia. Is she in danger of arrest?"

The frog leaping in her stomach was joined by its closest friends. Her hand immediately dropped to her belly.

Knox looked between them. "My instincts say no. While she was part of the team on the station, she was working with the rest of the medical staff treating the station's casualties. She didn't interact with the Setarips or the human conspirators at all, at least not while they were alive. Her presence had no effect on the course of events. Well, other than saving a lot of lives, which she certainly did. Even for the Sovereign, she'd be a tough person to implicate, and going after her might weaken the case against Aurora."

The breath she'd been holding squeezed out of her lungs. "Is there anyone else the Teeli could have turned against Aurora and your dad?"

"From the discussions I've had with the team," he indicated Justin, Gonzo, and Bella, who stood like statues, with Cade's rigid form visible between them on the screen, "it seems like the Teeli manipulative effect is short-term, but cumulative. That's why they had to get Isabeau to the Embassy, and then into Teeli space. It's like a twisted version of an immersion course. The longer and more intensive the contact, the stronger and more lasting the result."

Lelindia's dad propped his elbows on his knees. "Then how do you explain the Teeli's inability to manipulate any of us when we were on Feylahn?"

"They couldn't?" That was news to Knox.

"That's right," her mom agreed. "We were in close contact with them for much longer than Magee, but we weren't even aware the Teeli had that ability until the girls brought it up."

"Lelindia?"

She turned to meet Cade's gaze on the screen. "Yeah?"

"Do you remember having any strange reactions to Reanne at the Academy, especially when she touched you?"

Did she? She searched through her store of memories for times she'd interacted directly with Reanne. "I'm not sure. I always felt weird around her, unsettled, not quite myself." And Reanne's physiology had always bothered her. She'd seen internal inconsistencies from human norms, but hadn't been able to ask Reanne about them without revealing her Nedale abilities. "I saw odd behavior in others, but I can't say whether I was acting strange myself." She turned to Jonarel. "Do you remember me doing anything out of character while I was around her?"

"No." He reached up and stroked her hair. "You were always loyal and kind to Aurora. And me. I could tell you did not care for Reanne."

"Which means you're probably immune," Cade said. "I guarantee Reanne resented your close bond with Aurora. She was jealous of anyone who claimed Aurora's attention. She would have wanted to put distance between you but clearly she wasn't able to manipulate you like she did me and Jonarel."

She wrapped her arms around herself. "But we know she manipulated many of the Suulh we rescued on Gaia. Why did it work on them and not me or you?" Her gaze slid over her parents and Libra.

They looked as baffled as she was.

She turned to Knox. "What about you?"

He shrugged. "If the Teeli I've encountered have tried to manipulate me, it either hasn't worked or it was in a way I never noticed."

"Your dad was immune," she said. "You could be, too. Kire was. And Cade is, now."

"That's helpful." Knox's gaze circled the group. "The fewer people who could potentially flip to trial counsel's side, the better. Thankfully it's painfully obvious when someone you know has been affected."

She caught the hitch in his voice. This situation had to be a slow-drip torture for him.

"And you don't think you're one of the Sovereign's targets for arrest or attack?" Celia asked him.

"No. She needs me to play my assigned role, remember? Implicating me would take the pressure off Aurora, since she was under my command at Persei Primus. And since I'm a witness for my dad's defense, if anything happened to me now, it would cast serious doubts on the fiction the Sovereign's spinning. How about you?" he asked Celia. "How do you respond to the Teeli?"

"I have no idea." And she clearly didn't like that lack of intel. "I've never met one. Aurora made sure I never came in contact with the Teeli we encountered during our survey mission."

"Then make sure you continue that streak."

Celia looked like Knox had shoved a lemon slice in her mouth.

"I know you hate ducking danger," Knox continued. "But it would be far worse if you fell under Teeli influence, even short-term."

"That's what Aurora said." Celia folded her arms. "So how about the other elephant stampeding through the room? What's the likelihood I'll be the next one arrested? I was the lead security officer for the Persei Primus mission, and on Gaia."

"I'd say it's a toss-up right now. It might depend on how much of a danger the Sovereign thinks you pose to her plans."

Celia's dark eyes shot sparks. "A big one. But she may not realize it. We only met briefly on Gaia."

"That's in our favor. Anyone who's spent any time with you knows getting in your way is unwise."

"Especially if she's carrying a spoon," Cade said.

Judging by Celia's reaction, it was an inside joke. Celia tilted her head in his direction. "Is there any indication Cade's on that short list for arrest?"

"No one's approached the team," Justin said, "and we haven't seen any sign of surveillance. Admittedly we've been pretty isolated out here, but I guarantee the Sovereign knows where we are.

We're not hiding, and it's not like we tried to conceal our movements to get here from *Gladiator.* That being said, Reynolds and I have been monitoring FS communications, just in case something new pops up."

"So this time we'll get some warning before anyone's arrested?" Micah asked with more than a touch of irony.

Justin smirked. "Assuming the orders go through normal channels. It's always possible the Sovereign's working with a select group of loyalists who she communicates with directly, but so far that doesn't seem to be the case. We were able to find the digital trail for both the Admiral's and Aurora's arrest warrants. Now that we know what to look for, we can flag anything similar."

Knox rubbed his fingers along his beard, a sign he was deep in thought. "Which brings up another point." He looked to Cade. "My dad made it clear during my last visit that he didn't plan to have your team testify in his defense. Too many ways for trial counsel to turn your actions into a conspiracy. However, he thought trial counsel might go after you for the same reason. The Sovereign certainly knows a lot about you. But none of you are on trial counsel's witness list. The omission struck him as strange."

"Could we know something that might unravel the Sovereign's case?" Cade asked.

A ray of hope pushed back the gathering gloom.

"I don't know. Just give it some thought, see if you come up with any insights that might be helpful."

Cade spread his hands. "I appear to have plenty of time."

Thirty-Six

Cade wanted desperately to believe he had the power to bring the Sovereign's house of cards crashing down. He wanted Aurora and the Admiral sprung yesterday.

He caught movement in his peripheral vision. Unity had drifted closer, spinning back and forth to get his attention. He held up a finger in front of the camera feed. "Hang on a second." Switching off the video and audio, he turned to Unity. "What's up?"

"We want to help."

"How?"

"Monitoring is one of our primary functions. If you need to know what's being said during the Admiral's trial, we could facilitate that."

He exchanged a look with Celia.

"That would mean revealing yourself to Knox and Siginal," she said. "They'd want to know how we're getting that intel. Aurora asked us to keep your presence a secret."

"We know. But we want to help."

"It's your call, Unity," Cade said. "Well, yours and Ifel's. Are you prepared to have Siginal and Knox know about you? About what you can do?"

"Siginal will be fine," Unity assured them. "The Kraed created Star. They will understand. And you all trust Knox. Why shouldn't we?"

"And Ifel's okay with this?"

"It was her idea."

That pulled him up short. "She's listening in to this discussion?"

"We're translating it for her, yes."

"Could have given us a heads up," Celia murmured.

"You didn't know? You thought this meeting was secret?" Unity swayed like the end of a clock pendulum. "But we are always in communication with Ifel."

"Which is fine," Cade assured them. "This is on us. We should have realized."

"Secrets are complicated."

"Tell me about it." He turned back to the camera. "Okay, here we go."

Switching the audio and video back on, he cleared his throat. "Sorry about that."

"Is there a problem?" Brendan asked.

"Nope. I was talking to Unity. They want to help."

Brendan looked eager, but Micah, Lelindia, and Jonarel all stared at him with wide eyes. "Is that wise?" Micah asked, his gaze darting to Siginal, then Knox.

"Ifel thinks so."

"Ifel?" Knox sat up straighter. "The Yruf leader? Who's Unity?"

Lelindia's parents and Siginal looked puzzled, too.

"They're..." Cade gave Unity a sidelong glance. The mobile unit was staying out of sight of the video pickup. "Part of the Yruf," he answered slowly, sending a pointed look to Micah. If anyone could explain Unity, it was him.

"They were helping us with communication while we were in Teeli space," Micah said.

"A specialized comm team?" Knox asked.

Micah's mouth twitched. "You could say that."

"And how do they want to help?" Knox asked Cade.

"For starters, they're offering to monitor your dad's trial."

Knox's brow furrowed. "How could they do that?"

Cade shot Unity another sidelong glance. "We haven't gone into the specifics, but if they say they can, they can."

Knox took that in with a slow nod of his head. "That would certainly help even the playing field." It was clear he knew there was a ship's worth of info they weren't telling him, but he didn't push. "Unfortunately, obtaining that intel would violate Union law."

"Not necessarily," Cade said. "The Yruf aren't part of the Union. They're an alien species who is curious about life on Earth. If they choose to use their technology to observe human behavior to better understand us, that's perfectly acceptable. The Fleet has done the exact same thing regarding other species on planets we've explored."

Knox gave a startled laugh. "That's an interesting argument." He rose and plucked his wine glass off the coffee table. "Lelindia, Jonarel, can you please help me in the kitchen?"

Lelindia looked utterly confused by the non-sequitur. A couple beats later her mouth formed a silent "oh" and she popped off the couch, holding her hand out to Jonarel. "Absolutely."

"Celia, you might want to go get a snack, too," Knox added.

Celia stood immediately. "I think I will." She strolled through the opening leading to Brendan's kitchen, leaving Cade alone in the front room.

As soon as Aurora's crew and Knox had moved out of earshot – although Jonarel wasn't actually out of earshot – Marina waved her hand in the air to get Cade and Micah's attention. "Can one of you please explain Unity to me. They're not just a comm team, are they?"

Micah lowered his voice. "They're a non-biological being the Yruf created to help maintain their biosphere in space." His gaze flicked to Siginal. "They're somewhat like the Nirunoc, in that they have a symbiotic relationship with the Yruf and have a similar role in their society."

Siginal's yellow eyes went flat. "Do the Yruf know of Tehar's existence?"

"Yes. We introduced them to each other before we entered Teeli space. It's what encouraged the Yruf to tell us about Unity. And just so you know, Unity adores Star. They've been working well together, although Unity's a lot more..." he searched for the right word, "exuberant than Star."

"Exuberant?" Siginal seemed scandalized.

"Exuberant?" Unity echoed, drifting beside Cade's shoulder so they showed in the vid pickup. "Is that a compliment?"

Micah grinned, but Siginal, Marina, and Gryphon all looked startled.

"That's your voice," Marina said.

"I know. I was doing most of the talking onboard the Yruf ship, so Unity recorded my voice and used it as the basis for their communications with us."

"You'll get used to it," Cade assured Marina. "This is U-2, one of many mobile units Unity uses."

"And yes, Unity, it was a compliment," Micah assured them.

"We are exuberant?"

"Compared to Star, yeah. You're very outgoing and social. Star's more reserved."

Siginal seemed to take that description of Star as a personal compliment. "The Yruf do not act like typical Setarips." His brows drew down. "Do you trust them?"

To Cade's shock, Siginal directed the question to him. "Completely. They're an honorable, honest, and compassionate race.

And they've placed their trust in us. Unity's onboard the *Starhawke* right now."

Siginal's frown deepened. "They are not on the Yruf ship?"

"They're on both," he clarified. "Unlike Star, Unity's not a single entity, but a multitude all working and speaking as one."

"Like a hive?" Marina asked.

"Sort of. But without the singlemindedness. Because they're a multitude, their communication ability is incredible. They can be lightyears apart and yet what one mobile unit knows is transmitted almost instantaneously to the rest. They were designed that way."

Marina and Gryphon looked impressed.

Siginal looked wary. "Did Tehar allow Unity onboard, or was that Aurora's decision?"

"Star's." Cade reined in a flare of irritation. At least Siginal seemed to be asking because of concern for his family rather than suspicion of the Yruf. "Aurora never would have coerced Star into accepting Unity. And Unity would never do anything to harm Star."

"No, we would not!" Unity said. "Star's our friend."

Siginal's dark brows rose.

"Ask Jonarel, if you don't believe me," Cade said.

Siginal glanced toward the kitchen. His gaze slid back to Cade. "I... believe you."

Well, that admission seemed to take a Herculean effort.

"So, Unity," Gryphon said, cutting through the tension, "how would you go about getting us intel on the Admiral's trial?"

Unity spun a quarter turn. "We're very good at infiltrating. It's how we took control of Cade's ship, *Gladiator*. We could access the building where the Admiral's trial is being held and infiltrate their tech."

"Uh, that may not work," Brendan said. "The Justice building won't have cameras or any other tech in the courtroom. There won't be anything to tap into."

"Then we'll be the tech. Once we access the room, we'll — what's the phrase? — be your eyes and ears."

"You can do that without being noticed?" Gryphon asked. "There will be security in the building."

Unity chuckled. "Nothing we can't handle."

Brendan's mouth curved in a smile. "Cade, I think Unity just solved your lack of activity problem. I assume you'd like to take the lead on this project?"

Exactly what he'd been thinking. "You assume correctly." Unity had provided him with a perfect Plan B. "Unity, would Ifel be okay with my staying on the Yruf ship? That way I can be hands-on with the operation and as a bonus, I won't need a bodyguard."

Celia poked her head around the archway, confirming she was listening to every word.

"Though my bodyguard is excellent," he told her.

Her lips quirked before she ducked back into the kitchen.

Unity spun. "Of course. You're always welcome with us."

"What about Aurora?" Libra asked. "If Unity can infiltrate the courthouse, can they access the detention center, too?"

Adrenaline surged into his veins, clearing a path through the exhaustion settling into his bones.

Unity bobbed so they brushed the sleeve of Cade's shirt. "You want us to access Aurora's cell?"

"If you can."

"Oh, we can. We will start working on the plans now."

Cade wanted to hug the egg-shaped unit. His night was definitely looking up.

Libra's lips pursed. "Cade, will you keep us updated on what's going on after you leave the house?"

"Of course."

"He could do that." Brendan's jaw worked, like he was chewing on his tongue or the inside of his cheek, something Aurora did when she was thinking hard. "Or, maybe we could stay on the *Starhawke*. I know you'll want to keep in close contact with Unity and Cade, and I'm guessing Marina and Gryphon would like to be with Lelindia."

Marina beamed at him. "You know me well." Her gaze moved to the kitchen. "This is a very special time."

Cade mentally smacked his forehead with his hand. How had he spaced all thoughts of Lelindia and Jonarel's kid? Of course Marina and Gryphon would want to be on the *Starhawke*. They were going to be grandparents soon.

Libra looked torn. "We'd be so far from Aurora."

"But more protected from the Teeli," Signal pointed out. "Your family is at risk." He looked pointedly at Micah.

Micah stiffened, clearly not appreciating being identified as a weak link. But without Aurora by his side, he *was* the most vulnerable member of the family.

"The *Starhawke* would be a safe sanctuary for your family," Signal said to Libra, "and allow us all to remain close together."

Libra's gaze shifted to Micah. "Are you okay with going back to the *Starhawke*?"

He shrugged. "I'm not doing anyone any good planetside."

Brendan cupped Libra's hand in his. "It's the smart move. We can visit Aurora tomorrow then all go up together. We won't be able to see Aurora again until next Friday, anyway."

Gryphon tossed his two cents into the pool. "I think Aurora would feel better knowing you were staying on the *Starhawke*."

Libra huffed, shooting an annoyed look at Gryphon and Brendan. "I'm starting to feel like a vagabond."

"You're forgetting you'll have a job on the *Starhawke*," Marina said matter-of-factly. "The Nedale needs a Sahzade."

Thirty-Seven

The room the FS officers took Aurora to was even less welcoming than the visitor room where she'd talked with her family. Light shone down like a spotlight from the recessed bulb set in the middle of the ceiling. No windows, and only the one door she was led through. The space would have made a decent-sized walk-in closet, but it barely gave clearance for the small metal table positioned at the exact center — attached with the requisite bolts to the cement floor — and two wooden straight-backed chairs facing each other, one of which was occupied by Aurora's lawyer.

She stood as Aurora entered.

She had a youthful appearance, probably late-thirties or early-forties. Her tawny skin, perfectly shaped dark brows, and the locks of hair at her nape suggested she was a natural brunette, but she'd dyed the top layers of her sophisticated shoulder-length hairstyle a golden-blonde a few shades lighter than Aurora's.

Her makeup was similarly polished, and her pantsuit fit with the precision of a tailored garment. The overall impression was one of confidence, competence, and authority. She stood silently, her gaze on the FS officers until they exited the room and closed the door.

She held up a finger to Aurora, picked up her tablet, tapped a command, then set it back down. "Generated privacy screen," she explained. "These rooms are supposed to be secure and unmonitored, but under the circumstances, it seemed a justified precaution. It generates audio and visual white noise so no one will be able to hear or see anything that transpires between us."

In the rational world, rules meant something. In the psychotic world where the Sovereign reigned, anything was possible.

Two seconds in and the woman had already shown she was intelligent, resourceful, and honest. Her emotional field was as clear and direct as her greeting as she stuck out her hand. "Captain Hawke, I'm Phoebe Liddell, retired Lt. Cmd., and former COJ trial counsel."

The use of Aurora's title wasn't an accident, either. She was making a statement on where they stood. Aurora clasped her hand. "Thank you for coming, Lt. Cmd. Liddell."

She waved her free hand in the air. "You're welcome to call me Phoebe if you prefer. Most of my clients do. I'm in private practice now."

Aurora smiled at the woman's openness and candor. Another positive sign. "Aurora's fine for me, too."

"Good." Phoebe gave a sharp nod and reclaimed her chair, waiting until Aurora settled into the empty chair across from her before pinning her with a stare as direct as a laser. "Your father has retained my services to meet with you, and he and your mother stated they believe your arrest was a tactical move by someone who was seeking to discredit you. That's a bold charge, one I likely would have discounted if your father wasn't the owner of Far Horizons

Aerospace, and if you weren't one of the most respected officers in the Fleet. Do you agree with their assessment that someone is attempting to discredit you?"

She could feel Phoebe treading carefully, trying to separate facts from fiction to get a read on whether Aurora could be trusted. "Yes, I do."

"Do you know who this person is?"

"Yes."

"Can you give me a name?"

"If we decide to work together, yes."

"Smart answer." Approval shone in Phoebe's eyes. "And you're right, trust is earned. It's also a necessity in a criminal defense. If I don't trust you, or you don't trust me, we won't make a good team. So let's build that trust. Ask me a question, any question, and I'll tell you the truth."

She was gutsy. Another mark in her favor. "Why do you want to take this case?"

Phoebe drew in a breath, considering the question before answering. "I served as trial counsel in the COJ for fourteen years before opening my private practice. I've seen the worst and best of human behavior, from ensigns to admirals. Those experiences have made me a good judge of character. That's why Admiral Schreiber's arrest stunned me. I have always admired and respected him, in and out of the courtroom. Sedition seems very out of character."

"It is. He would never betray the Union."

Phoebe's head tipped. "You have no doubt about that?"

"None."

"Why are you so loyal to him?"

Phoebe was testing her, too. "He's an honorable man who has put his life on the line countless times to defend the ideals of the Fleet. Anyone who doubts his loyalty to those ideals doesn't know him at all." She held Phoebe's gaze. "But you haven't finished answering my question."

"You're answering it for me. I agree with you. The Admiral's arrest didn't sit well with me. Your arrest is no less unsettling. Something's off about this whole situation, and I want to know what it is. I want to make sure justice is done."

"And if I'm guilty?" Might as well toss the big bomb out there before they got any farther.

"I studied your service record during my trip here. You don't fit the pattern for criminal behavior. And I seriously doubt your Fleet psych evaluations indicate delusional or megalomaniacal tendencies. Those behaviors wouldn't fit with the rest of your record. That being said, if I decide you're the most accomplished slow-con player in galactic history, then you'll be finding yourself new representation."

"Fair enough." The matter-of-fact way Phoebe had said it drew a clear boundary, one Aurora approved of wholeheartedly. Dishonesty would not be tolerated.

So far, Phoebe's emotional field exactly matched her words and body language. She'd also already passed Aurora's dad's rigorous empathic tests, or he never would have sent her down here.

Which meant the next trust step had to be hers. "Now you get to ask me any question you want, and I'll tell you the truth."

The faintest hint of a smile curved Phoebe's mouth. "What's your greatest fear?"

Aurora's eyes widened. Not at all the kind of question she'd been expecting. But a brilliant one. The answer could reveal more than any dry facts Phoebe could have extracted. "That I'll fail to keep the people who depend on me safe from harm. That the malevolent forces bent on destroying the Union, the Fleet, everything I've fought to protect, will outthink, outmaneuver, or overpower me." Her throat tightened, but she pushed through. "That they'll leave a scorched path of death and destruction in their wake."

Phoebe sucked in a breath. "Damn." She blinked once, twice, her face slack. "You're telling the truth, aren't you."

Not really a question, but it deserved an answer. "Yes."

Phoebe's eyes took on a piercing gleam. "And this malevolent force is responsible for your incarceration? And the Admiral's?"

Aurora nodded. "If you choose to represent me, you'll be going up against adversaries more powerful than you can possibly imagine. And defending me might put you personally at risk." The sickening thought made her stomach plummet into her boots. "The better you do your job, the more they'll want to neutralize you."

Phoebe held her gaze. "I've been threatened before."

Aurora stared right back. "These people can make good on those threats."

A frown line appeared between her brows. "You've seen it firsthand?"

"Yes. They don't care who they hurt. Even children." *Like Keenan.* Which generated another stomach gravity drop to the floor. "Do you have kids?" That would be an excellent way for the Sovereign to manipulate her.

But Phoebe was already shaking her head. "Never felt the need to procreate. Also, FYI, my husband is former FS and I'm licensed in four types of firearms and have a martial arts background. We can take care of ourselves." She looked pointedly at Aurora's hands on the table.

They were curled into tight fists, white showing at the knuckles.

She forced them open, flexing her fingers. "I don't like the idea of others being hurt because a psycho's after me."

"I can see that." Phoebe slid her tablet to face her and tapped the screen. "Does that mean you're ready to tell me everything you know about this psycho so we can get this defense off the ground?"

She studied Phoebe's emotional field. No hints of fear or anxiety, just focused determination. Would that change as the tale unfolded?

Only one way to find out.

"Her name is Reanne Beck, and she was my roommate at the Academy."

Thirty-Eight

Considering the comet-sized bundle of information Aurora threw at Phoebe, the lawyer handled it pretty well. She balked at the idea of the Teeli as aggressors rather than the pacifists they claimed to be, but as Aurora laid out the story of the attack on Gaia, the role the Setarips had played, and the discovery of the enslaved Suulh, who had provided first hand knowledge of the Teeli's actions, the doubt cleared from Phoebe's gaze.

"And where are these Suulh now?"

"Hidden where the Teeli and the Sovereign can't get to them."

"Can you tell me where?"

"No. I won't risk their safety. But there are a number of people besides my crew who can confirm what I've told you is true. Ambassador Siginal Clarek, leader of Clan Clarek on Drakar, for one."

Phoebe's eyes widened. "They're in Kraed space?"

Aurora simply stared at her.

"Okay. So what about Reanne? Where is she?"

It took a lot longer to tell the story of the Admiral's journey to Gallows Edge to track down proof of the Setarip-Teeli alliance, Aurora's search for him and eventual capture by Tnaryt, and the resulting confrontation at the river with the Sovereign. By the end, Phoebe was visibly rattled, her emotional field twisting like a tornado.

"You're saying Reanne Beck has done all of this just to capture you?"

"Yes and no. I'm the catalyst, but my demise is not her only goal. If she had to choose between gaining power and destroying me, I honestly think she'd choose destroying me, but it'd be a slim margin. She derives great emotional and psychological pleasure from seeing me suffer. But she also wants to prove I'm helpless to stop her. That's why I'm here." She swept her arms to encompass the room. "It's an elaborate game to her. She doesn't care who she hurts or kills to achieve her goals. She's irrational and psychotic, which makes her very, very dangerous."

"I'm getting that. I'm amazed you've been able to make it this far."

"I'm tougher than I look."

Phoebe scrutinized her for several seconds. "I believe you."

Although she didn't have all the facts. So far, Aurora had omitted any mention of her mixed heritage, her connection to the Suulh, or her abilities. And for good reason.

Her hours of isolation had given her time to think about the Sovereign's prosecution strategy. It seemed unlikely she wanted this trial to reveal Aurora's Sahzade abilities. Doing so would shine attention on the Suulh, something the Sovereign would want to avoid. They were her secret weapon, after all.

Also, any knowledge of Aurora's abilities might incite the scientific community to demand Aurora become a test subject in a Fleet facility. That wasn't the Sovereign's goal, either. Her vengeance was personal. She wanted Aurora directly under *her* thumb, neutralized and helpless, not showing a bunch of scientists what the Suulh were capable of. That meant keeping the knowledge of Aurora's Suulh abilities a secret.

On that one point, they were in agreement.

Eventually she might choose to make her skills known to others, but not like this, and not when it could cause a ripple effect that could endanger those she loved. Her mom, for starters. She was a Sahzade, too. And then there was Lelindia to consider. If Aurora made her Suulh heritage known, someone would figure out the connection between her and Lelindia. And Lelindia's baby.

She couldn't let that happen.

"I'll need to work up a list of witnesses for your defense." Phoebe typed on her tablet. "I'll have a better idea who to bring in once I receive trial counsel's list of witnesses and evidence, but Dr. Forrest is top of my list since you've served together all your career."

"When do you expect to receive trial counsel's list?"

"Now that I have your signed agreement for representation, I can contact COJ. I should have the materials by tomorrow at the latest. Then we'll prepare for your Article 32 hearing."

Article 32 hearing. The unreality of her situation settled over her like a layer of dust, leaving her feeling dried out and itchy. "Will I be speaking at the hearing?"

"No. Depending on what trial counsel hits us with, my focus will be on getting you out of here," she gestured to their austere surroundings, "so you're not stuck here through your trial."

Aurora shrugged. "I probably am stuck here." The Sovereign would make certain of that, just like she had with the Admiral.

Phoebe's eyes narrowed, then she nodded slowly. "That may be true, but I'll do my best to fight it. A lot will depend on which judge we're assigned."

The Sovereign would probably have a say in that, too.

And then the real fun would begin.

Thirty-Nine

Cade wasted no time packing his bag, tossing things in as he laid a hand on them. Even so, Celia was waiting for him at the top of the stairs, her bag over her shoulder.

"What took you so long?" she taunted with a straight-faced expression that turned into a smirk when he flicked his jacket at her.

"Keep that up and I'll leave you behind."

"I'd like to see you try."

She beat him down the stairs in three graceful hops, even loaded down with her bag.

He grinned as he followed. They were both feeling like they'd been let out of school a week early. Not that he didn't appreciate Brendan's hospitality, but as soon as Unity and Ifel had offered him an alternative that gave him an important job *and* the ability to get a visual on Aurora, he'd been full steam ahead.

Unity was waiting for them in the foyer. Cade locked up the house as Celia and Unity headed for the shuttle. No telling when anyone would be returning, although Iolana and Kai would check in periodically.

Cade wanted to believe they'd all be celebrating here after Aurora was acquitted of all charges, but the image had the gossamer quality of a dragonfly's wing.

The flight to the *Starhawke* took all his focus as he navigated through the cross-traffic that couldn't see him. The shuttle's relatively small size helped, and the fact that speeds were strictly regulated this close to Sol Station. He didn't have to worry about a rookie pilot racing in unexpectedly... like he was doing.

Kire and Kelly strode into the *Starhawke*'s bay right after the shuttle docked. Unity had already informed them of the broad strokes of the new arrangements. "Didn't expect you two to be back so soon," Kire called out as Celia stepped off the shuttle ramp, Cade and Unity close behind.

"Didn't expect to be here," Cade replied. "But thanks to Unity, turns out I can be useful while still staying hidden."

"Lucky you." Kire grinned, but it didn't reach his eyes. Cade sensed dense layers of worry and irritation in Kire's emotional field.

Aurora's first officer would crave intel on Aurora just as much as the rest of them. But with Aurora off the ship, his place was here. He couldn't take an active role in obtaining that information like Cade could.

Kire bumped Cade's arm with his fist. "Knock it off, Ellis. I know that look. Stop probing my psyche."

"Would I do that?"

Kire gave him another tap, amusement whisking away his heavier emotions.

"Okay, yeah, I would." He gestured back toward the shuttle and glanced at Kelly. "You ready to give me a lift over to Ifel's ship?"

Kelly folded her arms, turning to Kire. "I could, but what do you think, Commander? Maybe it's a better idea for him to hang onto the shuttle for the time being. Keep our options open."

Kire's brows rose a fraction.

Cade studied the young navigator for a moment, though her body language and emotional field gave no clue as to what was going on in her head.

"That *would* keep our options open," Kire agreed with a slow nod.

"But that will leave you with only one shuttle." Cade felt compelled to point it out, even though he loved the idea of keeping the shuttle with him. "That narrows your options."

Kelly shrugged. "Not really. With the *Rowkclarek* here, we have a whole bunch of Kraed shuttles at our disposal."

He'd watched this woman play poker — and win handily — by paying attention to every detail and staying one step ahead of the other players. While everyone else had been focusing on the big changes Aurora's arrest had wrought, Kelly seemed to have assigned herself the task of managing the minutiae the rest of them were missing.

If she thought his keeping the shuttle was the smart play, he wasn't going to argue. "Then I guess Unity and I will head out." He turned to Celia. "That is, if you're ready to hand off the bodyguard duties to the Yruf. I know how much you've enjoyed the role."

That earned him a smile. "Even I will bow to the superiority of the Yruf's security skills."

Cade pressed a hand to his chest in exaggerated shock. "Did you just admit that someone is *better* than you?"

She laughed, the sound lighter and more relaxed than any he'd heard from her. "I hate to say it, but I'm beginning to understand why Aurora likes you."

This time his shock wasn't feigned. His jaw hit the deck.

"And on that note, I'll leave you to it." She gave a brisk wave and headed for the exit.

No one spoke until the doors closed behind her. "Micah has definitely had a positive effect on her," Kire murmured.

"No kidding." And to think she'd started off hating Aurora's brother with a passion that bordered on obsession. But Micah was bringing out a side of her Cade hadn't imagined could possibly exist. "I thought it was a win after she stopped threatening to cut my heart out. I never expected her to be... nice."

Kire snorted, and even Kelly smiled. "These are strange times, my friend." Kire clapped him on the back. "Do you need anything before you go?"

"I don't think... wait. Can I stop by the greenhouse for some supplies?" He'd sampled Yruf cuisine during the binary star mission, and while it was edible, he still preferred the flavors he was used to.

Kire swept out a hand. "Help yourself. With Lelindia, Libra, Marina, *and* Gryphon onboard, replenishing our greenhouse produce will not be a problem."

Less than an hour later he was back on the shuttle, Unity in the charging niche above him as they exited the *Starhawke.* Unity had given him coordinates for the rendezvous with the Yruf on the dark side of the moon, where Earth's telescopes and orbital satellites couldn't see them. The Yruf ship would have to open the bay to admit the shuttle, which would make that section momentarily visible, just as it had when they'd delivered him a few days ago.

"Do you have a plan for how you'll infiltrate the Justice building?" Cade asked Unity after the shuttle had cleared the station traffic, heading toward the glowing orb of the waxing moon.

"We have multiple plans," Unity assured him.

"How soon will you implement them?"

"That partially depends on you. Do you want to participate?"

"Participate? What do you mean?"

"Do you want to work with our pilots like you did during the reconnaissance missions at the binary star system?"

"You mean fly with them?"

"And assist them in navigating the atmospheric air traffic, yes. We've analyzed the data we've gathered, but your cultural knowledge of the flight patterns would be extremely helpful."

Excitement surged through his veins. "Hell, yeah!" He wasn't about to pass up another ride in a Yruf two-seater. "Absolutely I want to do that."

Unity chuckled, sounding exactly like Micah. "We had a feeling you might. We'll meet with Ifel as soon as we dock to arrange it."

A short time later, as he walked down the shuttle's ramp into the Yruf bay, the familiar feel of the space made him smile. The first time he'd been brought onboard, he'd been quietly freaking out, certain his crew were all going to die. And he'd had good reason for that belief. Justin had been in bad shape from an unknown ailment and Unity had taken control of the explosives Gonzo had planted on *Gladiator* to repel an invasion.

How far they had come.

He followed Unity up to the ship's main bridge. He still couldn't have navigated there himself, despite the numerous trips he'd made there during his time onboard. Unity had confirmed they handled the undulating passageways, but the path they laid out never looked the same even when he took the same route. He no longer feared getting lost or trapped – Unity would never let that happen – but he'd given up trying to figure out where he was at any specific point as he walked the black and gold deck.

The Yruf he passed on the way all greeted him with the subtle head and neck tilt Justin had told him equated with a human's nod of welcome. He couldn't replicate the movement if he tried, since his neck didn't have as many vertebrae as theirs, so he nodded in return.

That was another change. He was seeing the Yruf going about their daily lives. When he'd first stepped foot on the ship as a captive, it had felt like a ghost ship, all the Yruf invisible except for Ifel and her guards. Now, the ship teemed with life, including Yruf children with their parents who looked at him with open curiosity — but no fear — as they passed.

Collectively, the Yruf had accepted him as someone to be trusted. Another sign of how far they'd come.

He spotted Ifel as soon as he and Unity emerged from the multi-colored lighted tunnel onto the primary bridge. She stood a head taller than anyone else, the colored lights of the bridge displays playing off the glossy emerald-green, black, and gold scales of her face.

She turned toward him, her tongue flicking out and her head tipping in greeting.

He nodded back as he stopped next to her. "Thank you for offering me this opportunity."

"You're welcome," Unity translated her reply. "I'm very sorry to hear of Aurora's incarceration."

His throat tightened. "Thanks. But if Unity can do what they say they can, that will be a big help."

"We told you we could," Unity replied, sounding amused as they bobbed up and down. "Ye of little faith."

That startled a laugh out of him. "Really getting a handle on those idioms, aren't you?"

"Yep." Unity pivoted slightly toward Ifel. "Cade has agreed to join us on the expedition."

He knew the words were for his benefit. He hadn't heard any of the mobile units speak until Unity revealed themselves using Micah's voice. Vocalizations seemed unnecessary for Unity to communicate with the Yruf. Yet another point he didn't understand.

"The moonlight and aerial traffic over the target site are obstacles we need to avoid," Unity translated. "The optimal time to make our approach is late tomorrow night after the moon sets."

"Why is the moon a problem?" He'd thought their camouflage was like the *Starhawke's*, rendering the ship invisible no matter what the conditions.

"Our camouflage was designed for space, not terrestrial landings. In atmosphere, shadows and reflection are a concern."

"Ah." So not like the *Starhawke's*. Good to know. Speaking of which... "We could take the *Starhawke's* shuttle instead. The camouflage works just fine in atmo."

"But we can't function in the shuttle the way we do with our ships," Unity replied, bobbing twice and speaking for themselves. "To reach the targets, we need our ships."

"Fair enough." He'd gladly wait a day if it ended with him getting a visual on Aurora. "One other question. Is there any way we could talk to Aurora and the Admiral through you, not just observe them?"

"Interesting idea." Unity was silent for a moment, pondering. Cade and Ifel waited. "The dampening technology used at the facility to prevent unauthorized comm signals would not affect our ability to communicate. But we've never tried a direct audio connection with a biological before. In theory, if we physically entered the ear canal, we should be able to speak with them and allow others to speak through us while remaining undetected."

"I like the sound of that."

"So do we. We should probably test communicating with Aurora first, since she wouldn't be alarmed by our presence or voice."

Cade smiled. Unity was starting to think like one of the crew. "Good call." He stifled a yawn with the back of his hand.

Ifel's head moved in the sinuous, alien way of hers as she studied him. "You need to rest," Unity translated, gliding closer. "Come on. We'll show you to your cabin."

"Cabin?" He hadn't even considered where he'd sleep. Last time his team had used the bunks on *Gladiator*. On his first visit, they'd stayed in the containment area. "You have cabins?"

Unity chuckled. "Of course."

Now that the prospect of seeing Aurora had been pushed back a day, the fatigue he'd been fighting sank into his muscles. A cabin sounded wonderful. He nodded to Ifel. "Thank you."

She gave an answering head tilt before returning her attention to her crew.

He followed Unity into the undulating corridors, stopping when Unity did, the walls closing in to create the Yruf's unconventional lift. To his surprise, they rose, the deck of the lift pushing against his boots. Ordinarily he traveled to levels below the main bridge.

Out of habit he counted the seconds, which lasted longer than any trip he'd made so far. The bulkhead peeled back differently, too. Rather than opening onto one of the winding corridors he was used to, he found himself stepping into a vaulted circular space. The deck had the same black and gold pattern as the rest of the ship, but the walls didn't ripple here. Instead, the curved bulkhead was inset with circular hatches at regular intervals, maybe twenty in all. It gave the impression of the galaxy's most meticulous rabbit warren — if the rabbits were two meters tall.

The domed ceiling of the open space stretched at least eight meters high, with a miniature jungle of verdant trees, lush ferns, and mossy knolls at the center. Yruf of all colors and sizes lounged on the carpet of vegetation and curled around the branches of the trees. The males' neutral tones mostly blended with the surroundings while the more jewel-toned hues of the females stood out with the vibrancy of peacock feathers and tropical fish.

Every single Yruf glanced his way.

He paused, his gaze sweeping left and right, taking it all in. "What is this place?"

"A residential circle." Unity floated forward along the curving wall to their left.

Cade lengthened his stride to catch up. "I'm staying where the Yruf live?"

A couple Yruf children moved to the edge of the grove of trees to get a better look at him as he passed. He nodded at them and gave a little wave.

Their heads tilted in unison in the Yruf greeting, then one of them imitated his wave.

"You sound surprised." Unity paused in front of the sixth door they came to.

"I am, a bit. I figured I'd be staying in a room like the one I had the first time I was onboard."

"A containment unit? Why would we put you there?"

He shrugged. "I don't know. This just seems... private."

"It is private." Unity bobbed. "You are the first non-Yruf to ever enter this space."

His mind spun at the enormity of what Unity had imparted. And the degree of trust they'd placed in him. "I'm... honored."

"You took us to stay with Aurora's family. Why wouldn't we allow you to stay with ours?"

That choked him up. He didn't have a good response, either. He cleared his throat and pointed at the door. "Is this one mine?"

"Yep. We can open it for you, but we have also added a touch pad similar to Star's. We figured you might be more comfortable using that." The emerald bulkhead shimmered slightly to the right of the circular door. A very good imitation of one of the *Starhawke*'s door controls appeared underneath.

Since Unity had gone to the effort, he tried it out, placing his fingertips on the smooth surface. The circular hatch rolled open.

He stepped across the threshold into the most unusual cabin he'd ever seen.

The bulkheads spread out like wings, giving the space roughly the shape of a pie slice with the doorway at the narrow end. The room he entered was separated from what he assumed was the bedroom and bathroom at the back by a curving bulkhead with a circular opening on the left side.

The front room was dominated by several bowl-shaped pieces of furniture, some twice his size, all grouped on raised platforms. "What are those for?"

"The Yruf equivalent of a couch," Unity replied. "They're not designed for your physiology, but well padded. You should find them quite comfortable. And this is your food station." A three-meter-wide section of the bulkhead to his left was lined with large circular compartments. "Touch one."

He did as Unity instructed. The scaly covering parted. Inside he discovered a selection of citrus he'd taken from the *Starhawke*'s greenhouse.

"We took the liberty of moving your provisions to your room, and separating them so we can optimize their care to maintain nutritional value. We can talk you through cooking instructions whenever you're ready." Unity hovered over the raised serpentine counter that ran parallel to the food compartments.

A quick glance confirmed the counter had colored light displays built-in that resembled what Cade had seen on the bridge. He didn't see anything that looked obviously like a stovetop or oven, but he'd deal with that later.

He gestured to the circular opening in the bulkhead at the back of the room. "And that's the bedroom?"

"Yes." Unity glided forward, Cade right behind.

This looked more alien than the front room. An even larger bowl-shaped piece of furniture took up most of the space. The colorful patterns on its side made it resemble a giant's teacup, with no discernible opening for getting in and out.

He set his pack with his clothes and toiletries beside it.

"This is the bed," Unity confirmed, "and the bathroom is over here." Unity hovered to a partitioned alcove on the opposite side of the room. "But we should warn you, the Yruf don't shower. You may find the soaking channel a bit... challenging."

He stepped around Unity and inspected the room. The sanitation station looked similar to the one he'd used in his cell back when he'd been a prisoner on this ship, though this one was more decorative and had shelving on one side. But the soaking channel Unity had referred to gave him pause.

It spanned the entire length of the alcove, long enough that he could stretch out with his arms overhead and probably not touch the edges. It was about a meter wide, but only an eighth of a meter at the deepest point, which was at the center. Knobby bumps pebbled the bottom, the sides sloping up to about ten centimeters deep at the edges.

Even if it was filled completely with water, and he laid flat on his back, the water wouldn't cover him more than halfway. Not that he'd want to lie down for long on all those bumps. Did the Yruf use the pebbled surface to slough off the skin covering their scales?

"Washing my hair should be interesting." But he'd figure it out. No way was he going back to the wilderness look he'd had to tolerate during his first visit onboard.

"We can work on an adaptation," Unity assured him.

Cade waved the offer away. "Don't worry about it. Humans got along fine for millennia without showers. Do you think you can get me a pitcher or some other container for water? That would help with rinsing."

"Of course." Unity twirled. "Are you hungry? Should we show you how to prepare food or drink?"

He exited the alcove and gazed at the giant teacup. "Honestly? I think I'd rather get some shuteye. I just need you to tell me how to get in."

"Oh, that's easy." Unity floated toward the oversized cup-bed. "Place both palms flat on the side where you want it to open."

Cade did as instructed, choosing the curve closest to the interior bulkhead.

It rippled and slid down like melting wax under his hands until it was flush with the bedding inside the curve, leaving an elongated U-shaped opening wide enough for a Yruf.

"Will this configuration work for you?" Unity asked.

Cade stepped onto the platform, turned, and boosted himself up until he sat on the padding. It felt slightly warm to the touch. "Cushy. How do I close it back up?"

"Place your hands on either side of the opening and it will fill in."

Taking his boots off and dropping them on the platform, he tucked his legs inside the cup and followed Unity's instructions. The opening rippled closed.

Unity rose above the lip of the cup. "Are you comfortable?"

The warm padding made him want to stretch out like a cat dozing in sunlight. "Very. Thank you."

"Do you need anything else?"

"No, I'm good." But when Unity disappeared below his line of sight he rolled up onto his knees. "Where are you going?"

Unity hovered in place. "We have an alcove in the front room. Why? Do you need us to stay in here?"

"Oh. No. Just wondered."

"Did you think we were leaving you?" The amusement in the question made Cade laugh at himself.

"Maybe. Probably. You are back home, after all." He swept an arm to encompass the room. "This is great, but I suddenly felt like a kid on my first night at camp. Having fun, but way out of my comfort zone."

"We *are* home," Unity agreed, "but we are *always* home. Whenever we go with you, we are also still home."

He rubbed a hand along his cheek, where whiskers were beginning to sandpaper his skin. "Yeah, still haven't fully wrapped my head around that one. Obviously. I'll get there eventually."

"Take your time. We're not going anywhere."

Cade chuckled. "Got it. Goodnight, Unity."

"Goodnight, Cade."

He took his time washing up, changing into a pair of lounge pants and a T-shirt before settling back into the Yruf bed. The curved surface would take some getting used to, but the padding was plenty big enough for him to stretch out with room to spare, and the Yruf version of pillows were soft as clouds.

He sighed, his thoughts turning to Aurora. A twinge of guilt caught him as he compared his surroundings to hers.

It's okay. You're here to help her. And starting tomorrow he'd be gathering intel from the detention center and the Court of Justice. With the Yruf's help, he'd make sure Aurora didn't spend one more night isolated and alone.

Forty

Lee-Lee?

Aurora had waited as long as she could stand it to reach out to her energy sister, who was apparently spending the night at Admiral Schreiber's house, along with Marina and Gryphon, Aurora's parents and Micah, Siginal and Jonarel, and Cade's team.

But that wasn't what had her perched on the edge of her cot, trying hard not to let her knee bounce every three seconds. Cade and Celia had left her dad's house and headed into orbit. Why? What had happened? She couldn't just *sit* here, wondering why the plans had changed.

Sahzade.

The connection immediately lowered her stress level, but questions swirled in her head like fat snowflakes caught in the winter wind. *What's going on? Why has Cade left my dad's house?*

Lelindia's chagrin came through loud and clear. *Sorry I didn't warn you. Cade's gone to stay with the Yruf.*

I know. She'd already figured out Cade was on Ifel's ship, which was very good news. The Sovereign couldn't touch him there. But she still didn't understand why he'd made the switch. *Why?*

He and Unity are working on a plan to get visual and audio access to the COJ and the detention center.

That pulled her up short. Of all the scenarios bouncing around in her head during the past hour — most involving the Sovereign stalking Cade — that one hadn't made the list. She peered around the walls of her cell, curiosity taking root. *How?*

I don't have the details, but Unity's certain they can do it.

Her heartbeat picked up the pace. *Do you know when?*

No. But we'll all be heading back to the Starhawke *after your folks and Micah visit you tomorrow. I can talk to Unity then.*

Wait, what?

My parents and Micah are going to the ship? For how long?

At least until the next visiting day at the detention center. Is that a problem?

No, of course not. From a safety standpoint, there was nowhere else she'd rather they be. But the move was unexpected. She hadn't gotten any hints of it when her family was visiting today. *When was that decided?*

During the discussion this evening. Libra took a little convincing. She wanted to stay close to you.

That fit with what she'd been sensing from her mom. But the one she felt guilty about was her dad. This abrupt change had to be wreaking havoc with his work commitments.

Not that she knew what his job situation was at the moment. Micah had taken a semester sabbatical to join her on the *Starhawke*, but her parents had still been figuring out the logistics of how they were going to move forward. She didn't know their long-term plans.

With a sigh, she allowed her head to fall into her hands to hide her face. If she was being watched by the Sovereign's minions — best to assume she was — any inexplicable expressions at this late hour would rate as odd and worth investigating.

What about my dad's work?

He doesn't seem concerned about it. I'm sure the university has been understanding about giving him time off, considering.

Considering his daughter was in the brig on sedition charges.

Her teeth scraped together. When she'd made this decision, she'd been so focused on protecting her crew and Cade, she hadn't given the impact on her parents and Micah enough thought. She'd shaken up their lives like a toddler with a rattle without even consulting them. She should have contacted her parents before turning herself in, at least given them a chance to share their opinions.

I can hear you thinking.

Lee-Lee's gentle chide put the brakes on her guilt train.

None of this is your fault, Sahzade. Don't let the Sovereign's actions get to you.

Easier said than done in these stark surroundings. She shook her head to clear it, then moved to the sanitation station and splashed water on her face. The cool glide of the liquid on her skin helped to calm and center her. The connection to Lee-Lee helped, too, like a supportive hand on her shoulder.

She took her time patting her face dry, the towel continuing to act as a screen.

Having her family and Lee-Lee's together on the *Starhawke* was a best-case scenario. Well, best-case in which she was still stuck in this cell.

And in the next few days, Cade would be implementing whatever plan he and Unity were working on, which hopefully would lead to his being able to see and hear her.

Eagerness injected her veins. She made sure it didn't show on her face as she replaced the towel on the narrow shelf. After changing into her sleepwear and sliding under the covers, she closed her eyes, focusing on a happier topic. *How did your parents react to the news of the baby?*

Like you'd expect.

An image of Marina and Gryphon's reaction played in her mind's eye.

Her internal smile was bittersweet. If she hadn't been stuck in the detention center when the reveal had occurred, the strong emotions the scene had generated would have lit up her emotional field like a lightning flash. But the emotional quagmire of her surroundings continually forced her to dampen her normal receptivity. She hadn't figured out Cade had moved locations until she'd done a brief sweep to pinpoint everyone after dinner. *Have you finalized the list of potential baby names?*

Not even close. It's growing like desert lilac in monsoon season. But I'm going to take Jonarel's suggestion and discuss it with my mom and Libra. Maybe Siginal, too.

A warm feeling curled up like a kitten on her chest. *I'm glad he came around.*

You and me both.

Good to know at least one hurdle had been cleared. *So tomorrow you'll let me know what Unity says?*

Yep. You can pass on any questions to me that you have for Cade, too.

A subtle smile touched her lips as she visualized the game of telephone they'd be playing – her questions to Lelindia relayed to Unity on the *Starhawke*, then to Cade on the Yruf ship, and finally looping back through the chain to her.

Which sparked another thought. *What about the Admiral? Will Cade and Unity be accessing his cell, too?*

I have no idea, but I'll ask.

She could sense the Admiral, but couldn't decide whether he knew she was here or not.

Knox will be visiting him tomorrow. He didn't say anything specific to me, but I know him well enough to guess his intentions. I believe he'll be filling the Admiral in on the broad strokes of tonight's discussion.

Thank goodness for the coded communication system the Admiral and Knox had created long ago. They could convey covert messages in their normal speech or written communication with each other. Or with her, for that matter, since Knox had taught the system to her when she became his first officer.

Knox had told her the Admiral originally came up with the idea for the system as a way to test and sharpen Knox's communication skills, but considering all that had happened in the past year, she suspected the real reason was wanting a way to talk freely about the Teeli threat without danger of discovery.

It showed a lot of foresight, although she seriously doubted either Knox or the Admiral had envisioned they'd need it for this type of scenario.

Make sure he tells the Admiral I'm okay. I don't want him worrying about me.

She almost heard Lee-Lee's sigh. *Sahzade, he's been worrying about you from the day he learned of your existence. He's not going to stop now.*

Forty-One

Jonarel awoke to the murmur of low voices in deep discussion, the sound coming from the direction of the Admiral's kitchen.

"...protest scheduled for this morning," Justin said. "The comments Bella's finding are getting really scary."

"I don't know if local law enforcement is prepared for this kind of event." Knox sounded worried. "Bringing in the Federal Coalition might enflame the issue, but they certainly can't ask for backup from FS."

"Damned if they do, damned..."

Lelindia gave a little snuffle and tucked her body more firmly into the curve of his, nestled in the bed they had shared in one of the Admiral's guest rooms.

Tightening his arms around her, he nuzzled the top of her head, her hair tickling his lips.

She sighed in contentment, her eyelids fluttering open.

He rested a hand on her abdomen, circling her navel with his thumb. "How is our daughter this morning?"

She tipped her head back, tracing the outline of his lips with her finger. "Very happy."

"And how is my checana?" he purred.

"Also very happy."

They both knew it was a qualified statement. She would not be truly happy until Aurora was free. At least her parents' arrival had given her a much-needed boost yesterday.

She turned toward the east-facing window, where diffuse early-morning sunlight struggled to break through the marine layer. Her muscles stiffened, lines of tension clouding her beautiful face. "I need to get up."

He loosened his hold immediately, watching as she gathered the clothes she'd worn the previous day and disappeared into the bathroom.

Sliding out of bed, he pulled his tunic over his head as he tuned into the sounds of the household. His father was awake but still in the room next door, the quiet rumble of his voice in their native language indicating he was talking to someone on the *Rowkclarek*. He didn't try to make out the words of the conversation. Years of training as a child to respect the privacy of others — eavesdropping for a Kraed was as easy as breathing — had made it a habit to ignore his father's personal conversations.

He followed the same rule with everyone else, especially his checana and Aurora, although he made exceptions for any situation that indicated potential danger, like the discussion that had woken him.

He didn't hear any sounds coming from the two rooms Lelindia's and Aurora's parents had slept in. Knox was still in the kitchen talking with Justin.

The bathroom door swung open, drawing his attention to his mate.

Lelindia ran her fingers through her thick dark hair, trying unsuccessfully to push it back from her face where it spilled over her shoulders. "I didn't think to bring a hair tie."

He captured her face in his hands, his fingers stilling hers. "Your hair does not need adornment."

Her lips tilted up. "No, it needs *taming*."

"I like you wild," he murmured, sinking his fingers into the silken strands and massaging her scalp. "Then I can do this." He leaned down, brushing his lips over hers.

Her reaction was gratifying. Her lips parted on a moan.

He gave into the urge to stroke her lips with enough pressure to quicken her breath, and his. When he lifted his head, the look in her eyes almost made him whimper.

"I wish we were in our cabin," she whispered.

Not only would that mean he would have time to follow up on his kiss, but the bulkheads in their sleeping quarters were soundproofed.

She ran her hands down the front of his tunic, eliciting sparks at every point of contact. "Later."

Yes, later.

They passed the closed door to his father's room on their way to the kitchen, his voice still a low rumble on the other side. Jonarel picked out a soft snore and the relaxed breathing of at least two of the members of Cade's unit coming from the media room on the opposite side of the house. Cade's team had insisted on giving up the bedrooms for the night.

"Morning." Justin raised his mug in greeting from his seat at the small dining table in the kitchen nook. The wide windows behind him provided an expansive view of the white-capped grey-blue ocean waves stretching to the horizon.

"Morning," Lelindia replied, approaching Knox, who was seated at the high-top counter of the kitchen island. "Mind if I make a pot of tea?"

He smiled. "Your mom beat you to it. It's in that carafe over there." He pointed to a bright red container sitting on the kitchen counter.

Jonarel slipped past Lelindia, snagging a couple mugs from the cupboard and filling them from the carafe. The brew didn't smell as enticing as the teas Lelindia made on the *Starhawke* — his checana had a gift for unusual blends — but he had grown extremely fond of sharing morning tea with her whenever their schedules allowed.

"Where is my mom?" she asked, accepting the mug from him with a mouthed *thank you.*

Knox pointed toward the glass sliding doors leading to the backyard. "Your folks went with Aurora's family for a walk on the beach."

"Good." She settled into the chair to Justin's right. "That gives us a chance to talk about Raaveen and Paaw."

"And that's my cue to be somewhere else." Knox stood. "Considering our current circumstances, the less I know the better."

After Knox retreated toward the Admiral's study, Justin rested his forearms on the tabletop, his voice low. "Are you wondering what we should tell them about Aurora?" His gaze flicked to where Jonarel stood leaning against the granite counter of the island. "I assume we don't have any communication problems anymore?"

"You are correct." During his banishment, they had worried that his father might intercept or redirect any communications they sent to the Suulh colonists on Azaana. Thankfully that restriction was no longer an issue.

"It's more that I don't know if we should tell them at all," Lelindia said. "The last time I saw them, it wasn't exactly a fun and relaxing social call. And then you had to truncate your communications because of Siginal. I don't want our next message to freak them out more than we already have."

"But they'd want to know," Justin countered, taking a drink from his mug. "Remember, they've been captives themselves."

"Which is precisely why I'm worried how they'll react. They might assume Aurora's incarceration is like theirs was on the Setarip ship. They'd go ballistic."

"We could explain it so they'd understand." He grimaced. "Probably."

"Explain that the leader of their race, their shining hope for the future, is locked away in a sterile box with no idea when she'll be released? I see them having a PTSD reaction to that news rather than calm understanding."

"Yeah." He scrubbed a hand down his face. "You're probably right. But I can't lie to them, either. Which begs the question — what do we tell them?"

Lelindia chewed on her bottom lip. "Could we be vague? Tell them we've encountered a problem on Earth that we're working through?"

"If we go that route, should I be assuring them everything's okay?" Justin's brows rose with obvious skepticism.

"I guess. Maybe." She dropped her chin into her hands and stared at the opposite wall like it was an ancient text she was working to decipher. "We could tell them Aurora's family has been reunited. That's the truth, and will give them something positive to focus on."

Jonarel cleared his throat. "What about our daughter?"

Lelindia's gaze snapped to his. "You think we should tell them?"

She sounded hesitant. A flicker of unease wound between his shoulder blades. "Unless you do not believe they would be pleased that you mated with me."

She blinked, then shook her head in a firm negative. "Are you kidding? Your clan provided them with a new home where they're safe from the Teeli, and you designed and built the ship that allowed us to rescue them. The Suulh adore you. I think they'll be thrilled."

"You do not think they would wish you had mated with one of them?" While most of the Suulh on Azaana were mated pairs with children, he recalled a few unmated males who had looked on Lelindia with a favorable — if deferential – eye.

Lelindia's undignified snort almost made him smile. "That was never an option." She turned to Justin. "I hadn't really thought about when I would tell them about her, but Jonarel's right. Now that we aren't hiding anything from Siginal, we should definitely let the Suulh know a little Nedale is on the way."

"Paaw will love hearing that." Justin ran a finger around the rim of his mug, his expression wistful. "She respects Aurora, but she's in awe of you."

"And she loves you." Lelindia's hand rested on Justin's forearm, stilling the repetitive motion. "You should have seen how she, Raaveen, and Sparw lit up when they talked about you during our last visit."

"Yeah?"

"They miss you, too. But they're thriving on Azaana, in large part because of all the work you did with them while you were on Burrow." Her gaze swung back to Jonarel. "I don't know when, given all we're dealing with right now, but the next time we visit Azaana, we need to make sure Justin's with us."

Justin perked up like Lelindia had given him a stimulant injection.

Jonarel heard the soft click of the door to his father's room opening and his steady tread. "Agreed, though perhaps a more immediate option would be asking my father to arrange to bring the trio here in one of our ships."

He used *our* on purpose, reestablishing the clan bond between them. Being cut off from his clan had felt like losing a limb. Lelindia's and Tehar's presence had made the pain bearable, but waking this morning with his checana in his arms and his father nearby had made him feel whole again.

"The trio?" his father asked.

"Raaveen, Paaw, and Sparw," he replied.

"Ah." His gaze swept over them, then he bowed his head slightly to Lelindia. "If you wish them to be brought here, I would be happy to arrange their transport."

Lelindia looked a little flustered by his obvious obeisance. "Not right now, obviously, but depending on how long the *Starhawke* is stuck here, it might be a good idea. Zelle and Ren could look after the colony while they're gone. They'd get a chance to meet my parents and Aurora's family, and see for themselves what we're dealing with. I know they'd be safe from the Sovereign on one of your ships."

His father's gaze held hers. "Our ships. You are of Clan Clarek now."

Honeyed warmth spread through Jonarel's chest. His father felt as he did.

Lelindia's mouth opened and closed like a fish. "I... I guess I am." Her smile was tentative. "It's still so new."

His father brushed a loving hand over her head in a familial caress. "For us both."

Jonarel filled another mug with tea and handed it to his father. "Are you planning to remain at Sol Station?"

His father accepted the mug with a nod. "For now. I have not yet decided where my presence is most beneficial. I am also uncertain whether I will be called to testify."

"With trial counsel's case focused on Persei Primus and Gaia, you probably won't be," Justin said. "You weren't involved in either."

His father growled softly, taking a drink of tea. "But my clan provided Aurora with the *Starhawke*. Following the trial counsel's reasoning, that would make us either accomplices or imbeciles."

An answering growl rumbled in Jonarel's throat. "I challenge them to make a case for either."

"Which they probably won't." Justin held up his hands, palms out, as their combined growls filled the space. "That's my point.

The Sovereign's being strategic about this. If she wants to turn public opinion against the Kraed, which would be in her best interests, casting a shadow of doubt over you could be more effective than making a direct accusation of wrongdoing or ineptitude. There's a segment of the population that already fears your physical strength and technological superiority. Given what we're seeing from the protestors so far, it would be a small leap for the Sovereign to fan the flames of that mistrust. That would encourage people to draw fear-inspired conclusions about the Kraed that paint them as enemies rather than allies."

"Are you saying she wants to discredit the Kraed?" Lelindia's indignation sharpened her tone.

Justin shrugged. "It's just a theory, but she's already turned the public against the Fleet by tagging the Admiral and Aurora as traitors. The protestors are demanding investigations into all Fleet activities and personnel. It's put the Fleet on shaky ground with public opinion. There's significant unrest within the ranks, too, with people being singled out for being loyal to the Admiral or for *not* being loyal. It's a mess. If the Kraed fall under suspicion, that would leave—"

"The Teeli." Jonarel spat the name as a curse.

"Exactly." The irony in Justin's voice could cut steel. "The paragons of peace."

Forty-Two

"Do you know what Ifel wants to talk to me about?" Cade asked Unity as he followed them out of his cabin.

"Yes."

He waited as they continued past the jungle grove to the lift section. "Are you going to tell me what it is?"

Unity bobbed twice. "No."

Cade blew out a breath. Unity was getting better at keeping secrets.

He halted when Unity did, the walls closing in, creating the Yruf lift. The release of pressure on the soles of his boots let him know they were going down. When the bulkheads peeled back moments later, they revealed the ornate circular hatch for Ifel's throne room.

"This is a formal meeting?" He hadn't spent any time in the room since his visit with Aurora.

"A... private one," Unity replied.

His steps slowed. "You're freaking me out a bit here."

Unity spun halfway and hovered. "Don't worry. It's a good thing."

The massive door rolled back. The interior was already lit with the chasing light pattern that reminded him of five giant snakes steadily circling the perimeter of the room. A new light source he'd never seen before lit Ifel's throne from within, making it glow like polished amber.

The Yruf leader reclined with a sinuous ease, her cloak draped around her in luxurious folds. She watched him as he approached, Unity by his side.

The other change in the room was the addition of a solid bench at Ifel's feet that was table height for him. The same amber glow emanated from within.

Ifel's long fingers pointed at the bench.

"Sit," Unity confirmed.

He boosted himself onto the raised surface, facing her. The material was warm to the touch and remarkably comfortable, as though it was conforming to the contours of his body.

The height of the bench still put him below eye-level with Ifel, forcing him to tilt his head back to meet her gaze.

She curled forward, slowly reaching out. When he made no move to stop her, she rested one hand on his cheek and the other at his temple, the skin covering her scales as smooth as glass.

"You have great potential, Cade Ellis," Unity translated as Ifel's gaze held his. "But you fight against it, resisting the full scope of your abilities."

He felt the tug of Ifel's mind touching his. Again, he offered no resistance. Whatever she wanted from him, she could have. He owed her that. He waited, expecting her to project images to him, but none came.

"Aurora allowed me to assist her in stepping from behind her walls. Will you do the same?" Unity translated.

It was bizarre, but talking to Ifel like this felt a lot like talking to an older, more experienced version of Aurora. Despite their obvious differences, the two had a lot in common.

He glanced at Unity out of the corner of his eye, swallowing the anxiety creeping up his throat. Aurora had described the direct link conversation she'd had with Ifel, how they'd freely communicated, not with images, but words they both had understood despite speaking different languages. "Why?"

He didn't even know he was going to ask the question until it popped out.

"Because Aurora needs you."

Gut punch. He sucked in air. "How will this help her?"

"By fully opening your connection to each other."

Fully opening? His mind spun, grappling for the meaning of her words. "Are you saying..." He cleared his throat, tried again. "Are you saying you can help me to communicate with Aurora? Telepathically?"

Unity chuckled, matching the amusement Cade felt from Ifel. "The Human concept of telepathy is a bit... outdated," they said. "Limited. What Ifel's offering is to help you connect with Aurora the way the Suulh do."

Really having trouble breathing now. "How is that possible?"

Unity's voice took on the more measured pace they used when translating Ifel's words. "My race has sought this form of communication since long before I was born. I have learned a great deal from my time with Aurora, Micah, and Lelindia. And I have studied you, as well. Biologically, you have the same adaptation for this form of communication that they do, but much of it is latent, underdeveloped. The part you allowed to become fulfilled is what enables you to see Suulh energy fields. I am offering to help you develop the rest, the gifts that are inherently yours."

His mouth opened, but no words came out. The fact that his heart was slamming against his ribs like a rabbit with a jackhammer might have something to do with that.

"Breathe, Cade," Unity said softly.

He sucked in air, the resistance in his lungs letting him know how much tension had coalesced in his chest.

Why was he so tense? This should be great news. He should be exhilarated. Ifel was offering the possibility of a connection with Aurora he'd never imagined.

Instead, he felt like he was about to skydive with a parachute that had a fifty-fifty chance of opening.

Images flickered in his mind then, the sensation familiar as Ifel sorted through his memories.

"Not just underdeveloped," Unity murmured. "Traumatized."

He flinched as an image flashed by.

Ifel paused her memory sift, slowly returning to the image and allowing it to hover on butterfly wings.

He didn't want to look at it. Didn't want to see what she was showing him.

She waited patiently, her mind gently holding space with his, allowing him to adjust to the uncomfortable emotions the image evoked.

He recognized the child in the image – no more than four – cowering on the floor. He had *been* that child. He could still feel the wetness of the tears streaking his chubby cheeks as he stared at the monster looming over him.

His father's face was a twisted mask of rage, the fury focused like a knife's point on him. His mother was a blurry figure in the background. Her face was ghostly pale but slightly averted, as though she couldn't bear to look at him. She was hunched over, her arms wrapped protectively around her torso.

Every instinct screamed at him to run to her, to beg her to protect him. But he didn't. Because she wouldn't. Just like all the other times. She wouldn't stand against his father, especially now. Not when it was so much worse.

The image hung suspended in time as the seconds ticked by. He finally realized Ifel was giving him time to process his emotions, to begin seeing the image through the eyes of an adult rather than the trauma of a child.

"You were a child," Unity confirmed. "These are your parents?"

"Yes." He sounded like he'd swallowed a mouthful of sand.

A crest of anger rose in Ifel like a cobra's head, a hiss escaping her lips.

He could easily imagine why. He knew without a doubt that no Yruf would ever consider raising a hand to strike a child.

"This was not the first time?" Unity asked.

"No." He cleared his throat twice before he continued. "But it was the last." At least until his father found out he'd applied to and been accepted by the Academy.

"What changed?"

"I did." If anyone else had asked him about that day, he honestly wouldn't have been able to answer the question. But with Ifel plucking the image deftly from his mind and allowing him to really look at it, all the details he'd suppressed came flooding back.

"You were picking up on their thoughts." Unity translated. Clearly Ifel wasn't asking. She already knew.

"I made the colossal mistake of telling them what I heard."

The cobra head of anger flashed its fangs, somehow moving to create a barrier between his child self and his father. "What did you hear?"

Cade drew in a shuddering breath.

Ifel's fingers on his face pressed more firmly, anchoring him, silently reminding him she was with him, supporting him, protecting him.

A single tear slid from the corner of his eye and rolled down his cheek. "It didn't make any sense to me then. But when I reached adolescence, I understood. By that time I'd convinced myself I'd overheard my dad say something out loud. I'd forgotten about the voices in my mind."

Hearing the words in his own voice gave him a moment of vertigo, the world abruptly spinning on the wrong axis.

The feeling of physical support from both the bench beneath him and Ifel facing him increased.

"We've got you," Unity murmured, this time speaking for themselves.

He should probably question what exactly that meant, but he'd deal with it later. "My father was having an affair with a co-worker. He was thinking about their latest... meetup, in graphic detail. I was a child, innocent. The words and images I was getting confused me, so right in front of my mother, I asked him what it meant to do those things with Cynthia."

A wretched sickness filled his stomach, the same sensation he'd felt when his father's backhand had knocked him to the floor. It was the most brutal blow he'd ever received. And his father hadn't stopped with one.

"My childhood ended that day, at least as far as I was concerned. My parents kept me home for two weeks afterward, locked in my room. They told anyone who asked I had a bad case of the flu. In reality, they were waiting for the bruises to fade. I spent all day, every day, alone, except for when my mother brought me food. I hated those moments most of all. She wouldn't look at me, or talk to me. She acted like I was invisible – just set the tray on my bedside table and left."

The memory made him tremble. Her antipathy had hurt far worse than the bruises on his face and body. "It gave me a lot of time to think. To make choices. By the time my face had healed enough that I could go out in public, I'd created a veneer that fit with their expectations of who they wanted me to be." And he'd held onto it until the day he'd boarded the train that took him to the Academy. "That also meant locking the voices and images away in a vault and never thinking of them again. Until I met you."

He allowed the mental image of that traumatic moment to fade into the background as he focused on Ifel's diamond-pupiled gaze. "I'd forgotten that part of me even existed."

The cobra still swayed behind her eyes, its flared hood protecting him from any who dared harm him. "I am sorry for your suffering. No child should have a memory like that."

Pressure built, more tears dripping down his face and off his chin. "I agree."

And maybe that was something else that had drawn him so strongly to Aurora and the Suulh. As Aurora had reminded him recently, every Suulh birth was planned, every child cherished and nurtured as a precious gift. On some level, he must have sensed that from her, known that with her, a child would be safe.

She would protect her child with the fierce loyalty and love his mother hadn't... even against him.

Was that part of their dynamic, too? Did he secretly wonder if he would turn out like his father, domineering and cruel to his own child? The very idea made the sickness in his stomach surge, coating his throat. But if the worst happened, if he ever did lash out at his child, Aurora would stop him. Contain him. Neutralize him. She was the one woman he could trust completely to save him from himself.

The look in Ifel's eyes changed, sorrow and tenderness filling her emotional field. "You are not your father."

He tried to shake his head, but she still held him firmly in place. "We don't know that."

Her pupils widened, her tongue flicking rapidly. "*I* know that."

The declaration in Unity's translation came with an emotional push from Ifel that stilled the air in his lungs. In that moment, he wasn't talking to Ifel, his Yruf friend. He was talking to Ifel, the formidable leader of the Yruf. "If you posed any threat to Aurora, or her future children, you would not be here."

The meaning of her words soaked in, icy-hot. He wouldn't be here. Or anywhere near Aurora. Ifel would have made certain of that.

Which meant she believed in him. No doubts. No reservations.

He blinked rapidly, fighting to clear his vision as her face wavered.

"You have never valued yourself as you should, Cade Ellis. Now I have a better understanding why." Ifel dipped her head, her tongue flicking twice. "But if you reconnect with the lost parts of yourself, you can become the person you were meant to be, and the mate Aurora deserves."

His heart thumped unsteadily as Ifel gave voice to his deepest desire. And his greatest fear. He could sense how invested she was in the outcome, how determined she was to help him.

But the thought of facing his demons left him quivering like a leaf. What pain awaited him down that road? What if he couldn't defeat the monsters of his past? What if he wasn't as strong as she believed him to be? What if he failed?

Her pupils contracted, her tongue flicking again.

"The choice is yours," Unity said into the silence.

Choice. She was giving him a choice.

He could take the clear and easy path, remain the man he was today, the man Aurora already loved.

Or...

...he could take the murky and difficult road, fulfill his potential and earn his place at Aurora's side.

Taking a ragged breath, he squared his shoulders.

"How do we begin?"

Forty-Three

"You're sure you'll be able to get a message to your dad about the Yruf potentially monitoring him?" Micah asked Knox.

Since Knox was visiting his dad at the detention center, he'd offered to drive them all in from the beach house when they went to see Aurora. Lee-Lee, her parents, Jonarel, and Siginal had taken Siginal's transport to the Kraed Embassy. Knox would be dropping Micah and his parents off there afterward so they could take Siginal's shuttle to Sol Station.

He wished Aurora was coming with them.

Knox changed lanes as they approached the exit for the detention facility. "He'll definitely get the message. A very vague message."

"And no one will figure out what you're telling him?"

Knox shot him an amused glance as they exited onto the main road for Seaview. "We've been using this coded system to communicate with each other since before I graduated from the Academy. No one has ever even questioned it, let alone figured out how to crack it."

"And Aurora knows it, too?"

"Yep. I started teaching her the day she arrived on the *Argo*. She's good with language and analysis, so she picked it up fairly quickly once she understood the system."

"And she didn't find it odd that you wanted her to learn it?" his mom asked from the backseat.

"Not at all. Coded messages aren't uncommon in Fleet communications. This one just happened to be specific to communications with me and my dad. Since she reported directly to me and I reported directly to my dad, it made sense."

His mom sighed, resting her head on his dad's shoulder. "I'm glad I didn't know about any of this while she was still serving on Fleet ships. I would have been even more of a nervous wreck."

Micah tended to agree with her. Aurora facing danger when he was beside her to help was one thing. Aurora facing danger when she was lightyears away scared the stuffing out of him.

His dad's mouth quirked in a smile as he slid his arm around Micah's mom. "She's an adventurer. Exploring new places and learning new things is in her blood."

His dad's blood, too. The two were a lot alike.

Micah had a taste for adventure too, otherwise he never would have gotten into competitive surfing. But he recognized his mom's attitudes when it came to the lifestyle he'd chosen — staying in one place, building a sense of community around a topic he was passionate about. If his mom had been in his life when he was growing up, she might have helped him find his career faster, without all the searching and false starts that had filled his post-teen years.

The stop at the entrance gate's security checkpoint was a different experience with a Fleet captain behind the wheel. The Fleet personnel snapped to attention. But walking through the grass-covered courtyard and into the detention center for the second time was every bit as unpleasant as the previous day.

Scratch that. It was worse. The number of people waiting in line had tripled, but that wasn't the problem. Now he had a clear visual in his mind of the miserable place his sister was living in. Standing here, thinking of her in there, had parked a black cloud over his head.

He surveyed the growing crowd filing in through the front entrance. His mom had insisted on arriving early, although they'd still been behind several larger groups. A few looked like they may have been camped out in the parking lot all morning.

The makeup of the crowd was different, too. Yesterday it had been all adults. Today children were added to the mix. No school on a Saturday.

Their presence dug at his gut. He couldn't imagine being a child visiting a parent in the brig.

To their credit, the kids were taking it in stride. The younger ones looked eager, even excited, like they were at grandma's house, not a Fleet detention center. They were probably too young to understand the implications of where they were. The older ones showed a stoic acceptance of their surroundings, no doubt a result of being raised in a Fleet household.

Micah glanced over his shoulder at Knox, who was drawing a few stares from the other visitors waiting in line. There was a morbid curiosity vibe to their interest in him. Knox wasn't dressed in uniform, but unlike Micah and his parents, his face was clearly well known to people connected with the Fleet. Or maybe his picture had been on the news when the story broke about his dad's arrest.

Knox met his gaze from the side of his eye, a silent acknowledgment of their mutual discomfort passing between them.

The line moved forward. He followed his parents as they stepped up to the window and gave their names. The same Fleet employee from the day before checked them in, but the man gave no sign of recognition. Knox, however, triggered a stiffening of the man's spine and a crisp "yes, sir, thank you, sir" when Knox handed over his ID.

They were directed to the same door and into the same waiting room, though Knox was placed in a different numbered group. "I'll be heading to the men's visiting area," he murmured at Micah's questioning look. "I'll meet you three outside afterward."

Knox's group exited through the side door first, then Micah walked with his parents down the depressing bland hallway to the women's visiting area.

His mom seemed calmer and more focused than she had the day before, her gaze sweeping their surroundings with an analytical look that reminded him a lot of Celia. Planning a jailbreak?

He wouldn't doubt it. Or maybe she was making mental notes of things she wanted to ask Unity about after they'd infiltrated the detention center.

That was the thought that kept the cloud from dropping a torrent of rain on his head. By tonight he'd be back on the *Starhawke*, back with Unity, and the Yruf would be on the job of making a direct connection to Aurora.

The visitor area door clanged shut behind him, startling him out of his thoughts. The guard directed them to bench number four this time, in between a middle-aged woman to the left and a man close to his age with two little boys by his side on their right.

After they sat down, his mom gave his hand a squeeze, her gaze locked on the door on the opposite wall where Aurora would enter.

He squeezed back, appreciating the steady reassurance. It was getting harder and harder to believe he'd spent most of his life not knowing she and Aurora were still alive. Their presence in his world now seemed as vital as the air he breathed.

The far door opened and the prisoners filed in. Aurora was last in line. Her closed-mouth smile looked more natural this time, the sparkle in her eyes as she sat down breaking up the hanging cloud like rays of sunshine.

"Hey there." Her gaze swept across them, her slightly unfocused look indicating she was reading their emotional fields. Whatever she found must have pleased her, because her smile grew. "Thanks for coming."

"Wouldn't miss it." Their mom propped her elbows on her knees, leaning toward the transparent barrier. "We came in with Knox."

"Oh?" The cadence of surprised interest in the response was off by a fraction from normal. Aurora must have sensed Knox's presence when they'd all arrived. "How is he?"

"Concerned about his dad, and you, but handling it like you'd expect. He said to tell you hello."

"Please tell him hello back. I assume that means the Admiral is being detained here, too?"

This time Aurora nailed the vocal cues and it was their mom who missed a beat before responding. "That's right. I forgot you didn't know that already."

Aurora's mouth flattened to a line, but the somberness didn't reach her eyes. "No news feeds in my cell. But I'm glad he's visiting the Admiral. Isolation is tough for a sharp mind. Having someone to talk to helps."

"Yes," their mom agreed. "I'm sure he'll appreciate having some interpersonal communication."

Micah had to work to keep his thoughts from showing on his face. To anyone listening, it was a banal interchange. To anyone who knew about Unity and Cade's plan, it was full of meaning.

"I had a visit from Phoebe Liddell yesterday. I was impressed by her, and we got along well. She's agreed to represent me."

"So we heard," their dad confirmed. "She notified me last night. I'm glad you liked her. I had a good feeling about her when I spoke with her."

Micah suppressed a snort. That comment coming from his dad wasn't a figure of speech.

"You were right." Aurora's gaze flicked to his, her lips twitching. "She's great."

"Did she give you any indication of next steps?" Micah had exactly zero knowledge of Fleet legal procedure, a fact that he needed to remedy in the days to come.

"She's requested the files from trial counsel. After she's looked them over, she'll begin gathering relevant witnesses. She expects my Article 32 hearing to take place next week."

Thunder rumbled through the cloud over his head, erasing all levity. "Will we be able to attend the hearing?"

"No. But she can notify you when it's been scheduled."

He projected his next question rather than asking it out loud. *Are you worried?*

She met his gaze with the calm he'd seen her exhibit on the bridge of the *Starhawke* when facing a thorny issue. *Worry is a misuse of imagination* she projected back.

Forty-Four

When Lelindia had been on the grounds of the Kraed Embassy the previous day, she'd been so focused on meeting with President Yeoh and seeing her parents that she hadn't given her surroundings much attention.

Not that Signal had given her time to. After the *Rowkclarek*'s shuttle had landed on the rooftop shuttle pad of the Embassy's transportation center, Signal had left his attendants in charge of the shuttle, whisked her and Jonarel to his transport, and departed. She hadn't encountered anyone.

Now, as the transport entered the dense grove of trees that surrounded the Embassy, she scooted closer to the window. Nope, still couldn't catch more than a glimpse of the earth-toned structure tucked within the jungle atmosphere.

The vehicle swung into the open-mouthed cave of the transportation building, blocking out the midday sun. It took a moment for her eyes to adjust, but her Nedale senses were already soaking up the verdant pulse of life all around her.

A cool breeze greeted her as she, Jonarel, and her parents stepped out of the vehicle after Signal. Breathing in the fresh aroma of rain-dampened earth and sun-warmed leaves helped to tamp down the squiggles of anxiety that had unsettled her ever since she woke up.

"Come." Siginal beckoned them toward a sunny archway and a curving path that wound through the lush vegetation, leading to what she assumed was the entrance to the Embassy. "I wish to introduce you to the others."

A slight breathiness in his voice indicated this moment might have more significance to him than his casual words let on. Who exactly would they be meeting?

She and Jonarel walked beside her parents as Siginal led the way along the path. She studied the artfully natural greenery that concealed at least ninety percent of the Embassy's exterior. "You have an excellent gardening crew."

Siginal slowed his steps to walk beside her. "I am honored you think so. My people do not possess your abilities, but there are many who share your passion for plant life."

"It shows."

The double doors of the Embassy's entrance reminded her of the cabin doors on the *Starhawke* – beautifully grained thick wood panels carved with intricate landscape imagery. Lush flora provided a background to the fantasy-like animals of Drakar, only some of which she could name.

The doors opened silently as they approached, a waft of warm moist air sweetened with the scent of blooming flowers pushing aside the winter chill with a gentle hand.

Stepping inside was like being transported to another world, though not the one she'd expected. The non-linear walls with their knotty barked surface gave the impression of a wooded grove rather than an administrative building, but it didn't reflect the Clarek compound the way the *Starhawke* did. The flooring was unusual, too – it had the packed earth look of a forest trail or glade, but without the granular texture under her shoes. Blooming flowers, moss, and ferns appeared to grow right out of the floor, providing the source of the floral scent.

Doors of inlaid colored glass similar to the style of the *Starhawke*'s observation lounge were inset at intervals and angles that gave an organic feel, but a single piece of furniture anchored the enclosed space. Technically it qualified as a reception desk, though in its former life it had clearly been part of the base and root system of an enormous tree. The serpentine roots had been put into service holding various technical items she couldn't begin to identify but recognized as Kraed designed.

However, it was the Kraed sitting behind the unusual desk who gave her pause. All the Kraed she'd met on Drakar had Jonarel's coloring – forest green skin with brown tendrils twining across it, and mahogany hair. This female's skin was the yellow-green of savannah grass, and her short, layered hair and the patterns crossing her skin were auburn.

The female rose, stepping around the barrier, revealing the trim physique of a runner. She met Lelindia's gaze straight on, a look of anticipation in her eyes, which were a saturated violet rather than gold.

"Remar." Siginal embraced her, the moment lasting longer than a typical hug, but not as long as experience had taught Lelindia it would have if their whole group had been Kraed.

Siginal stepped back, his thick arm sweeping toward Lelindia. "Come, checala. I wish to introduce you to Daymar's clan."

Lelindia's brows rose. Daymar's clan? Siginal hadn't prepared her for this. Neither had Jonarel. The ground felt a little unsteady under her feet as she stepped forward.

"Lelindia, this is Remar Terfeli, daughter of Harvan, Daymar's brother, the leader of Clan Terfeli. Remar, this is Lelindia Forrest, Nedale of the Suulh and beloved mate of Jonarel."

The look in Remar's eyes as she opened her arms to Lelindia showed this was not news to her.

Questions collided like popping corn in her head as Remar embraced her.

"It is an honor to welcome you." Remar's accented Galish had a different rhythm and tone than Jonarel and Siginal's, her diction less pronounced, so that *honor* sounded like *owner.*

"Thank you." She returned the embrace, which bought her a little time to gather her thoughts. "I'm sorry I'm a little flustered," she said as Remar released her. "I wasn't expecting this."

Remar gave Siginal a wry look that was quite familiar. Lelindia had seen Daymar look at Siginal the same way. "My uncle does love spectacle." She met Lelindia's gaze, amusement in her eyes. "But you already know this."

"I do." A smile curved her lips. "It's a pleasure to meet you, Remar. These are my parents, Marina and Gryphon Forrest."

Remar greeted and embraced them as well, then hugged Jonarel with obvious enthusiasm and affection. "I am very happy for you."

Jonarel's gaze met Lelindia's over Remar's head. "And I am very happy."

"So I see."

Movement to Lelindia's left made her turn. One of the doors had opened, revealing a small anteroom and a beautifully carved wood staircase rising out of view.

"Come." Remar motioned them forward. "The others have gathered in the immersion room."

"Others?"

"Immersion room?" her dad asked.

"My clan wants to meet you. The immersion room is our private space in the Embassy for... communion. Come."

As they climbed the solid curved treads of the staircase, Lelindia nudged Jonarel with her shoulder. "You could have warned me."

"Why would I spoil my father's surprise?" He slid an arm around her. "This was more fun."

"Fun?" she said in mock bewilderment. "Who are you and what have you done with Jonarel?"

His snort of laughter startled Siginal and Remar, who both paused on the stairs. Siginal looked at them with concern, but Remar looked delighted. She gave Lelindia an approving nod before continuing up the staircase.

Judging by the number of steps, and the slight burn in her calves, they were heading to the top floor.

Jonarel's hand moved to the small of her back, giving her a slight boost with each step.

She turned her head and lowered her voice. "Why is Remar's coloring different than yours?" she murmured. "I thought all Kraed had the same coloring."

"It is a common misconception," he replied, his voice loud enough that her parents could hear him. "Clan Clarek made first contact with Humans—"

"Which they never let us forget," Remar commented in a teasing tone.

"—and we have served as the Kraed's GC representatives and ambassadors ever since," Jonarel continued smoothly. "We were the first to remodel and staff this embassy, and are still the public face of our people."

"Allowing the rest of us to retain our privacy," Remar added. "But at a cost to Clan Clarek. My clan, and others who enjoy traveling beyond our borders, realized it was unworthy of us to expect so many from Siginal's clan to remain away from our homeworld for so long. The clans set up a rotation to manage the tasks that are necessary for us to accomplish here, but which do not require us to leave the Embassy. Members of my clan currently serve at this post and will continue to do so for another three of our years. Then we will return home and the next clan will begin their period of service."

"So everyone working here is part of your clan?" her mom asked, sounding as out of breath from the climb as Lelindia.

"Or Siginal's, yes."

"That doesn't explain why your coloring is different," Lelindia said, circling back to her original question.

"Yes, it does." Remar paused on the landing at the top of the staircase. "Clan coloring is distinctive."

"But—"

The doors behind Remar parted. Whatever Lelindia was going to say flew right out of her head as she gaped at the room before them.

She'd spent enough time on the *Starhawke*'s walking track to recognize the projections on the walls for what they were, but it was still an impressive representation of a vista that certainly wasn't on Earth.

Towering, gnarled trees whose bark perfectly matched the walls of the reception area and stairwell stretched their limbs up, down, and sideways, creating natural platforms of intertwined branches. The tiered levels of the room appeared to sit on those natural platforms, a view of what looked like garden groves peeking through from below, while a sparkling sea beckoned in the distance.

At least seventy Kraed stood as one and faced the door. The combined effect of that much focused attention temporarily rooted her where she stood.

The majority had Remar's lighter coloring, though a few had the familiar coloring of Clan Clarek.

"Welcome to Drakar," Remar said with pride.

"This is Drakar?" Her mom's brow furrowed, confusion clouding her eyes as she glanced at Lelindia. "From your descriptions I expected it to be more... jungle-like."

Siginal led them forward. "My clan's home fits that description. We live at the equator. The hill lands are further north. This is the home of Clan Terfeli."

What followed was a whirlwind of introductions that made Lelindia's head spin. Many of the Clan Terfeli members were related to Daymar – cousins of one type or another – and all were eager to meet Lelindia. Either Siginal had paved the way with alacrity, or Daymar had been her champion to the Terfeli all along. Maybe both.

No one asked about her pregnancy, though. Siginal might have held onto that nugget for now. She was happy to take her cues from him when it came to relations with the clans.

At some point Jonarel brought her a wooden mug filled with a brew she'd enjoyed on Drakar that was similar to tea. She took the opportunity to draw him aside to a secluded nook of one of the trees out of view of the gathering. While most of the trees were projections and sleight of hand illusions, a couple were living specimens growing right through the floor of the building. The feat of engineering boggled her mind. "Okay, explain to me how clan coloring can be distinctive when your mother's matches yours and your dad's, even though she came from Clan Terfeli."

Jonarel stroked a finger along her cheek, leaving a trail of warmth. "Because our coloring is adaptive."

"Adaptive? You mean it can change?"

"Yes, if we choose."

She caught his hand in hers, mulling that over. "Why didn't you ever tell me you could change your coloring?"

"You never asked."

The sound that came out of her throat was exasperation laced with laughter. "Why on Earth would I ever ask? It never would have occurred to me. I know your skin and hair tones changed when you went through adolescence, but I figured that was a permanent hormonal shift."

Jonarel shook his head. "It is what gave me the ability to choose. Children cannot change, only adults. But I am of Clan Clarek and will remain so all my life. I have no reason to alter my appearance."

She held his hand up, studying his skin with her fingers and Nedale senses, trying to pick up on the biological elements that would make what he was saying possible. "So you could change right now?"

"No."

The slight huskiness in his voice made her realize her tactile inspection was having an unintentional consequence in other parts of his body.

"Our coloring is of deep significance. We do not change it lightly. Even if that were not true, making the change takes time and concentration. My mother told me it was a process of many days to alter her skin tones and eye color, and months for her hair to grow in darker. She did not make the change until after she and my father had pair bonded and spent their first year with the Terfeli. Only when they returned to our clan did she embrace our colors as her own."

What he was saying captivated her, especially when the rumble of his voice combined with the warmth from his body. "If she hadn't changed her skin tone, would you have developed her coloring after adolescence?"

He shrugged, the tendons in his hand flexing under her gentle caress. "I do not know. To my knowledge no child has been conceived of parents who were not officially part of the same clan with the same coloring." The liquid quality of his golden eyes sharpened. "You are wondering about..." His gaze dropped to her belly.

She lowered her voice to a whisper, although the buzz of conversation in the room should prevent even the Kraed from overhearing. "Yes. I admit I've been hoping she'll have your coloring. It's so beautiful, and it would be a visible bond between our races.

But based on what you're saying, what if she doesn't have your coloring?" Worry gnawed at her. "What if she doesn't have the ability to change her coloring as an adult? Will that hurt her chances of being accepted by your people, of having a Kraed mate if that's who she chooses?"

"No." He captured her hands in his, pulling her close. "She is part of Clan Clarek, and will always be. Her position in our society, like yours, will ensure that any Kraed mate she may choose would become part of our clan. Her coloring at birth, or her ability to change her coloring as an adult would never be a concern."

She released her breath – and her tension – on a sigh. Leaning into him, she rested her cheek against his chest. "I love you."

He stilled for a moment, like she'd startled him. Then his arms wrapped around her, drawing her into the nurturing warmth of his body. "And I, you, checana."

Forty-Five

If someone had asked Micah that morning which experience of the day would push him the farthest out of his comfort zone, he would have laid all his money on the visit to the brig to see Aurora.

He would have lost that bet.

Walking into the immersion room at the Kraed Embassy where Lee-Lee's family was waiting for them had knocked him off-kilter, but stepping off Siginal's shuttle onto the *Rowkclarek* took first prize.

Funny, really. After spending so much time on the Yruf ship, he should be used to alien starships not being anything like the ships that came out of Far Horizons. Except he'd never imagined that a starship that looked so much like the *Starhawke* on the outside would look nothing like it on the inside.

Also, unlike at the Embassy, what he was seeing weren't projections. It was all very, very real.

"So this is what a typical Kraed starship looks like?" his dad asked, his voice reverent.

"A Clan Clarek ship, yes," Siginal answered, clearly pleased by their reaction.

"I made modifications for the *Starhawke*," Jonarel explained, "so the design would have many of the familiar Fleet style features Aurora was used to. If I had brought her a ship with this design, she and the rest of the crew would not have been comfortable."

No kidding. Micah was just visiting and the intimidation factor made him want to tuck his arms close to his body so he wouldn't accidentally touch anything.

While his dad and Gryphon peppered Signal and Jonarel with technical questions, Micah pivoted in a slow circle, taking it all in.

The vaulted space where he stood had trees – mammoth, alien trees – growing up through a series of planked walkways and staircases that linked the trees together. He could hear the bubbling patter of water over stones that sounded like a small river – a *river* – below him, though he couldn't see the source.

The warm air pressed against his skin, humid enough to make his clothes stick to his body. A slight breeze wicked at the beads of moisture trickling down the side of his face.

A bump against his shoulder made him glance down.

Lee-Lee grinned up at him. "You look the way I felt the first time I saw Jonarel's home."

"His home? This is what the Clarek compound looks like?"

"Pretty much. Definitely what it feels like." She waved a hand in front of her face, fanning herself as she surveyed their surroundings. "Kelly had mentioned that their ships blended with the compound on the interior, but I'd thought she meant like the *Starhawke* does. This is... more."

"Yeah. Much more."

He couldn't even begin to guess where they were standing in relation to the layout of the ship. A shuttle area, obviously, since the shuttle had docked here, but the sections above and below them offered no indication of their functionality. He could have been next to engineering or the med bay or the bridge. He couldn't tell the difference.

The Kraed crew who were working all around them in the enclosures and ramada-style sections at the various junctures were keeping a respectful distance, though he was aware of the curious glances they kept shooting him and Lee-Lee. Their parents, too.

"Do you know any of them?" he asked her.

"Some look familiar, but I'm not seeing anyone I can name. I'm sure Kelly could. She was befriending every pilot and engineer who would talk to her. I spent my time with the horticulturists."

He examined the trees. "I'm sure they need horticulturists onboard too, to keep these trees and the rest of the vegetation alive."

"Good point."

And there was quite a lot of vegetation. Flowering vines twined around the tree trunks, and ferns grew right out of the bark. He took a step closer to the nearest one. "Is this the same bark as what's on the *Starhawke*'s walls?"

"Uh-huh. These are denglar trees, the dominant species in the area where the compound is located. Many of the furniture pieces on the *Starhawke* are made from these trees, too."

He rested his palm lightly on the uneven surface. A sensation of calm, of grounding, swept over him, acutely obvious in contrast to the unsettled feeling that had been dogging him the rest of the day.

"See?" Lee-Lee came to stand beside him. "You are Suulh."

The comment confused him. "What do you mean?"

"You may not be able to generate an energy field, but the tree is reacting to your touch the way it would with any Suulh. It... likes you, for want of a better description."

"Really?" For some reason that pleased him enormously.

"Really. Plants are incredibly receptive. The tree is responding to the nurturing energy that's part of who you are. And judging by what I can see in your body's reaction, it's feeding you, too."

"Feeding me? Is that why I feel calmer?"

"Uh-huh. I'd never thought about it, but that might be one reason you're drawn to the ocean. The lifeforce of the plant and animal life probably nurtures you the way being in the middle of a forest affects me. And the animals sense your nurturing energy in return and want to be near you."

"So Streak and Cutter are energy junkies?" he asked with a grin.

She shot him a quizzical look. "Streak and Cutter?"

He shook his head. "Sorry. I forgot you weren't with Aurora and me when she met them. I've gotten so used to having you around that it feels like you've always been there. Streak and Cutter are a pair of dolphins who like to surf with me."

"Ah. It wouldn't surprise me if you give off a lot of energy when you surf. I'm sure they enjoy it."

"So when—"

"Checala."

They both turned as Siginal approached.

"It would be my honor to present you to the clan this evening. Would you, your guests, and crew do me the pleasure of joining us for the evening meal?"

Lee-Lee's smile lit the room like a Hawai'ian sunrise. "We'd be delighted."

Two hours later, Micah was back onboard the *Rowkclarek*. He'd stowed his things in his cabin on the *Starhawke* – which he was coming to think of as *his* regardless of the fact that it was on the guest deck – and joined everyone else for the short walk to Siginal's ship.

They drew strange looks from passersby, and with good reason. Siginal had provided every single one of them with a Kraed outfit to wear for the event.

The leggings and tunic he wore weren't as skin-tight as a wetsuit, but close. The calf-high boots were comfortable but still felt odd on his feet after years of beach footwear that was easy to slip on and off. He'd needed Celia's help to lace these up. She hadn't teased him too much when he'd contacted her, asking for help. And now she was walking beside him as they stepped off the airbridge from the station onto the ship.

The otherworldly interior fascinated him. It was a marvel of ingenuity, and visual proof of how differently the Kraed approached their environment compared to humans.

But what startled him the most was how pleasant the temperature felt this time. "They must have cooled things down for us," he murmured to Celia as they followed Siginal, Jonarel, and Lee-Lee along one of the planked walkways.

"I doubt it." Celia gestured to his clothes. "Their fabric is temperature-regulating."

"Really?" He ran a hand down his tunic. "I thought this was ceremonial or something."

"It is. They don't give their clothing to just anyone. It's a sign of acceptance, of trust. But it's also practical. And I would guess it's Siginal's way of encouraging your family and Lelindia's to visit Drakar."

"You think so?" He hadn't considered that possibility.

"Definitely. He's wanted a bond between his people and the Suulh for a decade. The only thing that would make him happier is if Aurora came, too."

A knot tightened in his gut. "Not an option at the moment." And didn't that make him feel like a louse? Here he was, off to an incredible dinner on an alien starship, and she was stuck alone in her cell—

A sharp jab in his ribs caught him off guard. "Ow."

"Knock off the guilt trip." Celia's tone was teasing but the look in her brown eyes was serious. "Aurora wouldn't want you to beat yourself up. She'd want you to experience all this to the fullest."

He rubbed the spot where she'd nailed him. "That's going to leave a bruise."

"Probably. But you'll heal quickly. And you needed the reminder."

"Tough love?" His smile froze. Talk about a terrible word choice.

Emotions he couldn't label flickered behind her eyes. "Something like that."

Forty-Six

The *Rowkclarek's* dining hall had provided Jonarel with a template for the observation lounge on the *Starhawke*, with two key alterations. He had reduced the size to a fifth, to better match the *Starhawke's* dimensions. He had also taken Aurora's preferences into account, replacing the *Rowkclarek's* sprawling tree canopy with floor to ceiling windows that gave a breathtaking view of the stars.

But his father's ship still produced a flutter of joy in his chest, the walkways and workstations as familiar to him as his parents' home on Drakar.

He slid his arm around Lelindia as they entered the crowded dining hall. Every member of the crew appeared to be in attendance.

Her focus had been on the bevy of trees surrounding them, but when she smiled up at him, the beauty of her beloved face filled his heart to the brim. She snuggled closer, giving him the tactile connection he craved.

What a gift. His checana always responded to his unspoken cues as effortlessly and willingly as if she were Kraed, as though she too yearned for the physical closeness that was a hallmark of his people.

How had he ever lived a single day without her by his side?

He honestly couldn't imagine, but he knew his world had been a somber, colorless place before her emerald-green energy field had filled it with life.

Tehar's image appeared to his father's right, standing beside Rowk, his father's Nirunoc brother, who had bonded with the *Rowkclarek*.

The sight of them together pushed a lump into Jonarel's throat. He had wondered if Rowk would allow it, as Tehar's presence onboard his ship was a very personal connection, one that had been severed when his sister had helped the crew escape Drakar. But the affectionate look in Rowk's eyes as he gazed at Tehar made it clear he had absolved her of blame and welcomed her back into his midst.

"Clan Clarek, my son and daughter have returned!" His father's voice boomed to the treetops, filling every knot and bower.

A cheer of approval reverberated through the gathered crowd. Jonarel expected them to surge forward, as would be customary on Drakar after such a declaration, but his father held them in place, his arms raised.

He waited for silence to descend once more. "That in itself would be a great boon to our clan. But another blessing has been bestowed upon us, one rare and precious. My son brings with him his checana." His voice caught, emotion evident in every syllable. "The mate of his heart."

His father's words evoked looks of startled surprise, which rapidly changed to awed reverence directed at Lelindia and Jonarel.

His fingers curled around Lelindia's hip, locking her in tighter. She responded by resting her hand on his chest, directly over his heart.

His father noted the action with an approving nod. "It is my honor to present to you the newest member of our Clan, Lelindia Forrest, Nedale of the Suulh."

The silence suspended above them, marking the collective inhalation. Then the first whispers of a chant reached him, soft at first, but rising like a tide as more voices took up the call. The low hum moved in undulating waves, lapping over them – *pirareath, pirareath, pirareath.*

Lelindia tilted her head up, meeting his gaze. "What are they saying?"

Brushing a curl of auburn hair away from her face, he caught her jaw in his hand. "A blessing, which requires a response."

Her eyes widened as he lowered his head. Then all he knew was the exquisite taste of her lips and her happy sigh.

Nothing in his life had ever felt so right.

The pounding of drums finally brought his head up.

Lelindia looked dazed, her beautiful brown eyes slightly unfocused and a tender smile on her lips. She blinked. "They're drumming."

"Yes, checana. They are welcoming you."

A slight blush reddened her cheeks but her smile was bright as a star. "Then I guess we should mingle."

"Not yet. When they have finished."

She nodded, tucking her head against his chest.

He rested his cheek on her hair and closed his eyes. This was what he had yearned for all his life. Incredibly, impossibly, he had found a way to bridge the gap between who his clan needed him to be, and who he wanted to be. He had followed his heart and finally recognizing the mate who loved him for who he was at his core.

As the drumming drew to a close, his father's hand landed on his shoulder. He didn't need to open his eyes to know the clan was moving in. Humans called this type of gathering a group hug. The Suulh called it a nurturing circle. He called it home.

Which is why the loving touch of Lelindia's energy field as it surrounded him felt as natural as taking his next breath. He lifted his head, meeting her gaze. Judging by the reactions of those closest to them, she was expanding the field outward through the group. Another energy field, similar but not identical, slipped over him from his left, where Marina and Gryphon stood next to Lelindia. He recognized Gryphon and Libra's energy fields as well, weaving in and out of Lelindia and Marina's.

Lelindia giggled, her hand dropping to her belly. "Little Nedale wants to join the fun," she whispered.

In a room full of Kraed, the whisper might as well have been a shout. He could feel every head turn, every gaze locking on him and Lelindia.

He kept his focus on his checana. "Our daughter must enjoy being surrounded by her kin."

Sharp inhalations like microscopic hull breaches swept the crowd.

His mate remained oblivious, her delight in the energetic response of their daughter holding her attention. He rested his hand over hers. "Would you like to make the announcement official?"

Her gaze leapt to his, her mouth hinging open. "What?" Then she noticed the taut expectation on every face. "Oh." For a moment she seemed at a loss for words. Then she cleared her throat, the calm demeanor that served her so well in the med bay settling into place. She raised her voice – which was not necessary with the room holding its breath – but the action unwittingly emphasized her leadership role in the clan. His father would approve. "Jonarel and I have conceived a child. A daughter."

He had expected the roar that filled the room. Lelindia clearly had not. She cringed against him, her hands flattening protectively over her stomach.

He dropped his head close to her ear so she could hear him. "Do not fear. This is how we welcome new life."

Marina and Gryphon looked equally startled. Then he felt the firm presence of Libra's energy field coalescing around them, creating a barrier.

He met her gaze and shook his head.

She stared back, unmoving, but the warm pressure dissipated.

The roar ended as abruptly as it had begun, though the echo continued to pulse around them.

"Clan Clarek," his father trumpeted, "our clan, our people, are blessed this day. Come!" He swept a hand to the tables laden with food and drink. "We have much to celebrate."

Forty-Seven

"The pilots are already heading to their ships," Unity informed Cade as he stepped onto the lift. "Yrlef is expecting you."

Yrlef — the blue and gold scaled female pilot who'd taken him on the wildest ride of his career. "Pilots and ships, plural? How many are going?"

"Six."

"Six?" He'd assumed they'd send one, maybe two.

"You think we should bring more?"

"No. No, that wasn't what I was thinking at all. I just didn't expect you to put that many resources behind this."

"Why wouldn't we?" Unity sounded puzzled. "Aurora's well-being is important to us. And the Admiral is important to her."

"That's very generous of you."

"It's what she would do for us."

"You're right, she would." Without a moment's hesitation.

Strapping into the two-seater Yruf ship called to mind the twisting, turning roller coasters he'd loved so much as a teenager, before he'd gotten his pilot's license. He'd mentally prepared for the virtual spacewalk experience this time... at least until Yrlef rocketed the ship toward Earth like a meteor on a collision course.

Cade hissed as they streaked past an orbiting satellite and entered Earth's atmosphere with the five other Yruf ships.

Thanks to the panoramic projection the ship's cockpit gave him, it felt like he and Yrlef were sitting in the middle of a blazing inferno. Nothing showed between his feet and the flickering flames surrounding the ship except a hair's breadth of clear air. What a rush!

He was pretty sure he was grinning like a fool by the time they dropped into the troposphere. Too bad the Yruf's neural tech wouldn't work with his brain. He'd love to give that a try from the pilot's seat.

Yrlef banked, spun, and dove to avoid the various privately-owned craft and Fleet vessels between them and the rapidly-approaching ground. This close to the Fleet's busiest transportation hangar, there were quite a few.

He'd briefed Ifel and Unity on the traffic patterns for other vessels they were likely to encounter that would intersect their planned flight path to the COJ building and detention center. Yrlef was making the task of avoiding them look easy. A quick glance to either side confirmed the other ships were doing the same. The cover of darkness and the Yruf tech allowed them to remain invisible to his eyes and the aircraft in the area, but their exterior outlines showed as multi-colored geometric shapes on the interior projection.

He hadn't seen the shapes representing the other ships during the previous reconnaissance mission, so either it was something the Yruf only used in atmosphere, or it was something Unity had come up with specifically for his benefit since he wasn't part of the neural link the Yruf shared with the non-biological entity.

"Having fun?" Unity asked him from their niche embedded in the back of Yrlef's chair facing him.

"Oh, yeah." He could do this kind of flying all night.

Yrlef's amusement wafted over him like a breeze. Maybe she'd picked up on his unconscious image or emotional projections, or maybe Unity had translated what he'd said. Last time they'd flown together she'd been closed off emotionally — not unfriendly, but reserved. This time her flying style told him she was allowing herself to relax and have fun, while still staying on mission.

He picked out the collection of buildings that served as the Union's governing hub near San Diego's Gaslamp Quarter. The building that housed Fleet HQ was the largest and tallest, but the Court of Justice wasn't much shorter. Its Victorian architectural details gave it more curving lines than the squared angles of the twentieth century Modern design of the Fleet HQ building.

He was pretty sure both had been built nearly a hundred years ago, shortly after the Galactic Council had been formed and the Union established. In all honesty, he'd never paid much attention to the Court of Justice before. Legal matters weren't part of a pilot's purview. Now he was wishing he'd taken a tour of the building during one of his many layovers in between missions so he'd be of more help to Unity now.

Yrlef slowed the ship and brought it into a looping flightpath that steadily circled the area. Four of the other ships spread out to the points of the compass about a kilometer away, while a quick glance up showed the fifth was hovering roughly the same distance above him like a giant hummingbird.

Now he understood why they wanted six. They were essentially creating a bubble of monitored airspace so he and Yrlef could focus on the task at hand. The move fit with the Yruf style, reminding him of the way they'd trapped the Ecilam ship in the hopes of opening negotiations.

A semi-transparent projection formed in front of Cade depicting a 3D model of the courthouse.

"Did you generate this?" The image had an alienness to its form similar to the geometric projections of the Yruf ships.

"Uh-huh. We needed the high-resolution scans from our current location to complete it. We used publicly available data to identify the interior elements."

"The detail is impressive."

"Thank you. You can use your hands to manipulate the projection. We based the interface on technology Celia used on the *Starhawke* when we were helping her create a plan to handle the Teeli armada."

Reaching out, he rotated the image, studying the layout. "It looks like the courtrooms are all located on the interior of the middle floors." The lower levels looked like public administrative with the upper floors functioning as private offices. The judges' chambers and panel deliberation rooms attached to the courtrooms filled out the exterior. "Couldn't make it easy, could you," he mumbled. He'd been hoping the courtrooms would be on the exterior walls, with nice big windows. "So, what's your plan?"

"These conduits." 3D lines appeared on the model in purple. "They're for ventilation, correct?"

He zoomed in and studied the pathways. "Yep."

"Our scans indicate they're composed of metal. Do you know what type?"

"Usually steel or aluminum."

"Excellent. Our presence will be impossible to detect as a foreign object in that environment."

"So you're thinking you'll infiltrate the ventilation system to reach the Admiral's courtroom?"

"Yes."

"How are you going to get in?"

"The ventilation system is connected to the circulation units on the rooftop. We'll use a dart to enter from there."

"Dart?"

"It's the closest Galish term for describing our tech. We used a space-modified version to infiltrate *Gladiator*."

"Ah. But won't that leave your tech exposed on the roof where someone might find it?"

Unity chuckled. "No. We *are* the dart. We'll be delivered in an organic gel that will break down in your star's rays. The residue will be indistinguishable from bird poop."

"Bird poop?" Cade grinned. "Micah actually taught you that term?"

"We learned it during a particularly funny story Micah shared about a seabird who flew over him while he was on his surfboard. Made quite a mess."

Cade's bark of laughter made Yrlef turn and stare at him.

He waved a hand in the air, still chuckling. "It's all good," he told her, then looked at Unity. "Maybe you can tell me that story when we get back to the ship."

"We'd be happy to."

"Okay, so the tiny versions of you get delivered via this gel as a sort of dart that attaches to the ventilation unit, then you make your way into the ventilation system through the ducts. How long before you'll have eyes and ears on the Admiral's courtroom?"

Unity was silent for a moment. "We'll have to determine which room they've assigned for his trial. That should be relatively easy once we're onsite. After that it depends on which room it is. We can't cover distance quickly in that form. But we'll be ready before the trial begins."

Cade peered down at the courthouse as Yrlef guided the ship toward one of the large ventilation units visible behind a substantial clay-red turret.

Her hand position changed, her long fingers twitching as multi-colored lights danced across her interface. A red mark appeared in the projection over the ventilation unit in Cade's projection. Yrlef flicked one finger, and a blue dot appeared in the center of the red mark.

"We're on the ventilation unit."

Cade blinked. "That's it?"

"That's it," Unity confirmed. "We'll let you know when we've accessed the assigned courtroom."

Yrlef banked the ship and changed course, heading north, the other five ships joining her in a tight formation.

"Now we'll access the detention center."

His heart pounded in an unsteady rhythm as his mind jumped tracks. The emotional resonance they raced toward shone as bright as a searchlight.

Aurora.

Forty-Eight

Aurora jerked awake from a restless doze, her hands up by her shoulders, palms out like she was reaching for something in her sleep. Her senses on red alert, she searched the darkness for any sign of what had woken her.

The door to her cell was closed, the air still. Her energy field hadn't engaged, indicating the tightness in her belly wasn't due to a physical threat.

Then what—

She clutched her blanket to keep from leaping to her feet. Instead, she bored holes in the ceiling with her eyes. Cade!

Even if she hadn't known what to expect thanks to the intel Lelindia had given her earlier in the day, she would have figured out he'd arrived, and that he was in an aircraft of some sort. His resonance was a significant distance above her.

Alarms weren't going off and searchlights weren't sweeping the night sky, indicating the Yruf ships were pulling off their stealth maneuver.

Being this close physically to Cade was triggering internal fireworks for them both. His emotional field wasn't any steadier than hers. She didn't recognize the resonances of any of the Yruf she was sensing. Their emotional fields were subtle compared to the pyrotechnics she and Cade were setting off.

She turned her head slowly, peering out her narrow window at the sliver of darkened sky visible from the bed. A moment later a wellspring of tenderness swept over her like an emotional hug. Her eyes drifted closed of their own volition, her body soaking up every drop like Cade was an oasis in the desert.

She drew in a few deep breaths, pretending to go back to sleep. But all her focus was on Cade's presence above her. She'd resigned herself to their prolonged separation – or thought she had. Sensing him so close was torture and bliss combined.

She felt the echo of her emotions in his, the delight in the connection and the yearning for more. But this was far more than she'd expected or dared to hope for. Knowing he'd be keeping an eye on her lowered her stress level by a factor of ten. She rolled so her back was to the door and buried her face in her pillow to hide her smile.

The Sovereign had her pawns and minions, but Aurora had the best damn crew in the galaxy and the backing of a Setarip faction the Sovereign couldn't manipulate. Her chances of getting out of this unscathed were looking much brighter, indeed.

Forty-Nine

Cade held his breath as Unity brought up the projection of Aurora's cell. The color was off – Unity had to compensate for the low lighting – but Cade immediately zeroed in on the figure lying on the narrow cot at the far end of the rectangular space.

Aurora.

His hand passed through the projection as he unconsciously reached out to touch her. He could feel the joy blooming inside her, dispelling the darkness that had shrouded her when he'd first arrived. But he couldn't see her face, or anything except her shoulder and the tumble of her blonde hair partially covered by the sheet.

A moment later, she shifted, slowly turning as if in her sleep, now facing him.

His heart stutter-stepped. She looked so... normal. And beautiful beyond measure.

He wasn't sure what nightmare vision he'd imagined, but the image Unity was relaying wasn't the horror show he'd feared. In fact, except for the presence of the sanitation station and the shrunken size of the window, her cell wasn't that different from the small bedroom she'd had in the dorm room she'd shared with Reanne at the Academy. This one was narrower and devoid of character or personal touches, but still recognizable as a Fleet layout.

"Thank you, Unity," he murmured, his fingers outlining Aurora's face in the image.

"You're welcome."

Aurora's expression softened, the barest hint of a smile on her lips. No doubt she was reading his emotions, knew he was watching her.

He sighed, completely absorbed by the visual, by the deep sense of connection that linked them. Her courage and her selflessness continued to humble him. He'd known since the day they met that she was special, but the amazing woman she'd become blew away all his expectations. That she felt the same way about him still stunned him. And made him love her all the more.

"Unity, could you loop this projection into my comband?" Then he could pull it up no matter where he was.

"We can arrange that, but you'll probably prefer the life-sized display in your cabin."

"Huh?" His gaze sharpened through the projection, focusing on U-2. "What display in my cabin?" He hadn't seen anything that looked like a screen.

Unity laughed softly. "What you call a bulkhead that separates the sleeping area from the front room is also a dual-sided display. You'll see when we return."

That sounded *very* promising.

Another projection popped into focus on his right. The cell looked identical to Aurora's except for the occupant. Admiral

Schreiber lay on his back on his cot, eyes closed, chest rising and falling steadily. But even in sleep, a crease lined his forehead, and his fingers clutched the fabric of his blanket like a lifeline.

He looked worn out and weary in a way Cade had never seen before. Even when the Admiral had been sedated in the *Starhawke's* med bay, recovering from his near-fatal injuries, there had been a vitality to him that seemed absent now.

He dragged his gaze away from the Admiral and checked Aurora's projection. She hadn't moved, but he could feel the concern in her emotional field.

He studied the Admiral's image again. The Admiral had been in his cell a lot longer than Aurora, close to a month. Cade hated seeing him looking so vulnerable. And unlike Aurora, they didn't have any way to communicate with him through Lelindia.

"Are there surveillance devices in their cells?" Not that he'd expect anything less from the Sovereign.

"Oh, yes. We've been analyzing them in both rooms. They're not tied to the surveillance lines in the rest of the building. The feed isn't going to the security center with the others. It looks like it's being fed directly to one of the administrative offices."

"The CO?"

"CO?"

"Commanding Officer."

"Oh. We're analyzing... no, this office belongs to the Executive Officer."

"Are there any other cells sending feeds to that office?"

"Not that we've detected."

Great. The Sovereign had the XO in her back pocket. "You ready to act as the galaxy's tiniest earpiece?"

"We'll have to reach Aurora first. That'll take a while. Yrlef recommends heading back to the ship."

Cade blinked. He'd completely forgotten Yrlef was still circling over the detention center. The image of the buildings underneath his feet was largely obscured by the projections of Aurora's and the Admiral's cells.

He hated the idea of the physical separation from Aurora, but the prospect of the life-sized display Unity had mentioned was some consolation. Besides, they'd accomplished what they'd come here to do. The rest was up to Unity. "Okay."

The ship changed course immediately, banking away from the detention center and settling into formation with the other Yruf ships as they streaked toward the star-strewn sky.

Cade kept his attention on Aurora's image. He felt the shift in her emotions when she sensed him moving away, the corners of her mouth tightening.

I'm still here, Rory.

She couldn't hear him, but he knew she could feel the emotions he projected. The pang of loss mellowed for them both, the feeling of connection reasserting itself.

With any luck, soon they'd be able to communicate using Unity as a conduit. Well, one-sided conversations, anyway. Aurora would have to be circumspect about any responses she made to him.

If Ifel was right about his latent abilities, maybe eventually he and Aurora would be able to communicate on their own.

That sent a fizz of excitement through him, partially eclipsed by a shadow of fear. He still had to conquer his demons first.

He was so focused on Aurora during the flight that he completely missed Yrlef reconnecting their ship with the Yruf ship's core. It was only when the displays winked off that he looked up.

Unity detached from the back of the pilot's seat and hovered by his side as he stood. He followed Yrlef and Unity as they entered the undulating corridor. Yrlef gave him the head tilt gesture of parting. He nodded back, then continued in the opposite direction with Unity, arriving at his cabin not long after.

"Are you ready to see the display?" Unity's enthusiasm practically bubbled out.

He grinned, just as excited. "You bet."

"Follow me." Unity led him to the bedroom, stopping between the giant cup-bed and the bulkhead that separated the bedroom from the main room. "Watch the bulkhead."

The surface shimmered like sunlight on water for a moment, then the wall disappeared.

He gaped as he stared into Aurora's cell.

He didn't realize he'd walked forward until his hand touched the cool surface of the bulkhead. Still there, but it was like his cabin and Aurora's cell were separated by a glass wall.

She was lying on her cot, her eyes closed, her chest rising and falling like she was sleeping.

He crouched by her bed, which gave him the best view of her face. She didn't look like a projection on a flat surface. She looked like she was centimeters from his fingertips. "The image quality is amazing." He looked at Unity over his shoulder. "What do you normally use this type of display for?"

"Observing."

"Observing what?"

Unity hesitated, somehow managing to look uncomfortable. "Ifel used it when you and your team were in the containment area. It allowed her to study you from all angles, to pick up on every nuance of your behavior, no matter how small."

"From all angles?" He flinched inwardly. "I knew I was being watched, that I didn't have any privacy, but I'd assumed it was just from your mobile unit in the ceiling of my cell."

Unity dropped closer to the deck so they were at eye-level. "Your views on privacy are very different than the Yruf's. This type of monitoring is normal onboard our ship. It's one of the ways Ifel keeps tabs on the wellbeing of our society. Our integration throughout the ship allows her to see what's happening anywhere at any time."

"And the Yruf don't find that invasive?"

"Never. Their trust in Ifel, in each other, is absolute. No Yruf would ever abuse that trust."

He rolled that over in his mind. "Given that scenario, I could see how it could be a net positive. Not that different than having Star onboard the *Starhawke*, I guess." Though he'd never worried whether the Nirunoc was paying attention to their private activities. Maybe because she was the soul of discretion, too.

His gaze returned to Aurora. "But Aurora values her privacy. When you make contact, the first thing I want to ask her is if she's okay with this setup. I don't want her to feel uncomfortable. Well, more uncomfortable."

Unity bobbed. "We can give her privacy whenever she would normally want it. But somehow we don't think she'll mind having you watching her."

"I hope you're right." Because now that he'd seen the visual Unity had created, he didn't want to give it up. "Have you had time to make physical contact with her?"

"We've set ourselves up as — how did you put it? — the galaxy's tiniest earpiece. We don't know if Aurora's aware we're there. We haven't tried speaking with her yet. We thought you would want to do that."

His breath came a little faster. "What do I need to do?"

"Talk to her. We'll open a channel now."

He worked to calm his pounding heart. "Aurora?" he whispered. "Can you hear me?"

Her head jerked on the pillow, her eyes flying open. Startled excitement flooded her emotional field, hitting him like a microburst.

He chuckled, an answering wave of happiness rolling through him. "I'll take that as a yes." He grinned at Unity, then turned back to Aurora. "Just so you know, Unity has managed to set up a 3D projection of your cell for me. I can see you like I'm looking right through the wall."

Her emotions fluctuated, her gaze moving around the room as she processed what he'd told her. The emotion that rose to the top was a yearning that pulled at his heart.

He swallowed. "I'm guessing you wish you could see me the same way. I wish you could, too." This had to be a special kind of torment for her, so close and yet so far. "But I need to know if you're okay with me watching you. I don't want to creep you out."

Her mouth twitched, amusement and tenderness overlaying her emotional field.

That was a good sign. "Unity assures me they know your habits well enough to give you privacy when you'd want it." In fact, Unity was probably a better judge than he was. Aurora's modesty always seemed to take a hike when she was around him. Still, it was one thing to be in the same room with your lover, something else to be watched from outside. "So, is it okay? That I'm watching you? If so, close your eyes for a five count."

Aurora gave a small sigh, her eyes drifting closed, opening five seconds later.

"You're beautiful."

Her subtle smile flitted across her lips again.

He wanted to make her really smile, or better yet laugh, but that would be foolish. Small movements she could pass off as restless insomnia. Laughing out loud would shine a spotlight.

He studied her image. "So, the way Unity has oriented this, I'm looking at you from the blank wall between your bed and the sanitation station. If you want to be looking at me, face that direction."

She rose onto her elbow, punched the thin pillow in a futile attempt to fluff it, and settled back down with her gaze on the wall he'd identified. She wasn't looking right at him, but it was close.

"I'm staying in a cabin the Yruf gave me in one of their residential areas. It's really something. Your image is projected life-size on the bulkhead between the bedroom and the front room."

The giddy excitement returned to her emotional field, threaded with aggravation.

"I know it's not ideal. You can't talk to me. But Ifel's working with me on a possible solution to that, too. It just might take a while. Oh, and the XO has you under surveillance. You and the Admiral. I assume there's a direct line from the XO to the Sovereign."

Concern overrode her excitement.

"Speaking of the Admiral, now that we've successfully tested this method of communication with you, we'll see about trying the same thing with him. Unity's infiltrated his cell, too."

Her nose twitched and she sighed again.

Her frustration tugged at him. Her inability to take action had to be eating away at her. Aurora had patience in spades except when those she cared about were in danger. And the Admiral was most definitely in danger.

But there was nothing more they could do about it tonight. He certainly wasn't going to wake the Admiral from a sound sleep by whispering in his ear. And Aurora needed a decent night's sleep, too. "It's late," he murmured.

Even as he said it, her eyelids drooped.

"I'm going to sign off now. But know that I'm here, watching over you." He glanced at Unity. "So's Unity. They'll alert both of us if there's anything we need to know." His fingertips brushed the bulkhead, the smooth surface slightly warm to the touch. "Sleep well. I love you, Rory."

An emotional surge like a cresting wave rolled over him, taking him by surprise. Fierce longing and exquisite tenderness surrounded him, holding him in their embrace. Wow. Aurora could really project when she wanted to.

The wave ebbed as Aurora took a shuddering breath and rolled to her back, her face now in profile.

He stood, gazing at her, their connection tethering him like a boat rocking gently against the dock. He had to get her out of this. Had to get *them* out of this.

He turned as Unity hovered at his shoulder.

"We closed the audio channel," Unity said, answering his unspoken question.

"Thank you." He glanced at the Yruf cup-bed. "Guess I should try to get some shuteye, too." Though as wired as he was now that he could see Aurora, he couldn't imagine falling asleep.

"Yes, you should. Ifel has you scheduled for another session tomorrow."

He swallowed. If it was anything like the last one, he'd need his strength and his rest. "Good to know. And Unity?"

Unity stopped partway across the room. "Yes?"

"Thank you." He gestured to Aurora's image. "For everything."

Unity twirled slowly. "You're very welcome."

Fifty

Bright lights woke Aurora from a sound sleep. She squinted, lifting a hand to block her face from the harsh glare of the overheads. But as she sat up and pushed the rough blanket away, her gaze landed on the blank wall to her right.

She fought back the smile that wanted to burst forth. That would be a completely inappropriate reaction to waking up in a stark detention cell, even for an optimist like her.

Cade had promised not to invade her privacy, but that concern wasn't even a blip on her radar. She trusted their emotional connection to let him know if she was uncomfortable with him watching anything she was doing. Right now she was far too excited to be uncomfortable.

After washing up at the sanitation station and changing into her exercise clothes, she stood facing the blank wall and did a few simple side stretches. She kept her gaze on one particular spot on the wall, and felt a zing through Cade's emotional field when, from his perspective, their eyes met.

"Good morning, sunshine."

Keeping her cool was a lot harder this morning than it had been lying in her cot last night. With his voice in her ear and the flow of his emotions running through her, she was on sensory overload.

But she couldn't respond, no matter how much she wanted to. In fact, this situation had the frustration factor she'd faced the past two days during her visits with Micah and her parents ramped up to a thousand percent. She loved hearing Cade's voice, but her inability to reply had her biting her tongue with enough force to leave teeth marks.

She needed to come up with some way to communicate back, something non-verbal...

Or very verbal!

Leaning into a forward bend, she started to sing softly to herself, choosing a song her dad had taught her. It was one of his favorites, *I Can See Clearly Now*, about the rain ending and sunshine appearing in blue skies.

"I could get used to you serenading me in the morning."

Cade's chuckle made her shiver. Another emotional zing struck when she apparently looked right at him. It was a heady experience. She paused, holding her pose to elongate that tantalizing connection.

She could get used to this, too. Which was a bizarre thought, considering her current circumstances. She should be miserable, and worried, and furious. And she was, at least on some level, but not enough to dampen the natural high of the gift Cade and Unity had given her.

Judging by Cade's emotions, he was watching every move she made as she went through an abbreviated yoga sequence. He'd watched her stretch before, in their shared cabin on the *Starhawke*, and on more than one occasion, it had led to more strenuous exercise in the bedroom.

She couldn't tell if her thoughts triggered his emotional response, or vice versa, but by the time her breakfast tray arrived, she'd warmed up more than her muscles.

Rather than sitting at the desk, which would put her back to Cade's point of view, she settled onto the floor, leaning against the shelving unit. She placed the food tray in front of her like she was on a picnic.

"Hang on," Cade said. "I'm going to go grab something so we can eat together. Be right back."

Unity's voice — well, Micah's voice, actually — replaced Cade's a moment later. "We wanted you to know we've infiltrated the facility's surveillance and communication systems. If there's anything you need to be aware of, we'll alert you."

Thank you. The words rose to her lips but she swallowed to keep from saying them out loud, ducking her head and picking up her coffee mug.

No doubt about it, not being able to respond was going to test her patience to the limit.

"Aurora?" Cade's voice again. "You okay?"

She sipped her coffee, keeping her gaze steady on the wall like she was lost in thought. Which was partially true. She was definitely thinking, trying to figure out some way she could turn this into a dialogue rather than a one-sided conversation.

"You're frustrated. I get it. I don't have to talk if that's making it tougher for you."

Not what she wanted. She flipped her head toward the door like she'd heard a noise, then back to neutral.

"I think that was a no. If I'm right, pick up your muffin."

She followed his instruction.

"Okay, this is good. We just need to create a system for establishing yes and no responses. How about this. One tap of your finger for *yes*, two taps for *no*. Okay?"

She tapped her finger once on her knee.

She could hear the smile in his voice. "And since I know you well, if your answer is *maybe* or *it depends* rather than *yes* or *no*, spread your index and middle finger apart."

He did know her well.

"So, is this the best breakfast you've ever had?"

She almost laughed. To cover it, she bit into the dry muffin, which had the most flavorless raisins she'd ever tasted. She tapped her left index finger twice.

He did laugh. "Why am I not surprised? But I know it's not your worst breakfast, either. Or mine. Did I ever tell you the story about…"

Cade regaled her with tales of his team's exploits while she ate, some funny, others harrowing, but always with an upbeat ending. The familiar cadence and timbre of his voice made the walls of her cell seem less bleak, the floor not as cold and unforgiving, though she still chafed against the limitations on her own responses.

She couldn't laugh, or even smile without ducking her head. She had to wait for him to ask her questions she could answer with their coded system. He was pretty good at picking up on her emotional cues and following up, but not being able to communicate her thoughts and ideas made her feel gagged. Not pleasant.

Of course, the Sovereign wanted her gagged. And trussed up, too. That was the point of this whole drama she'd concocted.

Which brought her focus to the Admiral. She could sense him in his cell. He'd been melancholy ever since Knox's visit to the detention center yesterday. She figured Knox had told him about her incarceration.

"I'm going to take a wild guess that you're thinking about the Admiral."

Her gaze sharpened onto the plate in her hand. She'd risen to start washing and drying her dishes and must have tuned out what Cade had been saying. She tapped her finger once against the side of the plate.

"Unity's prepared to set themselves up in the courtroom where the Admiral's trial will be held. When the trial begins, we'll have eyes and ears on everything. I'm also planning to try communicating with the Admiral today the same way I'm talking to you now."

Her heart thumped painfully in her chest, driven by a flash of anger. The injustice of it all made her want to pound her fist into the wall. Through the wall, actually.

"I know," Cade said softly. "I feel it, too."

And he did. She could sense it. His understanding helped her keep her own response under wraps.

She finished cleaning her dishes, set the tray by the door, and then stood in the middle of the room, unsure what to do next. She'd already made her bed and folded her clothes.

"How can I help?" Cade asked. "Unity says your family and Lelindia aren't awake yet, so we have some time before they try to contact you." He was silent for a moment. "I know. Why don't I read to you, like we used to do at the Academy."

The suggestion caught her by surprise, her gaze swinging to the blank wall. She'd mostly forgotten about those cozy winter evenings spent curled up together in her dorm room reading out loud to each other. She'd loved every moment, but those memories had been obliterated by all the pain and heartache that had followed.

"Are you still a Charles Dickens fan?" he asked softly, clearly picking up on the echo of past emotions, a tinge of guilt in his emotional field.

She tapped her finger against her hip.

"Then *A Tale of Two Cities* it is."

She allowed herself a tiny smile before she moved to her cot. Slipping off her shoes, she propped the pillow against the opposite wall so she was facing Cade's viewpoint. Stretching out, she leaned against the meagre padding of the pillow and closed her eyes.

Music filled her senses first, something hauntingly orchestral that set the perfect tone. Then Cade's velvety voice flowed over her.

"It was the best of times, it was the worst of times..."

Fifty-One

"Cade's been talking to Aurora," Unity informed Lelindia as soon as she stepped into the med bay on her way to the greenhouse.

She halted as U-1 dropped from the charging station installed in the ceiling, coming to hover next to her. "So the mission last night was a success?" she asked them.

"Big success." Unity spun in a circle. "Now we can talk to her, and so can anyone else onboard, at least when Cade's not talking to her. He's been reading to her and playing her music."

"That's brilliant. I bet she loves that." Aurora would be handling the isolation better than most, but anything they could do to break up the monotony had to help. "What about the Admiral?"

"We've placed ourselves in his ear canal, but Cade hasn't tried making contact yet. He's waiting until the Admiral has his yard time. He wants to take advantage of the ambient noise to make his voice in the Admiral's ear less startling."

"Smart man."

"Yes, he is." Unity swayed. "Where are you going?"

"I'm meeting my mom and Libra in the greenhouse. We're going to discuss baby names." She'd broached the topic during the celebration the night before, and had gotten an enthusiastic response.

"May we come?"

"Of course." She always enjoyed Unity's company, and their outside perspective might help her narrow down her choices. "Tehar's joining us, too."

"What about Jonarel?"

She smiled. "He's heading over to the *Rowkclarek* with my dad and Brendan." They'd been enraptured with the *Rowkclarek's* design, spending almost the entire night talking to Siginal and the crew about the ship. "Jonarel and Siginal are giving them a tour. I don't expect to see them until later today. Come on."

Unity followed her as she stepped into the greenhouse. Her mom and Libra were already there, their hands buried up to their wrists in the thick soil of one of the vegetable beds. Their energy fields twined together as they unearthed radishes and carrots with deft movements.

Looked like her mom had the same idea she'd had, finding ways to distract Libra. Brendan was taking the separation from Aurora in stride — his ability to sense her emotions probably helped — but Libra had always struggled when it came to handling a perceived or real threat to Aurora's wellbeing.

That's why she'd come up with this plan. Yes, she wanted Libra's help with choosing a name, but it wasn't a priority. She'd made it one when her mom had pointed out that the Nedale needed a Sahzade. Having Libra focus on her and the baby gave Libra a job, something to temper the pain of Aurora's absence.

Her mom glanced over her shoulder and winked. "Thought we'd get a little work done while we talked."

Lelindia chuckled. "Why am I not surprised?"

"Because you're my daughter and a very insightful woman."

"Like mother like daughter," Lelindia said. "I assume Celia gave you the same list she gave me of produce and herbs she wanted gathered for her upcoming meal plans?"

"You assume correctly."

Celia had declared herself and Micah as the official cooks — with help from Brendan and Gryphon — while Lelindia's and Aurora's families were onboard. She'd also taken point on keeping Micah occupied. Right now they were in the hydrotank. Kire and Kelly had staked a claim to the bridge, monitoring system traffic and communications, particularly anything relevant to the Admiral or Aurora, and sharing their findings with Justin.

In many ways, the crew's current situation felt a lot like the waiting game they'd endured in Teeli space — perched on a perpetual knife's point until the Sovereign made her move. Coming up with strategies to get through this with their sanity intact meant being creative, especially since in this case, they didn't even have scientific work to accomplish.

Grabbing a trowel off the potting bench, she knelt beside her mom. "Tehar? Are you ready to join us?"

Tehar materialized to her left, her dark hair wrapped into a topknot and her casual clothing almost identical to Lelindia's. She looked like she could physically join the work party. "I am. Would you like me to keep a log of your options and choices while you discuss names?"

"That would be great." She dug her fingers into the soil, the lifeforce of the plant responding to her energy field. "To start, it would help me if you'd share your thoughts on how the Kraed might react if I do or do not use the Clarek clan name."

"Certainly." Tehar folded her hands. "There is no record in our history of a new member of a clan not taking the name of that clan, either at birth or pair bonding. But there is also no record of anyone mating with a non-Kraed. Last night my father introduced you as Lelindia Forrest, even though you are Jonarel's mate and a member of the clan. I noted the clan's reaction. They did not seem unnerved by the duality."

"So you don't think they expect me to become Lelindia Clarek?" Her tongue tripped over the pairing, creating a hiccup between the first and last name.

"I do not."

"Good." She loved Jonarel with all her heart, and wanted to be accepted as part of Clan Clarek, but she didn't want to be absorbed by them. She was and would always be Lelindia Forrest. "Which brings up a question for you, Mom. Do the Suulh have last names and if so, what was our family name before you left Feylahn?"

Her mother's lips pinched for a moment, tension running like a taut string from her jaw to her neck. She set her trowel down and brushed the soil from her hands. "No, we don't. On Feylahn, you would be known as Lelindia, Nedale of the Suulh. No last name. Our energy fields are our family markers, so there's no need for a name. The concept of a family name was one we struggled with when we first came in contact with Humans. When we chose Galish names — first and last — we found names that were close to our own but also tied to something in the natural world that held meaning for us."

"But a gryphon is a creature of myth."

Her mom's lips lifted at the corners. "Your father was never one to follow the crowd."

"True."

Libra sat back on her heels. "What you're really asking is whether your daughter should be a Forrest like you, right?"

"Pretty much."

Her mom and Libra exchanged a look. "Your father and I wouldn't be bothered if you chose to give your daughter the Clarek name," her mom replied. "We've gotten used to having Forrest as part of our identity, but from a Suulh perspective, it's not significant. And your child is half-Suulh, half-Kraed. Her name should reflect both. If being a Clarek is important to the clan, and you like that idea, then I say go for it."

She turned to Tehar. "What do you think?"

"I think my father would be very pleased if your daughter is a Clarek." The solemnity in her golden gaze emphasized how incredibly pleased Siginal would be. And if he was pleased, the rest of the clan would be, too.

"Okay, then that part's settled. Her last name will be Clarek. Which means I want a Suulh first name. Mom, Libra, you're up. I need suggestions."

That prompted another shared look between them. "You want to go with an actual Suulh name?" Libra asked. "Not a Galish version of one?"

"As I understand it, you chose Galish names to prevent the Teeli from finding you. But the Teeli already know who I am and where I am, so trying to hide my daughter's lineage seems pointless. I'd much rather honor her heritage with an authentic Suulh name. And not one that anyone at the Azaana colony already has. That would be confusing."

Her mom picked up her trowel again, focusing on the fluffy green top of the next carrot plant. "What kind of meaning do you want it to convey?"

"I'm not sure. She's going to be an unusual child, so I guess I want her name to reflect that somehow. But I don't want to pick something just because of its meaning, either. What does your birth name, Maaree, mean?"

Her mom gave her a rueful smile. "It's a tree species on Feylahn."

"Really? So we're both named after trees? Wait a minute. Is Breaa a tree species, too?"

"Yes."

She chuckled. "Now I know why you chose the last name Forrest. We're a family of trees."

Libra grinned at her. "I've always wondered if someday you'd figure that out."

"Took me long enough. So, if we're trees, what about you? What does your birth name mean?"

Libra sobered, a flash of pain crossing her blue-grey eyes. "Mine's more abstract. But it basically means *taking flight*."

"Hence the last name Hawke."

Libra nodded.

Lelindia would bet money that Libra's mother's name, Sooree, had a meaning related to something aerial, just as Aurora's did, but she wasn't about to probe a sore spot by asking. "So, if I stick with tradition, I should choose the name of a Feylahn tree, assuming there's a name I like." She settled cross-legged onto the deck, giving her mom and Libra her full attention. "What are my options?"

They began offering one name after another in a steady stream. She allowed the flowing sounds to wash over her, the lyrical beauty of the Suulh language enchanting her as it always did. Many of the names were beautiful, elegant, evocative, but nothing felt quite right.

A flutter in her belly made her inhale sharply in surprise.

"Lelindia? What is it?" her mom asked, peering at her.

"She moved." She rested her hand on her abdomen, but the sensation had passed. "What was the last name you said, Mom? It sounded like rain?"

"You mean raehn?"

Another flutter. Definite movement. "Uh-huh. That one."

"Galish speakers probably would pronounce it as rain, since there's no Galish vowel equivalent to the Suulh vowel."

"She's reacting to it?" Libra asked.

"Yeah. In a way I've never felt before." She leaned over, bringing her lips closer to her belly. "What do you think, little Nedale? Do you like the name Raehn?" She laughed at the sensation that followed. It felt like her daughter was wriggling with delight. She looked back at her mom. "What kind of a tree is a raehn?"

"They're strong trees," her mom answered, looking equally delighted. "Tall, with thick but supple outstretched branches and broad green leaves. They grow in widely spaced groups, with smaller tree species clustered around them like children gathered around a storyteller."

"And when they flower in the spring," Libra added, "their entire canopy turns gold."

"Sounds lovely."

"It is. We had a small grove that grew near the sonea laanaa. In fact, one was quite close to the laalindeeaa tree your mom loved so much."

"The one I'm named after?"

"Uh-huh."

"The fruit the raehn produce were one of your Aunt Amethyst's favorite treats as a kid," her mom said. "But she had to work to get them, since they're mostly in the upper branches. I ended up healing various minor injuries and one bone break as a result of her tenacity."

"I can believe that. She strikes me as the stubborn type."

Her mom rolled her eyes. "You have no idea."

She hadn't considered all the people who might have an opinion about the name she'd select, including her relatives on Gaia. But it sounded like they had a winner.

She turned to where Tehar was quietly watching them. "Any objections you can think of?"

"None at all." Tehar's eyes had the luminous quality of liquid sunshine. "Trees are highly valued in our culture as they are in yours. The name is an honorable one."

"Then it's settled." Lelindia sighed, resting both hands on her belly. "Raehn Clarek." Her daughter wriggled again, eliciting a chuckle. "Your family is eager to meet you, checala."

Fifty-Two

"He's on his way to the yard."

Unity dropped into Cade's peripheral vision from the charging station in the main room of his cabin.

Cade turned from the food prep station where he'd been studying the Yruf version of a cooktop and stove. He'd debated whether to make a sandwich or actually try to cook a meal. The controls were giving him trouble. Like the systems on the Yruf bridge, the patterns relied on a wider visual color range than the human eye could differentiate. Even with Unity's help, it felt like a quagmire. Maybe his first foray should be something simple, like baking a potato.

The bulkhead that separated the main room from his bedroom displayed the feed from the Admiral's cell the same way the flipside in his bedroom showed Aurora's cell.

As the Admiral exited his cell, the image switched from the 3D projection to a flat feed from the detention center's security cameras.

The Admiral descended the stairs of the common area for his assigned wedge, following his security detail out the door to the corridor that eventually led to one of the exercise yards. The image flipped again, going to an exterior camera that had an elevated view of the grass and dirt enclosure.

The guards unlocked the gate, then stepped back, motioning the Admiral to enter.

"Thank you." The Admiral's voice came through clearly, though it sounded deeper than normal, a result of Unity's location within the Admiral's ear canal.

The Admiral gave the guard a polite nod, which was not returned. Unperturbed, the Admiral strode into the exercise yard, taking a moment to look up at the sky. The camera angle didn't give Cade a view of what the Admiral was looking at, but the strong shadows indicated a clear day.

The Admiral wore a standard-issue Fleet sun hat, which shaded his face, preventing Cade from seeing his expression. On the plus side, anyone watching the brig's security feed wouldn't be able to see the Admiral's face, either. This was the perfect time to initiate direct contact.

The Admiral began walking the perimeter at a steady pace, like an athlete taking laps around a track. Cade waited until he'd made four and a quarter circuits, putting him with his back to the guard gate, before he spoke.

"Admiral?"

The Admiral's stride hitched, like he'd caught his toe on a rock or depression in the dirt, but to his credit, he kept moving without any other outward sign of surprise.

"It's good to see you, sir. I won't go into the details of how we set up this communication, but suffice to say the Yruf were involved. We have audio and visual on you and Aurora. The tech in your ear is Yruf designed."

The Admiral had completed half a lap, bringing him around to face the guard gate. Cade waited until he'd made the turn and was moving away again. "I've already been in communication with Aurora. She's fine, by the way. Lelindia said Aurora doesn't want you to worry about her."

The Admiral snorted, which brought a smile to Cade's lips. "Yeah, I know. But she really is okay. She and I worked out a system of yes and no responses, with one tap of her finger to mean *yes* and two taps to mean *no*. A *maybe* or *it depends* is indicated by spreading the index and middle finger apart. It's limited, but better than nothing."

"Mm-hmm." The Admiral's vocalization was subtle, a low hum of understanding that the guard's wouldn't be able to hear even if they were listening for it.

"Good. I also wanted you to know we'll have eyes and ears on the courtroom during your trial. We thought it was prudent since your trial is restricted to prevent observers."

Another hum of agreement.

"I'm with the Yruf, but my team's with Knox." He paused. This next part was tougher. "He told us Magee's testifying against you. I'm sorry."

The Admiral's steps slowed for a few beats, then resumed their steady pace.

"After she testifies, we'll do whatever we can to prevent the Teeli from taking her off-planet again." He glanced at Unity. "I think the Yruf would agree to help if we asked."

Unity bobbed. "Of course we would."

Cade gave Unity a thumbs up. "I don't know if you heard that, but Micah's been teaching the Yruf how to communicate in Galish. They're using his voice recordings to respond to us." It was the simplest explanation he could give without getting into who and what Unity was. "I'm staying on their ship to monitor you and Aurora, but also because Aurora was concerned that I'd be the Sovereign's next target."

"Mmm." Definite agreement in his tone.

"So far there's no indication that I'm in danger of arrest. Aurora's and Lelindia's families are on the *Starhawke* docked at Sol Station, and I have one of the *Starhawke's* shuttles with me, just in case."

The Admiral's sigh seemed to carry the weight of the cosmos.

"Not exactly a scenario either of us planned for." He held back his own sigh. "But there's good news, too. Siginal finally saw reason and accepted Jonarel and Lelindia's mating with open arms. From what I hear, they had quite a celebration on his ship last night. And Lelindia's pregnant."

The Admiral's stride slowed.

"I was stunned, too. The baby's due sometime in the next three to five months. She doesn't know for sure since this is the first Suulh-Kraed child ever conceived." He was more than a little curious to see what the little girl would look like. And whether she'd have her daddy's sharp claws. "On a personal note, Siginal's animosity toward me seems to have taken a backseat. I won't consider the change permanent until I see how he reacts when Aurora and I are together, but it's a good sign."

And he and Aurora would be together again. Soon. He wouldn't accept any other outcome.

"The Yruf have linked the *Starhawke* to the communication system I'm using to talk to you, so Aurora's crew will be able to talk to you as well. We'll make sure you're in the loop on everything we find out."

The Admiral continued to circle the yard as Cade talked. Maybe it was his imagination, but it seemed like the Admiral's steps had a little more bounce to them, his head held a little higher. Cade wasn't tuned in enough to the Admiral to sense his emotions the way he could Aurora's, but he wanted to believe he'd lightened the Admiral's load a little bit.

"I'll touch base with you when you're back in your cell, but before I sign off, you need to know one final item. Your cell and Aurora's are being monitored with audio and visual by the detention center's XO using a direct feed that's not hooked up to any other cells. We're assuming the Sovereign is getting the same info."

"Mmm." That time it sounded like he'd already suspected what Cade had confirmed.

"Good to see you, sir. Talk to you soon." Cade made the hand gesture he and Unity had agreed on for closing the channel.

Unity bobbed closer to Cade. "He seemed pleased."

"I would be, too. After a month of no contact other than Knox's monitored visits, we've broken through his isolation." He was feeling lighter, too.

His stomach rumbled, reminding him of his food dilemma. Walking back to the cooking area, he reached into the pantry alcove and pulled out a sweet potato. "Okay, Unity, walk me through how to bake a tuber."

Fifty-Three

"Emoto to Cardiff."

Micah paused the steady motion of the kitchen knife, the somberness in Kire's tone putting him on alert.

Celia had the same reaction, her body taking on a coiled tension. "Yes?"

"The Admiral will be leaving for the courthouse soon."

Micah's fingers tightened on the knife handle. He'd known this was the next step in the proceedings, but for some reason he wanted to bare his teeth and snarl. Maybe because he knew his sister's trial would soon follow.

Celia met his gaze, understanding flashing in the depths of her eyes. "Have you told Lelindia?" she asked Kire.

"Yes. She and Jonarel are meeting Signal in the cargo bay, then will be heading for the observation lounge. Kelly and I will be down in a bit. Unity's going to start the projection feed as soon as the Admiral's in the courtroom."

Celia's mouth curved in a smile that looked predatory rather than friendly. "We'll wrap up here."

"Emoto out."

Her smile lost its edge as she pointed at Micah's cutting board. "That broccoli won't chop itself," she chided.

"Neither will the potatoes." He used his knife to point at the mound next to her.

"I'm on it." She resumed the fluid slicing motion, turning her cooking into a ballet he loved to watch. But it wasn't as free-flowing as it had been before.

"You're worried."

She paused, glancing at him. "Concerned."

"Because?"

"They're trying to frame the Admiral and Aurora for a crime they didn't commit, and we don't even know what information they're using to do it, at least not yet. I want to help them, but right now I'm useless."

"You're not useless." That term could never apply to her.

"Well, I feel useless. I know the Sovereign is manipulating the truth. I've dealt with plenty of liars and cheats, but never in a legal setting." She sighed, her grip on the knife rounding into a fist. "I'm out of my depth, and I hate it."

The level of trust, of openness, in that statement made his heart stutter. Setting down his knife, he closed the distance, stepping behind her and resting his hands lightly on her shoulders. When she didn't resist, he began a slow massage, working out the knots between her shoulder blades. "I hate it, too. But you're the most observant person I've ever met, and a shrewd opponent. You'll figure out a way to help them. Give yourself time."

One of the knots released, her groan doing funny things to his equilibrium. "Thank you."

"For the massage?"

"For being... here."

He swallowed, focusing on the movements of his fingers to keep his hands from shaking. It was the closest she'd come to acknowledging the bond they'd been developing. "You're welcome."

He worked out another knot, but as the silence stretched between them, his fingers detected a new tension starting to build in her lithe body. With a soft brushing motion across her back, he dropped his hands and retreated. "Better?" he asked, picking up his knife and watching her out of the side of his eye.

She rolled her shoulders and neck. "Much. Aurora should keep you on as the crew's masseuse." It was a playful comment, meant to break the tension.

He let it. "I'm not sure she could afford me."

She chuckled. "No family discounts?"

He spread his arms and fluttered his eyelashes. "A man's got to make a living."

That earned him a laugh, followed by a flick of one of the dishtowels.

He almost grabbed it, the impulse to pull her close rearing up on its hind legs and pawing the air. He reined it in.

Instead, he joined in her laughter and backed up out of range.

She pointed the tip of her knife at him in mock warning, then resumed her chopping, a smile that turned his insides to mush still lingering on her lips.

She reminded him so much of the marine animals he'd loved since he was a child — alert, cautious, potentially dangerous, but also curious and playful once he'd established a relationship of trust.

Maybe that's why he was so drawn to her. She shared the duality that intrigued him about the underwater world. And like that world, her exterior beauty had drawn him in. But it was the mysteries within her psyche that held him in thrall. Every time she revealed something new — in this case, admitting her fears — it added another layer of color, her inner beauty glittering like gemstones.

Fifty-Four

"They're escorting the Admiral to the transport."

Aurora pressed her palms and the pads of her feet against the cold concrete, a burn starting between her shoulder blades as she held the yoga posture while Cade gave her the play by play.

"The transport's heading for the gate."

She inhaled on a forward sweep of her leg, coming into a lunge. The Admiral's imminent departure had triggered a nagging sense of unease that made staying still impossible. She was more than half an hour into her practice, but at this rate, she couldn't imagine stopping, not without wanting to crawl out of her skin.

"Unity will let me know as soon as the Admiral's brought into the courtroom." Cade was silent for a few beats. "He's going to be fine," he said softly.

She blew out an aggravated breath as she twisted to face the blank wall where she knew Cade was watching. She let her expression and emotions speak the words she couldn't say out loud.

"I get it. Not being able to take action sucks."

No kidding. Every muscle in her body screamed at her to do something, anything, yet here she remained, locked away in a tiny box, waiting for the next blow to fall.

"Unity said your family talked to you yesterday."

He was trying to distract her. Good luck with that.

"And I heard Lelindia has settled on a name for the baby, but she's not telling anyone."

Aurora dropped her hands and her gaze to the floor in a forward fold, but not quickly enough.

"She told you, didn't she?"

Of course she did. In any normal scenario, Lelindia would have come to her for help in deciding the little Nedale's name. Instead, her mom and Marina had stepped into that role. But Lelindia had reached out to her as soon as the decision was made and told her what she'd chosen.

Raehn Clarek. It was perfect.

Maybe that's why she was in such a foul mood this morning. The impact her incarceration was having on the important moments in her life had cast a shadow she couldn't get out from under.

"Rory?"

Cade's voice caressed her, the concern clear even without her empathic senses.

She glared at the floor, struggling to get her emotions under wraps. She couldn't afford to yell or cry, two options that sounded really good right now.

"Ordinarily I'd say *talk to me*, but since that's part of the problem, I'll just say I love you."

She blinked furiously, but a drop of moisture still hit the concrete.

"I know this is hard for you. I can feel it. There's nothing I'd rather do right now than bust you and the Admiral out, take off, and never look back."

For someone who couldn't read her mind, he was doing a damn good job. Hearing her thoughts out loud helped. Her shoulders loosened, air filling her lungs – in and out, in and out.

And maybe that was part of the problem, too. She couldn't *say* anything. Not to Cade, not even to herself. Not with the Sovereign listening. All her thoughts kept swirling like a cyclone, with nowhere to go. She was a captive in her own head.

Talking with Lelindia was her only outlet, but their interactions kept reminding her of what she was missing.

"I do have one bit of news that might help. I wasn't going to say anything because it may not work."

The anxious excitement in his emotional field caught her full attention. Settling onto the floor facing the wall, she went into a straddle pose, bending forward to rest on her forearms.

He cleared his throat, his hesitancy piquing her interest even more. "The thing is, Ifel's been working with me on my latent abilities. She tapped into something from my past, a trauma, that kept me from developing them."

That fit. She'd always sensed there was a part of himself he'd held in check, kept hidden from the world, even from her. Since she'd had a closet full of secrets, many of which she'd concealed from him while they were at the Academy, she hadn't pushed him for answers.

Apparently Ifel had.

"She believes that if she keeps working with me, I may develop the ability to talk to you the way Lelindia does."

Her breath caught. For a moment she forgot she was being watched, forgot she was staring at a wall and not into Cade's eyes. "Wh—" But she stopped herself before her lungs could finish pushing air through her vocal cords to create the word. Instead, she turned it into a gusty exhale, then followed it up with two more for good measure to cover the lapse.

"I have no idea how long it might take, if it works at all. She's pushing hard. I think she knows how much that would mean to both of us."

She closed her eyes, the hint of a smile finally tugging at her lips. The next time she saw Ifel, she was giving the Yruf leader the biggest hug in the universe.

"I'm glad I told you. We—" He cut off abruptly.

She opened her eyes, staring at the wall.

"Sorry about that. Unity just let me know the Admiral's transport has arrived at the Court of Justice and he's being led inside."

Fifty-Five

"The government will demonstrate that Admiral William Schreiber conspired with Captain Aurora Hawke to usurp the lawful authority of the Galactic Union. The government will demonstrate that Admiral William Schreiber and Captain Aurora Hawke collaborated with two separate factions of the Setarips to inspire widespread panic, with the intent of militarizing the Fleet and dissolving the Galactic Council and General Assembly, thereby replacing them with an autocracy that would be led by Admiral William Schreiber. Furthermore, the government will show that Admiral William Schreiber and Captain Aurora Hawke then intended to collaborate with the Kraed and use the combined military power of the Setarip, Galactic, and Kraed fleets to invade the sovereign territory of the Teeli to subdue them and make them part of the new autocracy."

Stellar light.

Aurora's mind snagged on the phrase *sovereign territory of the Teeli* as her blood flash-chilled in an instant, making her shiver. She should have been better prepared for this after the way she'd been treated since her arrest. She'd known what she was up against. But the trial counsel's words still hung in a thick cloud before her, harbingers of the approaching storm.

A galactic empire – Humans, Suulh, Teeli, Setarips, and Kraed – all under the Sovereign's dominion. That was the Sovereign's end game. Well, that and tormenting Aurora for the rest of her days.

Guilt pricked her like porcupine quills as images tumbled through her mind in reflecting raindrops – Reanne as an eager cadet determined to befriend her, Reanne's delighted smile when she'd seen her in the RC tent on Gaia, the cloaked figure of the Sovereign standing imperiously over her as she knelt in manacles beside the riverbank, and the hatred in the Sovereign's eyes when she'd unmasked her.

Bile rose at the back of her throat, choking her.

The Sovereign's attacks were personal, certainly, but the pivotal reason behind hers and the Admiral's incarceration was the Sovereign's determination to remove the largest obstructions to her goal. Permanently.

If she and the Admiral were convicted, the Sovereign would make certain the reasons for their incarceration were publicized. According to Lelindia and Celia, public opinion toward the Fleet was already falling fast. With the specter of a militarized Fleet hanging over their heads like a shroud, the Federal Coalition and General Assembly could push for even stricter limits on the Fleet's use of weapons. Or more oversight onboard Fleet ships. Both would weaken the Fleet's ability to do its job of defending against an attack.

Leaving the Union ripe for an invasion by Setarip and Teeli warships. The Fleet wouldn't even recognize the Teeli ships for what they were. No one except her crew had seen them before. As far as the Union was concerned, the Teeli fleet was exclusively passenger ships.

But the Teeli would know exactly how to strike the Fleet where it would do the most damage.

Or maybe the Sovereign wouldn't need to invade at all. How many members of the Council did she have under her thumb? How much sway did she already have over the Fleet? Maybe not enough to achieve her goal quickly, but given time, that could change.

Although the Sovereign wouldn't want a slow transition. Patience wasn't one of her strong suits once she had her target in sight. She'd want pageantry, drama, all attention focused on her as she ascended to her throne.

And with Aurora out of the equation, she could finally bring to bear the most dangerous weapon at her disposal, the one that would ensure her continued survival and dominion.

She could unleash the Suulh.

Fifty-Six

"Aurora, it's okay." Cade sensed the glacier that slid down Aurora's spine in reaction to the trial counsel's opening statement. It chilled him to the bone.

The display in the main room of Cade's cabin showed a triple screen that wrapped around half the room — Aurora in her cell on the left side, and two viewpoints on the courtroom to his right. He fought a slight sensation of vertigo as his gaze moved from one 3D image to the other. They all looked like rooms he could walk right into, but the difference in perspective and depth of field was messing with his head.

One viewpoint was positioned above the Fleet panel's seating area, providing a clear view of the witness stand, the judge's bench, and the side door where the Admiral had been led in. The second view was positioned from the front of the witness stand facing the tables for the trial counsel and defense. Both lawyers had been seated before the Admiral was brought in, which had given Cade a chance to study them.

The trial counsel's dark hair was pulled back in a tight, military-style bun that emphasized her strong features and the grim slash of her mouth. Streaks of grey at her temples matched the grey of her uniform and added to her austerity. The fit of her uniform indicated she spent a significant number of her off hours doing weight-bearing exercises that had turned her muscles to stone. If she threw a punch that connected, you'd probably feel it all the way to your toenails.

The Admiral's lawyer was her polar opposite. Petite in stature and slight of build, his tailored suit was all clean lines and simple detailing. With salt and pepper hair and visible laugh lines around his eyes, he gave the impression of calm competence and warmth, but the look in his eyes as he listened to the trial counsel's opening statement made it clear how sharp the mind was inside the unassuming exterior.

Aurora was listening just as intently. Her mouth tightened as she rose to her feet. The slight stiffness in her walk as she went to the sanitation station and got a drink of water spoke volumes about how much pressure she was under.

Unity was also projecting the video and audio feeds in the *Starhawke's* observation lounge for everyone there. He could imagine the uproar the opening statement had caused, especially after the mention of the Kraed.

Judge Ottoman surveyed the room like a king on his throne, his black robes swirling around his heavy-set form. Something about his attitude made Cade wary. He couldn't possibly be sensing anything from the judge at this distance, but that didn't stop his instincts from poking him. The judge's demeanor struck him as wrong, but it wasn't anything he could put his finger on.

The trial counsel wrapped up her statement and sat.

Dale Copeland rose, his demeanor radiating calm certainty and absolute confidence. He approached the panel as though he was greeting old friends.

"Trial counsel paints a compelling picture, but…"

He delivered his opening statement with an easy manner that had a visible effect on the panel. Their shoulders relaxed and their postures became less rigid in their chairs the longer he spoke.

Even better, he was having the same effect on Aurora. She'd returned to her cot and was reclining facing Cade, arms folded in a relaxed pose. By the time Copeland finished his statement, her gaze had softened considerably.

"Commander Adams, call your first witness."

"Trial counsel calls Timothy Holcomb."

He sensed Aurora's reaction, heard her audible inhalation. The tightness around her eyes returned, expanding to her jaw.

She knew Holcomb. How? The name rang a bell for him, but not one he could place.

He didn't recognize the reedy man who was led into the courtroom. Whoever he was, he didn't look at the Admiral or the panel. His gaze remained pinned on the witness stand like everyone in the room had the power of Medusa if he met their eyes.

After he was sworn in, the trial counsel walked leisurely around the table to face him. "Mr. Holcomb, can you please tell the court your current title and position?"

"I'm the Director of Persei Primus space station."

Now the man's significance locked into place.

"And how long have you held that position?"

"Nine years."

"So you were the Director at the time of the Setarip attack two and a half years ago?"

"Yes, I was."

"And as Director, who do you report to?"

Holcomb's gaze slid partway toward the Admiral before darting back to Adams. "The Fleet Director."

"Are you a Fleet officer?"

"No, I'm a civilian administrator."

"Then why do you report to the Fleet Director?"

"Because Persei Primus is a Fleet-operated R&D facility. Fleet personnel and their families account for the majority of our population. The administrative staff and service providers on the station make up the rest."

"So at the time of the attack you were reporting to Admiral Schreiber?"

"Yes." A trace of bitterness tinged the words.

Adams took a step closer to the witness stand, giving Cade an excellent view of the gleam in her eyes. "Mr. Holcomb, do you recall the days leading up to the Setarip attack on Persei Primus?"

Holcomb swallowed, the audio picking up the sound as the man's jaw worked like he was fighting to keep hold of his emotions. "Vividly."

"And do you recall if you had communications with Admiral Schreiber during that time?"

"Yes, I did."

"What was the topic of those communications?"

"Prior to the... attack," his lips twisted around the word, "it was standard administrative comms — status updates, resource requests, staffing queries, and performance reports. But as soon as we spotted the Setarip ships in the system, we sent out a Fleet distress call. The Admiral would have received it, along with any ships close enough to respond."

"And did any ships respond?"

"Yes. We received confirmation from the *Argo* shortly before our communications went down."

"Who was the commanding officer of the *Argo* at that time?"

"The same as now, the Admiral's son, Captain Knox Schreiber."

"What about in the days following the attack? Were you in communication with Admiral Schreiber then?"

"Yes."

"And was the topic of those communications the same as before the attack?"

"No."

"What changed?"

"The Admiral was focused on the attack, in particular the item the Setarips had stolen from the station."

"And what was that item?"

"A prototype for a winged propulsion pack."

The trial counsel touched her tablet. Several diagrams and a photo appeared on the display screens before the panel and the witness stand.

Cade had been expecting it, but his stomach still twisted at the sight of the device. The last time he'd seen it, it had been all but embedded into the backs of the Suulh who had been forced to carry it during their Necri existence.

"Is this the prototype that was stolen?"

"Yes. It was a classified project, but was declassified during the investigation by the review board following the attack."

"Tell me, Mr. Holcomb, how many of the Fleet personnel and civilians of Persei Primus died or were never recovered after the Setarip attack?"

For the first time Holcomb looked directly at the Admiral. Holcomb's face looked chipped from ice, but his voice burned like fire. "One hundred forty-two."

Fifty-Seven

Lelindia shuddered as the faces of the deceased rose like specters in her mind's eye. Persei Primus had been a painful test of her Nedale abilities, the first time she'd faced a multitude of horrific injuries, the first time she'd seen lives lost before her eyes.

She'd worked as hard and as quickly as she could, pulling people back from the abyss. But she'd been one person amid hundreds of casualties. Even with the help of her medical team, it had been impossible to get to everyone in time.

Jonarel's arm wrapped around her shoulders, his warmth chasing away the chill.

They'd all gathered in the *Starhawke*'s observation lounge. Tehar had rearranged the seating and blacked out the windows to create a mini-theatre, with Unity's projections of the courtroom at center stage.

"Were you aware that the prototype was the objective at the time it was taken?" The trial counsel had a calculated delivery that set Lelindia's teeth on edge.

"No."

She'd spoken to Director Holcomb a few times while the *Argo* was at Persei Primus. She remembered him as a straightforward, compassionate man who had been deeply affected by the heavy losses.

"Where were you during the attack?"

"I was in the command center, coordinating with our security chief, trying to stop the Setarips from invading and destroying the station. I knew what they were capable of if they managed to dock. Repelling Setarip attacks is precisely why our station is so heavily fortified."

"Was this a typical Setarip attack?"

"It seemed like it when their ships arrived in the system, but to my knowledge this is the first time Setarips ever used a frontal assault as a diversion. The squad they sent to infiltrate the station and steal the prototype used an old RC freighter as a decoy, docking with the station right before the Setarip ships attacked. We weren't even aware Setarips were on the station."

"Do ships normally dock without communicating with your crew?"

Holcomb scowled. "Of course not."

"Then how did the Setarips manage to dock the RC freighter without your realizing who they were?"

"Because they had two human collaborators working with them who knew RC protocols and did all the talking. They claimed they needed repairs, which was not an unusual request. We gave them clearance to dock."

"Why didn't anyone stop the Setarips when they left the freighter?"

"They timed it perfectly with the arrival of the Setarip ships. Normally one of our station security officers would have met them at the airlock. That's protocol. But our security personnel were scrambling to get to their defensive posts on the opposite side of the station and all civilians were being evacuated to the protected bunkers in the hub. The freighter wasn't a priority. They were rescue personnel. Their job is to help in crisis situations. I assumed they could take care of themselves and hopefully help our people, too."

"But there were Setarips on that freighter?"

"Yes."

"How many?"

"I don't know for sure, but more than twenty, along with the two humans."

"Why didn't anyone notice the Setarips once they were on the station?"

"None of us were watching for an attack from personnel wearing RC uniforms with thermal hoods." A note of defensiveness crept into his voice. "I remember seeing the group on the command center security feed moving down the concourse toward the hub, but at quick glance, with their faces concealed by the hoods, they all looked human. I assumed they were coming to help. I had no reason to suspect them. Neither did anyone else."

"Where was the prototype that they stole located on the station?"

"In one of the secure research sections of the hub."

"What did they use to break into the area where the prototype was stored?"

The Director's voice turned arctic. "They didn't break in. They had our command access codes to override the command center and central hub lockdown." His gaze flicked to the Admiral.

"How many people are authorized to use those access codes?"

"Four. Myself, my two senior officers..." He gave the Admiral a long, hard look. "And Admiral Schreiber."

"Where were your senior officers during the attack?"

"In the command center with me."

"Could the command override have been sent from within the command center?"

"No. The security system clearly logged that the code was entered manually at the access terminal for the secure room."

"Is there any way that the log for the security system could have been altered to hide that the code was sent from the command center?"

"No. Command center logs and terminal logs are on separate parts of the system. It's one of multiple redundancies to ensure accurate data monitoring. The type of alteration you're describing would create a gap in the terminal log and an overlap in the command log. Neither log shows any signs of tampering."

"Were the codes used for anything other than accessing the section with the prototype?"

"Yes. Before they stole the prototype, they used the codes to override environmental systems and release a gas into the ventilation system that knocked out the command center personnel and the civilians in lockdown. I saw the assistant director slump to the ground right before I blacked out. The next thing I knew the *Argo's* medical team was reviving me."

Lelindia hadn't been present for that. She'd been busy working triage for the wounded pouring in from the rest of the station.

"How did the medical team get in if the command center was locked down?"

"All Fleet cruiser and frigate captains have override codes for this type of eventuality, where a ship's or station's crew has been incapacitated while under lockdown, but it requires voice authorization and direct bio scan. It can't be done remotely. Captain Schreiber overrode the lockdown when he came onto the station."

"Were your primary access codes used for anything else besides dispersing the gas and stealing the prototype?"

"Yes. After we were incapacitated, they deactivated the station's shields, weapons, and internal communications. That's when the casualties escalated." His lip curled in a snarl. "The Setarips docked one of their ships, but they didn't count on the resourcefulness of our people. Or their willingness to sacrifice themselves. After the FS officers lost contact with the command center and the shields went down, a small group sealed the interior blast doors, closing off that section from the rest of the station. As soon as the Setarips opened the airlock, the officers blew the dock from the inside. They took out the Setarip ship and every Setarip who'd infiltrated, but at the cost of their own lives."

A dull ache throbbed in Lelindia's chest, an echo of remembered pain. The patients she'd been treating on the station had shared that story, with tears of sorrow and pride in their eyes as they described the courage of their fallen comrades.

"When did you discover the prototype had been stolen?"

"After I first met with Captain Schreiber and Commander Hawke. The Commander described the case she'd seen the Setarips take onto the RC freighter. There were only a few items on the station that would fit that description. A search revealed the prototype was missing."

"You're referring to Commander Aurora Hawke, now captain of the *Starhawke?*"

"That's correct."

"Was Commander Hawke the only one who saw the case?"

"No. Several members of the *Argo's* response team confirmed they had also seen it."

"What about security footage?"

"We didn't have any security footage after they used our access codes to sabotage the internal communications. We don't have a single image where you can identify the Setarips while they're on the station."

"If you didn't see through their disguises when they arrived and there's no video footage afterward, then how can you be so sure who they were?"

"Because one of the human collaborators and nine of the Setarips died on the station. That's how we confirmed they were Ecilam faction."

"Were they killed during the fighting?"

"No, poisoned by a device embedded under their skin. According to the medical team who witnessed the simultaneous injection, they died instantly. Our scientists tried to analyze the device that delivered the poison, but the components had dissolved into trace minerals. Completely unidentifiable."

"When did this injection occur?"

"According to the medical team, during the tail end of the fighting, around the time the RC freighter detached from the station with the prototype onboard."

"Was anyone able to question the human collaborator before they died?"

"Not to my knowledge. The official report states he was screaming obscenities and then keeled over."

Lelindia shivered. She'd been treating the injured members of their team when she'd heard the shout of alarm from one of her nurses. She'd rushed to the downed collaborator and enveloped him in her energy field, but the poison had acted quicker than anything she'd ever seen. His body had been a barren wasteland before she'd even touched him.

Jonarel rested his cheek on the top of her head, offering silent support.

She leaned into him, his nearness soothing the emotional pain.

She glanced to her left, where Celia was seated beside her, with Micah on her other side. Her friend was watching the proceedings with rapt attention, her lips pulling back ever so slightly from her teeth whenever the trial counsel spoke.

Clearly she didn't like the woman any more than Lelindia did.

"...*Argo* was unable to stop the Setarips?"

She turned back to the projection.

Holcomb looked like he was chewing nails. "I understand that they tried, but according to the reports from the FS officers who were still conscious during the battle, the *Argo* was focusing on defending the station rather than attacking the Setarips."

He said it almost grudgingly, like he didn't want to say anything positive related to the *Argo* and its crew.

Adams rested her hip against her table. "Let's talk more about the access codes used to obtain the prototype and disable the station. How often are those codes changed?"

"We receive encrypted updates every week."

"And who sends those updates?"

"The Fleet Director."

"So until recently you received them from Admiral Schreiber?"

"Correct."

"How long had it been since you received the most recent update before the attack occurred?"

"Less than a day."

"And there were only three of you on the station who knew those codes?"

"That's correct."

"Did a Security Council review board question the station's personnel after the attack?"

"Yes." Holcomb's jaw tightened. "They were on station for two months."

"And what were their conclusions?"

His gaze shifted to the Admiral, his tone turning condescending. "They didn't find cause for any charges to be brought against any member of my staff. Instead, forty-seven of them received Fleet commendations for their bravery and dedication to duty. Most posthumously," he added in an undertone.

"Was the review board able to determine how the Setarips obtained your access codes?"

"Not to my knowledge."

"But the only other person with access to those codes was Admiral Schreiber."

"That's correct."

"Thank you, Mr. Holcomb. No further questions."

Fifty-Eight

Aurora was breathing fire.

Which was really a problem because she couldn't let it show on her face or in her body.

All that anger dove inward, generating flaming coals that roasted her insides.

The trial counsel was making the case that the Admiral had given the access codes to the Setarips. Nothing Holcomb had said proved it, but Aurora got the impression Holcomb was the setup man, laying the groundwork for what was to follow.

"I know," Cade whispered softly in her ear. "I know."

She stared at the wall, visualizing a charred, smoking hole carving into the bland surface.

Less than half an hour into the proceedings, and she already knew everything she needed to know about the trial counsel. Commander Adams wasn't a woman who was interested in justice. She was looking to make a name for herself by taking down the most powerful man in the Fleet.

What had the Sovereign promised her? Wealth? A judgeship? Something even more despicable?

She was so focused on her anger it took a moment to realize the Admiral's lawyer had already started his cross-examination.

"...those codes travel a great distance through multiple relay points to reach the station?"

"Yes," Holcomb said slowly, like he was testing the ground beneath his feet.

"Has a new access code ever failed to arrive?"

A brief pause. "Yes."

"Has a new access code ever been delayed in its delivery, arriving late?"

Another pause. "Yes."

"Do you know the cause of these failures and delays?"

Holcomb's irritated sigh filled her ear. "It's always an issue with a relay station. Solar flares, asteroid collisions, a systems glitch, something that's physically affecting the hardware or software — slowing it down, causing it to reboot, or taking it completely offline."

"And how are those issues resolved?" Copeland's voice was relaxed, conversational.

"We'd send a test comm through the system. It's designed to send a message back the moment it encounters a problem. As soon as the faulty relay is identified, messages are temporarily routed away from that relay until the ICS techs handle any needed repairs."

"How many relay beacons would a typical message from Earth to Persei Primus pass through?"

"I don't know the exact number off the top of my head."

"Approximately how many?"

"Around thirty."

"Thirty relays, each one having the potential for a problem that could delay or stop delivery, is that correct?"

"Yes." Holcomb sounded less antagonistic than he had when the cross-examination began. Copeland's delivery seemed to be coaxing him to mellow without his even realizing it.

"Are the codes sent at the same time each week?"

"Yes."

"So you receive the codes at the exact same time each week?"

"Not exact, but within a two-hour window, yes."

"And if the codes don't arrive in that two-hour window, that's when you send the test comm?"

"Yes."

"Did the access codes you received prior to the Setarip attack arrive on time?"

A beat. Two. "I don't recall."

Silence fell. Aurora strained to hear anything that would give her a clue as to what was happening.

"Can you please tell me if this is the access code message you received prior to the attack?"

A chair squeaked in the background, Holcomb's breathing becoming audible, like he'd leaned closer to where Unity was hidden.

"That looks right," Holcomb finally answered.

"Can you please check the time stamp on this message and tell me if it was delivered in the expected two-hour window?"

Another creak. Holcomb might be getting restless. "No, it wasn't," he huffed.

"How long after the two-hour window did it arrive?"

"The timestamp shows seventeen minutes after the window closed."

"Can you please take a look at this second document, and confirm if it is the log from a test comm sent from Persei Primus to Earth the day before the Setarip attack?"

"Yes, it is."

"What is the difference between the timestamp on this test log and the first document?"

"The test log's timestamp is seventeen minutes prior to the timestamp for the access code message."

"And can you please describe what the test log tells you regarding how the relays were functioning at that time?"

Aurora held herself in suspended animation as she waited for his answer.

"The test log doesn't show any issues with any of the relays." A note of uncertainty had crept into Holcomb's voice.

"Is that an unusual log report for this type of test comm?"

"Yes."

"If I'm understanding you correctly, you're saying the access code comm was delayed, but the test log doesn't show any issue that would have caused that delay. Would you agree with that statement?"

"He's concerned," Cade whispered into the silence.

"Yes," Holcomb answered.

"In your time as Director of Persei Primus, have you ever encountered that situation before?"

"Not that I recall."

"What might cause that situation to occur?"

"It shouldn't be possible."

But it happened.

Communications had been Aurora's chosen specialty at the Academy. The facts pointed to one inevitable conclusion, one that should be impossible but clearly wasn't. Someone had figured out a way to intercept the message at one of the relay stations, hanging it up long enough to duplicate it and cause the seventeen-minute delay.

Someone with a tie to the Rescue Corps and a close working relationship with the Ecilam Setarips. Someone named Reanne Beck.

Fifty-Nine

Cade could feel Aurora's anger through their connection — a snarling, snapping creature with pointy teeth. He could also see on the visual of her cell how hard she was working to keep those flares of anger from showing as she sat on her cot, staring at the wall.

But her eyes widened and her lips parted as she picked up on something in Copeland's line of questioning Cade hadn't.

However, Copeland didn't follow up. He switched topics. "Let's discuss the device that was embedded under the skin of the Setarips and the human collaborator who died on the station. You said your scientists tried to analyze the device that delivered the poison, but the components had dissolved into trace minerals and were completely unidentifiable, is that correct?"

"Yes."

"As director of a research and development station, how much knowledge do you have about the projects being worked on at the station?"

"I have full knowledge of all of them."

"So there's nothing under development you don't know about?"

"Of course not. I'm responsible for the wellbeing of every person on that station. It's my job to make sure they're not exposed to unnecessary risk. I can't do that if I don't know what's happening in our labs."

"And the scientists who work on your station, how accomplished are they in their given fields?"

"Very. We have some of the brightest minds working at our station."

"Were the scientists able to provide any insights as to the origin of the device that was used?"

"No. As I said, it dissolved into trace minerals before they could examine it."

"Did any of the scientists discuss with you whether they had seen a component that dissolved like this before?"

"We discussed it at length, both among ourselves and with the review board. No one had seen this type of technology before."

Cade snorted. That's because only a psycho like the Sovereign killed everyone she left behind.

"Have you ever heard of such technology being used by the Fleet?"

"No."

"Have you heard of or encountered anything similar since the attack?"

"No."

"Have you ever heard of Setarips using devices like this before?"

"No."

Copeland made a note on his tablet. "How many Setarip ships attacked the station?"

"Five."

"How violent was their attack?"

"Extremely."

"What was the impact of their attack on the station's shields?"

"They were taking a beating, but holding. We have shielding that rivals any starship's."

"Were your weapons having any effect on the Setarip ships?"

"Yes. We got a solid hit on one of their destroyers. It was withdrawing from the battle right before I blacked out."

"But the other four ships were still actively attacking the station when you were incapacitated?"

"Yes."

"And according to witness accounts and the station's command logs, at some point after you were incapacitated the station's shields and weapons went down completely?"

"Yes."

"After you were revived by the *Argo's* medical personnel, were any of the Setarip ships still in the system?"

"No."

"Did you inquire about any damage the *Argo* had suffered during the battle?"

"Yes."

"What did you learn?"

Holcomb's lips pressed together. "They'd suffered some damage."

Some damage? More like *a lot* of damage. Cade had poured over those reports after the Admiral gave him access. His team needed to keep apprised of all Setarip activity, but that wasn't the real reason he'd requested the Persei Primus reports. Even though he hadn't interacted with Aurora in years at that point, some part of him had needed to know what she'd gone through. To confirm she was okay.

Copeland tapped his tablet. A document appeared on the panel box and witness stand screens. "I have here the official Fleet damage and repair order for the *Argo* which is signed by the *Argo's* chief engineer on the day following the battle. The repair order is also signed by the crew chief at Spiral Bay shipyard, where the repair work was done. Director, can you please read the list of damaged components to us?"

Holcomb coughed, leaning toward the screen. "Dorsal plating missing from sections F – J. Number six and seven aft cannons inoperable. Port thrusters two and five inoperable. Starboard thruster seven inoperable. Hull breach section E-6–"

"That's far enough, thank you." Copeland held up a hand. "Earlier in your testimony you stated that you allowed the decoy RC freighter to dock because the human collaborators claimed the ship needed repairs. How often do ships dock at your station for repairs?"

"Usually about once or twice a week."

"As director, do you have oversight on these repairs?"

"Of course."

"What types of repairs does your station provide?"

"For small to mid-sized vessels — yachts, freighters, personnel transports — just about anything they need. For larger vessels, it depends on the nature of the problem."

"Based on the damage list currently before you, would your crews be able to provide the necessary repairs for a large ship with those issues?"

"No."

"Why not?"

"The damage is too extensive."

"Too extensive for your crews to handle?"

"Yes."

Cade caught the light in Copeland's eyes as he nodded. "Thank you, Director Holcomb. No further questions."

Sixty

Micah shifted in his seat. Normally the chairs in the observation lounge were comfortable, but at the moment it felt like he was sitting on a bag of rocks. Might have something to do with what was happening on the projections from the courthouse.

His imagination easily conjured an image of Aurora sitting at the defense table, facing witnesses who firmly believed she was a traitor to the Union. He didn't want to acknowledge that soon he'd be watching her fate decided by the courts.

Celia rested a hand on his arm.

He instantly stilled, sparks of tingling awareness shooting out from the point of contact.

"You okay?" she murmured, her focus on the projection as the next witness approached the stand.

Not even close. Her hand on his arm worked great as a distraction, but now he was uncomfortable for a different reason. He forced his voice into a semblance of normalcy. "Yeah."

Her gaze flicked to his, assessing. To his dismay and delight, she left her hand where it sat on his sleeve as she returned her attention to the proceedings.

"Mr. Pataconi." Commander Adams strolled toward the witness stand. "What is your current job title?"

"I'm the SGQ2-F team leader for the ICS's software security."

Pataconi looked a lot more relaxed than the last witness. Younger, too, maybe in his mid-to-late thirties, with a trim frame and reddish-brown hair that matched his beard.

"How long have you been the team leader?"

"Seven years."

"How many people are on your team?"

"Fifty-seven."

"What specifically does your team do?"

Celia's fingers tightened slightly on Micah's arm. He took a peek at her, but her focus remained entirely on the projections, alert and analyzing.

"We manage the data security for the Fleet side of the ICS relays in SGQ2, overseeing all Fleet communications, to or from Fleet accounts. We're responsible for protecting the system against hacks and infections, making sure all messages are routed correctly, identifying and patching weaknesses, and monitoring system updates."

"How many messages are routed through the relays you oversee?"

"Our quadrant processes millions of messages each day."

"And what types of security do those messages have?"

"It depends on the message." Pataconi leaned forward, resting his elbows on the arms of his chair, and lacing his fingers together. "There are three distinct security levels. The lowest security settings are for general delivery, which includes messages from family and friends to Fleet personnel or personal correspondence between Fleet personnel. The middle level of security is Fleet standard, which is used for things like personnel orders and resource requests. Standard has several layers of added security. The top level is restricted delivery, which is available to authorized personnel only. Classified documents, administrative and ship access codes, and sealed orders are sent restricted delivery. All communications have multi-factor authentication and top-end encryption. There's also a fail-safe for standard and restricted messages that will instantly shred any message that is opened by anyone other than the intended recipient, simultaneously pinging the sender to alert them to the breach."

Celia's fingers twitched again, warmth spreading up Micah's arm and down into his palm from the unintentional caress. He gritted his teeth. Apparently Pataconi's response meant way more to her than it did to him.

"What happens in the case of a breach?"

"My team immediately tracks down the source of the breach and implements a patch to seal it. We send our findings to Fleet HQ and the Federal Coalition. They handle the criminal investigation."

"Can a standard or restricted-level message still reach its intended recipient if it has been intercepted, manipulated, or altered after being sent?"

"No. Any attempt to do so would result in the message being shredded and the alert triggered."

"Could a standard or restricted message be fabricated and sent by someone without the necessary Fleet credentials?"

"Objection, Your Honor," Copeland interjected. "Calls for a conclusion."

"Mr. Pataconi is an expert, Your Honor," Adams countered, straightening her spine. "He should be allowed to answer."

"Objection overruled," the judge replied. "Mr. Pataconi, please answer the question."

Celia stiffened. A quick glance showed her lips were pressed together.

"What is it?" Micah murmured.

She shook her head, her gaze locked onto Judge Ottoman.

Something about the judge's response had triggered a reaction, but he'd have to wait to find out why.

Pataconi turned back to Adams. "No, ma'am. The scenario you describe is not possible."

A document appeared on the witness and panel screens with several blocks of black covering lines of the data. "Mr. Pataconi, can you identify what type of message this is?"

Pataconi bent toward the screen, his gaze scanning the message. "It's a restricted communication from Fleet HQ to Persei Primus station."

"How can you tell?"

"The symbol encoded on the message here," he pointed to the upper left of the document, "indicates it's restricted, for the recipient's eyes only. The sender code indicates it originated at Fleet HQ, and the recipient code indicates it was received at Persei Primus."

The trial counsel touched her tablet and a second document appeared beside the first. The message's content was entirely blacked out. "What about this message?"

"This one's Fleet standard, sent from Fleet HQ, but the recipient code is for the starship *Argo*."

One of the blacked-out lines on the first message disappeared. "Can you please read the sender's name for the first message?"

Pataconi's gaze slid briefly to Admiral Schreiber, but without animosity. "Admiral William Schreiber."

A line of text cleared from the second message. "Who's the sender for the second message?"

"Also from Admiral William Schreiber."

"Who is the recipient for the first message?"

"Director Timothy Holcomb."

"And the second message?"

"Commander Aurora Hawke."

"What is the difference in the delivery time stamps for the two messages?"

Pataconi glanced between the two messages. "The first message was delivered four hours, twenty-six minutes before the second."

The remaining black disappeared from the first message. "Can you identify the content of the first message?"

"These are Fleet access codes for the space station."

"Persei Primus space station?"

"Correct."

"Sent by Admiral Schreiber to Director Holcomb?"

"Yes."

The black over the second message vanished. "Can you please read the content of the second message sent by Admiral Schreiber to Commander Hawke?"

Pataconi cleared his throat. "*Our mutual friends are in your area and dressed for a night out. They look forward to seeing you soon. Let me know how the meet up goes.*"

Sixty-One

Lelindia's jaw hit the deck.

Kire's reaction was more vociferous. He launched out of his chair beside Jonarel, a stream of curses she'd never heard him use flying out of his mouth like shotgun blasts.

"...asteroid-kicking morons!" he finished, his face flushed, spittle spraying from his lips. "You're being tricked!"

"They cannot hear you." Jonarel's voice held a healthy dose of irony, but the fire in his eyes matched Kire's as he glared at Pataconi's image.

Kire shoved both hands into his hair, making it stand up in dark spikes. "The Admiral did not send that message."

Lelindia whole-heartedly agreed, but she couldn't seem to get her vocal cords to work.

"Of course he didn't." Celia's voice was cool water on a hot stove, the tension in the room sizzling and popping. "It doesn't sound anything like him."

"...authenticate both messages prior to appearing here today," trial counsel said. "What..."

Kire's attention swung back to the projection, his hands falling to his sides and curling into fists as Pataconi spouted technobabble in response to the trial counsel's question.

Lelindia had never seen Kire so overtly irate before. He was one of the most cool-headed people she knew. It was one reason he was a great commander and comm specialist. But his frustration level had clearly reached epic proportions. Ever since Aurora had been taken off the ship, his normal smile had slowly been replaced with a scowl that deepened day by day.

She understood his outrage because she shared it. Having two of the people she respected most in the galaxy on trial for treason, implicated under falsified evidence, had eaten away at her self-control, too. The growing civil unrest regarding the Fleet wasn't helping, either. If she didn't have Raehn to focus on, she probably would have been the one spitting fire.

"So, here's the real question," Celia continued, drawing Kire's gaze before throwing down the gauntlet. "Are you going to get angry, or get even? Use that Fleet-trained communication-minded brain of yours to figure out how the Sovereign did it?"

Kire stared at her for a moment, anger buzzing around him like bees. Slowly, a subtle self-mocking smile crept across his face. He dropped back into his chair. "Challenge accepted."

"Good." Celia returned her focus to the projection, a slight pinch to her mouth the only outward sign that she was as upset by the proceedings as the rest of them.

"...professional opinion as an ICS security expert, what is your assessment of the authenticity of these two messages?"

Pataconi straightened in his seat like he'd been waiting for the question and was glad the moment had finally arrived.

A part of her wanted to hate him. Whether he knew it or not, he was working for the Sovereign, and that made him either a menace or a pawn.

But dressed in his blue button-front shirt and tie, his beard and hair neatly trimmed, and laugh lines bracketing his intelligent eyes, he didn't look like an agent of evil. He looked like someone she'd enjoy talking to.

She still hated every word out of his mouth.

"I thoroughly reviewed all available data and digital forensics related to these messages, including transmission logs, relay diagnostics, and account security. No breach alerts were triggered by either message, nor were they shredded. They successfully reached their intended recipients without any indication of unlawful access by an outside source. Based on those findings, it is my professional opinion that these communications are authentic."

"Thank you. No further questions."

Kire, she noticed, had his head bent over his comband, typing furiously, his fingers stabbing the surface with much more force than necessary. "Unity!" he barked. "I need a recording of that testimony sent to my comband."

U-1 floated into view. "Right away."

"Thanks," Kire murmured absently, his gaze shifting to the projection as the Admiral's lawyer stood and rounded the table.

"Mr. Pataconi, can you please identify this document for me?" The screens switched to a single document, this one without any blacked-out sections.

Pataconi glanced over it. "This is a comm test log."

"What is a comm test log?"

"It's generated when a test comm is sent to one of the relays to determine if there's a software or mechanical problem that's causing a service disruption."

"Right track, keep going," Kire murmured.

Copeland took Pataconi through the same series of questions he'd asked Director Holcomb regarding the delay in delivery of the access code message, bringing it back to what the test comm indicated – that there were no issues with the ICS relay that should have caused the delay.

"Mr. Pataconi, given your experience and knowledge as a security expert, do you have an explanation for this apparent contradiction in the data?"

Pataconi looked irritated, but more at himself for not having an answer to the question than at Copeland for asking it. "Not at this time."

"What would prevent someone from gaining access to one of the ICS relays, either physically or through the software, and temporarily holding a message?"

"The relays all have heavy shielding to prevent damage from space debris and radiation. To manually access them, that shielding would have to be switched off, which would light up our system like a star. And any attempt to access through the system software would trip the fail-safes and alerts I've mentioned earlier. They're not just set up to protect individual messages from being hacked. They would also activate if the system detected an internal security threat."

The gleam in Copeland's eyes signaled he had an ace up his sleeve he was about to play.

"If the system were accessed without triggering the fail-safes and alerts, would it produce the data in front of you?"

Pataconi chewed on his bottom lip as his gaze scrolled over the documents like he'd find the answers written there.

Copeland waited patiently.

Lelindia waited much less patiently.

Pataconi finally lifted his head. His nod was short, but definitive. "Yes, I think it would."

Kire, she noted, was grinning like the Cheshire Cat.

Sixty-Two

The cramped room where Phoebe Liddell was waiting for Aurora felt like a breath of fresh air despite the lack of windows and ornamentation. The time spent with her lawyer was the one chance she got to talk without fear of being overheard.

Unity had already confirmed that Phoebe's privacy screen was necessary — the room was being monitored by the detention center's XO. As soon as Phoebe switched the privacy screen on, Unity had also confirmed the screen was functional, though with Unity being Unity, it had zero effect on them. "That's impressive tech," Unity whispered in her ear. "There's no way the Sovereign's minions will break through. Oh, and Cade's listening in."

Good to know.

"I've examined all the information trial counsel provided." Phoebe flipped through several screens on her tablet. "They've focused on your involvement with the Setarip attacks on Persei Primus and on Gaia."

Not news to her thanks to Unity's audio feed of the Admiral's trial, so she'd have to tread carefully. She didn't want to give any hints that she already knew what Phoebe was here to tell her. That would do serious damage to the trust she'd established. "What do you mean, my involvement?"

"They're accusing you of helping the Setarips steal a prototype from Persei Primus, then working with them to create the crop destruction on Gaia to incite panic among the populace, both under Admiral Schreiber's orders."

"To what end?"

"Trial counsel is trying to prove Admiral Schreiber plans to militarize the Fleet, overthrow the Union, and install himself as an autocrat with you as his right hand."

"That's insane." She didn't hold back on the vehemence in her voice. It felt cathartic to finally let her feelings have free rein.

"I agree. But they have compelling evidence that's going to be a challenge to refute."

"Like what?" She needed Phoebe to tell her what she already knew so they could talk about it without fear that she'd trip herself up.

"Comm messages, for one. The first one's between you and Admiral Schreiber." She pulled up a message on her tablet and turned it so Aurora could read it.

She recognized it instantly as the one the ICS specialist had read during the Admiral's trial earlier. She studied it, looking for any clues Pataconi had missed. "The Admiral never sent this to me," she said out loud. But the delivery timestamp nagged at her. Something about the date—

"But he did send me happy birthday wishes on this date."

Phoebe's perfectly manicured brows rose. "It was your birthday?"

Aurora shook her head. "No, it was the beginning of my birth month. I made a comment to the Admiral way back when I was at the Academy that I didn't believe in celebrating for one day, I celebrated the entire month. So, he got in the habit of sending me a happy birthday message – or more accurately a happy birthmonth message – on July first rather than on my actual birthday. The timestamp on this message looks like a match for that."

"So you think this might be a real message between the two of you that was altered in the comm records to change the content?"

"That seems likely."

"I didn't think that was possible."

"It's not supposed to be, but every system has weak points that can be exploited, especially by someone in a position of authority. Kire would have some theories, I'm sure."

"Kire Emoto, your first officer?"

"Yes. He knows more about the ICS than anyone. Well, except maybe the Admiral."

"Admiral Schreiber's an expert on the ICS?"

"Uh-huh. He helped create it. That's what makes this supposed evidence even more ludicrous. If the Admiral wanted to send a subversive message through the ICS, to me or anyone else, that no one would recognize as his, I'm sure he could find a way.

Doing something like this?" She pointed to the message on Phoebe's tablet. "It's blatant and stupid. And he's not stupid."

Phoebe's mouth curved a fraction. "I don't think I'll use that argument in court, but it's an excellent point. You're both much smarter and more detail-oriented than the evidence portrays you as being. There's also an arrogance that doesn't fit your personalities."

"Thank you."

"For what?"

"For believing in us. If the attitudes I've encountered in here are any indication, public opinion isn't on your side."

"Our side."

Now it was Aurora's turn to smile. "Our side."

"No, it's not, but public opinion doesn't matter in the courtroom. Evidence does. So, we need to figure out what evidence we can bring to bear to counteract what's being fed by trial counsel." Phoebe tapped her finger against her lip. "Is there any chance you have a copy of the Admiral's original message – the birthday message – that's not stored in the Fleet ICS servers?"

"Yes!" Bubbles of excitement raced from her stomach to her head like overflowing champagne, making her a little giddy. "Yes, I do. In my cabin on the *Starhawke*. I have a data clip where I store copies of all my birthday messages from my friends and family."

"So you would also have copies of the Admiral's previous birthday messages, all coming in on July first?"

"Yep."

Phoebe made a note on her tablet. "That's a good start. If you're right about this being a converted message, and the delivery timestamps on the two are identical, that would be a powerful argument for falsified evidence. Do I have your permission to visit the ship to retrieve the data clip and talk to the crew? I need to talk to them anyway, especially Dr. Forrest and Lt. Cardiff, since they were on Persei Primus with you. I'm hoping they'll be good defense witnesses."

"Absolutely. Lelindia knows where I store the clip. And you can pose our *what if* scenario to Kire about the ICS, see what he can come up with."

"We'll also need to hire an outside ICS specialist to go over everything. There are additional comm messages in the evidence packet, sent from your personal ICS account."

Aurora blinked. "What personal account?"

Phoebe looked up sharply. "You don't have a personal ICS account?"

"No. I never needed one. I always used my Fleet account."

Phoebe spun the tablet so Aurora could see the first message.

Neither the sender nor recipient account meant anything to her. "I've never seen either of these accounts before."

"Well, according to the evidence I was given, the first one is registered in your name."

Aurora gritted her teeth. "Reanne." She read the name of the recipient. "Who is Michael Bryant?"

"You've never heard of him?"

Aurora shook her head.

"He's the man you encountered·on Persei Primus who was leading the Setarips."

Aurora gulped. "I didn't think they'd ever identified him." But he'd figured prominently in her nightmares for several months following their confrontation. "Wait a minute. This message is about the RC freighter they used as a decoy. It's giving him instructions on how to obtain it." Her heart thumped in her chest. "You said this sender account is registered to me?"

"According to the records. Clearly I'll need to have the specialist look into that with a fine-toothed comb."

She swallowed past the constriction in her throat. "What about the other messages?" She saw five open tabs.

"More instructions, including how to meet up with the Ecilam before the attack."

Aurora flipped to the second message, then the third. "These are Reanne's messages." Now that she was looking for it, she recognized her former friend's writing style. "This is how she coordinated the attack."

"So you think this account was originally hers?"

"More likely one of her puppets who she was dictating the messages to. If this account originally tied directly to Reanne, I can't see her submitting it as evidence no matter how well she altered it to point to me. She's too focused on self-preservation for that."

"Hopefully a specialist will be able to uncover the original owner's identity. That would give us reasonable doubt. What about Gaia? I'm assuming you don't want to bring any of the Suulh here to testify, but is there anyone besides your crew and Knox Schreiber who could provide evidence to support your version of events?"

She dropped her gaze to the tabletop. She'd omitted any mention of Cade's team when she'd told Phoebe about the attack on Gaia during their first meeting. She'd been vague on the details of the crew's movements and Phoebe hadn't questioned how a crew of six had managed the complex op, in particular how they'd flown both the *Starhawke* and the Setarip ship back to Gaia with only one official pilot available. She'd allowed Phoebe to assume Jonarel had piloted the *Starhawke*.

"It's okay, Aurora," Cade murmured in her ear. "Tell her."

Her jaw tightened. Of course he would say that. He'd do anything, give up anything, to free her, just as she would do anything, give up anything, to keep him from being captured. They were at cross purposes.

"Aurora?"

She glanced up.

"There is someone, isn't there?" Phoebe's gaze was penetrating but kind. "Someone you're protecting besides the Suulh."

"Tell her."

She shivered, Cade's voice setting off mini quakes that made her teeth click.

She couldn't drag him into this. She just... couldn't. But maybe there was a way to keep him safe while still getting the help she needed with her defense. "Several someones, actually, but introducing them will complicate things."

"Complicate them how?"

She took a deep breath and dove in. "Admiral Schreiber has an elite unit, specially trained officers who are all experts in their fields. I wasn't aware of their existence until Gaia. The Admiral sent them as our backup. They're the ones who helped my crew deal with the Setarip threat."

Phoebe frowned, typing rapidly on her tablet, pages flipping back and forth. "I don't recall any mention of them in the official reports."

"There isn't. The Galactic Council isn't even aware of their existence."

Phoebe's eyes widened. "Why not?"

"I got the impression Admiral Schreiber didn't want to put all his trust in the Council after the Teeli joined."

"I can understand that but..." Apprehension shadowed Phoebe's eyes. "This isn't good."

"I know how it looks. I had the same reaction when I found out about them. But we wouldn't have been able to stop the Setarips on Gaia without their help." A different kind of shiver passed over her. If Cade hadn't pulled her and Lelindia out of that orchard before the Necri and Setarips had reached them, the Sovereign might have achieved checkmate before the game barely began.

Phoebe leaned back in her chair, her nails tapping lightly on the tabletop. "So this elite unit reports only to Admiral Schreiber?"

"Yes."

"Do you know where they are now?"

"Last I heard, acting as a security team for Knox."

"So you've kept in touch with them since Gaia?"

She forced herself not to squirm under Phoebe's unrelenting gaze. "Yes. They helped my crew recover the Admiral when he was kidnapped by the Etah at Gallows Edge."

"So their loyalty is to the Admiral?" Phoebe spoke slowly, enunciating each word clearly.

No doubt what that question was digging at. "Their loyalty is to the ideals of the Fleet and the Union. The Admiral has dedicated his life to upholding those ideals, so they're loyal to him. But if he suddenly turned on the Union and tried to do what trial counsel has accused him of, they'd give their lives to stop him, or anyone else with the same agenda. So would I."

Phoebe stopped the soft tapping on the tabletop. "So if I contact Captain Schreiber, will he put me in touch with this elite unit? Or deny their existence?"

"He'd probably talk to you first and decide for himself how to proceed."

Phoebe nodded. "Unfortunately, you're not describing the kind of witnesses I was hoping for. Bringing them into this would be a risk. Their testimony could do more damage than good. It might reinforce the perception that you and the Admiral are operating without oversight on your own agenda."

Aurora dropped her chin into her palm. "Which we are, except our agenda is trying to stop the Sovereign and the Teeli from doing what we've been accused of. All our actions have been in response to moves she's made, which keep escalating and weakening the Council and Fleet." She rubbed at her temple, where tension coiled into tight bands. "What evidence are they using to implicate me regarding the attack on Gaia?"

"There are communication records like the ones from the Persei Primus incident. But what concerns me the most is that Lt. Magee, the Admiral's former PA, is set to testify against you. Do you know why?"

She sighed. "She's under Teeli influence."

"What do you mean?"

During the long recitation of her history with the Sovereign and the Setarips, she must not have mentioned the Teeli's manipulative ability. "We've learned that the Teeli have the ability to influence the behavior of some people, push them to act in ways that are out of character. Reanne can do it, too. I'm immune. So is the Admiral, which is another reason we're big obstacles to her plans. She can't nudge us out of her way. But Magee is clearly susceptible. That's how she ended up at the Teeli Embassy working for Bare'Kold. The Admiral and I were captives of the Etah at Gallows Edge at the time, and the Teeli took advantage of our absence, using their abilities to convince her to join them."

"Do you have any proof of that?"

"Other than Magee's completely uncharacteristic decision to leave her post shortly after the Admiral had gone missing? And now testifying *against* me? No. But I've known Magee as long as I've known the Admiral. She loves him like a father, and she loved working with him. The fact that she's supporting these allegations tells me she's not thinking for herself anymore. The Sovereign and the Teeli are thinking for her."

"You said you and the Admiral are immune to the Teeli's influence. Why?"

"I'm not sure. We haven't figured out a common denominator yet. But it seems like they have to touch you to exert a strong influence. It either works or it doesn't."

"How do you know?"

"Because my friends observed Reanne's influence while we were at the Academy together. They didn't mention it at the time, accepting it as normal youthful angst, but recently we've been putting the pieces together. I also watched Sly'Kull try it on Kire when we were at the Teeli Embassy. He failed spectacularly, much to Kire's delight."

"Why were you at the Teeli Embassy?"

She gave Phoebe a rundown on the proposed Teeli mission to the binary star, the potential trap there, and Siginal's arrival to warn them of the Admiral's arrest. "The Sovereign used the mission to get us out of the way so she could move on the Admiral. If Siginal hadn't alerted us, we'd still be in Teeli space, oblivious to what was happening here."

"What about the Admiral's elite unit? Why weren't they protecting him?"

"Because he sent them with us as backup, like on Gaia, except this time we knew they were there Only one member of the team stayed behind, and she's the one who alerted Siginal when the Admiral was arrested."

"Are there any official records to corroborate the stated purpose of your mission to Teeli space?"

"The Admiral would have filed paperwork, but considering what we're seeing with the comm messages, my guess is those files are now either missing or altered."

Phoebe sighed. "You're not making it easy to mount a defense."

"I know." And there were plenty of secrets she hadn't shared with Phoebe that would make it even harder. "The Sovereign is very good at setting traps."

Sixty-Three

Jonarel stood as close to Lelindia as he could without actually touching her, watching Aurora's lawyer walk down the airbridge to the *Starhawke.*

Intellectually he knew Lt. Cmd. Liddell was on their side but having a stranger onboard the ship who wanted to talk to his mate — alone — shoved his protective instincts into overdrive.

His father, standing on Lelindia's other side, was no better. His expression was as welcoming as a greewtaith's.

Liddell eyed them both as she stepped onboard, her gaze shrewdly assessing. "Dr. Forrest, Ambassador Clarek, and Lt. Clarek, I presume?"

"You assume correctly." Lelindia smiled, cutting through the tension as she stepped forward to shake the woman's hand. "Thank you for making the trip, Lt. Cmd. Liddell."

"Aurora said you have physical evidence for me onboard. I wasn't about to miss the opportunity to see a Kraed ship up close. Or meet the crew Aurora holds in such high regard."

The ice thawed with a steady drip, drip, drip. His father held out his hand. "She is an extraordinary captain." The pompous note in his father's voice drew a sidelong look and bemused smile from Lelindia.

"And an even more extraordinary friend," Jonarel added, clasping Liddell's hand in his. She had a firm, confident grip, without any hint of the underlying fear he and his father often inspired in Humans. That earned her points as well.

"The crew's gathered in the observation lounge." Lelindia led the way toward the cargo lift, walking side by side with Liddell, leaving Jonarel and his father to follow behind.

Liddell turned to him after they stepped on the lift. "Aurora wanted me to assure you that she's fine." Her gaze included his father and Lelindia. "She knows you're upset that you can't visit her."

"Is there any way to change that order?" his father asked.

"Unlikely, but I'll review it, see if there are any loopholes we can—" She cut off as the lift doors opened, revealing the curving corridor leading to the observation lounge to their left. Liddell gazed at their surroundings with frank appreciation. "I'd heard that the Kraed favored curved designs over straight lines, but I had no idea that it applied to the interiors of your ships as well." She touched the knobby denglar bark façade of the bulkhead lightly with her fingertips. "Or that you'd have such an organic feel on a starship."

If she was trying to get on their good side, it was working. "We wish our ships to feel like home."

"That's the impression I got from Aurora, that this ship is her home."

"It is," he agreed.

"Then let's see what we can do to get her back here."

When the observation lounge doors parted, all eyes focused on Liddell. Brendan and Libra stepped forward first, followed by Micah, then Kire. Cardiff and Kelly hung back, acknowledging Liddell when Kire introduced them, but not moving from where they stood on the far side of the ovoid table. Only Marina and Gryphon were absent, since their presence might generate questions they'd rather not answer.

"So, how do you want to handle this?" Brendan asked as they all took seats around the table.

Liddell had chosen a chair between Brendan and Lelindia. "I thought I'd start by giving you an update. I'm sure you're eager for news."

Libra and Brendan nodded, while everyone else schooled their expressions, taking care not to reveal that they already had more news than Liddell could possibly imagine.

"I'm happy to answer what questions I can, though I can't share any details of Aurora's case. Then I'll need to interview Dr. Forrest and Lt. Cardiff individually, in private, since they're the two crewmembers who have relevant testimony."

"What *can* you tell us about Aurora's case?" Libra asked with an appropriate level of motherly concern.

"That trial counsel is focusing on events surrounding the Setarip attacks on Persei Primus and Gaia. They're attempting to prove that Aurora helped orchestrate those attacks, in conjunction with Admiral Schreiber, as a precursor to a military overthrow of the Union."

"That's ludicrous." Kire rested his forearms on the table, the gleam of battle in his eyes. "They're loyal Fleet officers. Neither of them would ever knowingly do anything to harm the Union."

Murmurs of assent passed around the table.

Jonarel watched Liddell, who was observing the crew's reaction to Kire's statement.

A tiny smile turned up the corner of her mouth. "I happen to agree, which is why I'm defending Aurora. But my job is to prove that to the Fleet panel. To do that, I need evidence and witness testimony that contradicts what trial counsel is presenting."

Lelindia reached into a pocket and pulled out a slender data storage device. She set it on the table in front of Liddell. "Those are the copies of Aurora's birthday files that you requested. Can you tell us why they're relevant?"

Liddell picked up the device and tucked it into the sleeve of her tablet. "Unfortunately, no, but they could be very helpful. Thank you."

"How's Roe doing?" Kire asked.

Liddell's brows rose at the unfamiliar nickname, but she did not falter. "She's doing better than I'd expect from someone in her situation. But I get the impression resilience is one of her strengths."

"Definitely," Lelindia and Brendan said at the same time.

"She asked me to tell you all that she misses you."

"We miss her, too." Kire's voice came out a little tight.

"But otherwise, she's healthy, in good spirits, and ready to fight this. One other thing." She focused on Kire. "Before I leave, I'd appreciate a few minutes of your time. I have some questions regarding the ICS and Aurora said you're the man to talk to."

Kire perked up. "Absolutely."

"Great." Her gaze shifted between Lelindia and Cardiff. "So, who wants to go first?"

Sixty-Four

"What's your current post on the *Starhawke*, Dr. Forrest?"

"Medical officer." Lelindia studied the woman seated across from her at the small table in the galley. She could understand why Brendan had chosen Liddell. She radiated intelligence and competence while remaining friendly and approachable. "And please, call me Lelindia."

"Lelindia." Liddell made a note on her tablet. "I've never heard that name before."

"It's a family name." Which was true insomuch as all her family members were named after Feylahn trees.

Liddell nodded. "Call me Phoebe." She looked back at her tablet. "How long have you held your current post?"

"Since last July."

"And what was your posting prior to accepting the position on the *Starhawke*?"

"I served as the Chief Medical Officer on the *Argo* for two years."

"Who was the first officer on the *Argo* during that time period?"

"Aurora. We transferred together from the *Excelsior*."

"How long after your transfer did the Ecilam Setarip attack on Persei Primus occur?"

"About two weeks." She got the feeling Phoebe already knew the answers and was checking to make sure what she said matched up.

"How did you first learn about the attack?"

"I was in the med bay when I got the call from Aurora. She informed me that Setarips had attacked Persei Primus. She requested that I assemble a team of my top medics. After the *Argo* arrived in the system, my team and I joined Aurora and the FS team on a shuttle to reach the station."

"Why didn't the *Argo* dock directly with the station?"

"The debris field from the battle with the Setarips prevented it. Even if it hadn't, we weren't receiving any response from the station. There was no way to coordinate docking a ship as large as the *Argo*. A shuttle was our only option."

"Were there any Setarip ships in the system at that time?"

"Not that we detected."

"And what did you find when you arrived on the station?"

"At first, nothing. None of the station personnel were visible from the airlock, so Aurora split us into four teams to search the station."

"Who was assigned to your team?"

"Aurora, Lt. Cardiff, and two of her security personnel. We headed down one of the main corridors toward the command center while the other teams secured the docks and investigated the RC freighter." The chill of that day crept over her.

"Did you see anyone in the corridors?"

"Not until we got word from one of the other teams that they'd encountered casualties. We abandoned our search and ran to the central hub. That's where we found most of the wounded."

"What types of injuries did they have?"

She suppressed a swell of anger as the images of their wounds flashed through her mind, accompanied by echoes of their pained groans and whimpers. The senseless brutality of the attack still dug at her, more so now that she knew the Sovereign had been behind it and used the stolen prototype to force the Suulh into their Necri existence. "All types. Burns, abrasions, broken bones, internal bleeding, nerve damage."

"Were these injuries consistent with what you'd expect from a Setarip attack against the station?"

"Yes."

"Were there any injuries that seemed unusual or out of place?"

She swallowed. "Just the way the Setarips and their leader died."

Phoebe's head came up. "Are you referring to the Setarips who had snuck onto the station by impersonating RC personnel?"

"And the human male who led them, yes."

"So you saw them personally?"

"Yes."

"When?"

"My team and I had been in the hub, working to stabilize the station's casualties, when one of the teams searching the docks reported they'd encountered Setarips. Fighting broke out between them. The Setarips were trying to reach the RC freighter docked on the concourse. Aurora and Celia took off to help, but I stayed with the casualties. A couple minutes later I received a report that we had team members down. I left three of my medics in charge of the hub and took the other three with me. By the time we got there the Setarips had been subdued. They were lying on the ground with various debilitating injuries. The FS officers were securing them and their leader, a human male in his late thirties or early forties."

"Who was he?"

"I never found out his name. But he was screaming obscenities at the FS officers when I arrived. I rushed to help two of our team members who had been badly injured. Then I heard a shout from one of my nurses. When I looked up, I realized the leader's litany of abuse had stopped and he'd slumped to the ground. All the Setarips were prone, too. They'd died instantly."

"And you weren't able to revive them?"

"No. A subcutaneous device had injected a toxin I'd never encountered before. It destroyed their nervous systems and brain stems in seconds. We were *right there*, and there was nothing we could do." That failure haunted her even more now than it had then.

If she'd been able to save their leader and question him, they might have been able to prevent all the destruction the Sovereign had wrought since.

"Where was Aurora at that moment?"

"She and Celia were in the airbridge to the RC freighter, trying to stop the rest of the Setarips and the female human collaborator from leaving."

"How long were they in the airbridge?"

"I saw them run in right as we arrived. I didn't check the time, but I think they were gone two or three minutes."

"Did the injections trigger before they returned?"

"Yes."

"So you didn't have eyes on Aurora at the time the injections went off?"

"No."

Phoebe sat back, her posture more relaxed. "How would you describe your relationship with Aurora?"

"She's like a sister to me."

"How long have you known each other?"

"All her life. Her mother and my parents have lived in the same house together since before I was born."

"So your families are close?"

"Very."

"Would you say you know Aurora well?"

"Better than anyone."

"How would you describe her character?"

"She's a protector at her core. Helping and defending others from danger is her first instinct. It's why she wanted to join the Fleet and why she's such an excellent commanding officer. Her dedication to serving others and her willingness to put herself on the front lines has earned her the respect and loyalty of her crew on every ship we've served on together."

"Why did you choose to leave the Fleet's flagship when she asked you to serve on the *Starhawke*? For a lot of Fleet personnel, serving on a smaller privately owned ship might seem like a step down."

Lelindia lifted her brows. "You're on the *Starhawke*. Do you think anyone who's been on it would think serving on this ship was a step down?"

Phoebe's lips twitched. "Point taken."

"Although that's not why I said yes. I wanted to see Aurora in her first command, to work closely with her every day. This ship and this crew was a dream come true for both of us."

"How long have you known the other crewmembers?"

"Aurora and I befriended Jonarel and Kire at the Academy, and Celia after we joined the *Argo*'s crew. Kelly, our pilot, is our newest crewmember. She came onboard right after we reached Gaia on our first mission."

"And Lt. Clarek designed and oversaw the construction of the *Starhawke*?"

"That's correct."

"So he owns it?"

"No. Aurora does. He gave it to her."

"He gave it to her?" Phoebe stared, clearly baffled. "Why would he do that?"

Answering this question had become considerably easier in the past couple months. "At the time, he and his father expected he'd pair bond with Aurora. Things didn't work out that way, but the ship's still staying in the family, so to speak. Jonarel and I pair bonded in January."

"I was wondering." Phoebe bobbed her head. "Congratulations. The vibe I got from the Clareks when I came onboard was very protective of you."

Lelindia smiled. "Protective is their defining characteristic."

Phoebe laughed. "Noted. Okay, so is the *Starhawke* considered part of the Kraed fleet?"

"Officially, we're an independent science and exploration vessel. We're not strictly a Kraed or Galactic Fleet vessel. That gives us flexibility, which is one of the reasons the Galactic Council liked the idea of having us as an adjunct. We can be available to whoever needs us most."

"And who determines where you're needed?"

"We accept missions from both the Galactic Council and the Fleet."

"Who do you report to?"

"Admiral Schreiber."

Phoebe's mouth thinned, her amusement drying up. "Let's talk about your mission to Gaia. What orders were you given?"

"We were asked to investigate severe and unexplainable crop destruction that was threatening the long-term viability of the planet."

"And who gave you those orders?"

"We were briefed by Admiral Schreiber, but the order came from the Galactic Council."

"And why was your ship given that mission?"

"We were uniquely qualified to handle it. I have an extensive background in botany, as does Celia. We also have Kraed technology at our disposal, something no Fleet ship could provide."

"What did your investigation reveal?"

"The crop destruction was being carried out by a group of Etah Setarips."

"How did you figure that out?"

"It took a while. When we engaged them on the planet, they were all dressed in mesh full-body suits that concealed their features. But we were able to unmask the ones who died during the fighting. All of them were Etah."

"Were you able to capture any Setarips for questioning?"

"No, unfortunately. Our crew disabled the Setarip ship's engines, but the remaining Setarips attempted to flee in shuttles.

After exiting the ship, the shuttles exploded, we suspect from auto-destruct devices."

"Why do you suspect auto-destructs?"

"Because we encountered a similar device on the Setarip ship. Aurora was able to neutralize it, or it would have killed everyone onboard."

Phoebe's eyes widened. "Does she have explosives training?"

Tip-toe, tip-toe. "She has knowledge in a lot of different areas. She took the risk of disarming it because if she didn't, it was going to detonate."

"But the ship did explode later?"

"Yes. Four Fleet officers were flying the ship back to Earth to be studied, but they never made it out of Gaia's atmosphere."

"Another auto-destruct?"

"Yes, although this one was planted by rogue Rescue Corps personnel."

"You're referring to the two RC officers mentioned in the official report, the ones who attempted to kidnap Director Beck and died on the scene?"

"Yes."

"And where was Aurora when that occurred?"

"On the island where we'd taken the Setarip ship after we captured it. We'd set up a temporary base of operations there while we waited for the *Argo* to arrive."

"And the *Argo* crew oversaw the investigation into the actions of the Rescue Corps personnel and the destruction of the Setarip ship?"

"That's correct."

"Where did you go after you left Gaia?"

"To Kraed space. The *Starhawke* had taken heavy fire during the confrontation with the Setarips. A trip to Drakar seemed prudent before we accepted any new missions. Fleet shipyards aren't equipped to repair Kraed vessels."

Phoebe gave her a long look.

She knew what Phoebe wasn't asking. Phoebe knew about the Suulh. Aurora had told her. But Aurora had also made it clear the Suulh could not be brought in to testify.

Lelindia wholeheartedly agreed. Not because the Suulh would object. Raaveen and Paaw would do it in a heartbeat. Zelle and Ren, too. But it would expose them to the Sovereign's machinations and destroy the safety net currently surrounding Azaana.

Besides, they couldn't provide any credible evidence. Their physical injuries had all been healed. The only way they could disrupt the Sovereign's sedition narrative would be to give a demonstration of their abilities to the court. That was a bridge Aurora would never allow them to cross.

"Can you think of any witnesses who could help Aurora's case?"

She chewed on her lip. "Siginal could be a character witness. He was Aurora's mentor at the Academy."

"He's credible, but we need people who can give evidence, not opinions."

And that was the rub. She could name a hundred Fleet personnel she and Aurora knew who would swear Aurora was innocent, but none who could provide evidence to prove it.

Including Admiral Payne.

Kire had received a message that morning from Payne asking about the status of Admiral Schreiber's trial and offering to come out of hiding to testify.

Unfortunately, Payne hadn't played any part in Persei Primus or Gaia. She hadn't been caught by the expanding wave of destruction until after the events at Gaia were over. Her testimony would be irrelevant.

The lack of evidence had always been their sticking point, starting with Gaia and continuing through their recent mission to Teeli space. Now it had become the Achilles heel of Aurora's defense.

Which left them chasing their tails while the Sovereign wove a tapestry of lies that smothered the truth.

Sixty-Five

"Well, that was fun."

Micah's shoulders relaxed at the dry humor in Celia's voice. She'd been in the galley with Liddell for more than an hour. Not that he'd been checking the clock. Much.

Celia watched Aurora's lawyer leave the observation lounge with Kire, their heads bent in quiet conversation. "Not as brutal as I'd feared, but still a challenge. I think she suspected I knew more about Aurora's and the Admiral's cases than I should, but she didn't ask and I didn't say."

"What *did* she ask about?"

"Mostly the Setarip attacks on Persei Primus and Gaia. Of course I dodged any reference to the Suulh. Liddell's reactions indicated she's aware of them, but again, she didn't push."

"Probably doesn't want them mentioned on any official record."

"Exactly. She and I don't have attorney-client privilege." Celia stretched her arms toward the ceiling, her spine popping. "Ah, that's better." The stretch also emphasized every curve in her body.

Micah focused on the door to the galley like it held the secrets of the universe, willing his body *not* to react the way it wanted to. "You up for cooking? I think my dad and Gryphon already slipped into the galley."

"Now that *does* sound like fun." She flashed one of the smiles that turned his bones to rubber. As usual, she didn't notice his impairment. "Star, do you and Unity have the recording of the Admiral's trial feed we missed during Liddell's visit?"

"Yes, Celia," Star replied. "It will be ready for you to review after Liddell has left the ship."

"Great, thanks. Unity, please let Aurora know Lelindia and I have both met with her lawyer, and currently Liddell's talking to Kire about the ICS."

"Will do," Unity replied.

Celia turned toward the galley door while Micah followed behind her like a balloon on a string. She glanced over her shoulder. "You know, I've gotten used to the two of you using the same voice. Although it's not exactly the same. Unity's delivery and inflections are different. If I closed my eyes, I'd still be able to tell which of you was speaking."

Now why did that comment make his chest warm like honey on a summer's day? "Prove it. I dare you," he teased to keep from blurting out something far more damning as she strode into the galley.

She laughed, but her pupils widened like a cat preparing to pounce on a mouse. "I think I will."

"Dare her to what?" Gryphon asked, deftly dicing up an onion half and dumping it in a bowl.

Celia produced hair ties from one of the mysterious pockets she always seemed to have in every garment she wore and wrapped her hair into two topknots. "I'm going to prove I can tell the difference between Micah and Unity when they're speaking. Micah doesn't think I can."

"Oh, really?" The look Gryphon shot Micah's dad carried more meaning than Micah would have liked, but Celia didn't react. "To make it official, you'll need a moderator. I'll do it."

Celia snagged an apron and slid it over her head. "Works for me. We can't trust Brendan to be impartial."

"Hey!" His dad shot her a mock glare.

She widened her eyes in exaggerated innocence. "He's your son."

"And I'm a licensed therapist. Impartiality is part of my job."

Celia pointed a finger at him. "Another strike against you. You're trained *not* to judge."

Micah chuckled, earning him a wink from Celia.

His dad sent him an imploring look. "Back me up here."

He held up his hands. "Uh-uh. No way am I going to be accused of favoritism. Gryphon gets to officiate."

"Then maybe I'll rethink that batch of brownies I was going to make."

"You wouldn't."

"I would."

"Then I'll make them," Gryphon practically crowed. "I'm the one who taught you the recipe, after all."

His dad pressed a hand to his sternum. "And this, the most unkindest cut of all."

Silence fell for two seconds, and then they all burst out laughing.

"I assume everyone else will be allowed to view this battle royal?" Gryphon asked.

"Absolutely," Celia agreed. "I want plenty of witnesses to my victory over the sadly deluded Micah."

He grumbled in protest at her boast, but internally he was throwing a party. If she was that confident about her abilities, she was paying *very* close attention to him, way more than she even realized.

He'd still do his best to confound her during the competition, but he'd already achieved his real victory.

She'd just given him a glimmer of hope that their friendship might be ever so slowly evolving into something more.

Sixty-Six

Cade stumbled out of the Yruf lift on legs that barely supported him. Exhaustion dragged at every cell in his body and his head felt like his brain had been sucked out and replaced with dandelion fluff.

He hardly noticed the curious looks from the Yruf relaxing in the park area as he made his way to his cabin, Unity by his side.

Unity must have figured out he was mentally compromised because the door opened before his hand reached toward the controls.

Lead weights pulled at his feet with each step to the bedroom. As soon as the curved surface of his bed parted under his touch, he sank to the mattress without bothering to take off his boots.

His eyes drifted closed, but his mind spun with the imagery Ifel had coaxed from him during their session.

She was a compassionate but persistent teacher, pushing him at every turn, refusing to allow him to back away from the challenges she presented. Facing the traumas of his early childhood hurt like hell, and he'd shed more tears in the past few days than in his entire adult life.

But it was worth it.

Because it was working.

Today he'd caught snippets in his mind of Galish words and phrases spoken in a voice he recognized as Ifel's even though it lacked the sibilant accent he associated with her.

And judging by her emotional reactions, she'd been getting some words from him, too.

The concept still freaked him out a bit, the idea that two beings without a common language could somehow communicate mentally across those barriers. Ironically, it hadn't bothered him when Aurora and Ifel did it, but they both had experience communicating with their own people in a similar way. He didn't. This was much, much stranger, and much harder for the part of him that still yearned for his father's respect and approval – as ludicrous as he knew that to be – to accept.

Which is why he and Ifel spent so much time examining his formative years and reframing the trauma his parents had inflicted.

It helped that he got a maternal vibe from Ifel. He had no idea how old she was, but considering her brother had a grown daughter, she was probably at least as old as his parents.

His own mother had never defended him, never protected him – not when he was a child and not since he'd become an adult. He hadn't realized how much he'd come to expect that lack of support until Ifel was there, sharing his memories. She'd made it clear that the abuse he'd endured didn't have to define him, that the lessons his father had beaten into him could be unlearned, and a new path charted.

He'd had no idea how badly he'd needed to hear that, feel that, accept that. Physically he might be an immovable jumble of bones right now, but emotionally, he'd never been more at peace with himself.

The one part of his body that didn't require any effort to function – his ears – tuned into a wistful melody being sung in a lovely soprano.

His eyes popped open. *Aurora.*

It spoke to the depth of his exhaustion that he hadn't even glanced at the bulkhead to check on her when he'd staggered into the room.

He turned his head without lifting it from the mattress, looking through the gap in the curving shell of his bed to the projection of Aurora's cell.

She was seated on her cot, angled toward him, her legs tucked into what he was pretty sure was called a lotus pose, her wrists resting on her knees. Her eyelids were at half-mast, her lips tenderly shaping each word of her song.

He didn't recognize the melody, but the lyrics captivated him. She sang of the moon, the stars, the ocean, of being lost, of not being together, but always moving, looking for answers.

Moisture rolled over the bridge of his nose and dripped onto the mattress. Whether they were tears of exhaustion or tears of appreciation for the beauty of her song, he let them flow without resistance.

When the last note faded, she sighed, her gaze unwavering, as though she could see him as clearly as he could see her.

"That…" The word came out guttural and incomprehensible. He shifted on the mattress and cleared his throat. "That was beautiful."

She blinked slowly in acknowledgment, but it was her emotional field that surrounded him like a cozy blanket.

Nice. "I just got back from a session with Ifel. I'm a little tired." Yeah, like Mt. Everest is a little hill.

Sleep.

"What?" His head jerked off the mattress, making his neck crack, though he barely heard it as his heart revved up like a racecar. "Did you just project something to me?"

Her brows drew down, and her index finger and middle finger spread apart.

"Maybe?" What did that mean? He peered at her. "Were you thinking something after I told you I was tired?"

Her index finger twitched once.

"You were. Okay." He licked his suddenly dry lips. "Try thinking it again like you're saying it directly to me."

Her frown disappeared, replaced with a look of concentration.

You. Sleep.

His exhaustion got kicked out of the room by a rush of adrenaline. He lurched to his feet. "I heard the words *you* and *sleep.*"

Her eyes widened for a split second before she brought them back to half-mast.

"You were thinking something that had those two words in it, weren't you?"

Her finger twitched once at the same time he heard another word.

Yes.

Forget the racecar. His heart was in a cage match with his ribs. "I heard you. I *heard* you!"

The excitement in her emotional field spiraled with his, almost lifting him off his feet.

"Okay, I'm going to try projecting to you." He took a deep breath because his lungs needed more air. *You make my heart sing.* Corny, but it was all his brain could come up with on short notice.

Her eyes widened for a split-second.

"You heard something, didn't you?"

One finger twitched.

"I projected five words. Tap your finger to let me know how many you heard."

One, two, three taps.

"I projected *you make my heart sing.* Does that match up with what you heard?"

Yes.

And he'd just heard her again.

He probably looked like a lunatic with the goofy grin on his face, but only Unity could see him. Meanwhile Aurora looked cool as a comet, although her emotions were just as heightened as his.

He blamed his exhaustion for what popped out of his mouth next. "You do realize we're going to have to name our firstborn after Ifel, right?"

Aurora didn't control her reaction this time. Her anxiety punched him as her eyes rounded into twin moons and her mouth sagged open.

She snapped it shut, her emotional resonance cutting off like a slammed door.

He winced, smacking the side of his head with the heel of his hand. *Way to go, Ellis.* What a stupid, stupid thing to say, especially right now. As if she didn't have enough on her mind. Now he'd unwittingly struck a nerve. "I'm sorry, Rory. That was meant to be a joke. Did I mention I'm very tired?"

Her chest rose and fell rapidly. Frustration leaked through their connection, and a dollop of anger.

He sat on the edge of the bed and buried his head in his hands. "Forget I said anything." He should shut up and get some sleep before he made this situation even worse. "Why don't I have Unity—"

Maybe middle.

He lifted his head. "What?"

Amusement nudged aside her frustration, a hint of a smile curving her mouth.

Middle name.

"Middle name?" he parroted.

One brow rose, her green eyes sparkling with mischief.

"Middle name," he said again. It took his beleaguered brain a few beats to catch on. Then he got it. Or hoped he did. "Are you saying we could use Ifel as our firstborn's middle name?"

Aurora's mouth curved a little more, and her index finger tapped once.

Yes.

Despite the humor in her emotional field, she wasn't kidding. She was giving him a serious answer to his bumbling, badly-timed, off-hand question.

The enormity of that answer rendered him speechless.

A lump the size of a small moon filled his throat, bringing a new trickle of tears with it. "I—" He couldn't get another syllable out. His heart was too full and his body too drained. So he projected what he wanted to say instead, praying she'd hear him. *I love you.*

She heard him. He knew by the sheen coating her eyes, turning them into mirror pools. She blinked rapidly, but her emotional response came through even more clearly than her words.

Love you.

He closed his eyes, holding this moment in his heart.

He was living on an alien starship. She was trapped in a Fleet detention center. And the woman who wanted to destroy everything they held dear was out there, stalking them.

But right now, none of that mattered. As he opened his eyes and gazed at Aurora, a sense of determination settled over him.

The Sovereign wouldn't win. No matter what challenges she threw in their path, he would move the moon and stars to bring Aurora back to his side. And together, they would fight for their future.

Sixty-Seven

"You've got to be kidding," Micah said.

"You've got to be kidding," Unity repeated.

Jonarel glanced at Gryphon and Brendan, seated beside him, while they awaited Celia's response.

He could not see Celia, or any of the members of the audience, including his mate. After Lelindia and Marina had heard about Micah and Celia's competition, they had decided they wanted to play along. So had Libra, Kire, and Kelly. Tehar had erected a denglar bark screen in the observation lounge to shield Micah and Unity from view. Celia was the main participant, but everyone else was submitting their guesses, and would receive a score at the end.

As the officiant, Gryphon was keeping Celia's tally, while Brendan was marking the correct answer to each pairing.

Since Jonarel could easily tell the difference between Micah and Unity based on the sound vibrations they produced – a benefit of his Kraed hearing and a lifetime interacting with Nirunocs – he had chosen to join Gryphon and Brendan on the shielded side of the screen to watch the proceedings. He did not want his body language to unfairly tip the scales in Celia's favor. She was far too adept at reading unconscious cues.

"Micah spoke first," Celia declared.

For reasons Jonarel could not fathom, Micah grinned like Celia had given the wrong answer. In fact, he had been grinning almost non-stop since answer number twelve.

Gryphon added another mark to Celia's tally. Forty-seven correct answers out of forty-nine tests. Impressive. Apparently Jonarel's concern about giving her an advantage was irrelevant. She was doing fine on her own.

One more before the competition ended.

"Pair number fifty," Gryphon announced.

Micah sank down on his haunches as Unity glided over to hover where Micah's head had been.

"That's a wrap!" Unity said, then scooted to the side.

Micah stood, sliding his hands into the pockets of his jeans and rocking back on his heels. "That's a wrap!" he repeated.

A hush fell over the room for a three count.

"Micah spoke second."

The bright smile that lit Micah's face was in direct contrast to his extremely lopsided loss.

A shadow of concern flitted briefly over Brendan's face as he studied Micah, but it did not linger.

"We have the results," Gryphon announced as he stood. Brendan and Jonarel joined him as Tehar lowered the screen into the deck.

Celia pivoted to face them, confidence in every line of her body.

"With a final score of forty-eight to two, the overwhelming winner is..."

Celia's gaze flicked to Micah, a smug smile already curling her lips.

"Celia!"

Applause and cheers broke out. Lelindia whooped the loudest, and Kire generated a piercing extended whistle through his teeth.

Micah laughed at their enthusiasm. Walking over to Celia, he stuck out his hand. "Congratulations. I guess you really can tell us apart."

She accepted his handshake, using her grip to pull him closer. "I could have made it fifty to zero," she murmured quietly enough that only Jonarel could overhear them. "But I didn't want to embarrass you."

The gleam that lit Micah's eyes did not look like embarrassment. "I'll keep that in mind."

Brendan lifted his tablet in the air. "Star checked the rest of the scoresheets. The person who had the most correct answers after Celia was Libra, with thirty-seven."

"I should hope so," Libra harrumphed. "I'm his mom."

Micah released Celia's hand and pulled Libra into a hug. "Lucky, lucky me."

"Kire was next with thirty-two." Brendan said. "Lelindia and Bronwyn tied at twenty-three, and Marina had nineteen."

Marina laughed, shaking her head. "This is why I'm a healer, not a linguist."

"And the galaxy is better for it," Gryphon proclaimed to the entire room.

Lelindia slipped past her parents, moving to Jonarel's side. He tucked her against him, breathing in her delightful scent.

"That was fun," she murmured, resting her head against his shoulder.

"I am glad." His mate had needed a distraction after Liddell's visit. Everyone had. Only his father had bowed out, the competition holding no more challenge for him than for Jonarel. They had agreed to wait until the early morning to watch the remainder of the day's testimony from the Admiral's trial.

Lelindia met his gaze. "You really can hear a difference between the two of them all the time?"

He stroked a finger down her cheek. "You can tell the difference between two nearly identical plants."

Her lips softened in a smile, but her gaze warmed at his touch. She dropped her voice to a whisper. "How about we head to our cabin?"

Heat spread through his body like wildfire, his vision arrested by the sultry look in his mate's eyes. Clasping her hand, he pulled her toward the galley entrance, the shortest route to the personnel lift.

"Goodnight, everyone!" Lelindia called out with a laugh.

Chuckles followed her announcement, but Jonarel did not pause. As soon as they were through the galley and in the corridor, he swept her off her feet, cradling her to his chest.

Her lips pressed against his neck and along his jaw, drawing a rumble of pleasure as he stepped onto the lift. But when she nibbled on his earlobe and scraped his skin lightly with her nails, he almost sank to his knees.

By the time he carried her into their cabin, her ministrations had heated his skin to the boiling point. The fire in her eyes and the swipe of her tongue when she kissed him stripped away his remaining restraint.

They tumbled to the bed, his body caging her in as he rocked against her. Her answering moan unraveled him. "My checana." He pulled at her clothing as frantically as she pulled at his.

Their joining lit up his nerve endings, suffusing him with pleasure as her energy field caressed every millimeter of his skin. Her cries blended with his, her nails digging into his back, the room exploding with joy. *Yes!*

He caught himself as his body surrendered, rolling her on top of him to keep from crushing her. She quaked with aftershocks, her skin slick with sweat, her dark hair covering her face.

His checana. More precious than the air they breathed.

"That was... perfect." Lifting her head, she pushed her hair back with one hand, then propped her chin on her fist. "How do you always know exactly what I need?"

He smiled, his hand cupping the curve of her hip. "You are very clear about what you desire."

"Am I?"

"Yes."

"Mmm." Her contented hum vibrated against his chest. She traced his mouth with her fingertips. "I desire you. Always."

The joy her words inspired filled his heart to the point of pain. "I am yours. Always." Capturing her finger between his teeth, he licked and nibbled, bathing in the intoxicating depths of her eyes.

"Always," she repeated, her brows puckering, her rosy glow fading.

"You are thinking of Aurora?" He already knew the answer. He had watched this transformation overtake her many times in the past few days.

Lelindia sighed. "Sorry."

He twined his fingers through her hair, stroking the smooth strands. "Do not apologize. I understand."

"I know." Pressing onto her forearms, she brushed her lips over his before snuggling into the crook of his neck. "It's just... Liddell's visit made Aurora's trial more real somehow. I'm worried that..." Her voice hitched, tugging on his heart. "That she won't be here for Raehn's birth."

An ache radiated through his torso. "I share that fear." He had never witnessed a Suulh birth, but based on his knowledge of his mate's culture, their daughter's birth would be celebrated with fanfare, just as it would be in his culture. As it was, his mate was holding off announcing their daughter's name to the crew and the clan. He cherished the name she had chosen, a perfect pairing of their two cultures, but he understood why she wanted Aurora with her before sharing it. Aurora *needed* to be present to greet their daughter as she joined this world. Any other outcome was unacceptable.

"We will find a way," he promised her.

She blew out a breath, lifting her head to meet his gaze. The gritty determination in her eyes struck an answering chord in his heart. "Whatever it takes?"

He slid his hand behind her head, his claws lightly pressing into her scalp. "Whatever it takes."

Sixty-Eight

"Lt. Magee, what is your relationship to Admiral William Schreiber?"

Until the trial counsel asked the first question, Aurora hadn't been certain the unbalanced emotions she'd detected in the Admiral's courtroom belonged to Magee. The familiar tones of Magee's voice in her ear through Unity's feed clashed with the emotional resonance Aurora sensed from her.

"I was his PA for thirteen years."

Brittle fear crackled like kindling beneath a cauldron of bubbling rage in Magee's emotional field. She'd never associated either emotion with Magee.

But fear and rage were the Sovereign's stock in trade. Somehow she'd embedded them in Magee's psyche like a festering wound.

Aurora shuddered. Reaching to the shelving unit beside her cot, she pulled out the scratchy blanket and draped it over her legs, tucking her hands under the folds.

"Are you his PA currently?"

"No."

"When did your posting with him end?"

"Last October."

"Did you accept another job at that time?"

"Yes. I took a position as Delegate Bare'Kold's assistant at the Teeli Embassy."

"Did you terminate your contract with Admiral Schreiber or did he?"

"I did."

"Why did you terminate your contract?"

The rage popped and spurted in Magee's field like a smoking volcano. "I felt my safety and physical health were in jeopardy continuing to serve with him."

What? She hadn't expected that.

"Are you currently working at the Teeli Embassy?"

"Not directly. Delegate Bare'Kold offered me a position on Ways'lend, the Teeli homeworld. I've been serving there since late December."

"When did you return to Earth?"

"Two weeks ago."

"After you returned to Earth, did you undergo a medical exam?"

"Yes."

A medical exam? Where was trial counsel going with this line of questioning?

"Who requested that you receive a medical evaluation?"

"Teeli Delegate Sly'Kull."

"Do you know why he made this request?"

"Yes. Last year I had been subjected to repeated low-voltage electrocution as a form of torture. As a result, I've been suffering from visual impairment, joint stiffness, numbness, and severe migraines."

Aurora's stomach twisted, a sense of foreboding rearing its head. The symptoms she was describing were an apt description of the damage Kreestol could have inflicted if she attacked Magee with her energy field.

"Lt. Magee, who tortured you?"

"Captain Aurora Hawke."

The lie hit Aurora like a dagger to the gut, the pain bright and startling. She quickly shuttered her expression, but the wound continued to bleed. Magee's emotional field made it clear she believed she was telling the truth. Her certainty twisted the blade.

"When did this occur?"

"July and early August of last year, after Captain Hawke resigned from the *Argo* and returned to Earth to become captain of the *Starhawke*."

Aurora's toes curled under the blanket. She had seen Magee repeatedly during that timeframe. But her memories involved friendly chats in the Admiral's office and sharing drinks in a local bar while she and Jonarel filled Magee and the Admiral in on the progress they'd made getting the *Starhawke* mission ready.

"How specifically did she torture you?"

"She shocked me. I don't know what type of device she used. But it hurt. A lot. Like being trapped against an electrified fence."

Aurora squeezed her eyes shut, willing away the mental images that assailed her. Magee's remembered pain vibrated through her, difficult to block out.

Magee had clearly been assaulted, her mind reprogrammed. Had Kreestol been a stand-in for Aurora during those sessions? Had the Sovereign convinced her Kreestol *was* Aurora to make the lie the Sovereign was creating more convincing and believable to Magee's subconscious? Aurora's resemblance to her aunt was strong. In a weakened and terrorized state, Magee's mind might have made the leap to stop the pain.

"Why would Captain Hawke torture you?"

"Admiral Schreiber told her to. She was his right hand, his enforcer and liaison. The torture continued until I did what Admiral Schreiber wanted." Magee's voice scraped through Unity's connection, the impotent rage of an adult combined with the whisper of an innocent terrorized by the monsters lurking in the shadows.

"What did Admiral Schreiber want you to do?"

"Falsify reports, reroute messages, conceal his movements from the Fleet and Council, especially those involving the Kraed."

Aurora's teeth clicked as her jaw tightened. The best lies were those based in truth. The Admiral had asked Magee to do some of those things during his search to obtain proof of the Teeli's duplicity. But his actions and Magee's had always been within the bounds of Union law.

Now the judge's pre-testimony announcement to the panel that Magee was testifying in exchange for immunity made perfect sense. In the Sovereign's version of events, Magee was admitting her guilt to several Union felonies.

"Did Admiral Schreiber tell you why he wanted you to take those actions?"

"He told me he planned to overthrow the Union and militarize the Fleet."

Aurora's stomach curdled.

"Did he specify how?"

"He'd begun collaborating with the Setarips." Bitterness shoved aside Magee's rage and fear. "He wanted to prove to the GC and General Assembly that the Setarips could cause planet-scale destruction. If he could convince everyone that the Setarip threat was growing exponentially, inciting fear and panic in the populace, he could push forward his agenda to militarize the Fleet."

The Admiral's emotional resonance turned to granite. She'd never sensed that from him before – complete emotional immobility. But at the moment, he was suppressing emotional distress the size of Jupiter.

She wasn't far behind.

"How would a militarized Fleet benefit him?"

"As Fleet Director, it would give him the right to usurp the Federal Coalition's enforcement authority. Every planet, station, or colony in Fleet space would no longer be under Federal jurisdiction, they'd be under Fleet jurisdiction. His jurisdiction."

The plan Magee was outlining was ludicrous to anyone who knew how honorable and humble a man the Admiral was. Or how strongly he believed in the Union's guiding principles.

One of the reasons the governing body that later became the Union had decided *not* to militarize the Fleet was to prevent the potential for overreaching domination. By putting law enforcement throughout Fleet space in the hands of the Federal Coalition instead of the Fleet, the Fleet remained a mostly exploratory branch. The Fleet's charter stated that Fleet ships and personnel could only use their weapons for defense, never for attack.

Unfortunately, if the panel believed the Admiral was a power-hungry despot, Magee's tale switched from ludicrous to plausible. Judging by the emotional resonances near Magee, she was successfully tapping into the panel's base emotions, unlocking fears and sparking outrage.

"Was that his only goal?"

"No. He was also working to convince the Kraed to make a joint invasion of Teeli space."

"Why would Admiral Schreiber want to invade Teeli space?"

"To expand his dominion, subjugate the Teeli, and strip them of their resources."

Aurora fought to keep from reacting. If the Sovereign had reason to suspect she was hearing any of this, she'd have even bigger problems. But Magee's words were so, so, so much worse than she'd anticipated.

"When you decided to terminate your contract with Admiral Schreiber, were you concerned about the danger for retaliation that would pose?"

Magee drew in an audible breath. "Yes. I had to wait for the right moment. When it came, I grabbed it. Admiral Schreiber and Captain Hawke both left the system for a couple weeks. I decided my best hope for an ally were the Teeli. I went to see Delegate Bare'Kold at the Teeli Embassy. I didn't know if he'd even see me, let alone believe me. But I took what proof I had and told him the whole story. Thankfully, he did believe me."

"Is that when he offered you a position as his PA?"

"Yes. I was safe at the Embassy. Admiral Schreiber had no authority there. And Delegate Bare'Kold promised to get me off planet and to Teeli space as soon as he could arrange it."

"Did you see Admiral Schreiber or Captain Hawke after that?"

Magee's voice hardened. "I saw the Admiral. He came to the Embassy."

"Did he come to see you?"

"Not according to him. But I made sure he saw me. I wanted him to know I wasn't afraid of him anymore. I knew the security personnel Bare'Kold had hired would make sure he couldn't hurt me."

"What reason did Admiral Schreiber give for coming to the Embassy?"

"He was pushing for a Fleet scientific mission in Teeli space. He asked the Teeli to allow the *Starhawke* to study a binary star system near the border. But because of what I'd told Bare'Kold, he understood the dangers. I'd warned him about the *Starhawke's* camouflage ability, and that Captain Hawke wanted to gather intel on the Teeli that they could use to plan their invasion."

Aurora barely held in a screech. Magee's description of events neatly flipped the facts to implicate the Admiral as the mastermind of a takeover plot and cast Magee and the Teeli as the valiant resistance.

"How did Delegate Bare'Kold respond to Admiral Schreiber's request regarding the *Starhawke's* proposed scientific mission?"

"He told them he'd contact his superiors on Ways'lend. That enabled him to put them off for a couple weeks, long enough for him to escort me on his yacht to meet up with a Teeli transport that took me back to Ways'lend. I didn't expect to return to Earth. But when the Admiral was arrested and charged with sedition, I agreed to testify. I had to make sure justice was served."

Aurora's pain ignited into fury. The Sovereign's twisted fingerprints were all over Magee, warping her mind, making her see enemies in her friends, and friends in her enemies.

Just as the Sovereign had done to Kreestol.

As she would do to anyone she could bend to her will.

"Lt. Magee, when did you first meet Captain Hawke?"

Aurora tensed. What harrowing road was this new line of questioning taking them on?

"The year I became Admiral Schreiber's PA. Ambassador Siginal Clarek had joined the faculty of the Academy that summer, and the Admiral wanted to introduce me to him. I also met several of the cadets, including the Ambassador's son, Lt. Jonarel Clarek, Captain Hawke, and Dr. Mya Forrest."

"Is that Dr. Lelindia Forrest, former Chief Medical Officer of the *Argo?*"

"Yes. Mya's the name she goes by."

Used to go by. But Magee wouldn't know that.

"Did Admiral Schreiber or Ambassador Clarek show any particular interest in Captain Hawke at that time?"

"Definitely. They both seemed quite impressed with her academic achievements. It was after that meeting that the Admiral began corresponding regularly with Captain Hawke, taking an active interest in her progress at the Academy."

"How old was Captain Hawke at that time?"

"Sixteen, I think."

"Did you see any of their correspondence?"

"Not directly, although the Admiral would often tell me what she was up to. He was clearly very proud of her, treating her like the daughter he never had."

The Admiral had felt that way about Magee, too. As painful as Magee's testimony was for her to hear, she could feel the soul-scraping agony it inflicted on the Admiral, his pain seeping through the granite façade he was struggling to maintain.

"Did Admiral Schreiber's interest in Captain Hawke's achievements strike you as strange?"

"Not at the time. The Admiral's wife had died four years before I met him, and his son Knox was already serving in the Fleet."

The judge interrupted her. ""The witness is reminded that during testimony proper Fleet decorum will be observed and commissioned Fleet officers will be addressed by their proper rank and name."

"Sorry, Your Honor." Magee's voice caught and stuttered. "C-Captain Schreiber was already serving in the Fleet. The Admiral didn't have a personal life to speak of. His work with the Fleet was everything to him. Scouting out talented future officers gave him a break from the challenges inherent in his job as a Fleet Admiral."

For the first time, Aurora sensed emotional dissonance from Magee. Talking about her early days with the Admiral had brought up healthy, positive emotions. Apparently the Sovereign hadn't delved that far back into Magee's past, hadn't overwritten those memories. Now they were conflicting with the contrived toxic timeline the Sovereign had created for her to regurgitate.

"Admiral Schreiber wasn't the Galactic Fleet Director at that time?"

"No. He accepted that promotion the following summer."

"Did his attitudes change after he became the Director?"

The positive feelings from Magee washed away in a wave of vitriol that seared through her like fire. "Yes."

So that's where the Sovereign started her reprogramming, with the Admiral taking over as head of the Fleet.

"How did his attitudes change?"

"It was subtle in the beginning. But in recent years he insisted I spend more and more time with him. He monitored my movements, wanted to know everyone I talked to, and gave me extra tasks we needed to work on together, so I had no free time."

That description fit someone all right, but it wasn't the Admiral. Reanne had behaved exactly like that after she and Aurora had become friends at the Academy. Aurora had foolishly shrugged it off as the personality quirks of an overzealous youth.

"What about his relationship with Captain Hawke? How did that evolve?"

"They continued their correspondence, and he met with her every year at the Academy when he attended the graduation ceremony."

"How did he describe Captain Hawke at that time?"

"He kept saying she was special and would do great things." The disgust and loathing in Magee's emotional field spread over Aurora like tar.

"Where was Captain Hawke assigned after she graduated from the Academy?"

"The *Excelsior*, the same ship that Lt. Clarek was on. It patrols NGQ2, the quadrant of Fleet space closest to Drakar."

"Was her assignment Admiral Schreiber's decision?"

"Actually it was Captain Hawke's. She graduated at the top of her class, which gave her the privilege to choose from the available posts appropriate to her rank. She chose the *Excelsior*."

"Did you have any concerns about her choice?"

"I did. She'd become close friends with Lt. Clarek, which greatly pleased Admiral Schreiber. But from what I saw, she was manipulating the Lieutenant and Ambassador Clarek."

"Manipulating them how?"

"Convincing them to give her whatever she wanted. That's how she ended up with the *Starhawke*. They gave it to her."

She winced. That had been a well-kept secret. No one in the Fleet besides Admiral Schreiber and Lt. Magee knew the ship belonged to her. Clearly the Sovereign had extracted that information from Magee. And counted it as another mark against Aurora.

"How long was Captain Hawke on the *Excelsior*?"

"Five years. She was transferred to the *Argo*, Knox's ship, three years ago—"

"Lt. Magee. Final warning," the judge boomed out. "One more breach of decorum and I will find you in contempt and have the bailiff place you in the brig."

"Yes, Your Honor. I'm sorry." Magee cleared her throat. "She was transferred to C-Captain S-Schreiber's ship," Magee stammered, "three years ago, shortly after Lt. Clarek returned to Drakar to build the *Starhawke*."

"Was there anything unusual about her posting to the *Argo*?"

"Absolutely. No one makes commander as young as she was, certainly not to the Fleet's flagship. But having her as the second in command on the *Argo* made it easier for Admiral Schreiber to communicate with her."

"Was Admiral Schreiber the person who approved her promotion and posting to the *Argo*?"

"Yes."

"Did he tell you why he approved the posting?"

"He told me he wanted her with Kn— C-Captain S-S-Schreiber. That it was the best place for her to learn what she needed to know."

Magee had caught herself before committing her third offense, but her stutter was getting worse.

The trial counsel worked to smooth it over. "Did Captain Schreiber offer any objections to her appointment as his first officer?"

"Not at all. He seemed delighted."

"How soon after she transferred to the *Argo* did the attack on Persei Primus occur?"

"Almost immediately. A couple weeks."

"When did you first become aware of the attack?"

"When the distress call came in. I alerted Admiral Schreiber at once."

"And how did he respond?"

"He sent a priority message to the *Argo*. He also dispatched one of our medical freighters to provide assistance."

"What about other ships?"

"There weren't any other ships nearby at the time."

"Why not?"

"Persei Primus is located just outside the border of the Central Zone in the Outer Rim. Those quadrants are vast stretches of space that are minimally populated and traveled mostly by freighters along the trade routes. The stations and settlements in the Rim rely predominantly on their own defenses for protection from threats, rather than the intervention of starships."

"There were no starships posted to the Persei Primus system at that time?"

"Just one, the patrol yacht that was assigned to the station. Unfortunately, it was temporarily docked at the station for an engine retrofit at the time of the attack and was destroyed."

"Did Admiral Schreiber travel to Persei Primus after the attack?"

"Yes. We both visited the station soon after the reconstruction began."

"Was the *Argo* still present at the station when you arrived?"

"Yes."

"What was the stated purpose for their remaining?"

"As a deterrent to the Setarips. There was a risk that they would make another assault while the station's defenses were weakened."

"Were you present when Admiral Schreiber talked to the *Argo*'s officers about the attack?"

"Yes."

"Who led the *Argo*'s response team on Persei Primus?"

"Captain Hawke."

"Who did Captain Hawke chose to lead the security team for that mission?"

"Lt. Celia Cardiff, a junior member of Fleet Security onboard the *Argo*."

"Captain Hawke didn't take the *Argo*'s security chief?"

"No."

"Did she say why she made that choice?"

"She said Lt. Cardiff was exactly the person she needed with her. That things would have turned out a lot worse for her if Lt. Cardiff hadn't been there."

Aurora wanted to smack her head against the wall. Those were her words, but in a completely different context than how she'd said them and without the background that gave them weight.

"Was the *Argo*'s security chief unfit to go on the mission?"

"No. He was a seasoned officer in his prime."

"What about Lt. Cardiff?"

"She was much younger and relatively inexperienced."

And the best hand-to-hand combat fighter on the ship, Aurora added silently, *who had just finished kicking my butt on the sparring mat.*

"Did Captain Hawke give any additional explanation for choosing Lt. Cardiff?"

"Only that she'd trusted her instincts."

"Did either Admiral Schreiber or Captain Schreiber question her decision?"

"No."

Sixty-Nine

"Let's move on to the attack on Gaia."

Cade rested his elbows on his knees, his attention switching between Magee and the Admiral. Magee kept shooting daggers at the Admiral, who was making a valiant effort to hide the pain Magee's words and vitriol were inflicting on him.

"Who recommended sending the *Starhawke* to investigate the planet's agricultural destruction?"

"Admiral Schreiber. He was adamant that the GC needed to send the *Starhawke*."

That was a lie. The Admiral had told Cade that members of the Council had lobbied for the *Starhawke* to be sent, and that if Aurora had still been on the *Argo*, he believed those same councilmembers would have pushed for the *Argo* to be given the mission. The Sovereign was the one who had wanted Aurora on Gaia.

"Why the *Starhawke*?"

"He said the talents of the crew Aurora had assembled were *uniquely* qualified to bring the situation to a resolution."

The Admiral's mouth thinned. Magee might be quoting him correctly, or she might be lying. Either way, the emphasis she put on *uniquely* implied the crew's talents were nefarious rather than beneficial.

"Did he elaborate on those talents?"

"No."

"How did Captain Hawke's presence on Gaia benefit Admiral Schreiber?"

"She was overseeing the investigation, reporting back on how the Gaians were reacting to the Setarips' actions. She was also in communication with the people the Admiral had placed in the Rescue Corps who worked for him."

Cade's heart thumped, adrenaline shooting into his bloodstream. Was this it? The moment the Sovereign had been waiting for? Was Magee about to expose the existence of his unit, drawing them into the Sovereign's net?

"Do you know their names?"

He almost didn't hear Magee's answer over the roaring in his ears.

"Officers Debora Marek and Ricardo Contreras."

His breath stuttered in surprise.

"Are those the same two RC security officers who instigated the hostage attempt on the RC Director and died at the scene?"

"Yes."

"Who led the investigation into that incident?"

"Kn– C-Captain Schreiber."

"Why Captain Schreiber and not a detective from the Federal Coalition?"

"Because the attack on Gaia involved Setarips. Any Setarip threat or investigation falls under the purview of the Fleet. Setarips are not Union citizens, so the FC has no authority."

"When was the *Argo* called in?"

"After Captain Hawke reported that her crew had successfully neutralized the Setarip threat and taken possession of the Setarip ship."

"Why was the *Argo* selected?"

"It's standard procedure for the Discovery-class ship assigned to the quadrant to be brought in whenever there's been a Setarip attack."

"So the *Argo* would be brought in following any Setarip attack in the SGQ2 quadrant?"

"That's correct."

The trial counsel pulled up a document on the screens. "Lt. Magee, is this the report Captain Schreiber submitted following the *Argo* crew's investigation into both events?"

Magee skimmed the document. "Yes."

"Can you please read the highlighted paragraphs for us?"

Magee cleared her throat. "It is the determination of this investigative team that Officers Debora Marek and Ricardo Contreras acted in concert with the Etah Setarips to disrupt Gaia's agricultural stability. While the ultimate goal of this attack has not been determined, the arrival of the *Starhawke*'s crew halted the Setarips' efforts and revealed the presence of the Setarip ship on Gaia. The

Setarips attempted to escape but failed and chose to take their own lives rather than accepting capture. After the ship was brought to Gaia, Marek and Contreras planted explosives onboard. The explosives detonated as the ship was leaving Gaia, killing the four Fleet officers in charge of the vessel and vaporizing the bodies of the dead Setarips who were being transported to Earth."

Magee's gaze cut to the Admiral, a snarl curling her lip before she continued reading. "Salvage attempts were unsuccessful as the debris from the explosion fell into the ocean and sank to the ocean floor. No evidence has been found to indicate any other Rescue Corps personnel participated in these events. All personnel have been cleared for a return to duty."

"Thank you. Can you also please read the highlighted section below that?"

"The presence of Setarips so close to Earth, and from a faction that was believed to be extinct, is cause for serious concern. Further investigation by the Fleet into the current whereabouts and movements of all known Setarip factions is strongly recommended."

"Is this document signed by Captain Schreiber?"

"Yes."

The trial counsel touched her tablet. "Lt. Magee, I have another set of documents I would like you to take a look at." The image on the screens changed to a document with columns and numbers. "Can you please describe what these documents are?"

"These are financial records for one of Admiral Schreiber's subsidiary accounts. He used this particular account for payments that he didn't want tracked through Fleet channels."

"What types of payments?"

"To personnel who were not part of the Fleet chain of command and who operated without Council oversight."

Cade's blood chilled. She was talking about his unit again.

"Why weren't the payments tracked through Fleet channels?"

"Admiral Schreiber needed to keep the activities of these people secret."

"Why?"

"The Council would have objected to their actions and put a stop to it."

"And who was in charge of processing these payments?"

"I was."

"Did you understand what these payments were for at the time you were processing them?"

"No. I thought the payments were going to Fleet officers who were working as covert operatives to protect the Union. I was told the reason the payments were being made in this manner was to prevent their identities from being compromised."

"Do you know the names of any of the people he was making payments to?"

A crease formed between Magee's brows, her voice faltering. "Y-yes." Confusion flitted across her face, like she didn't understand her own answer.

The trial counsel didn't seem to notice. "Let's start with the payments from three years ago." Several lines highlighted in yellow on the first document. "Can you identify who the highlighted payments were made to?"

Magee licked her lips, her head tipping like she was trying to catch the faint whisper of a voice in her ear. "All those payments went to Michael Bryant."

Wrong. Cade knew exactly what he and the members of his team were paid by Admiral Schreiber. Every single line highlighted on the accounting spreadsheet in front of Magee had been paid to him.

"Who is Michael Bryant?"

"He's the man who led the Setarip group that infiltrated Persei Primus. He pretended to be a member of the RC and was on the RC freighter that docked with the station right before the Ecilam attacked the station."

"Why was Admiral Schreiber paying him?"

"So he'd oversee the op to steal the prototype. He was in charge of outfitting the Setarips in RC gear, getting them safely to the station, and managing the access codes Admiral Schreiber gave him."

"Mr. Bryant was the one who entered the codes once he and the Setarips accessed the station?"

"Yes." Magee's face scrunched in distaste.

"What about these payments?" A new set highlighted on the document. "Do you know who they were made to?"

"Bryant's partner, Julie Cohen."

Wrong again. Those payments went to Justin. He was beginning to understand why his team had been excised from trial counsel's version of events.

"Who is Julie Cohen?"

"She was in charge of piloting the RC freighter to and from Persei Primus and transporting the prototype."

"What about these payments?" The trial counsel highlighted the lines for Gonzo's and Bella's base pay.

"Those were for Officers Debora Marek and Ricardo Contreras, the two RC officers who blew up the Setarip ship on Gaia."

"Do you know who these payments are to?" Williams' and Reynolds' payments highlighted on the document.

Magee's head twitched, a jerky movement he'd never seen her make before. She frowned at the spreadsheet, twitched again. "No." The single syllable came out robotic and monotone.

"When did you learn the names of the four people you've identified?"

"Not until last year, after Captain Hawke became captain of the *Starhawke*. Before then I believed the payments were going to legitimate Fleet officers. I didn't know Admiral Schreiber and Captain Hawke were behind the attack on Persei Primus and I didn't know what they had planned for Gaia."

"How did you learn of their involvement?"

"They told me. That's when the threats and torture began. During those sessions..." Magee paled, her hand drifting up to touch her face. "They gloated about what they'd accomplished. They ordered me to help them with their plans to bring down the Union. I didn't want to. I hated them for what they were doing. But I couldn't escape. And the pain–" Magee fell silent, her eyes staring at something only she could see.

Cade checked the feed of Aurora's cell. She was staring at the wall with a nearly identical expression on her face.

"Michael Bryant's payments continued after he died on Persei Primus station. Why?"

Magee's focus snapped back to the trial counsel, her mouth turning down. "He was replaced," she said slowly. "I don't know by whom. Admiral Schreiber only told me the names of the operatives who he'd had killed."

"Admiral Schreiber told you he ordered Bryant to be killed?"

"Yes. Bryant was supposed to take charge of the next phase after they got the prototype. He was expected to plan and lead the attack on Gaia, but when he didn't make it off the station he was terminated."

"Can you describe what you mean by terminated?"

Magee's voice turned clinically cool, detached. "Poisoned. Admiral Schreiber wanted to make sure anyone who failed to make it back to the Setarip ships wouldn't be left alive for questioning. He'd arranged for the boarding party to be injected with a device that would deliver a potent toxin, convincing them it was an immune booster that would help them heal faster if they got injured. The device had a built-in tracking dot. Any injector that didn't register as onboard the RC freighter when it detached from the station received an instant kill order. Bryant and any Setarips left on the station were expendable."

Seventy

Expendable.

Knowing it was coming didn't soften the blow. Aurora forced her body to remain still but her heart kept kicking her ribcage like a penned mustang determined to break free.

Magee had accused the Admiral of murder. M-U-R-D-E-R.

Her soul shrieked in outrage. The memory of Bryant and the Setarips lying at her feet, their eyes glassy and unseeing, made her stomach turn. She'd fought to stop them, not kill them. And Lelindia had done everything in her power to bring Bryant back.

She gritted her teeth as she stared up at the tiny window of her cell, where cold light filtered around the thick bar that bisected the angular cutout.

Clearly the Sovereign hadn't been able to conjure evidence – other than Magee's alternate-reality testimony – that would make a murder accusation stick. If she had, that charge would have been bundled in with the others against the Admiral.

"What about Julie Cohen? You testified that Admiral Schreiber only told you the names of people who were dead, but according to the reports, she made it safely off the station with the prototype, and her payments continued."

"She completed the job. But the Setarips had to eliminate her because she was kicking up a fuss about Bryant's death." A pause, like Magee was reading off a script and had to jump to the next line. "She was also replaced."

What a twisted tale. But the fact that Magee was telling it, a veteran Fleet officer who had served with the Admiral for years, gave it the weight of plausibility. It didn't help that Magee had no idea she was parroting the Sovereign's lies.

"Thank you, Lt. Magee. No further questions."

Aurora waited, a muffled cough and the scrape of a chair in the background the only sounds until Copeland spoke.

"Lt. Magee, you testified earlier that it was Admiral Schreiber's decision to transfer and promote Captain Hawke from the *Excelsior* to the *Argo*. Was that transfer processed through normal channels?"

"Yes."

"Were other admirals at Fleet Command aware of the transfer and promotion?"

"Yes."

"Did any of the admirals challenge Captain Hawke's promotion and transfer?"

"Not that I'm aware."

"Did the admirals have the right to challenge the transfer and promotion if they disagreed with Admiral Schreiber's decision?"

"Yes."

"You testified that Captain Hawke graduated top of her class at the Academy, which earned her the privilege of choosing her posting from those available to her, and that she chose the *Excelsior*. Why is the person who ranks top of the class at the Academy given that privilege?"

The silence stretched out. "Because it's a difficult honor to achieve," Magee said grudgingly.

"While Captain Hawke served on the *Excelsior*, did she receive any medals or other commendations?"

Another long pause. "Yes."

"Can you please read the highlighted section from Captain Hawke's service record on your screen?"

This pause lasted so long Aurora began to think Magee wouldn't answer. "Fleet Commendation Medal, Meritorious Unit Commendation, Promotion to Lieutenant, Humanitarian Service Award, Good Conduct Ribbon, Distinguished Service Medal, Promotion to Lt. Commander, Exploration Unit Award, Meritorious Service Medal."

"Were those promotions and medals received while she was serving on the *Excelsior*?"

"Yes."

"Are the promotions and medals Captain Hawke earned typical for a Fleet officer to receive during a five-year posting onboard a Fleet starship?"

"No."

"Is Captain Hawke's service record during that time exceptional?"

In the silence, Aurora could feel the pressure on Magee's emotional field, the programming acting like a giant hand clamped over her mouth, preventing her from answering the question.

"Lt. Magee?"

"Yes," came out on a hiss.

"Who recommended her for the medals and promotions she received while posted to the *Excelsior*?"

"Captain Warner."

"The commanding officer of the *Excelsior*?"

"Yes."

"Not Admiral Schreiber?"

"No."

"Lt. Magee, you testified that you visited the Teeli Embassy while Admiral Schreiber and Captain Hawke were away from Sol System for two weeks. Given your stated resistance to the alleged plans to overthrow the Union, and the method of enforcement you described to ensure your cooperation, why were you left unsupervised for so long?"

"They trusted that I would obey their commands."

"Trusted? What was the basis for that trust, given your stated objections to what you were being asked to do?"

Fear and confusion warred in Magee's emotional field. She was clearly struggling to reconcile the Sovereign's reprogramming with the core belief – only partially overwritten – that the Admiral and Aurora trusted her. "They... didn't believe... I would defy them." She phrased it more like a question than a statement.

"Were you restrained in some way?"

"No."

"Wearing a tether?"

"No."

"Then what prevented you from disobeying their orders as soon as they left the system?"

"I... nothing."

Seventy-One

Listening to Magee's testimony, and the medical examiner's testimony that followed, made it impossible for Micah to enjoy the meal he and Celia served everyone after the court adjourned for a lunch break. His mind kept spinning back to what the doctor had said.

Lt. Magee's injuries are consistent with repeated low-voltage electrical shock. The degree of healing to the damaged tissue indicates the most recent event occurred between six and nine months ago. It's unclear whether the chronic effects will ever resolve.

Up to that moment, he'd never considered his sister's and mom's abilities as dangerous. Not really. They were protectors, not aggressors.

But Magee's experience pointed out how their power in the hands of a warped mind could be destructive, even lethal.

He hadn't understood how the medical examiner could be so far off on her timetable for Magee's injuries until Lelindia provided a plausible explanation. After using his Aunt Kreestol to torture Magee into submission, the Sovereign had his aunt use her healing ability just enough to make the injuries look less recent.

That level of cold calculation made him shiver.

"You okay?"

He glanced at Celia, who had settled into her chair beside him after Unity had started the feed for the afternoon session.

"I noticed you didn't eat much," she prompted in a low tone.

Which was unusual for him. Ordinarily he had a healthy appetite. "I'm a little freaked out," he admitted.

Her gaze searched his, softly analyzing. "Witnessing evil deeds, even secondhand, will do that to you."

As usual, she hit the nail on the head. "Yeah. Thanks."

She gave him an encouraging smile that struck him like a prism of rainbows. "It shows you care. That's a very good thing."

So was her smile. He could soak up that glow all day long.

She'd smiled a lot after she'd won the competition last night. So had he. Proving how well-attuned she was to his vocal inflections had put him over the moon.

A figure appeared in the feed, drawing both their gazes as he strode toward the witness stand with the self-assurance of a diplomat.

Micah had seen vids of Teeli before, but not a life-sized projection. Somehow he'd expected them to be taller. Maybe some were, but this one was about the same size as Kire. His flowing grey robe added breadth to his shoulders, but also concealed what lay underneath. Celia could hide an entire arsenal in a getup like that.

The Teeli sat, his center-parted stark white hair falling straight to the middle of his chest. But it was his prominent electric blue eyes that startled Micah. He imagined chips of razor-sharp ice embedded within them, ready to be unleashed on the unwary, despite the Teeli's tranquil demeanor.

Commander Adams rose. "Delegate Sly'Kull, thank you for taking time out of your schedule to provide your testimony today."

"It is my honor to support the Court of Justice," he replied in Galish accented with a heavy drawl.

Celia made a gagging noise. Her bared teeth gleamed in the light from the projection. "The Teeli wouldn't recognize justice if it walked up and bit them on their pampered butts," she growled.

He had no doubt she'd happily sink her teeth into the pink-grey flesh of the Teeli who sat with entitled composure in the witness stand. Given what he'd been told about the Teeli's history, she was right.

"Delegate Sly'Kull, what is your current position at the Teeli Embassy?"

"I am the primary delegate to the Galactic Council for the Teeli."

"Was that the position you held on October eighth of last year?"

"No."

"What was your official position at the Teeli Embassy at that time?"

"I was serving as Delegate Bare'Kold's administrator."

"Did Lt. Isabeau Magee visit the Teeli Embassy on that day?"

"Yes."

"Did you see her on that day?"

The Teeli's eyes seemed to glow from within. "Yes. I greeted Lt. Magee when she arrived and escorted her to the reception room."

"How would you describe her behavior at that time?"

"She was quite agitated, fidgeting and looking around with a wariness I had not seen from her before."

"So the two of you had met previously?"

"At official functions, yes. She always accompanied Admiral Schreiber just as I accompanied Delegate Bare'Kold."

"Was her behavior on those previous occasions different from her behavior on October eighth?"

"Yes. On previous occasions she was composed. She always appeared very comfortable moving about in the crowd. But when she came to the Embassy, she was flustered, on edge."

"Did you speak with her?"

"Yes. I did my best to put her at ease. I had planned to leave when Delegate Bare'Kold joined us, but she asked me to stay. She said we both needed to hear what she had to share, that the future of the Teeli depended on it."

"What was the content of that conversation?"

"She detailed what Admiral Schreiber and Captain Hawke had told her about their plans to overthrow the Union and invade our sovereign space."

"Did you believe Lt. Magee's claims?"

"I was quite skeptical at first. Admiral Schreiber has been a respected leader and member of the Council for years. And my people are pacifists. We do not look for aggression in others."

Celia made a rude noise, drawing Micah's attention again.

The sparks shooting from her dark eyes as she glared at Sly'Kull would have set Micah's shirt on fire if she'd glanced his way. "Right, because in Teeli culture, *pacifist* is synonymous with *sadist*."

"Did Lt. Magee provide evidence to support her claims?"

"Yes. She gave us copies of written communications and payment ledgers — which have been submitted as evidence to the Court of Justice — that supported her assertions," Sly'Kull continued.

"Did Lt. Magee mention any concerns regarding her physical wellbeing?"

"Yes. She detailed the physical abuse she had endured after she refused to go along with Admiral Schreiber's demands. She also showed us the marks on her arms and legs."

"How did Delegate Bare'Kold react to the information she provided?"

"He was very concerned. We both were. Our people joined the Union in the hope it would give our citizens a better future. We had not imagined deception from those who claimed to be our allies."

"Look who's talking about deception," Lee-Lee grumbled from Celia's other side.

"Delegate Bare'Kold decided to offer Lt. Magee sanctuary at the Embassy while we investigated her claims. She accepted. We have endeavored to protect her ever since."

"Did you provide the results of your investigation to anyone?"

"Yes. We brought our findings to the Court of Justice."

"What were the findings of the Teeli Embassy's investigation?"

Sly'Kull dipped his head, his gaze shifting with studied reluctance to the Admiral, a sheen of moisture that looked like unshed tears coating his eyes. "Our findings supported Lt. Magee's claims."

"This guy should be on the stage," Micah's mom sniped, her words covered in barbs.

The derision and anger in her voice, paired with the way she flexed and curled her fingers, made him very glad he wasn't Sly'Kull. For many reasons.

"Or better yet, in a box."

Uh...

"Libra." His dad sent her a chiding look. "Violence isn't the answer."

Her eyes narrowed. "Sometimes it's the answer."

"You tell him, sister," Celia agreed.

His dad met his gaze over the top of his mom's head, a plea for backup in his eyes.

"It's not a good answer," Micah said slowly, keenly aware of the threat potential of the two women flanking him.

Both his mom and Celia scowled, dropping the temperature around his chair several degrees.

"But it's not like we could stop either of you, even if we wanted to," he added.

His mom shared a look with Celia that tied a knot in his stomach. "Glad we've got that settled."

"Yep," Celia agreed, turning back to the projection.

The alarmed look on his dad's face didn't help. Whatever he was sensing from them made it clear they weren't joking.

Seventy-Two

"…Lt. Magee when Admiral Schreiber visited the Embassy on December fourteenth of last year?"

Cade had been with the Admiral for that trip. They'd unexpectedly encountered Magee, who had acted happy to see them but also confused. It was the last time either of them saw her in person until she appeared to testify against the Admiral today.

"Lt. Magee was still at the Embassy at the time," Sly'Kull said in an apologetic tone. "We had not yet managed to arrange transport for her to Teeli space."

Translation — the Sovereign hadn't figured out where Magee would be most useful to her.

"Did Lt. Magee see Admiral Schreiber at that time?"

"Delegate Bare'Kold encouraged Lt. Magee to avoid Admiral Schreiber during his visit, but she was determined to *face her demons* as she put it. I was not there when she spoke with Admiral Schreiber, but both Delegate Bare'Kold and Lt. Magee shared their observations with me afterward."

"How did they describe the interchange?"

"Tense. Uncomfortable. They said Admiral Schreiber attempted to convince her to leave with him and Delegate Bare'Kold was forced to intervene. The presence of the security officers we had hired deterred the Admiral, but Lt. Magee was quite upset."

"Did Delegate Bare'Kold make any changes based on those interactions?"

"He decided we could not wait for the ship that had been sent from Ways'lend to reach Earth. A few days after Admiral Schreiber's visit, we took the delegation yacht and delivered Lt. Magee to the transport."

Cade's stomach cramped. He still felt responsible for Magee's captivity. He'd failed to stop her transfer to the Sovereign's ship. True, rescuing her hadn't been his unit's mission. In fact, the Admiral had specifically told him not to attempt to reclaim Magee. His team's priority had been finding out where and when the Sovereign and the Teeli were planning their next attack on Aurora.

Those facts didn't make him feel any better. His mind nimbly conjured vivid images of the living hell Magee had endured – was still enduring – since the Sovereign sunk her claws into her.

"Did Admiral Schreiber visit the Teeli Embassy again?"

"Yes."

"Do you recall the date of that visit?"

"January third of this year."

"And what was the stated purpose for that visit?"

"He claimed he wanted to discuss the possibility of a joint science mission in our space."

"Did you believe him?"

"No."

"Did you meet with him?"

"Yes. It seemed the prudent option."

"Did he arrive alone?"

"No. He brought Captain Hawke and her first officer with him, as theirs was the ship he wanted to send to the binary system."

Cade waited for Sly'Kull to add his name to the guest list, since he'd rounded out the quartet who had visited the Embassy.

But he didn't. Either Sly'Kull considered him not worth mentioning, or he was intentionally avoided bringing Cade's name into the discussion, just as Magee had.

"Did he say why he wanted the *Starhawke* to go on the mission?"

Sly'Kull sniffed like he'd smelled something distasteful. "It was a science vessel, and of Kraed design. That was supposed to make it superior."

"How did you respond to his request?"

"I negotiated a compromise. We allowed Captain Hawke's ship to enter our space and proceed to the binary star, however, we also sent freighters on a set schedule to deliver supplies, allowing us to visually confirm the ship, and Captain Hawke, were where they should be."

"Did you have any other methods for monitoring the *Starhawke*'s location?"

"Yes. One of our ships set up a monitoring system around the binary star to ensure we would be alerted if the *Starhawke* failed to arrive on time, or if it departed unexpectedly."

"Did the *Starhawke* arrive on time?"

"Yes."

"Did the *Starhawke* remain in the binary star system?"

"At first. The monitoring system was easy to detect. Captain Hawke would have known she was being watched." The barely contained glee in Sly'Kull's voice slid like rancid oil over Cade's skin.

"When did the *Starhawke* leave the binary system?"

"Five days before it arrived at ESS-1."

"Was that when the ship was scheduled to depart?"

"No. I had negotiated for Captain Hawke's ship to remain in the system for several standard Earth months, a reasonable timeframe for a scientific study of this scope."

"Was that the only reason you chose that timeframe?"

"No. It served the dual purpose of securing as much time for my people as possible with her ship and crew immobilized while our leaders decided how to handle the potential threat Admiral Schreiber and Captain Hawke posed to our sovereignty."

Sly'Kull's choice of words elicited a snort from Cade. What the Teeli delegate really meant was the threat the Admiral and Aurora posed to the *Sovereign*.

"Admiral Schreiber and Captain Hawke agreed to this timeframe?"

"Captain Hawke resisted the extended timeframe, but I made it clear that point was non-negotiable. She and Admiral Schreiber finally agreed."

"How long was the *Starhawke* in Teeli space?"

"Less than one standard Earth month."

"Was there any indication why the *Starhawke* left ahead of schedule?"

"Not that we detected, but another Kraed vessel accompanied the *Starhawke* when it arrived in this system."

"Did your monitoring system detect a Kraed ship other than the *Starhawke* in the binary system?"

"No. Sensors as unsophisticated as ours would not be able to detect a camouflaged Kraed ship."

Another snort. Sly'Kull was laying it on thick.

The tic around Sly'Kull's left eye gave away how much he hated admitting that fact. "That knowledge did not concern us before." He glanced significantly at Admiral Schreiber. "It does now."

Seventy-Three

"We have to bring Admiral Payne in." Kire's mouth set in a grim line, his gaze meeting Lelindia's. Everyone had gathered around one of the observation lounge tables after the Admiral's trial had ended for the day. "I could poke a few holes in Sly'Kull's testimony regarding our meeting with him and the mission to Teeli space, but Payne's the only one who can credibly refute Sly'Kull's testimony about that mission."

Lelindia's stomach did a somersault. "How can she testify without exposing the Suulh on Gaia? And her family?" She wanted the Admiral freed from the Sovereign's snare, but not at the expense of Keenan and his sister. They were innocents who'd already suffered enough collateral damage.

"The trial counsel will ask where she's been the past couple months," Celia pointed out. "And they'll want to know how she got Keenan out of the hospital."

"She won't have to answer those questions," Kire countered. "They aren't relevant to the Admiral's defense. What happened *before* we got involved in rescuing Keenan is very relevant."

"Payne's the one who first proposed the binary star mission to Aurora." Celia tapped her fingers lightly on the polished wood tabletop. "She also had direct dealings with Bare'Kold to set that up.

The question is, does she have any evidence to support her testimony?"

The image of Keenan lying still as death in his hospital bed sparked a flame of indignation in Lelindia's chest. "Other than her grandson landing in the hospital after Bare'Kold threatened her?"

"Unless she had recordings or written messages to prove it, that's circumstantial evidence at best. Unlike the documents the trial counsel is producing."

"False documents," Lelindia muttered.

"False documents," Celia agreed. "We do have our ship's comm log, which has a record of the request Admiral Payne sent for Aurora to meet with her back in November. But it doesn't give any details. It's only a request to meet for assignment. Since we didn't go on an assignment to Teeli space after that meeting, that wouldn't corroborate Payne's testimony or refute Sly'Kull's version of how the binary star mission was created. Without proof, any testimony Payne gave wouldn't hold up against a sedition charge."

"And the trial counsel might have false documents to prove Payne is collaborating with the Admiral and Aurora." Kire chewed on his lip. "It's what I'd do if I were the Sovereign and wanted to discredit Payne. Make it look like she's the one who tampered with Fleet records. She certainly had the access. Or the Sovereign might have figured out a way to implicate Aurora or the Admiral as the ones behind Keenan's accident. Then if Payne testifies, it will look like she's only defending them to prevent further retaliation against her family."

Lelindia dropped her head into her hands, digging her fingers into her scalp. "I am so sick of dodging lies that warp the truth into fiction."

Jonarel's hand rested on her back, the comforting warmth of his touch counteracting the bunched tension between her shoulder blades. "Perhaps this is a question we should allow Admiral Payne to answer for herself."

"I could send a message and ask her," Brendan offered.

She lifted her head, meeting his steady gaze. "And if she decides she wants to come?" Even the thought tied her in knots.

Brendan's blue eyes filled with empathy. He could feel exactly how much she hated the idea. "I doubt she will. Given the risks to her family and the unlikelihood of a positive outcome, it's not a smart tactical move. But she's a Fleet admiral. She'll want to make that determination herself."

"You're right." She sighed, glancing at Kire, who nodded in agreement. "Okay, Brendan. Send her a message and see what she says."

Seventy-Four

If Aurora had been living the life of a typical inmate in solitary, traveling to the courthouse for her arraignment might have been a welcome, if stressful, change of scenery. But thanks to Unity, the daily monotony of staring at the walls of her cell only defined her physical reality.

When she wasn't listening in on the Admiral's trial, she had a steady stream of one-sided visits with Cade, her crew, and her family. Even Siginal had surprised her by putting in an appearance. He'd been subdued, but also quick to assure her that he was watching over Lelindia and the baby and wouldn't let any harm come to them.

That had made her smile, something he must have seen on Unity's video feed of her cell, because the low-grade anxiety in his emotional field had melted away, replaced by the robust confidence she was used to.

The only voice she hadn't heard – the one she desperately wanted to hear – was Admiral Schreiber's. Unity could easily open a connection between them, but there was no way they could speak to each other without creating suspicion. According to Unity, she and the Admiral were being monitored far too closely by the XO already.

"This way."

She followed the two FS officers assigned as her escort as they led her down a narrow, unadorned corridor of the Court of Justice. She could sense the Admiral in one of the rooms above her. Unity was recording the proceedings for her so she could listen to them later.

Her escorts halted at a service elevator where two additional FS officers waited at a compact check-in station.

"Aurora Hawke for Article 32 Session."

The FS officer seated behind the desk flicked her gaze over Aurora, the calculating assessment reminding her of Celia. "Courtroom seven."

Her escorts motioned her to the elevator. It creaked and groaned as it rose, telling her the tales of the countless others who had traversed these halls.

The bland corridor on the level where they exited matched its twin below, except for the solid wood doors set at intervals along its length. Her escort opened the second door they reached.

Not the same level as the Admiral's courtroom — judging by the distance he was on the floor above — but it was the closest she'd been to him since returning to the Sol system. That knowledge soothed the raw edges of her psyche.

She smoothed her hand over her uniform jacket before following the escort into the courtroom.

Phoebe rose from her chair at the table for the defense, moving to greet her with a subdued smile. "Good morning."

She returned the closed-mouth smile. "Good morning."

Her gaze swept the room. The judge wasn't present, but the trial counsel, a tall man with a thin, gangly frame and an unremarkable face, was watching her like he'd spotted a cockroach sitting on his arm. His loathing was palpable even through the emotional dampening field she'd kept in place ever since her incarceration.

But that wasn't what raised the hairs on the back of her neck. His emotional field felt unnatural – unless he really was borderline psychotic. Unlikely, considering he was a COJ trial counsel. Which meant he was under Teeli thrall, his emotions enflamed until they were completely out of proportion with the situation.

She'd suspected that might be the case, but having it confirmed didn't exactly lift her spirits. Especially since the Sovereign was the one person in the universe she couldn't sense. Her nemesis could be standing outside the courtroom door, and Aurora would have no clue.

She sighed as she sat in the chair to Phoebe's left.

"Problems?" Phoebe asked in an undertone.

"Nothing new," she replied.

Phoebe met her gaze. "Just remember we're only getting started."

That's what worries me.

"All rise. The honorable Judge Sato presiding."

Aurora tuned into the emotional field of the middle-aged woman who strode into the room with brisk efficiency. Unlike the trial counsel, the judge's emotions were as straightforward and tamed as the dark hair wrapped in a neat bun at her nape.

After settling into her seat, she looked Aurora in the eye, taking her measure, before doing the same with Phoebe and the trial counsel. Her demeanor didn't change, but Aurora felt the hiccup in her emotional field as her gaze remained on the trial counsel, like there was something bothering her that she couldn't quite put her finger on.

That was a very good sign. It meant the judge wasn't in the Sovereign's pocket. If she was as sharp and observant as she appeared, that counted in Aurora's favor.

Aurora was so focused on the judge's emotional state and the implications of her reactions that she missed the opening comments until the trial counsel responded.

"Yes, Your Honor." He managed to keep the sneer off his face, but it was plastered all over his emotional field. "Docket number R-411-6592-Y12, the Galactic Union versus Captain Aurora Hawke."

"Thank you, Counsel. The charges?"

He rose, a towering scarecrow from a Halloween story, one where the seemingly benign toy suddenly sprouts claws and fangs and preys on hapless children. She managed not to flinch, but the emotions coming off him were disturbing, especially when paired with the preternatural calm of his voice.

"The charges against the accused are as follows. Count 1, Specification 1, Violation of UCFJ Article 81, Mutiny and Sedition. On or about July 2nd, 2241 the accused conspired with Admiral William Schreiber to create a revolt, violence, or disturbance against the lawful civil authority of the Galactic Council and Federal Coalition."

"Defense, how do you wish to plead to Count 1, Specification 1?"

"Not Guilty, Your Honor."

"So noted. The court record will reflect the plea of not guilty to Charge 1, Specification 1."

The recitation of charges continued, six in all, relating to the Setarip attacks on Persei Primus and Gaia. Then they got to the nitty-gritty point that would impact her immediate future.

"Your Honor, the government requests that Captain Hawke continue to be held in a Fleet detention facility until trial due to the seriousness of the charges against her and the flight risk she poses as a Fleet officer and captain of her own ship." The trial counsel flicked a look at her like she'd scuttled out from under a rock.

Phoebe stood immediately. "Objection, Your Honor. Captain Hawke's ship is currently docked at Sol Station and under surveillance by the FS, if I'm not mistaken. Surely the government has a higher opinion of FS forces than what trial counsel has expressed here." She looked pointedly at the trial counsel.

The trial counsel's neck flushed. "We have every faith in the FS. But the vessel is Kraed designed and built. We don't know definitively what it's capable of, or what degree of support Captain Hawke might receive during a flight attempt. Another Kraed vessel is docked beside it. FS has reported multiple crewmember visitations between the two ships."

"That's enough." Sato's gaze shifted to Aurora with equanimity as she held up a hand to forestall Phoebe's reply.

She sensed the judge's internal debate, felt the annoyance that had painted her emotional field at the trial counsel's mention of the Kraed. The Kraed were widely regarded as the saviors of Earth. Without their assistance, the human race likely would have perished a century ago. Accepting the trial counsel's implication that the Kraed would help an accused traitor of the Union flee didn't sit well with the judge.

But neither did letting an accused traitor slip through her fingers, apparently.

"So ordered. Captain Hawke is to remain in pre-trial confinement at the detention center." The judge struck her gavel on the bench.

Aurora held in the sigh that threatened to escape. She'd expected it, given the Admiral's situation, but the judge's decree snuffed out the little flame of hope she'd been keeping alive.

Seventy-Five

"Will's trial is not going well."

Jonarel shifted in the chair in his father's office on the *Rowkclarek*. His father had just confirmed the reason for this meeting.

He agreed with his father's assessment but was loathe to say so out loud. "The defense has not called any witnesses yet."

His father brushed the comment aside. "The Sovereign's lies have implicated our people in this farce as well."

Jonarel winced. Magee's testimony had been damning, especially her revelation that Clan Clarek had given the *Starhawke* to Aurora. In the twisted context of Magee's recitation, that action appeared insidious. "You will correct that misperception when you testify."

His father grunted. "Trusting this court is unwise."

Jonarel knew that tone far too well. He straightened. "What are you planning?"

"Contingencies."

His internal alert went from yellow to orange. "What kind of contingencies?"

His father steepled his fingers in a move Jonarel had seen the Admiral make many times. "All ships not currently on patrol have been recalled to Drakar and are being resupplied. A handful will join the current patrols along our border, but the rest will be ready to depart for Earth in eight days."

Jonarel's skin chilled. "Why are you sending them here?"

"In case they are needed."

"Needed to what?" He stayed seated, but his hands clutched the armrests with enough force to make them creak. "Fire on the Fleet?"

His father remained irritatingly calm. "I will not allow Will and Aurora to be detained while the Teeli overthrow the Union."

"Neither will I." He had promised his checana. *Whatever it takes.* "But if our ships show up in this system without provocation, we will trigger mass panic."

"They will not know we are here."

He stared. "They will if you attack the detention center. Or Sol Station."

"They will have no proof of our involvement."

Jonarel threw up his hands. "Our cloaked ships are their proof. As far as the Humans know, we are the only race with hull camouflage. And you are the Admiral's closest friend."

His father's eyes narrowed. "So you would have me do nothing?"

"I would have you think of the Union." His father's myopic focus on his own goals was proving to be a mountain Jonarel never crested. "The Sovereign is attempting to split the Union apart. If you bring our ships here, you will help her cause. You will force the Fleet to turn against us. Do you really want to attack Fleet ships? Fire on Fleet officers? Aurora and Lelindia have served with those officers. I have served with those officers."

That wiped the calm from his father's gaze, revealing the disgruntled impotence beneath. "Do you have a better solution?"

His father had capitulated far quicker than he had expected, almost as though he wanted to be talked out of this action.

Taking a breath, he allowed the pieces of the puzzle to settle in his mind's eye. "Having our ships prepared is a good strategy," he admitted. "We cannot predict what the Sovereign may do next." Which gave him an idea. "But rather than sending our ships here, our interests may be better served sending them into Teeli space."

His father's brows lifted. "Reconnaissance?"

"Yes. We have encountered armed Teeli ships on multiple occasions, but we do not have a clear idea of how many are in their fleet, where they are being constructed and berthed, and what type of supply chain they have created to support them."

"Important information to obtain." His father rose from his chair, moving to the viewport that gave a partial view of the starfield visible beyond the station. He surveyed the ships gliding past for several long moments before glancing over his shoulder at Jonarel. "How preoccupied have I been that I failed to notice my young son has grown into a wise leader?"

The compliment caught him off guard. "Then you agree?"

"I do." His father faced him. "But that does not solve the problem of Will's and Aurora's incarceration."

Jonarel exhaled. First crisis averted. Now to the second one. "You were at the detention center yesterday when you escorted Aurora's family. What is your assessment of the site's security and defenses?"

They spent the next hour discussing hypothetical scenarios, debating the relative merits of each based on information gleaned from Unity's vid feeds and his father's onsite observations. By the time Jonarel stood to leave, his confidence had increased exponentially in his father's willingness to keep a cool head if the Admiral and Aurora required extraction.

"I will ask Tehar to send Rowk all the information we gathered on Feylahn," he told his father. "You will let me know when our ships depart for Teeli space?"

"I will." His father rose. "Has Brendan received a reply from Admiral Payne?"

Jonarel paused at the doorway. "Yes. She reluctantly agreed with our assessment. She confirmed she does not have any evidence to provide, and her presence in the courtroom would put her family, and the Suulh protecting them, at risk."

"A prudent decision." His father stepped closer, his muscled arms wrapping around Jonarel's back. The tenderness and duration of the embrace said more than words ever could. "Then we will see what tomorrow brings."

Seventy-Six

The visit from her parents and Micah on Saturday was the one bright spot in an emotionally draining weekend. The antipathy in the cell block was growing exponentially, all the negativity of Aurora's fellow prisoners pressing down on her.

The reports she received from Cade made it clear why. The Fleet was under attack by the public, the Federal Coalition, and from within. The enraged women and men in the detention center — prisoners and FS personnel — blamed her and the Admiral for the Fleet's fall from favor.

The past few days hadn't improved the situation. By the time trial counsel wrapped up the case against the Admiral on Wednesday morning, the cascade of falsified evidence supporting the Admiral's guilt looked insurmountable.

Copeland had done his best to cast doubt during cross-examinations, but the emotional resonance of the panel — which was getting harder and harder for Aurora to detect through the quagmire of negativity around her — indicated the panel wasn't on the Admiral's side.

The defense would have a steep uphill climb.

Aurora settled onto her cot as Copeland called his first witness.

"Commander Elver, what is your current posting?"

"I'm Fleet Command's Ship Control Commander," she answered, each word spoken with crisp precision.

"How long have you held that post?"

"Four and a half years."

"As Ship Control Commander, do you oversee the movement of Fleet ships within Fleet space?"

"Yes."

"Does that include the eight Discovery-class starships?"

"Yes."

"Do all Fleet ships submit their planned flight paths to Ship Control?"

"Yes."

"How often do they submit their flight paths?"

"Every twenty-four hours."

"Do the ship captains have the authority to change those flight paths?"

"In certain instances, such as to answer a distress call, they're authorized to make discretionary changes. However, any necessary deviations from the path are immediately submitted by the bridge crew to Ship Control at Fleet Command."

"I like her," Cade commented in Aurora's ear.

So did she. The Commander's no-nonsense style radiated order and efficiency.

"Could a ship make a course change without submitting the change to Ship Control?"

"Yes, but we would still be alerted."

"How?"

"All Fleet vessels have an embedded tracking beacon. It emits a pulse that continually triangulates and logs their location using ICS relays. It's one way the Fleet coordinates movements in emergency situations. Any change a ship makes is logged by the ICS and by the ship's internal navigation."

"Does the beacon work when a ship enters an interstellar jump?"

"Yes. The tracking beacon still emits a pulse that's picked up by the ICS. It's distorted, of course, but the monitoring system accounts for that. We can still determine if the ship is following its projected flight path or if it's off course."

"What happens if it's off course?"

"The system immediately reports the deviation to us. It also notifies all nearby Fleet ships. My team and the neighboring ships will comm the displaced ship."

"What happens if there's no response?"

"If the next pulse indicates the ship is still off course, then the closest ships will be instructed to alter course to intercept."

Aurora had been on the receiving end of one of those alerts during her time on the *Argo*. A Fleet yacht had come under attack by two Setarip ships as it was entering the Osiris system. The crew made an unauthorized interstellar jump to evade capture, but not before the Setarips knocked out the yacht's comm. The shaken but otherwise unharmed crew had been delighted when the *Argo* had tracked them down in a neighboring star system and offered assistance.

"Could the ICS log be altered to prevent a ship from registering as off course in the system?"

"No. The two logs are independent. Even if the ICS log were altered, which to my knowledge is impossible, you'd still get a mismatch with the ship log, triggering an alert "

"Could the ship's log be altered to prevent a ship from registering as off course in the system?"

"No. The ship's log is integrated with the beacon. It cannot be altered."

"Why not?"

"Beacons and their dedicated logging servers are located in the most protected part of each ship. They're impossible to reach outside of space dock without cutting through multiple bulkheads and blast shielding."

"Could the beacon be disabled to disguise a ship's movements?"

"No. They have a dedicated power source. They'll transmit even if the ship's power fails. A beacon that stops transmitting creates a dark spot in the data stream, triggering a high-threat assessment alert. A dark spot indicates the beacon has been destroyed, which means the ship has been destroyed."

"Is there any way to alter a beacon's signal to disguise ship movements?"

"You'd have to change the laws of physics."

Cade chuckled. "I *really* like her."

Seventy-Seven

Cade leaned forward, the padding of the oversized cup-couch in the front room of his cabin adjusting to support his weight as his gaze flipped between Copeland, Elver, and Aurora.

Aurora's emotional field had been a dishwater grey when the afternoon session started, but Elver's responses seemed to be cleaning it up a bit.

"Cmd. Elver, using the information provided to Ship Control by the beacons and ICS logs, can the Fleet Director pinpoint the location of a particular Fleet ship at any given time?"

"Of course."

"Would the Fleet Director be able to use that information to calculate how long it would take a particular ship to travel from its current location to another destination?"

The *are you seriously asking that* look Elver shot Copeland made Cade snort. "The Director *must* be able to do that," she replied, as though explaining basic math to a child. "In a crisis, like a Setarip attack or natural disaster, it's imperative to know which ships can reach the destination quickly."

An image appeared on the panel and witness stand screens. "Cmd. Elver, can you please confirm these are the logs from the ICS and the *Argo* that detail the *Argo's* movements on the day of the Setarip attack on Persei Primus?"

Elver's gaze swept over the screen. "Yes, they are."

"Were you working at Ship Control that day?"

"Yes, I was."

"Based on these logs, is there any indication the *Argo* deviated from its scheduled flight path before the crew received the distress call from Persei Primus?"

"No, they did not."

"When did they deviate?"

"You can see it here in the data." Elver pointed to a row of numbers. "The course changes from the projected path, realigning them directly with the station."

"At the time the Setarip attack occurred, was the *Argo's* flight path taking the ship closer to or further away from Persei Primus?"

"They were traveling away from the station."

"If the attack had occurred fifteen minutes later, how much would that have increased the time it would have taken for the *Argo* to reach the station?"

"It would have been significant. Another hour at least."

"Thank you, Cmd. Elver. No further questions."

Adams rose and began the cross-examination. Cade got an inordinate amount of pleasure out of watching her struggle to gain any traction. Elver's testimony had been as succinct and orderly as her mannerisms, leaving Adams without anything to grab hold of. The trial counsel's face was pinched with irritation by the time Copeland called his next witness.

"Lieutenant Malecki, were you stationed on Persei Primus on July 2nd, 2241?"

"Yes, sir."

"Did Setarips attack the station on that day?"

The eyes of a veteran stared out of the lieutenant's boyish features. "Yes, sir."

"What position did you hold at that time?"

"I was an ensign, part of the FS team assigned to protect the station."

"Did your team attempt to repel the Setarips when they attacked?"

"Yes, sir, we did."

"Did you fire the station's weapons at the Setarips?"

"At first. We crippled one of their ships before our weapons and shields failed."

"Did the Setarips attempt to dock with the station after the station's shields went down?"

"Yes, sir."

"How did the FS team respond?"

"A group of senior officers sealed themselves off from the rest of the station, sacrificing their lives to blow up the dock the Setarip ship had attached to." The lieutenant delivered the line without emotion, but the tension around his mouth and eyes revealed he was reliving the pain of that moment. "The explosion destroyed the Setarip ship, and the resulting debris field made it difficult for any other Setarip ships to dock."

"The explosion killed all the Setarips onboard the ship and in that section of the station?"

"Yes, sir."

"Where were you when the explosion destroyed the Setarip ship?"

"Near dock three with the few remaining FS officers who were still ambulatory. We regrouped, working to move the casualties into corridor three to shield them from the next attack."

"Did the Setarips attack again?"

"No, sir."

"Could you see the Setarips?"

"I didn't have visuals on the Setarip ships when the blasts stopped rocking the station. I made my way to the dock three airlock port and saw the three remaining ships moving away from the station."

"Were the station's shields and weapons still inoperable?"

"Yes, sir."

"How soon after you saw the Setarip ships moving away did you first see members of the *Argo*'s crew?"

"About twenty minutes. I didn't know the *Argo* was there until I saw their response team coming down the corridor toward us."

"You didn't see the *Argo* arrive?"

"No, sir. The ship arrived on the opposite side of the station."

"So the Setarip ships left in the opposite direction from where the *Argo* arrived?"

"Yes, sir."

"Is there any method by which the Setarips could have known the *Argo* was approaching?"

"Yes, sir. Fleet protocol required the *Argo* to attempt to establish and maintain communication with the station after they received and responded to our distress call. Those communications generate a signal that can be detected by nearby ships. The Setarips wouldn't have been able to intercept the communications, but the wavelength of the signal would have indicated a ship in an interstellar jump that was moving rapidly toward the station from a particular point in space."

"Were you aware that Setarips from the RC freighter were on the station at that time?"

"No, sir."

"When did you become aware of their presence?"

"When the alert came over the *Argo* team's comm that fighting had broken out in the concourse."

"Did you join the *Argo*'s security team to repel the Setarips?"

"No, sir."

"Why not?"

Malecki's facial muscles twitched. "I was needed where I was. Casualties outnumbered medics and FS personnel six to one. I was helping with triage."

"Did you see the Setarips at any point later?"

"Yes, sir. I saw their bodies. All FS personnel did before the Setarips were taken to the morgue."

"Director Holcomb testified that the arrival of the decoy RC freighter at Persei Primus and the attack of the five Setarip ships was perfectly timed to ensure no one on the station knew Setarips were onboard the freighter. Would you agree with that statement?"

"I would."

"Was there anything about the station that would have made it more vulnerable at that time than at other times?"

Malecki shifted in his seat. "The patrol yacht assigned to Persei Primus was undergoing an engine retrofit. It was scheduled to be out of commission for nine hours."

"How many hours had it been out of commission when the Setarips attacked?"

"One and a half."

"So it would have been another seven and a half hours or so before it was ready to launch?"

"Yes, sir."

"You testified that you saw the Setarip ships moving away from the station prior to the *Argo*'s arrival. You also testified that at that same time the station's shields and weapons were down, and

Setarips from the RC freighter were on the station. What tactical threat did the *Argo's* arrival pose to the Setarips that would force them to pull their ships out of the system at that moment rather than pressing their advantage?"

"The *Argo* is a Discovery-class cruiser. Even three against one it outclassed the Setarip cruisers. It could have picked them off one by one."

"How did leaving the system and returning after the *Argo's* arrival change that dynamic?"

"Per Fleet protocol, the *Argo* had taken up a defensive position near the station. That limited their mobility and firing radius, especially with all the debris surrounding the station."

"Were you aware of the battle taking place between the *Argo* and the Setarip ships?"

"Absolutely. I could hear and feel the impacts on the station."

"Were those impacts commensurate with what you had experienced during the initial Setarip attack?"

"Yes, sir."

"Were you aware of the fighting on the concourse between the Setarips and the *Argo's* crew?"

"Yes, sir. I could hear the chatter over the comms."

"During the fighting, did any of the *Argo's* personnel act in a way that indicated they were not looking out for the welfare of the people on Persei Primus?"

Malecki's gaze shifted briefly to Admiral Schreiber, before meeting Copeland's gaze. "No, sir. They saved a lot of lives that day, including mine."

Seventy-Eight

After a week and a half of watching testimony for the Admiral's trial, Micah was developing a feel for the rhythm of the questions and answers. He was grateful that they'd moved on to witnesses for the defense.

Knox was testifying today, and they'd be seeing him in person tomorrow. Knox had invited Micah and his parents to stay at the Admiral's house tomorrow night so they could visit Aurora both Friday and Saturday without having to make two shuttle trips.

As he had the previous weekend, Siginal would be taking them down in his shuttle, and he would also be staying with them at the Admiral's house. Micah had a sneaking suspicion that Siginal's presence served a dual purpose – transport and extra security for him.

He wasn't used to being considered defenseless. Ifel certainly didn't think of him that way. Or Unity. But compared to the abilities his mom, Siginal, and his dad brought to the table, communicating with non-human animals and alien races didn't rank high on the self-defense scale. At least not in this scenario.

His sigh drew Celia's attention. She'd been sitting next to him during every testimony, cooking with him during breaks, and swimming and sparring with him most evenings. It was perfect... except for the fact he was in a perpetual tug-of-war with himself.

"Problem?" she asked.

He shook his head without looking at her. "Nope. I'm good."

She snorted. "Your *good* and Aurora's *fine* sound remarkably similar."

He was saved from a response by Knox's appearance on the courtroom projection as he approached the witness stand.

It was the first time Micah had seen him in uniform. And without a smile dancing in his eyes. The transformation into stern Fleet captain made it easy to picture him on the bridge of the Fleet's flagship. If this man had greeted him the first time they'd met, he would have been seriously intimidated. It made him appreciate how much Knox had worked to put him at ease.

The murmur of conversation in the observation lounge faded as Copeland stood.

"Captain Schreiber, what is your current Fleet posting?"

"I'm the commanding officer of the Discovery-class cruiser *Argo.*"

"And how long have you been the CO of that vessel?"

"Since she first launched, more than four years now."

"And what is your ship's primary mission?"

"We explore and defend the star systems in Southern Galactic Quadrant Two."

"Defend against whom?"

"Setarips, predominantly, although we run across criminal elements occasionally. We alert and work with the Federal Coalition in those instances."

"Is the planet Gaia part of your patrol area?"

"Yes."

"Do you spend much time there?"

"Not really. We stay mostly in the Central Zone and Outer Rim, areas that haven't been explored or where colonies are isolated. The Interior Hub falls under the purview of smaller Fleet vessels."

"Was your ship called to Gaia to investigate the Setarip attack that occurred last August?"

"Yes."

"Why was your ship called in rather than one of the smaller Fleet vessels you mentioned?"

"Discovery-class cruisers are always called in following Setarip attacks in their quadrants."

"Why?"

"It's been standard procedure ever since we lost several frigates and freighters to repeated Setarip attacks on the same target. The Setarips would wait for the smaller vessels to arrive with supplies and then descend with an even larger force. The Discovery-class cruisers are the best deterrent to that tactic."

Micah winced. Magee had alluded to the same point, but Knox's description gave him an entirely new perspective on how vicious some of the Setarip factions could be. And what Ifel was up against to achieve peace.

"Why wasn't the Federal Coalition in charge of the Gaian investigation?"

"Because Setarips aren't Union citizens. They can't be charged by the FC, but they can be detained and charged by Fleet Security."

"Have the Setarips ever attacked a target so close to Earth?"

"No. This is the first time. In fact, it's the first confirmation we've had of their presence in the Interior Hub. All previous encounters with Setarips have occurred in the Central Zone or Outer Rim."

"Where was the *Argo* at the time you received orders to report to Gaia?"

"The Outer Rim."

"How long did it take you to reach Gaia?"

"Three days."

"What was the situation when you arrived at Gaia?"

"The *Starhawke* was in orbit, the crew keeping watch for any sign of Setarip ships and awaiting the arrival of the transport crew who would take the captured Setarip ship to Earth."

"Was the Setarip ship also in orbit?"

"No, it had been secured on a remote island."

"Who was in charge of guarding the ship?"

"A security detail from the Rescue Corps."

"Did Admiral Schreiber visit Gaia during this time?"

"Yes."

"Was Lt. Isabeau Magee with him?"

Knox's reply came a little slower, his lips pressing together. "Yes."

"When did Admiral Schreiber and Lt. Magee arrive at Gaia?"

"A few days after we did."

"Did Admiral Schreiber remain during the investigation?"

"Yes. He stayed on the *Argo*, coordinating with the Galactic Council while I oversaw the investigative team."

"Was the Galactic Council kept informed of what was transpiring on Gaia?"

"Yes."

"Was there any other purpose for Admiral Schreiber's trip to Gaia?"

"He transported three of the Fleet crewmembers who were assigned to fly the Setarip ship to Earth."

"Who was the CO for that mission?"

"My first officer."

"Did the crew successfully deliver the Setarip ship to Earth?"

"No. The ship exploded over one of the Gaian oceans before it left atmosphere."

"What caused the explosion?"

"Based on our analysis and investigation, incendiary devices were placed on the ship and triggered when the ship attempted to leave atmosphere."

"Who placed the explosives?"

"Two rogue RC officers, Ricardo Contreras and Debora Marek."

"Did you send search and rescue teams to the crash site?"

"Immediately."

"Were you able to recover the crew?"

Knox's jaw flexed. "No."

"Were you able to recover the ship?"

"No. The wreckage sank into the ocean."

"Did Captain Hawke's crew participate in the search and rescue?"

"Absolutely."

"Did they remain on Gaia to help with the investigation?"

"No."

"Why not?"

"Their authority didn't extend to a criminal investigation."

"Where did the *Starhawke* go after leaving Gaia?"

"To Drakar. The *Starhawke* had suffered damage during the battle with the Setarips and needed repairs."

"Why Drakar instead of a Fleet shipyard or station?"

"The *Starhawke* is a Kraed-built vessel. Only the Kraed can service it."

Copeland paused, glancing at his tablet. "Did you and Admiral Schreiber discuss the Setarip attack while he was onboard the *Argo?*"

"At length. An attack so close to Earth from the Etah Setarip faction, a faction we had believed was wiped out, was disturbing, especially when we discovered RC personnel were involved."

"Was Lt. Magee present during those discussions?"

"Yes."

"How long have you known Lt. Magee?"

"Almost fourteen years, since shortly after she became Admiral Schreiber's PA."

"How often have you seen her during that time?"

"Several times a year."

"During official meetings with Admiral Schreiber?"

"Yes."

"Are you and Lt. Magee friends who see each other socially?"

A sympathy pang hit Micah as Knox tensed. He looked like he'd scraped against a coral reef.

"Yes."

"During the discussions about the Setarip attack on Gaia, did Lt. Magee show any signs of physical or emotional discomfort?"

"No."

"How would you describe her behavior during those discussions?"

"Calm. Focused. Professional. She was an active participant in the discussions, offering her insights and ideas."

"How would you describe Admiral Schreiber's behavior during those discussions?"

"The same. He and Lt. Magee would bounce ideas off each other, bring up points from their shared experiences overseeing the aftermath of Setarip attacks."

"Did their interactions with each other appear strained or tense compared to previous discussions you've had with them?"

"No."

"Did you spend any time with Lt. Magee on the *Argo* when she was not with Admiral Schreiber?"

Knox's shoulders flexed under his uniform as he shifted in his chair. "Yes."

"Were those professional or social interactions?"

"Social."

"How would you describe her behavior during those interactions?"

Knox's face looked brittle compared to the easygoing smile Micah associated with him. "She was relaxed. Happy."

"Did she express any concerns about her relationship with Admiral Schreiber?"

"No."

"Did she say anything to you about Captain Hawke?"

"Yes. She praised Captain Hawke and her crew. She also expressed concern for the damage the *Starhawke* had sustained during the fighting."

"Did she appear uncomfortable or agitated talking about Captain Hawke?"

"Not at all."

Seventy-Nine

Listening to Knox's testimony hurt Aurora far more than Magee's had. The pain in his emotional field cut through her like a laser, piercing her heart.

But despite the agony Copeland's line of inquiry caused him, Knox's voice maintained the stalwart tone that had always inspired confidence in those who served under him. Including her.

She needed that confidence, now more than ever.

Reining in her empathetic response to his pain, she focused on Copeland's new line of questioning.

"Was the attack on Gaia the first incident where Setarips and humans worked together against the Galactic Union?"

"No."

"What was the first incident?"

"The Ecilam faction attacked the Persei Primus science station three years ago with the help of two human collaborators."

"Is Persei Primus located in SGQ2?"

"Yes."

"Was your ship called in to investigate that attack?"

"Yes. We were the first responders. We received the initial distress call from the station."

"When the *Argo* arrived at Persei Primus, did you see any Setarip ships?"

"We didn't see any sign of intact ships. One of their destroyers was in pieces, floating near the station."

"How did you identify the ship as Ecilam faction?"

"There are aspects of Ecilam ship design that make them unique when compared to other Setarip faction vessels."

"How do you know about these design aspects?"

"The Fleet has had more contact with Ecilam vessels than any other faction. Videos and images were analyzed and unique characteristics identified. All Fleet personnel are taught these at the Academy, and Commanding Officers are expected to be able to differentiate between the various factions' ships on sight."

"Did the *Argo* dock with the station?"

"No."

"Why not?"

"The large ship docking ports were damaged and debris surrounded the entire station. We also didn't have communication with the station personnel. Our only option was to send a response team on a personnel shuttle."

"Was Captain Hawke a member of your crew at that time?"

"Yes. She was my first officer."

"What role did you assign to Captain Hawke during the mission?"

"She led the response team on the station."

"How long had she been your first officer at that point?"

"A couple weeks."

"Did you have any concerns about her leading the response team so soon after joining your crew?"

"No. She wouldn't have been under my command if she wasn't qualified to handle the duties assigned to her."

She appreciated the compliment, but she appreciated the smoothing out of Knox's emotions now that Copeland wasn't asking him about Magee even more.

"Lt. Magee testified previously that no one makes commander as young as Captain Hawke was."

Spoke too soon.

"How old was Captain Hawke when she received her promotion to Commander?"

"She turned twenty-seven a month after she accepted the post."

"Has any Fleet officer been promoted to the rank of Commander at a younger age?"

"No."

"Prior to Captain Hawke, to the best of your knowledge, what's the youngest age that a Fleet officer has been promoted to the rank of Commander?"

"Thirty-one."

"Did you request to have her assigned to the *Argo*?"

"Yes, although Captain Warner also recommended her for the post."

"Did her achievements at the Academy and onboard the *Excelsior* factor into your decision to make that request?"

"Absolutely."

"Was Captain Hawke the only Fleet officer who was qualified for that post?"

"No."

"Were there more experienced Fleet officers with similar qualifications who could have filled that post on the *Argo*?"

"Not the way Captain Hawke did."

"Why not?"

"Because she's extraordinary. What Mozart was to music Captain Hawke is to leadership. It's innate, a quality she was born with. My crew trusted her, followed her, respected her, because she always had their backs. Always. She's the best first officer I've ever had."

Aurora's throat clogged, her emotions threatening her equilibrium again. She'd always known Knox believed in her, trusted her, but she'd never heard him express it so clearly.

"Did you assign the *Argo*'s Security Chief to join the response team Captain Hawke led on Persei Primus?"

"No."

"Who was assigned?"

"Captain Hawke requested that Lt. Celia Cardiff head the security team instead."

"Is it standard procedure to have someone other than the Security Chief lead the security team in this type of situation?"

"No, it's not."

"What reason did Captain Hawke give for her choice?"

"Lt. Cardiff was the best hand-to-hand combat fighter on the crew. Lt. Cmd. Jeffries, the *Argo's* Security Chief, would be the first to tell you he didn't have her unarmed combat skills, or her quick reflexes. Captain Hawke believed Lt. Cardiff's skillset would be more useful dealing with the unknown situation on the station, while Lt. Cmd. Jeffries' experience would better serve the *Argo* in case the Setarips returned. I agreed with her."

"Did Lt. Cmd. Jeffries make any official objections to that decision?"

"No."

"Did he make any private objections you're aware of?"

"Never. He told me he understood Captain Hawke's reasoning and supported it. His extremely detailed incident report reflects that. We needed him at tactical to defend against the Setarips."

And he'd done a damn fine job in a challenging situation. Jeffries was one of the crewmembers she missed most from the *Argo*. Some of the crew found his no-nonsense attitude off-putting, but she'd resonated with the fierce loyalty that drove him. And with his willingness to put himself in the line of fire.

"How long had Lt. Cardiff served on the *Argo* prior to the Setarip attack on Persei Primus?"

"Ten months."

"So, she was not part of the *Argo*'s launch crew?"

"No. Her first posting was on the *Kepler*. She received her promotion to the *Argo* a year after we launched."

"Did Captain Hawke assign any medical personnel to the response team?"

"Yes. Dr. Lelindia Forrest, our Chief Medical Officer, who selected her top medics for the team."

"Was that standard procedure?"

"Yes. We anticipated heavy casualties on the station, especially after we got a look at the exterior. An entire section of the station had been obliterated."

The shadows of memory ghosted over Aurora, making her shiver. That moment had been nothing compared to what followed.

Eighty

Lelindia kept her focus on Knox. Repeatedly reliving the memories of the casualties she hadn't been able to save on Persei Primus wasn't a pleasant experience, but what he was going through wasn't a picnic, either.

"How long had Dr. Forrest been the Chief Medical Officer on the *Argo*?"

"Two weeks. She and Captain Hawke transferred together from the *Excelsior*."

"So Captain Hawke was familiar with Dr. Forrest's medical abilities?"

Celia snickered, earning a mock glare from Lelindia.

"Definitely."

"How soon after you arrived at Persei Primus did the Setarip ships reappear in the system?"

"About five minutes after the response team docked at the station."

"Did you alert Captain Hawke?"

"Yes."

"Did the Setarip ships attack the *Argo*?"

"Yes. They fired on us and the station."

"When did you learn there were Setarips on the station?"

"During the battle. Captain Hawke notified me when the RC freighter disengaged from the station."

"What exactly did she tell you?"

"That Setarips were escaping on the freighter, and that they'd stolen a case. She asked if we could stop them."

"Did you stop them?"

"We attempted to intercept the freighter, but we failed. The other Setarip ships formed a protective barrier between the *Argo* and the freighter. One of their ships maneuvered directly in our line of fire. The debris from the explosion prevented us from pursuing the RC freighter before it left the system."

Copeland touched his tablet. An image appeared on the screens.

"Captain Schreiber, can you identify this item?"

Lelindia gritted her teeth. She recognized the image as one Cade's team had taken while they were onboard the Setarip ship on Gaia. This particular device had been worn by an Etah Setarip. It was in much better shape than the hundreds of soiled devices she and Aurora had carefully extracted from the backs of the Suulh.

"That's one of the flight packs the Etah Setarips used for the agricultural attacks on Gaia."

"Does the design for this device match the prototype that was in the case the Ecilam took from Persei Primus?"

"Yes."

"Did you write the Setarip incident report regarding the attack on Gaia?"

"Yes."

"How many of the other Fleet Setarip incident reports have you read?"

"All of them."

"Why read all of them?"

"The Setarips pose a significant threat to Fleet ships, colonies, and outposts. Evaluating all prior incidents involving Setarips is part of my job."

"And in all those reports you've evaluated, have you ever come across evidence of Setarips working cooperatively?"

"No."

"Have you ever seen evidence of them trading or bartering with each other for goods or resources?"

"No."

"Director Holcomb testified that the two human collaborators working with the Ecilam Setarips on Persei Primus knew RC protocols. He also testified that the human collaborators spoke to the station personnel, claiming they needed repairs, and that their knowledge of Corps protocols and their presence onboard the freighter gained them clearance to dock. Did your crew question the presence of the RC freighter when you arrived at Persei Primus?"

"No."

"Why not?"

"We had no reason to believe it posed a threat."

"Nothing about it looked out of place or unusual?"

"No."

If it had, Lt. Reed, the one member of the response team Lelindia hadn't been able to save, might still be alive.

"Have you seen Corps freighters before?"

"Hundreds."

"Were the uniforms the collaborators and Setarips wore on Persei Primus unusual or inauthentic in any way?"

"The one slightly odd element was the thermal hoods worn by the Setarips to conceal their faces. Thermal hoods are typically only part of the cold weather uniform worn in extreme planetary environments."

"Returning to the attack on Gaia, were the humans who colluded with the Etah Setarips on Gaia employees of the RC?"

"Yes, they were." The arctic frost in Knox's eyes made it clear he wasn't talking about the two RC officers who'd taken the blame. He was talking about the psychotic mastermind who'd gotten away.

"Did anyone question their presence as part of the RC relief efforts on Gaia?"

"No."

"Did their knowledge of Corps protocols and their presence at the temporary RC headquarters help them obtain unauthorized access to restricted information?"

"Yes."

"Is the Rescue Corps under the governance of the Fleet Director?"

"No. The Corps is under the governance of the Galactic Council."

"Who is the head of the Rescue Corps?"

"The Corps Director."

"Do the two branches ever work together?"

"Absolutely. Cooperation is essential during disaster relief missions."

"Can Fleet personnel obtain Corps resources and equipment without going through the Corps chain of command?"

"No."

"Can the Fleet Director obtain Corps resources and equipment without going through the Corps Director?"

"No."

"Thank you, Captain Schreiber. No more questions, Your Honor."

Eighty-One

Aurora swiped the sleeve of her exercise shirt over her forehead, whisking away the sweat trickling into her eyes. Her feet kept a steady beat on the hard-packed earth, the chain link and block of the perimeter fence passing with monotonous regularity to her left as she circled the small enclosure in an endless loop.

Ordinarily she walked during her exercise time, but today she needed a way to release the pent-up energy that had built in her muscles as she'd listened to Knox's testimony.

She couldn't tell if the Admiral was gaining ground or not. Ordinarily Knox would be a highly credible witness, but he was the Admiral's son and her former CO. The panel knew that. They could consciously or unconsciously discount everything he said.

Their emotional resonances might have given her a clue, but it was nearly impossible to sense their distinct fields through the muddled mess surrounding her.

Keeping her head down, she gazed at the narrow strip of brown between the fence and the green grass. Despite the unseasonably warm day, she felt like she was running beneath thick gray clouds that blocked the sun.

"Hawke631!"

She stumbled, the sharp command catching her off guard. She halted, her hands dropping to her knees in a show of tiredness she didn't feel, buying time as she looked over her shoulder at the gate.

All four of her guards stood inside the enclosure – very unusual – and their body language conveyed aggression that was just a notch below combative. Even more troubling, their emotional states were raw and edgy.

What was going on?

Straightening, she walked toward them, keeping her hands away from her body. "Yes?"

"Time's up," the head guard barked, hand shifting toward her weapon.

Aurora didn't question her, despite the obvious lie. She always counted her circuits, and she'd barely surpassed the number of laps she made at a walk. At a run she should be able to complete three or four times as many. There was no way her hour was up.

But arguing wouldn't achieve anything.

She fell into step with them as they left the yard. But rather than directing her to the showers or back toward her cell, they walked her in the opposite direction toward the visitor center.

Interesting. Maybe Phoebe had news for her. "Is my lawyer here?"

No answer.

That gave her pause. If she was seeing Phoebe, they would tell her. And she'd be able to sense her. She didn't.

The stoic code of silence the guards maintained as they marched her into the building combined with the off-key notes in their emotional fields had her energy shield tingling beneath her skin.

The room they took her to was the same one she and Phoebe met in. But when they opened the door, the small space was empty.

Tension tightened her shoulder blades. She paused at the threshold. "Where's my lawyer?"

The guard gave her a flat stare. "Sit." She pointed at the table and two chairs.

"Phoebe's not in the building," Unity said in her ear.

She already knew that but the confirmation, combined with the level of wrongness in this situation, rang every internal bell she had. Too bad the cacophony of alarms clashed with the absolute certainty that the guards would gladly shoot her if she failed to follow orders. Not that they could hurt her, but the lightshow would unleash a tidal wave of new problems.

So she stepped into the room and took a seat.

The guard snapped the door closed, followed by a sharp click as the lock slid into place. A subtle hum started a moment later, the sound familiar although she couldn't place it.

"A privacy screen just activated," Unity informed her, answering her question. "The unauthorized video surveillance of this room can no longer see or hear you. Neither can the guards outside."

"This can't be good," she murmured, her gaze sweeping the room, searching for the threat she knew was coming.

"That all depends on your perspective," a mechanically modulated voice replied.

Goosebumps streaked across her skin, raising the hairs at her sweat-dampened nape.

A hooded figure in a shapeless brown cloak flickered into holographic life in front of her.

It took a tremendous act of will not to react. Her heart kicked into overdrive, but she managed to stay seated. Her fingers curled as she bared her teeth in a non-smile and mimicked her adversary's toneless voice. "Reanne."

"Sovereign," the cloaked figure corrected.

Aurora snorted to disguise her shudder, glancing up at the ceiling. The holoprojector was well concealed along the edge of the recessed light, only vaguely visible now because it was emitting an image. Had it been there the last time she was in this room? "You always did have delusions of grandeur."

"Says the woman with the superiority complex."

"Unity's working to track her signal to its source," Cade whispered. His tightly leashed anger ran beside her own, reminding her she wasn't the only one hearing this. "Keep her talking."

Not a problem. She had plenty to say. "So, frame anyone else for treason this week?"

"Oh, the stories you tell." The Sovereign waved her black-gloved hand, batting aside the question. "Then again, you've always had a talent for convincing people you're the hero of every story. But I know better. This is justice at its finest. You were born a traitor."

"*Born* a traitor?" She tried to wrap her head around that one and failed. "How did baby me manage that?"

"Simple. Your very existence is offensive. You're a half-breed. An *abomination*." The loathing coating those words could have covered the Taj Mahal.

A lot to unpack in those short sentences. But it gave her an opening she wasn't going to miss. "Isn't that the pot calling the kettle black?"

The Sovereign's cloak rippled like she'd jerked in surprise. "What?"

"You're a half-breed, too, aren't you? Your father's a Teeli, isn't he?"

No movement this time. The Sovereign stilled completely.

Aurora waited, the seconds ticking by. Had the feed been interrupted?

The response, when it came, could have sliced through tempered steel. "You have no idea what I am."

For once, she agreed with her. The girl she'd known as Reanne no longer existed. She'd accepted that after the last time they were face to face. Only her body remained beneath the cloak and hood. The Sovereign had consumed Reanne from within, twisting her into a wraith of death and hatred.

She sat forward, staring at where the Sovereign's ice-blue eyes — Teeli eyes — were shadowed by the hood of the cloak. "What do you want?"

"Come now, even you're not that stupid."

Her teeth clicked together as her jaw snapped tight. Cade's growl reverberated in her ear, followed by a word the Sovereign would definitely have taken exception to. "Pretend I am. Spell it out for me."

"Hmm." The Sovereign raised her gloved hand to her chin in a parody of thought. "Why don't you have one of your sycophantic crewmembers explain it to you? I know they're feeding you information about the Admiral's trial."

An unseen hand gripped her throat and squeezed.

"How could she know that?" Cade echoed the question looming in her mind.

The Sovereign's chuckle through the modulator sounded like glass scraping over metal. "Oh, Aurora, you forget how well I know you. Do you honestly think I can't tell you've been listening in on the Admiral's trial? I haven't figured out how you're doing it, but I'm certain your Kraed puppets are involved. That's the reason for the privacy screen." She waved her hand to indicate the ambient hum. "Didn't want them listening in on our conversation. Your annoying attorney proved how extremely effective these screens are. Although none of that matters. You can't hide from me."

"That's rich coming from you. You're the one who's hiding, not me."

"I'm the one who's *leading*. And soon I will lead you and your precious Admiral to your permanent home. With me."

Another wave of gooseflesh rippled over her skin.

"Over my dead body," Cade snarled.

Don't react. Work the problem. She wasn't certain if she was telling herself or Cade, but it was good advice. "You sound pretty confident. Some might say overconfident."

"And you're naïve. Do you honestly believe you can escape justice? That you can avoid punishment for your crimes against Nature? Against the Human race? Against me?"

If this was the time for airing grievances, she was up to the challenge. "Last time I checked, you were the one working with the Teeli and Setarips to overthrow the Union, not me."

Another chuckle. "My, my. Tnaryt must have been quite chatty with you before his abrupt end." She sighed. "It's a pity that I allowed him to die so quickly, but I just couldn't stand any more of his prattling. Still, he deserved so much more. I should have drawn it out, made him suffer. It would have been fun listening to him beg me to take his life. Ah, well." A flick of her hand. "What's done is done."

Bile rose at the back of her throat. She'd despised Tnaryt for the pain he'd inflicted on the Admiral and Nat. His death hadn't bothered her because he'd brought it on himself. But what the

Sovereign was describing chilled her inside and out. "Why are you here?"

"Why? To visit you, of course." The fake cheerfulness was more frightening than anger. "And to let you know your aunt can't wait to see you again. I understand you two had quite the conversation. If I'd known meeting you would incite this level of rage, I would have arranged it sooner."

"Why? Because you need her to be angry?" A dangling thread suddenly knotted and held. "Is that how you manage to manipulate people? By preying on their fear and anger?"

The Sovereign clapped her hands in a slow, rhythmic motion. "Gold star for you. I didn't expect you to figure it out. Though it's not nearly that simplistic, and far from the only way to help people see the truth."

"The truth?"

"The truth of your corrupting nature, the way you turn all those around you into mindless drones who do your bidding."

The ludicrous assertion rendered her speechless.

Cade didn't have that problem. "She's insane."

One hundred percent. Her warped perception of reality was based on a foundation of chaos.

Which made her unpredictable in the worst way. You couldn't outthink someone who wasn't thinking rationally.

She'd never been able to sense Reanne's emotions, but looking back on their history together, her behavior had always been emotionally driven — by jealousy, anger, and fear. Which might explain why those were the same emotions she used to alter the perceptions of others.

"The truth hurts, doesn't it?" No mistaking the glee in the Sovereign's voice.

Her internal thoughts swirled like a tornado. It took a moment to remember what the Sovereign was referring to. "How exactly do I corrupt people?"

The Sovereign spread her hands and shrugged. "If I knew how, I would have stopped you long ago. You're a plague against humanity. The fawning devotion you generate infects everyone you touch. But I'm immune. I see you for who you really are. And thanks to me, you and your precious Admiral will never harm anyone again."

The Sovereign stepped to the side, the holographic image focusing on the object behind her. She rested her hand on the front of it.

A clear box?

"What do you think of your new home?"

The air leaked out of her lungs.

Not a box. A cage.

Eighty-Two

"Beautiful, isn't it?" The Sovereign stroked the side of the two-meter-high cube. "The Teeli helped me design it. They've learned a great deal about the Suulh since your mother abandoned them. As you might imagine, Kreestol was quite eager to test it when she learned you would be the occupant. I can assure you that it's quite secure, even for you."

Aurora forced air back into her lungs as her mind raced. The Teeli had figured out a design that could nullify her Sahzade abilities?

"And because I didn't want you to be lonely…" The Sovereign took a step to the side, revealing a matching cage beside the first. "I had one built for your mother, as well."

Nausea swept through her, acid pooling in her abdomen.

Rising with slow deliberation, she planted her palms flat on the table, tilting her head in mock inquiry. "Remind me. How did that work out the last time you went after her?"

The Sovereign stiffened, the temperature in the room plummeting. But she shrugged with an unconcerned laugh. "You also forget that I've seen you two together. I know exactly how much your safety means to her. Do you honestly believe she won't do whatever I tell her to, if she knows it will spare you pain?"

"She'd never believe anything you said. She never has." Unfortunately, Aurora had been a headstrong teenage who hadn't listened to her mother's warnings about her toxic roommate. She'd brushed her mom's concerns off as overprotective paranoia.

Turned out her mom was right.

"True. She never liked me. The feeling was mutual, though I didn't understand why I hated her so much until I met Kreestol. But your mom will fall in line once I have you in here." She patted the first cage affectionately.

"Don't count on it. You'll have to catch me first."

That almost doubled her over with laughter. "Look around you, Aurora." She swept her arms wide. "I've already caught you. You're in the detention center I chose for you and soon you'll be convicted of treason against the Union. You and the Admiral both. I'll admit I had planned to have the Admiral in hand before you returned to Earth, but perhaps this is better. You're able to see and appreciate the fruits of my labors."

Aurora's energy field sparked beneath her skin, responding to the perceived threat.

"I have another bit of news for you," she continued in a stage whisper. "You've been reassigned to a new judge. Sato had an unfortunate accident."

Sick dread hit her like toxic sludge. She locked her elbows to keep her arms from shaking. "What kind of accident?"

"The foolish woman fell down the stairs. Can you believe it? So clumsy. Broke her neck. Died before the medics arrived. Sad, really. She had children."

Rage roared from her throat. "You monster!" Her hip struck the table as she lunged forward, her energy field igniting.

The Sovereign laughed. "Temper, Aurora. Don't let your emotions get the better of you."

Her whole body shook. Sato was dead. Murdered. If she hadn't been talking to a projection, she would have put the Sovereign through the block wall.

"Your new judge has a much better understanding of the situation. Soon you and the Admiral will be spending a lot of time together." The Sovereign walked a few paces away from the twin cages, the visual tracking her and settling on another pair of cages directly across from the first two. She rested her hand on the first one. "This cage is the Admiral's, conveniently placed directly across from yours. And because I didn't want him to feel left out, this one," she tapped the second one, "is for Lt. Magee."

Aurora's throat turned into sandpaper, her voice coming out in a rasp. "Is that where you've been keeping her?"

The Sovereign placed a hand over her heart. "Goodness, no. That would have been rude. She's been so incredibly helpful." Her tone changed, becoming dismissive. "But her usefulness is coming to an end. Maybe I should just kill her."

Aurora's heart thudded in her chest. It wasn't an empty threat.

"And someday I will. But this solution gives me so many more options."

Cade's sickened moan in her ear could have been her own.

"Oh, and let's not forget the best part!" The Sovereign waggled a finger at her. "You'll have to forgive me, because they're not quite ready yet. But it's your own fault. You've been so sneaky and secretive."

Aurora braced against the table again, unable to tear her gaze from the shifting holoprojection.

"Ta-da." The Sovereign swept an arm toward two partially completed cages that sat near the other four. "This is my gift to you. Or it will be soon. A way to honor our long acquaintance and prove my good intentions." She faced Aurora, her voice growing solemn. "I certainly wouldn't want to be responsible for splitting up your newly reunited family."

Understanding hit her like a sledgehammer.

Micah. Her dad.

The horror that followed held her suspended for a heartbeat, like a sudden updraft that carried her aloft. Or the push that sent her tumbling off a cliff.

She was vaguely aware that Cade was saying something to her, but all she could hear was the thundering of her heart and the Sovereign's delighted laughter.

"Oh, Aurora, you should see your face."

That broke the spell.

The heat from her energy field matched the burning in her chest. She jabbed a finger at the Sovereign. "You will never get your hands on them."

She couldn't see the Sovereign's smile, but she knew it was there. "Go ahead," the Sovereign said in a mocking tone. "Hit me with your best shot."

Energy surged in her hands. This was her waking nightmare, the one that had been haunting her ever since she'd learned the Sovereign's identity. She'd visualized this a thousand times, the Sovereign standing *right there*, right in front of her. But there was absolutely nothing she could do.

"Well." The Sovereign clasped her hands like it was time to get back to work. "I've given you a lot to think about, and you've given me a moment's entertainment. Now I must go. So much to do." She flicked her hand in the direction of the unfinished cages. "But don't worry, I'm not abandoning you. In fact, I promise that I will be watching you very, *very*, closely."

The projection blinked off.

The silence screamed.

Micah.

Air. She needed air.

Her dad.

Her knees gave way, dropping her into her chair.

The Admiral.

She slumped onto her forearms, staring at the scarred table.

Sato.

What had she done?

This was her fault. *Hers.*

When FS had come for her, she'd focused on protecting Cade and her crew. She hadn't considered the wider implications.

Now Judge Sato was dead, a casualty of Aurora's war with the Sovereign. She might not have been able to save her no matter what she did, but why the hell hadn't she extracted a promise from Micah, from her parents, that they'd stay far, far away from her? Why had she let them come here? The Sovereign hadn't known Micah and her dad existed. Now they were in the Sovereign's crosshairs.

And she couldn't protect them.

"Your family's fine," Cade said softly. "They're safe on the *Starhawke.* She's trying to get into your head."

His reassurance slid off her like water on a duck's back.

This wasn't a ploy. This was a checkmate move. The Sovereign wouldn't have revealed so much — told her about Sato — if she wasn't absolutely certain she'd trapped Aurora in a no-win scenario.

The lock on the door popped, making her jump.

The guards marched in, hands on their weapons. "Let's go."

Eighty-Three

Lee-Lee!

The wretched self-recrimination and anguish in Aurora's cry rooted Lelindia's feet to the deck of the greenhouse.

I'm here, Sahzade. I heard.

She'd been working in the greenhouse with her parents when Unity had alerted them to Aurora's unexpected visitor. They'd listened as Unity projected the conversation over the ship's speakers. By the time it ended, Lelindia was trembling with fear and rage.

Your family's fine. They're here, they're safe. Micah was in the galley with Celia, and she was pretty sure Brendan and Libra were in their cabin.

I know, but...

The fact that Aurora couldn't complete her thought told her how rattled she was.

We'll fig—

An enraged, feral roar from inside the med bay made her spin in that direction.

Jonarel charged into the greenhouse, nearly clipping the door edge with his shoulder before it could open fully. Fire and brimstone burned in his golden eyes as his gaze caught hers. Between one heartbeat and the next his arms swept around her, hauling her against the solid wall of his chest. He tucked her head into his shoulder so tightly she couldn't see.

His muscled body radiated barely contained violence. "I will kill her."

A shudder passed over her at the promise in those words.

Lee-Lee?

She pulled her head back, meeting his gaze. "I'm talking to Aurora."

He eased up a fraction, but the lethal panther who'd leapt into the room remained on guard.

I'm here she projected to Aurora. *Give me a moment.*

She shot a look at her parents, who were both wide-eyed. "Maybe you should get Libra and Brendan down here?" she asked her mom.

Her mom blinked. "Right. I—"

"Libra and Brendan are already on their way to the galley," Unity informed them. "As are Kire and Kelly."

Good. Unity had already mobilized the troops. "What's Cade doing?"

"He's talking to Aurora, though I'm not certain she's listening."

Her chest tightened. That behavior reminded her far too much of the near catatonic state Aurora had fallen into after uncovering the Sovereign's identity. She needed to pull her out of her tailspin before she sank any lower.

Sahzade, sit tight. I'm going to reach out to Cade, Ifel, and Siginal. I'll have Unity loop you into the discussion once we've gathered.

She could almost hear Aurora's sigh.

Thank you.

We'll figure this out. Talk to you soon. She turned to Unity. "I assume Ifel is aware of what's happened?"

Unity bobbed forward. "Yes. She is... concerned."

Unity's hesitation caught her attention. "Just concerned?"

Unity swayed. "She prides herself on her ability to maintain a steady emotional state. But this interchange has been... upsetting."

"So she's furious?" she guessed.

Unity bobbed once. "We'd say that's an accurate assessment."

"How about Cade?"

"Also furious. Right now he's pacing his cabin. Talking a blue streak, we believe is the apt phrase. Some of his words and phrases are unfamiliar to us, but by context we assume they're profanity."

"I'll bet." She'd have the same urge if she was alone. "Tell him we're going to have a conference call as soon as I can get Siginal over here. Tehar?"

Tehar appeared beside her. "Yes?"

"Can you ask your dad if he can come over here ASAP?"

Tehar made a strange, self-conscious movement of her hands. "He is already on his way."

"Already?"

"Rowk, Unity, and I made the decision to include him in the audio feed of the Sovereign's visit."

And she wholeheartedly agreed with their decision. They were looking out for the crew, and she was grateful. "Good. Saves us time. Tell him we're gathering in the observation lounge."

Tehar nodded and vanished.

Extricating herself from Jonarel's embrace took effort. He resisted her, his low growl and firm grip making her wonder if what he really wanted to do was sweep her off her feet and sequester her in their cabin.

Probably.

No way was that happening.

She shot him a stern look. He finally relented, but kept his hand tucked at her waist as she led her parents along the path through the greenhouse to the galley.

By the time they entered the galley, Libra was stalking the aisle like a caged lioness, Brendan and Micah watching her with concern. Celia was conferring in low tones with Kire and Kelly.

They all turned toward Lelindia, but it was Libra who cut her off, halting her in her tracks. "We have to act. Now."

Libra's tone left no room for discussion. She wasn't speaking as a concerned parent worried about her daughter. She was speaking as the Sahzade of the Suulh in full command mode.

Too bad. The past few months had helped Lelindia overcome the conditioning of her youth — largely thanks to Aurora — and she wasn't about to let any action move forward without Aurora's and the crew's input. Libra would have to cool her jets. "We will act," she assured her in an equally firm tone. "But first we need a plan. Siginal's on his way here, and Unity's going to connect us with Cade and Ifel."

Libra blinked, clearly shocked that Lelindia wasn't immediately falling in line. Brendan, on the other hand, gave her an encouraging nod.

She appreciated it more than she could say. She held his gaze. "Can you get everyone set up in the observation lounge while Celia and I make some tea?"

It was a multi-pronged ploy. She wanted Libra kept busy and everyone else out of the room. She needed a moment alone with Celia before tackling the group discussion.

He took the hint. "Good idea." He motioned to Micah and flicked a glance at Lelindia's parents as he coaxed Libra toward the door.

Jonarel's fingers curled around Lelindia's side, indicating he had no intention of leaving the room.

Her dad stepped in, clapping Jonarel on the shoulder and tugging gently but firmly. "Let's go greet your dad."

Jonarel resisted.

Then her mom clasped his free hand and pulled him toward the door. "Shall we?"

Jonarel's growl sounded like a grumble, but her parents hadn't given him an out. He wouldn't risk offending them by refusing. Releasing his hold on her with obvious reluctance, he allowed them to walk him into the observation lounge, followed by Kire, Kelly, and Unity.

Celia leaned her hip against the counter and folded her arms. "I'm guessing you want to know my unedited thoughts before we wade into this."

"Correct." Lelindia started the tea brewing and turned to her friend. "The Sovereign thinks she's already won."

"Which means the trials are a sham. She must have control of the panels. We know she has the judges. Now," she added with a disgusted scowl.

"Which leaves us with what?"

"I think you know."

"Yes, but I'd rather hear you say it."

Celia's dark eyes were deadly serious. "Looks like we're going to orchestrate a jailbreak."

Eighty-Four

Micah's head swiveled robotically as he took in the group seated around the elongated table in the observation lounge. He honestly couldn't decide who was the scariest person in the room.

Celia's composure provided an icy counterpoint to Siginal and Jonarel's fiery glares. Kire looked ready and willing to unload the ship's entire arsenal on anyone who dared approach the *Starhawke*'s airbridge. Even Lelindia's normally benevolent demeanor had taken on an air of menace. But it was his mom who had him on pins and needles.

When she'd stormed into the galley and rushed toward him, he'd backed up against the counter before he could stop himself. The hatred, the rage in her eyes had shocked him. Still shocked him. He never would have imagined his mom could seriously contemplate murder, but in that moment, he'd believed it to his core. His mom wanted the Sovereign dead.

And so he was taking a little extended mental and emotional vacay during this debate. Whatever he'd thought he was prepared for when it came to the Sovereign, he had been very, *very* wrong.

There hadn't been any visual to go with the disturbing audio, but that had made listening to it even worse. He'd clung to the galley's countertop, unable to move, barely breathing, his mind refusing to believe what he was hearing.

Even after the audio cut off, he'd remained locked in place until Celia snapped him out of it. Or more accurately snapped him into whatever state he was occupying now.

Cages. The Sovereign wanted to put his entire family in cages. She talked about it like they'd be part of her personal art collection.

A thread of emotion wormed its way through, coating his throat with sickly-sweetness.

Aurora had tried to warn him. She'd tried to send him back to his regular life, but he'd refused.

She'd known what she was facing.

He hadn't.

Not that it would have changed anything. If he'd grasped the depth of depravity the Sovereign was capable of, he still wouldn't have left Aurora's side.

"—can get her out of that detention center."

The hairs on the back of his neck stood at attention at his mom's tone. Utterly terrifying.

"No!" Siginal smacked his palm on the table, making Micah jump. "You will not leave this ship."

His mom's voice went subzero. "I don't need your permission, Siginal."

"You—"

"It's not about permission, Libra," Micah's dad interrupted, forestalling the battle. "It's about liability. We know we're targets — you, me, and Micah." His dad gave him a look that was probably meant to convey something. Unfortunately, he wasn't functionally processing anything right now.

His mom glanced at him. He hadn't noticed until that moment that her much smaller hand was firmly planted over his on the table, like she could pin him in place.

A hysterical laugh threatened to crawl out of his throat. He choked it down.

If she wanted to, she could.

"We need you with us, Libra," his dad continued. "No one can protect us like you can."

Way to use the psychology, Dad.

He'd scored a hit, too. Worry overwrote the aggression on his mom's features. Her hand pressed even tighter against his like she planned to fuse them together.

Another tickle of inappropriate laughter.

She could probably do that, too.

"Aurora agrees with you, Brendan," Lelindia said, her gaze shifting to Libra. "She's counting on you to keep them safe."

Swish. Nothing but net. He could see it in his mom's eyes. No way would she leave their sides after a statement like that.

"There are other options," Cade said from the projection hovering at one end of the table.

"Yes." Siginal nodded decisively. "My clan will extract them."

Lelindia's hand shot out. "Hang on. Your clan can't get implicated in this, either."

Siginal bristled. "Why not?"

"Because the Admiral and Aurora are accused of treason and conspiracy. If you break them out of the detention center, in the Fleet's eyes, that would be an act of war."

Funny how a word only three letters long could instantly change the atmosphere in the room.

"She's right," Kire agreed. "The Fleet would have to respond."

"And none of us want that." Lelindia took a breath. "It can't be Libra, and it can't be Siginal." Her gaze swept from Kire, to Kelly, to Celia, before resting on Jonarel. "But it can be us."

"Us." Jonarel's gaze dropped to Lelindia's abdomen. "But, checana—"

"Aurora's our captain," Celia said like that settled the matter.

"And we're Fleet," Kire added. "The Sovereign's already convincing everyone there are traitors in our midst. Our springing Aurora and the Admiral won't destroy anything that isn't already smashed to smithereens. It's not like we were going to keep working for the Fleet if Aurora was convicted." He turned to Kelly. "But that doesn't have to include you."

Kelly tipped her head, her eyes narrowing. "I'm not part of the crew anymore?"

"That's not what I meant."

"Good. Because I signed on with Aurora, not the Fleet. She's my captain just as much as yours. I go where she goes."

"Aurora is..." Lelindia's voice caught. "Very grateful. In her words, *best damn crew in the galaxy.*"

A tiny smile tugged at Kire's mouth. "Glad she noticed."

Cade cleared his throat, drawing everyone's attention. "My team's responsible for the Admiral's safety, so we'll be joining you. We're also going to have to get the *Starhawke* away from Sol Station."

Micah frowned. "Why is that a problem? I thought we weren't being held here." Maybe he'd missed something through his mental fog.

"We're not," Kire agreed, "that we know of. But now that the Sovereign's made her grand pronouncement, she'll be watching for any movement on our part."

"Exactly," Cade agreed. "If we don't want to telegraph our intentions, we'll have to time the extraction and departure to coincide. Since Brendan, and I assume Gryphon, will be staying on the *Starhawke*, I'd suggest they handle the ship's departure so Kelly's free to fly the *Starhawke*'s shuttle."

Cade's off-hand comment opened a crater the size of a stadium at Micah's feet.

Staying. They were *all* staying. On the ship.

Then what?

He'd been so focused on Aurora's situation he hadn't spun out the logic thread for himself or his dad. What all this meant for their lives, their futures.

What about his dad's house? Their jobs? Birdie and Kai? Could he even reach out to tell them what was happening? And how could his dad abandon Far Horizons? He couldn't just disappear… could he?

His gaze drifted to his dad's. Not surprisingly, his dad was watching him. He didn't seem nearly as freaked out, or as startled, by the turn of events as Micah was. Then again, he'd already flipped his life upside down several times — first when he met Micah's mom, then when he'd taken Micah to Hawaii, and then again when Aurora had shown up and their family had reunited.

Maybe it got easier with practice.

"—pilot the other shuttle. I can pick up my team and meet you at the detention center," Cade said. "Knox, too, depending on what he decides."

Right, Knox. Yet another future torpedoed. If the Admiral got busted out of prison, it was unlikely Knox's superiors would be sending him back to captain the Fleet's flagship.

He caught the glance Celia flicked at him, concern in her dark eyes.

She should be concerned. He felt like he was caught in an undertow that was steadily dragging him under.

Choosing to stay with Aurora's crew to help her defeat the Sovereign had been a decision he'd made willingly. But this situation wasn't a choice. For any of them. The Sovereign's sick plan to lock up his family and the Admiral in her demented revenge sideshow display had yanked his entire life — all their lives — out from under them.

Eighty-Five

"We have one more issue." Cade smiled grimly. "If we're going to rescue Magee, we have to do it now."

"Do we even know where she is?" Lelindia asked.

"We do," Unity replied in stereo. U-2 hovered beside Cade in his cabin, but U-1 bobbed at the opposite end of the observation lounge table in the vid feed. "We have been tracking her since her appearance at the courthouse. She is being kept at the Teeli Embassy."

A fact Unity had already relayed to Cade. Unity had been unsuccessful in tracking the Sovereign's signal to the source — apparently Ecilam tech was involved in the multitude of relays — but they'd talked to Ifel about potential roles for the Yruf in the extractions.

"Magee won't go willingly," Cade said, "not after what we saw at the Admiral's trial. But Unity has an idea."

Unity did an excellent imitation of Micah clearing his throat. "We gathered considerable data during Sly'Kull's testimony. We also observed Magee during her testimony. Based on our findings, we believe we can use her suggestibility to our advantage."

Celia leaned forward in the vid feed, looking intrigued. "How?"

"By impersonating Sly'Kull. We can infiltrate the Teeli Embassy and install ourselves in their security and communications systems. But unlike with you, we would be speaking as Sly'Kull, not with Micah's voice. We believe Magee is so conditioned to obey his orders that she would follow any order we gave her."

"What would you say?" Celia asked.

"We would tell her to leave the building. Then you can rescue her."

"What if she resists you?" Siginal asked.

Cade glanced at Ifel, who stood slightly behind him, looking more imposing than he'd ever seen her, including the day he met her in her throne room. Her diamond pupils widened, her tongue flicking twice.

"We do not believe that will happen," Unity translated her reply, "but we are prepared to offer additional assistance to extract her, as well as Aurora and the Admiral."

"Without being seen?" Lelindia asked. "Aurora's adamant that the Yruf's presence can't be revealed to anyone, especially the Sovereign."

"That's where things get tricky." Cade rolled his shoulders to work out the kinks in his neck. "We're only five days past the full moon, and skies are clear. We'll have a brief interval between lights out at the detention center and moonrise. Any role the Yruf ships play at the detention center would have to be completed in that time window. Otherwise, they'll be visible."

"But we'll have more time at the Embassy," Unity said. "We can be delivered as soon as the sun sets. Our scout ship will remain out of sight until it's time to rescue Magee."

"How will you deal with the physical security at the Embassy?" Celia asked.

"We can issue commands through the comms using Sly'Kull's voice. We could also order one of the guards to fetch Magee and bring her outside."

"What about Sly'Kull?" Kire asked. "He's no idiot. What if he catches on?"

"We'll be monitoring him. We should be able to contain him temporarily, if necessary. But we won't take any action until it's time to extract Aurora. Also, someone will need to physically intercept and subdue Magee after she leaves the building."

Cade ran a hand along his jaw, his gaze shifting to Celia. "Someone who can handle her when she gets hostile. Like—"

Knox.

Aurora's mental projection shot across his mind like a flare.

"Aurora thinks Knox should do it." Lelindia met Cade's gaze. "And I agree with her. He knows her better than any of us, and he's capable of physically overpowering her if necessary. He can secure her while we focus on freeing Aurora and the Admiral."

"Ifel's offered a transport for Magee," Cade added, "plus the scout ship that will deliver Unity. Assuming my team and Knox agree,

I can fly tandem with the Yruf transport to the Admiral's house, then we'll split off for the extractions."

"And what about the detention center?" Siginal asked, his gaze moving to Lelindia, pinning her in her chair. "Twice you have said you will focus on freeing Aurora and the Admiral." He somehow managed to loom over Lelindia without moving. "That is unacceptable. You cannot put yourself and your child at risk of capture by leaving the *Starhawke*."

Lelindia's tempered sigh was louder than a sonic boom. "Siginal..."

Eighty-Six

Lelindia loved Siginal dearly – she really did – but she was getting tired of being treated like an invalid incapable of taking care of herself.

Luckily for him, in this one instance, she agreed with him.

"I'm already planning to stay on the *Starhawke*."

Jonarel's gusty exhale matched the tenor of Aurora's projected *thank the stars* and the look of startled relief that swept across Siginal's face. In fact, every person at the table seemed to gain centimeters of space between their shoulder blades. In any other context, it would have been funny.

"The last thing anyone needs to be doing during this mission is worrying about me. If I stay on the *Starhawke*, I'll be an asset rather than a distraction. I'll take over as provisional captain so that Kire can lead Aurora's extraction team." She noted the spark that lit Kire's hazel eyes. "I assume you have no objections?"

His mouth turned up in a fractional smile. "None."

"Good. You can coordinate with Cade's team to fetch Aurora and the Admiral."

Celia raised her hand. "And how exactly are we getting them out?"

"Jonarel and I discussed this previously."

Lelindia's gaze leapt back to Siginal. "You did?" She turned to Jonarel. "When?"

"After Aurora's family last visited the detention center."

So that's what Jonarel had been doing on the *Rowkclarek.* "And?"

Jonarel gestured to U-1. "Unity?"

A projection appeared above the long table. It showed a detailed 3D map of an L-shaped building complex with triangular wedges radiating like spines on a dinosaur's back.

"We have control of all the facility's major systems," Unity informed them. "We deemed it a wise move given the uncertainty of the potential outcomes in this situation."

"Good thinking," Kire murmured, shooting Unity an approving glance.

"Aurora's cell is here." A blue dot appeared on the second level of one of the wedges near Lelindia. "The Admiral's cell is here." A red dot appeared in a wedge on the far side of the table. "As you can see, they are being kept on opposite ends of the complex."

"Because we needed a bigger challenge." Celia studied the projection. "What are the potential exit points from those two buildings?"

"Neither has a direct exterior exit. The Admiral's opens into an interior corridor that's connected to the administrative building. The corridor also has access to one of the exercise yards." A red dashed line showed the path. "So does the corridor that Aurora's wedge opens into." A dashed blue line appeared. "Unfortunately, they don't lead to the same exercise yard."

What looked like a twenty-five-foot solid block wall separated the two yards. "So we can't pick Aurora and the Admiral up from the same location?" Lelindia asked.

"Not without considerable risk. Getting them to the same location would be more complicated than extracting them separately."

I won't leave without the Admiral.

Aurora's assertion interrupted Unity's narrative, pulling Lelindia's attention away from the 3D display.

I know, Sahzade. She would never ask her to, and neither would the crew. Which meant they needed to focus on the Admiral's extraction first.

"—guard towers at these points."

"How do we get the Admiral out safely?" Lelindia asked. "He'll be in physical danger from the moment he leaves his cell." The FS personnel would be armed and wouldn't hesitate to use lethal force.

"Not if he goes through the ceiling," Jonarel said simply.

She turned and stared at her mate. "The ceiling? You mean crawl through a vent?"

"No, through the hole we will cut in the roof."

Eighty-Seven

It took every smidgen of willpower Aurora possessed not to look up. The roof? Really?

She had faith in Jonarel's structural engineering knowledge – he'd designed her ship, after all – but the detention center was a lot different from a starship. It was constructed of mostly cement and block that had been built to last. It wouldn't surprise her if the ceiling above her head was a meter thick.

Still, she liked the idea of plucking the Admiral out of his cell through the roof a lot more than having him attempt to make his way to the exercise yard. She wouldn't be there to protect him. Neither would anyone else.

"I will need to alter the shuttle," Jonarel's voice rumbled in her ear, "so that the cutter can be deployed through the shuttle's deck."

"Won't a cutter make a lot of noise when you operate it?" Lelindia asked.

"It is Kraed technology," Jonarel replied with a hint of reproach.

Aurora bit back a smile.

"Meaning it will be very quiet," Kire translated. "How long do you anticipate it will take to cut through?"

"Less than two minutes."

Impressive. But still an eternity if the guards heard something and decided to open the Admiral's door.

She projected a question to Lelindia. *Is there any way to prevent the Admiral's cell door from opening?*

"Aurora wants to know if there's a way to block the Admiral's door so the guards can't open it."

"We can help with that," Unity replied. "We can disable the electronic locking mechanism and obstruct the manual override."

"So we get the Admiral out, then we do the same thing to free Aurora?" Celia asked.

"Yes," Jonarel said with absolute certainty. "Our shuttle will move to Aurora's location while Cade's unit extracts the Admiral from his cell."

Aurora felt the flicker in Cade's emotional field. Not hard to guess the cause. He was torn. He couldn't rescue the Admiral and be the one to spring her from her cell, too.

You can't do it all she projected to him.

Wry amusement tinged his emotional field. *Neither can you.*

It was the clearest message she'd gotten from him so far, and it struck home.

He wasn't the only one trying to figure out how to be in two places at once. She'd briefly considered asking Lelindia to free her first and then drop her on the roof of the Admiral's cell so she'd be there to defend him.

But that assumed her extraction would go smoothly, which wasn't guaranteed. If they hit a snag getting her out, the Admiral would be in a world of hurt. She wasn't taking any chance on that happening. The cutter had to be deployed on his cell first.

"What about the Sovereign's surveillance?" Celia asked.

"Not a problem," Unity replied. "We've been gathering recordings and building a suite of feeds that we can use when the time comes. As far as the Sovereign will be concerned, the Admiral and Aurora will be sleeping in their cells long after they're gone."

"That will change if any of the guards sound the alarm," Celia countered.

"True, but the feeds will still only work for us. We will block communications, as well. That will make it difficult for the guards to coordinate."

"Unity." Kire's voice was uncharacteristically solemn. "Have I mentioned how glad I am you're on our side?"

No kidding.

"Cade brought up the possibility of help from Yruf ships at the detention center," Celia said. "But given the site layout and the extraction plan, it doesn't sound like there's much they could do without risking being seen."

"You're right." Cade agreed. "The Teeli Embassy has a lot fewer sight lines than the detention center. It'll be easier for their ships to stay hidden there. By design, the detention center is exposed. Having the Yruf there would be a significant risk. Not only is the moonlight a concern, but also the security lighting around the facility."

The Yruf can't come here.

She'd felt Cade and Lelindia leaning in that direction already, but she didn't want any arguments.

The Sovereign wasn't aware of the Yruf's presence, blaming Aurora's outside communications on the Kraed.

They needed to maintain that misperception. She wasn't about to gain her freedom by putting a target on the Yruf's backs.

Eighty-Eight

"We're breaking them out of the detention center?"

"That's right." Cade studied Justin's lean face on the vid feed. He looked like he hadn't had a decent night's sleep since the last time they'd spoken. This news wasn't going to make the situation any better. "I need you to gather the team and Knox. There's something you all need to hear."

Justin glanced over his shoulder, then nodded. "Okay, give me five and I'll call you back."

Ifel had already left Cade's cabin after the group call with the *Starhawke* had ended. She was coordinating with her pilots on the plan he was about to propose to Knox.

Five minutes later his unit and Knox were gathered in the seating area in the Admiral's house, facing Cade's feed. He watched their expressions as Unity replayed the interaction between Aurora and the Sovereign. The same shock, anger, and disgust showed on each face, but it was Knox he focused on the most.

His jaw was carved from stone, his blue eyes spitting fire by the time the recording ended. "I should have arrested her on Gaia when I had the chance," he ground out. "My gut told me she was involved. But I didn't have any evidence to prove it."

"None of us had evidence. We assumed she was a pawn in someone else's game. That's what she wanted us to believe."

Knox ran a hand over his jaw, his beard rasping against his palm. He stared at the floor for a moment, then met Cade's gaze. "There's no way my dad will win his case, is there?"

"No. You heard what happened to Judge Sato. Unity tapped into the COJ records and confirmed her death and Aurora's reassignment to a different judge. The Sovereign has removed all the obstacles to her goal. The Admiral's panel and judge are compromised. Aurora's will be, too."

He could see thoughts racing at lightspeed behind Knox's eyes. This situation had to be his friend's worst-case scenario. If Knox trusted to the system he and his father had fought to support and defend all their lives, the Admiral would end up as the Sovereign's prisoner. But if his dad escaped from the detention center, both their careers in the Fleet were over. His dad would be a fugitive and Knox would have to join him or risk becoming the Sovereign's next target.

"What about Isabeau?" Knox finally asked.

"We have a plan to get her out, too. But that will depend on you."

Knox straightened, morphing into captain mode. "What do you need me to do?"

He briefly outlined the plan they'd worked out. "You're the best person for the job."

Knox's gaze swept the semi-circle. "I can't ask any of you to do this. This mission will end your careers. You've already gone above and—"

"You're not asking," Bella said calmly. "We volunteered."

"It's our job to protect the Union," Gonzo added. "Even from itself."

"Especially from itself." Reynolds stared Knox down.

"And safeguard the Admiral." Tam laced his fingers together. "I am his doctor, after all."

"Face it, Knox." Justin leaned back, draping his arm behind Bella's shoulders with a grim smile. "You're stuck with us."

Knox looked at each of them in turn, then his attention shifted to Cade. "Are they always this stubborn?"

"Pretty much."

Knox sighed, but his mouth turned up in a smile. "Thank you. All of you."

"Don't thank us yet," Justin said. "We still have a jailbreak and kidnapping to pull off. And the small matter of survival after the fact. I don't know about the rest of you, but I'm not exactly sitting on a big ol' wad of cash."

"Are we taking *Gladiator*?" Bella asked, the first twinge of anxiety entering her voice. "We're not abandoning our ship at Sol Station, are we?"

"I hope not." Cade stared at the bulkhead, considering their options. "But that will complicate things. We don't have a spare pilot.

Maybe Gryphon could sneak over unnoticed and fly *Gladiator* out while–"

"Or we could." Unity slid into his peripheral vision.

"What?"

"We could reintegrate with *Gladiator*'s systems and fly the ship."

"Reintegrate? How? You extracted yourself from all the systems."

"We'll do it the same way we did the first time we took control."

Cade gaped at Unity. "You want to fire torpedoes at *Gladiator* while it's docked at the station?"

Unity's hearty laugh raised Cade's eyebrows. "No. That won't be necessary. We know exactly how to access *Gladiator*'s systems now. Just a simple insertion through the hull. We could be dropped off when the scout ship takes us to the Embassy."

He glanced at Bella. "What do you think?"

"I think it's a great idea. Unity can deliver *Gladiator* to the Yruf, assuming Ifel's willing to provide a docking bay again."

"I doubt that will be a problem," Cade answered.

Based on what he was picking up from Ifel, she was all in. If she could gather them all onto her ship and stop the destructive forces at work, she would. The only trick was keeping the Fleet – and the Sovereign – ignorant of the Yruf's presence.

He understood Aurora's vehemence on that point. The moment the Sovereign realized the Yruf were helping Aurora, she'd make it her mission to annihilate them. She'd unleash the vitriol of the other Setarip factions and the strength of the Teeli fleet to do it.

Ifel would assure them the Yruf could take care of themselves. And she was probably right. They'd survived on their own for longer than the Fleet had been in existence.

But keeping the alliance with the Yruf secret served another critical purpose, one that had long-range consequences. In the battle to stop the Sovereign and the Teeli from overrunning the Union, having the Yruf as their ace in the hole gave them an advantage the Sovereign couldn't account for.

Eighty-Nine

"Are we really going to do this, Dad?"

Micah sat in his parents' cabin, a mug of tea in his hands. He'd accepted the mug because his mom had needed something to do and making tea had occupied her for a few minutes. Now she was back to pacing the room.

"Do you see an alternative?" His dad looked calm. Unnervingly so. Like he'd anticipated this turn of events all along and had been planning accordingly. "Do you want to risk going back to the university? The Sovereign knows who you are now."

The memory of the harshly mechanical voice gleefully telling Aurora they were all going to end up caged together made him shudder. "No. But this isn't just about me. Or you." A fist squeezed his gut as he brought up the other potential casualties. "What about Birdie and Kai? Are they in danger now because of us?"

"Quite likely. Which is why I asked Siginal to send down a shuttle to fetch them."

"What?" He jerked so hard the tea sloshed over onto his hand. He licked it off. "They're coming here?"

"Yes. While you and Aurora were in Teeli space, your mom and I had several long discussions with Kai and Iolana. We wanted them to understand the potential risk being connected to us could bring them. We'd already seen how the Sovereign attacked Admiral Payne's family. I didn't want something similar to happen to them if you failed to capture the Sovereign in Teeli space. So, we set up a contingency plan that they agreed to. That's why they'll be joining us shortly."

Micah sat back, stunned. "I had no idea."

His dad's cheek creased in a wane smile. "This isn't the first time I've been in this type of situation. Juggling big secrets and shifting concerns has kind of been my norm. Although having our identities as common knowledge complicates things a bit."

"A bit?" his mom scoffed, sinking down beside his dad on the couch. "You have a gift for understatement. What's going to happen to Far Horizons?"

"Same thing that happened the last time I dropped off the radar to mate with you." He brushed a kiss on her cheek. "The management team will handle everything until we return."

"So you think we'll return?" Micah asked, gulping down half his tea. It could have been seawater and he wouldn't have noticed the taste.

"Don't you?"

"I honestly have no idea."

His dad shook his head. "Then you don't know your sister as well as you think you do. The Sovereign's attempting to take over the Union the way the Teeli took over Feylahn. Aurora will never let that happen. This battle's just beginning."

His dad's comment echoed in his mind as he entered the *Starhawke*'s shuttle bay a little while later. He recognized the shuttle sitting on the deck beside the *Starhawke*'s shuttle as one of the *Rowkclarek*'s, the more elaborate contours making it stand out compared to the streamlined *Starhawke* shuttle.

Siginal stepped onto the lowered ramp first, followed by Birdie, her long brown hair pulled back in a braid and a bulging duffel over one shoulder. She waved when she spotted him. "Stone!" Dropping the duffel to the deck she trotted over and threw her arms around him.

He pulled her close. "Hey, Birdie. I'm so sorry about this."

"Sorry?" She pulled back and swatted him playfully on the arm. "Are you kidding? This is the adventure of a lifetime." Her smile was genuine, but tension gathered around her eyes. "Besides, I want to see this hydrotank your mom raved about."

"It's pretty amazing," he admitted. "You won't believe you're on a starship."

His mom had waylaid Siginal, the two of them in deep discussion, while his dad greeted Kai. His dad grabbed Birdie's duffel, adding it to Kai's bag on the cargo glider that had risen out of the deck. Two Kraed exited the shuttle carrying additional bags that they added to the pile.

Birdie followed his gaze. "Your dad warned us to pack for an extended trip. We weren't sure what we'd need, so we brought everything."

"I don't think any of us know exactly what we need."

"Yeah." She rested her hand on his arm. "How's Aurora?"

He shrugged. "Livid. After what the Sovereign said..." He stopped that train of thought before it gained any steam.

"I'll bet. Your dad was vague in his message, but I gather things aren't going well."

"You could say that." He turned toward the exit. Celia stood inside the bay, watching them. His heart rate picked up at the look in her eyes.

She strolled forward, her focus on Birdie. "Welcome to the *Starhawke*."

"Thanks, Celia. Glad to be here."

"You two have met?" It hadn't happened on his watch.

Celia smirked. "Iolana and Kai stopped by the house to check on our food supplies after you and your folks left for the mainland."

"And Celia promised to teach me some sparring moves the next time we came over, but then she and Cade left."

"I'll make good on that promise," Celia assured her.

He wasn't entirely sure how he felt about Celia and Birdie spending time together. Birdie knew all his worst moments and biggest failures, and wouldn't hesitate to share them if Celia asked. He'd never minded that kind of open teasing with any other woman he'd introduced to Birdie, but Celia was... different.

And Birdie was watching him way too closely as he led her to the lift. The last time she'd looked at him like that, she'd been convinced he had a thing for Aurora. In that instance, she'd been way off base. This time? She was right on target.

Ninety

"Are you and Aurora certain about this?"

Lelindia met her mom's worried gaze across the table in the galley nook. Her dad wore a matching expression of concern. "Certain we need to get her out of prison and away from the Sovereign? Yes."

Her mom shook her head, her thick dark hair brushing her shoulders. "I mean are you certain you're prepared to live your lives as fugitives."

Lelindia set down her fork. She hadn't expected to be hungry, given the circumstances, but apparently Raehn was. Lelindia had been craving Celia's capellini pomodoro for the past hour. She'd finally given in. She wasn't good to anyone if she was distracted by cravings. "Were you prepared when you left Feylahn?"

"Not in the slightest." Her mom looked at her over the top of her mug of tea. "That's why we know what you're facing better than you do. We know what it's like to be constantly looking over your shoulder. We don't want that for you. Or your daughter."

Lelindia spread her hands. "Neither do I, but it's where we are. At least Aurora and I have resources you didn't. And allies."

"Will we be going to Drakar, then?" her dad asked.

She swirled her fork in her pasta. "I'm not sure." She popped the forkful in her mouth and chewed. "Uniting the Kraed clans to fight

the Teeli is essential in the long term. I think Aurora and I can do it."
They had to do it. If the Kraed waited for the Sovereign and Teeli to
show up on their doorstep, the consequences would be disastrous.
For everyone. "But we can't implicate Signal in the fallout from the
jailbreak. That could turn the Fleet and the Kraed against each other."

Her parents shared a glance. "Nobody wants that," her dad
agreed. "And on that note, I need to get to the bridge." He stood.
"Kelly and Star are taking Brendan and me through simulations,
prepping us for tonight."

And Lelindia needed to have a chat with Aurora to confirm
their game plan.

Her mom nodded. "Kire's giving me a rundown on the comm,
too. I'll be up shortly."

After her dad left, Lelindia focused on her food, popping
another forkful of pasta in her mouth.

Her mom's gaze turned thoughtful. "You're a lot more
relaxed about all this than I would have expected."

She shrugged as she chewed. As much as she disliked the
idea of being a fugitive – of her entire family and crew being fugitives
– she was counting the hours until Aurora would be by her side again.
"The theme of my life for the past few months has been *expect the
unexpected*. I guess I'm getting used to the deck dropping out from
under my feet."

Ninety-One

"How are the modifications coming?"

Jonarel slid out from beneath the shuttle when Kire's feet planted themselves right beside the gap.

He met his friend's questioning gaze as he stood. "Almost complete." In truth, he would have accomplished the task an hour ago if he had not been determined to finish a related project first.

"Any problems?" Kire folded his arms and peered under the shuttle's raised belly.

"No. The system is relatively simple." By Kraed standards, anyway.

"What happens to the falling debris during the cutting?"

He shot his friend a sidelong glance. Kire asking a question about engineering was definitely a smokescreen, meant to conceal the real reason for his visit. Engineering had been Kire's weakest subject at the Academy until Jonarel started tutoring him. "The system is self-contained. All debris will be gathered during the cutting process."

"Good, good." Kire placed a hand on the shuttle's hull, his fingers trailing across the smooth surface. "This isn't exactly what we'd anticipated when you, Roe, and I met up in that bar last summer."

"No. Things are… different."

Kire snorted. "Different. That's one way of putting it." He turned, propping his back against the shuttle. "I had a lot of wild ideas about what our future would look like working with Roe, but becoming fugitives from the Union didn't make the list."

Jonarel matched Kire's pose, his arm brushing Kire's shoulder. "At least it has not been boring."

Kire laughed, the sound flat, like he was standing by a dampening field. "That's very true. In fact, I think it's safe to say that boredom isn't something any of us need to worry about anymore." Kire eyed him critically. "How are you and Lelindia holding up?"

He considered the question. "Well enough." Although life as they had known it was about to be shredded. Working on the shuttle modifications and his special project had kept him from irritating Lelindia with an avalanche of *what if* questions about the future that neither of them could answer.

"And the baby?"

"Lelindia assures me she is fine."

"At least there's that." Kire rested the back of his head against the shuttle. "She might be the brightest spot we have to focus on for a while."

She certainly shone like a star in Jonarel's heart. "Are Brendan and Gryphon prepared to handle the *Starhawke*?"

Kire nodded. "Kelly's grilling them now on all the Fleet maneuvers in our database. I knew she was protective of this ship, but I've never seen her in full drill sergeant mode. If they get one scratch on the hull during departure, there will be hell to pay."

"Tehar is assisting, I assume?"

"Yeah. She's more easygoing about it than Kelly, which is funny. She IS the ship. I've already finished training Marina on the comms. She took to it like a duck to water." He tapped the heel of his boot against the deck. "Any thoughts on what we'll do after we get Aurora and the Admiral out?"

That was the question he had been waiting for. "My father will gladly welcome us on Drakar." Libra had been given the job of keeping in contact with his father during the extractions. Her stated purpose was to inform him of their progress, but in truth, she was responsible for making sure the *Rowkclarek* stayed put if things did not go to plan. His father would want to intervene if they encountered any problems. Jonarel had agreed with Lelindia that Libra was the one person his father would not dare to challenge.

"The Sovereign will expect us to go to Kraed space. Hide out there. So will the Fleet, given the evidence presented during the Admiral's trial. Which means that's the one place we *can't* go. We can't give the Fleet any excuse to enter Kraed space or fire on Kraed ships." Kire scrubbed his hand over his face. "How did everything get messed up so quickly? How did the Sovereign gain so much ground that we're—" he gestured between them "—now the enemies of the Union?"

"Not the Union. Only those who believe the lies she has spread. Many do not."

"Breaking Roe and the Admiral out of prison won't help with maintaining their innocence."

"Far better a tarnished reputation than allowing the Sovereign to gain physical control over them."

"Yeah, I know." Kire sighed, then pushed away from the shuttle. "I already set up a comm to go to President Yeoh's personal account as soon as the *Starhawke* leaves Sol Station. She's the one person who needs to know why we're taking these actions, to hear the Sovereign's threats to Aurora for herself, even if she can't share that information with anyone."

"Not yet, anyway." But they would defeat the Sovereign. They had to. "I have one additional item to show you."

Kire perked up, some of his typical good humor returning. "Oh?"

Jonarel led the way inside the shuttle, then crouched and opened the crate he had set beside the ramp. He unfolded the black garment sitting on top, holding it up.

Kire's brow furrowed. "Uh, what is it?"

"A battle suit."

"Battle suit? You mean some kind of armor?" Kire fingered the sleeve. "This fabric is pretty thin for armor."

"It is a rare Kraed fabric." His father had provided it from the *Rowkclarek*'s stores. Jonarel had been secretly working on crafting suits for the crew since shortly after Aurora's arrest.

Just in case.

"What can it do?"

"Deflect weapons fire and blades, regulate temperature, and protect from burns."

Kire whistled, smoothing both hands over the shimmering black fabric. "Seriously?"

"No."

Kire frowned, blinked, then grinned. "That was a joke."

"Yes. These suits are not as strong or adaptable as Aurora's shield, but they will provide protection if we encounter resistance during her extraction."

Kire's grin faded. "I expect we will."

"As do I."

"How many did you make?"

"Five." In theory, Lelindia did not need one, but he was not leaving the ship until she had it on.

No matter how much she protested.

Ninety-Two

"Jonarel, this is ridiculous!" Lelindia stared at the shimmering full body suit Jonarel had placed in her hands. "I'm staying on the *Starhawke*. I don't need this." She thrust it at him, but he backed away.

"You do not know what you may need. The suit will protect you."

"From what? If something happens on the *Starhawke* that this suit needs to deflect, we'll have way bigger problems than whether I've been injured."

Anxiety flashed in his eyes, his large body tensing.

Great. She'd made him more nervous, not less.

"Checana—"

"Besides, there's nothing to worry about. I can heal anything that happens to me as long as I remain conscious."

"And if you do not?"

"Then my mom will be right next to me at the comm station. I don't need a suit. I can—"

Jonarel moved so quickly she didn't have time to react. One moment he was standing with his hands tucked behind his back, and the next she was in his arms, the suit trapped between them as he captured her mouth with his.

Her body responded before her brain caught up, every muscle turning into warm taffy as his tongue slid along hers, stroking with deliberate intent.

She moaned – part desire, part aggravation. He was using his physical prowess to override her objections.

And he was good at it. He buried his fingers in her hair, delving deeper, using his other hand to pull her firmly against every hard, delicious plane of his body.

Damn him.

She nipped at his tongue, eliciting a low growl that she liked way too much. She wrested her mouth from his. "You don't fight fair," she grumbled, her lips marking a trail along his jaw of their own accord.

His fingers tightened in her hair, the tips of his claws lightly touching her scalp. He pulled back until their gazes locked. His eyes glittered like molten gold. "I fight to protect you. And Raehn."

Checkmate.

How could she possibly argue with that?

With a sigh, she surrendered. Touching her lips to his in a languid kiss, she murmured against his mouth. "Alright, Jonarel. I'll wear the suit."

Ninety-Three

"Admiral? Can you hear me? It's safe to talk now." Aurora waited with bated breath until his familiar tenor spoke in her ear.

"I hear you just fine, Captain."

She exhaled, releasing tension that had been building in her neck and shoulders ever since the Sovereign's unsettling visit.

Unity had done a test run on the dummy feed for both hers and the Admiral's cells right after lights out, confirming they could successfully spoof the audio and visual the Sovereign was receiving. It was running now, which allowed Aurora her first opportunity to talk to the Admiral directly. "Has Cade filled you in on what's happening?"

"The jailbreak tonight? Yes. He also played me the conversation you had with the Sovereign." He paused. "She doesn't seem to like us very much."

The unexpected joke startled a choked laugh from her. "No, she really doesn't." Her laughter faded. "But her plan's about to go up in smoke."

"So I heard. How soon are your crew and Cade's unit coming to fetch us?"

"Very soon. Cade's already left your house." She'd tracked Cade's movements ever since he departed the Yruf ship. Her crew —

minus Lelindia — had left the *Starhawke* a little later, both shuttles drawing closer by the minute.

"I understand Knox is going to intercept Isabeau as well?"

"Yes. The Yruf are helping with that part of the plan. It's easier for them to remain hidden near the Embassy. They'll transport Knox and Magee to their ship."

The Admiral fell silent for a moment. "I'm sorry, Aurora."

"Sorry?" She frowned. The Admiral's emotions had taken a decidedly melancholy turn. "For what?"

"For letting things get this far. For not being more proactive in exposing the Teeli. For not telling you sooner what I knew about you and Lelindia."

Actually, Knox had been the one to tell her, not him. But dwelling on "should haves" wasn't helpful. Her list was a lot longer than anyone else's. "You don't owe me an apology. But you do owe me a drink and a long talk when we're back on the *Starhawke*."

"The long talk I can provide. Your crew is about to clear my schedule. The drink, I fear, will be up to you."

She could feel his chagrin at the role reversal. Dependency did not sit well with him. "I've got you covered."

"Thank you."

The depth of emotion behind those two words brought a lump to her throat. She swallowed it down. "No thanks necessary. I'm the one the Sovereign's after. You're collateral damage." So was Sato. And Magee. And Keenan.

She shook her head, fighting off her guilt. "I should be apologizing to you."

"No, you shouldn't. I'm your CO. I'm the one person you absolutely cannot take responsibility for, no matter how hard you try. That's an order."

He wasn't joking. There wasn't even a hint of humor in his emotional field.

She said what he expected her to say, even though they both knew it was a lie. "Yes, sir."

He sighed. "Aurora, we—"

"Admiral?" Kire's voice broke into the comm. "We're maneuvering into position above your cell now."

"What about Aurora?"

That answered the question as to whether they'd filled the Admiral in on the timing of this rescue.

"She's next," Kire assured him. "Cade's team will get you out while we cut into her cell."

"You should extract her first."

"No, they shouldn't." Aurora shoved the scratchy blanket to the foot of her bed and stood, the cold of the concrete floor soaking through her socks. She could sense the occupants of both shuttles above, their nearness setting off little explosions of adrenaline. "I'm the one with an energy shield, remember?"

"Aurora—"

"No. My crew, my orders. You get out first." She wasn't budging on this.

Exasperation snapped through his emotional field. "I outrank you."

"Not on my ship, you don't," she shot back. "You're first."

"Admiral, move back against your door," Kire said diplomatically into the brief silence. "We'll be cutting directly above your cot."

"Understood."

Snatching her exercise clothes off the shelf, she dressed quickly, her gaze darting to the narrow window above her bed. No sign of movement. She knew the shuttle with Cade and his team was up there but she resisted the impulse to climb on her cot and press her face against the thick glass.

"Any indication they're aware of your presence?" she asked over the line.

"No," Kire and Justin responded in unison.

"But that's likely to change," Kire added. "Jon's starting the cutting now."

Ninety-Four

"The shuttles are approaching the detention center," Unity informed Lelindia, their voice coming over the ship's speakers since U-1 was on the *Starhawke*'s shuttle.

"Then we're up. Are you ready with *Gladiator*?"

"Yes."

Lelindia swiveled the captain's chair to face her mom, who'd taken over comm duties at Kire's station. "Let's see if they're feeling accommodating."

Her mom tapped her earpiece. "Station control, this is the *Starhawke*, requesting clearance for departure."

"One moment, *Starhawke*," a flat voice replied through the speakers.

Lelindia glanced at Libra, seated in the companion chair next to her. She looked as tense as Lelindia felt, her hand to her earpiece as she informed Siginal of their imminent departure. Lelindia's dad, sitting at tactical, and Brendan, seated at navigation, looked more eager than tense. That helped. She was counting on them to handle things if their plans went sideways.

Please don't let them go sideways.

Getting the *Starhawke* out of dock would be no small feat if station control didn't give them a green light. Not only would they have to navigate the heavy traffic in and out of the station, but the Fleet ships that had blockaded them when Aurora was arrested were still in loose formation around the station. Or more accurately, around the section of the station where the *Starhawke* and *Rowkclarek* were berthed.

As if that weren't enough, she was coordinating their movements with Aurora's and the Admiral's jailbreak at the detention center and Magee's abduction at the Teeli Embassy. While her mom and Unity handled communications with Kire and Justin during the brig extraction, Micah was in Aurora's office, serving as overwatch for Knox and the Yruf.

Libra glanced at her and gave a small nod. She'd promised Lelindia that if they hit a snag, she'd stop Siginal from doing anything rash to help them.

She needed that assurance. If any piece of their plan failed, they could all be in serious trouble. But having Siginal start an interstellar war in an attempt to save them wasn't a solution.

"*Starhawke*, this is station control. We're going to need you to wait on that departure request."

Lelindia's stomach tightened.

Her mom's lips thinned. "Is there a problem?"

"No problem. We have other requests ahead of you."

Lelindia didn't buy the excuse for a second.

"Can you give us an estimate on a departure time?" Her mom's voice didn't betray a hint of anxiety or annoyance, but the skin around her eyes and lips tightened.

"Not at this time."

So much for the easy path. "Unity?"

"Submitting departure request for *Gladiator* now."

She'd discussed this scenario with Unity and Brendan at length. So far, Fleet Security had ignored *Gladiator*'s presence at the station. The ship had arrived days before the *Starhawke* and was berthed in a different section of the station.

While the *Starhawke*'s larger flight profile required more space for a departure, Brendan had assured her that shouldn't cause more than a minor difference in launch times for the two ships. Station control's response to Unity's request should paint them a clear picture whether the station was holding the *Starhawke* in particular.

"We have a response," Unity said. "No mention of a wait. *Gladiator* is third in line for departure."

Her fingers curled around the armrests. "It's just us." She'd anticipated it, but that didn't mean she liked it. "What's the status at the detention center?"

"Jonarel has begun cutting into the Admiral's cell," her mom replied.

She took a deep breath. "Then we're switching to plan B." She turned to her dad. "What's the status on the Fleet ships?"

He studied his console. "They're moving." He met her gaze over his shoulder. "Tightening formation."

Dammit. Just what they didn't need. She swiveled to face Brendan. "Guess you'll get to do some fancy flying after all."

One corner of his mouth curled up briefly, easing some of the tension tightening her shoulders. "Are the charges set on the docking clamps?" he asked her dad.

"Set and ready," her dad confirmed.

That had been one small concession to Siginal. His crew had used one of their camouflaged shuttles to place the charges.

"Star, are the hull and shield reinforcements in place?" Brendan asked.

Tehar's image materialized in front of his console. "Yes."

Brendan's fingers moved over the console, the subtle hum of the engines vibrating up through the deck. "Then detonate the charges in three, two, one..."

Ninety-Five

A red outline marked the location of the *Starhawke*'s shuttle on Cade's display, the shuttle hovering above the roofline near one corner of the Admiral's wedge. Currently his shuttle was holding position parallel to where the *Starhawke* crew was carving a hole in the top of the Admiral's cell. His fingers twitched, ready to move in the second they finished.

The shuttle and the cutting mechanism remained invisible, giving no indication of the work in progress. Kraed technology doing what it did best.

Focusing on that outline was the only way he was able to resist the gravitational pull of Aurora's presence to his left. He felt like a comet being drawn in by a star, fighting the movement of his hands on the controls that wanted to nudge him closer to her.

Not your job, Ellis, he reminded himself. His unit was in charge of getting the Admiral out. They'd spring into action as soon as the other shuttle moved to Aurora's wedge. Her crew would make sure she got out.

But the sharp-edged anticipation in Aurora's emotional field whittled away at his concentration.

"Two guards are heading for the Admiral's stairway," U-2 informed them from the alcove above him.

"Routine check?"

"No."

Justin was already on the comm. "Any chance you guys can pick up the pace?" he asked Kire.

"Working on it."

"Unity, is the Admiral's door secure?" Cade asked.

"Yes. We have full control of the electronic locks and can slow the effectiveness of the manual overrides. But a colorless gas has started pumping into his and Aurora's cells."

"A gas?" Williams appeared behind Justin's seat. "What kind of gas?"

"Unknown. The Admiral has begun hyperventilating."

"What about Aurora?" Cade asked.

"Her shield is protecting her."

"Can you stop the gas?"

"No. The dispersal isn't tied to the ventilation system. It's seeping out from multiple locations on the sanitation station. The Admiral soaked his blanket in the basin and draped it over the dispersal points to slow the gas. He also covered his face with a wet towel, but he's in acute distress. We estimate he will be unconscious in less than a minute."

Cade swore while Justin slapped the comm. "They're gassing them. We need that opening now!"

"We know," Kire replied. "Ten seconds."

"Drew, help Williams prep for med evac," Cade ordered, his muscles tight as he hovered the shuttle a half-meter off the roof, as close to its invisible twin as he dared. "Reynolds, Gonzo, mask up."

The red outline abruptly darted away. A millisecond later the security lights from the adjacent parking area created a halo around the circular patch cut out of the flat roof.

"We're clear," Kire confirmed, but Cade was already in motion.

A gust of wind whipped the back of his hair as the shuttle's hatch opened. Two muffled thumps let him know Reynolds and Gonzo were on the roof, the shuttle between them and the nearest guard tower.

"Reynolds has eyes on him," Justin informed him. "Ladder's down, but the Admiral's having trouble standing and fastening his mask."

"The guards are attempting to break through our block on the manual override for the door," Unity warned. "We've jammed their comms, but—"

A siren split the air, making Cade flinch.

"—one of them pulled the manual alarm."

"Do we have the Admiral?" he yelled at Justin over the racket.

"Not yet," Justin yelled back, his hand pressed to his headset.

High-intensity spotlights flared to life like miniature suns, blinding him. He blocked the glare with his hand. A second later the lights cut out, leaving pulsing afterimages dancing across his vision. He blinked rapidly, trying to clear them.

"We cut power to the lights," Unity informed him.

"Can you do anything about the—"

"Snipers!" Gonzo shouted a split second before shots smacked into the shuttle's shields.

"Hang on!" Cade's restraints bit into his shoulders as he angled the shuttle and dropped it onto the roof next to the opening. The shuttle's shields deflected the brunt of the incoming fire.

A series of faint pops and louder hisses preceded a steady stream of thick smoke that obscured their surroundings. "Gonzo's tossing smoke bombs," Justin confirmed. "Williams!" he called into the cabin. "The Admiral's unconscious."

Cade's gut squeezed. "Gassed or shot?"

"Gassed. Reynolds is pulling him out now."

"How close—" The shuttle vibrated as footsteps pounded up the ramp.

"We've got him!" Gonzo shouted through his mask.

"Let's fly, Commander!" Reynolds yelled, the distant shouts and harsh siren cutting off abruptly as the hatch closed and sealed.

His gaze darted across the compound. "What about Aurora?" he asked Justin.

Justin met his gaze with obvious reluctance. "They've hit a snag."

Ninety-Six

A slight tremor through the deck beneath Micah's feet told him the charges attached to the station's docking clamps had triggered.

Plan B was underway.

The strident voice blasting over the ship's bridge speakers was a lot less subtle. "*Starhawke*, you have damaged station property! Hold position and await Fleet Security."

Micah did his best to block out the activity on the bridge, focusing on his earpiece. "Knox, what's your status?"

"We've left the transport," he replied. "Estimate seven minutes out from the Teeli Embassy."

"Unity, you're up."

"On it."

Now they'd find out if Unity could successfully impersonate Sly'Kull. The Yruf scout ship had delivered Unity to the Embassy right after nightfall. They had successfully tapped into the Embassy security and comms. But would Magee accept Unity's orders?

He glanced at the bridgescreen, visible from his seat in the upholstered chair near the office's open doorway. A checkerboard of images showed bits of debris from the destroyed docking clamps floating in front of several of the exterior cameras. Each camera gave a different view of the station and surrounding ships as his dad backed the *Starhawke* away from the berth.

They were committed now. No going back. Birdie and Kai, who'd insisted on sitting in the observation lounge so they could watch the departure, were likely to get quite a show.

"Magee is dressing."

He pulled his focus back to his earpiece. "Did she question you?"

"No. Her response is what I think you would call robotic."

At this point, he'd take it. "Knox, Magee is preparing to leave the building."

"Good. We'll be ready."

"*Starhawke*, this is your final warning. Hold position or we will fire." The voice over the speaker had gone from strident to threatening.

He squeezed his eyes shut, fighting the chill of unease creeping through his veins. They'd be okay. His dad was a hell of a pilot, and from what he'd heard, Gryphon was no slouch when it came to tactical. They could handle this.

He hoped.

Ninety-Seven

The siren stabbed at Jonarel's ears like a blade. Extending the cutting mechanism toward the rooftop above Aurora's cell meant temporarily sacrificing the shuttle's hull integrity and soundproofing, which had not been a problem until the alarm assaulted his senses.

Operating the cutter prevented him from covering his ears. His eyes steadily squinted shut as his head throbbed.

Just a little longer.

"You okay?" Celia shouted from where she was crouched beside him.

He grimaced in reply.

And then it got worse.

The piercing rat-a-tat-tat from automatic weapons filled his ears and lit up the shuttle's shields.

"Fire from the towers!" Kire called out from the cockpit.

"How can they see us?" Celia yelled over the noise.

"They can't. They're spraying the entire—"

A ricochet slammed into the sidewall of the cutter, sparks flying. Another clipped the opening, searing a line along the forearm of Jonarel's battle suit as it passed. He ducked, turning his head as a horrible grinding of metal added to the cacophony. When he looked back, the cutter was completely dark. And the hole was half cut.

"We have a problem!" he bellowed.

Celia looked at the unit, then turned to Kire. "Tell Aurora she's gonna have to break through from her side. The cutter's compromised." She grabbed a gas mask from the utility cabinet, pulled up the hood on her battle suit, and plucked the collapsible ladder from the deck. "I'll meet her out there."

He caught her arm. "I will go."

She shook him off. "I'm the security officer. You're the engineer." She pointed at the useless cutter. "You need to figure out how to get that thing back in the shuttle so we can break atmo."

Ninety-Eight

"*Starhawke*, this is your final warning. Hold position or you will be fired upon."

Lelindia admired the way Brendan's hands moved confidently over the navigation controls like he routinely flew under threat of obliteration. He'd give Kelly a run for her money in the calm and collected department.

"Eight Fleet patrol yachts are moving to intercept," Lelindia's dad informed them from tactical. "The frigates are closing in, too."

"Will they fire with so many ships nearby?" Libra asked, leaning halfway out of the companion chair, her gaze locked on the bridgescreen images.

"The yachts definitely will," Brendan replied. "They're maneuverable, with advanced targeting ability. Our design, actually."

Lelindia almost laughed at the pride in Brendan's tone. It struck an incongruent note considering the danger posed by the other ships. A danger his company had helped create.

"The frigates will wait until the station has halted all traffic and we've gotten further away," her dad commented, no trace of his usual humor in his voice. "Maximum damage at minimal risk of friendly fire."

"No, Siginal," Libra said, touching her earpiece. "Not so much as a twitch, do you understand?"

Lelindia felt a pang of guilt. Asking Siginal to remain immobile when the *Starhawke* was facing a threat was like asking her to ignore someone who was bleeding. But turning the Kraed into enemies of the Fleet wasn't in anyone's best interests. Hopefully Siginal understood the dangers of taking action.

And the consequences of crossing Libra when she used that tone.

"When can we engage the hull camouflage?" she asked Brendan.

"We'll need to wait until we've cleared most of the surrounding ships." Brendan glided the *Starhawke* between two small private vessels. "Which shouldn't take too long. A large, fast-moving ship in close quarters tends to make other pilots get out of the way."

Unless they didn't.

Movement on the bridgescreen caught her eye. A freighter appeared seemingly out of nowhere on their starboard side, near enough to touch. Before she could shout a warning, the image rolled – or more accurately, the *Starhawke* rolled – the ship's hull skimming past the freighter by what looked like a couple meters at most.

Stars praise Brendan Scott.

Except the roll had put them directly in line with two of the yachts.

The yachts opened fire.

Ninety-Nine

"Roe, the cutter's down. You're going to have to break the rest of the way through."

Aurora stared at the ceiling through the pearlescent glow of her energy shield. Her cell had begun to fill with gas shortly before the alarm siren started shrieking. She'd slowed the gas's expansion with wet linens, and her shield kept her in a bubble of clean air, but the clock was ticking. Exerting herself to break through the ceiling would use up her oxygen supply quickly and divide her concentration.

She examined the half-circle outline the cutter had made above her cot. At least she knew where to strike.

Climbing onto the cot's frame, she adjusted her stance to brace the sides of her feet against the walls. The banging on her door intensified, as did the shouted orders to stand down.

"Unity, how secure is that door?"

"We can hinder the manual override for a while longer."

Not the big assurance she'd hoped for — for her, or the guards. They would be hit with the gas if they managed to break through. She'd sensed the Admiral's fear when it overwhelmed him, the feeling of suffocation. It had ripped at her self-control. "Kire, tell

Kelly to move the shuttle away from the roof. This isn't going to be pretty."

"Acknowledged."

Balancing on the siderails of the cot, she took a few seconds to gather her energy field, focusing the power in her arms and hands. As the strength built, she swung upward, smashing her shield into the partial circle in the ceiling.

Chunks of plaster, wood, and concrete rained down like meteorites, striking her shield in flares of light and tumbling to the ground.

She flattened her palm against the wall to steady herself, examining the result. The neatly delineated partial circle was obliterated, replaced by a raw-edged crater. But she couldn't see sky yet. And the gas was trying to work through the weak points in her shield.

A loud bang reverberated from across the room, the door rattling.

"They're breaking off the locking mechanism," Unity informed her.

She braced her feet again, collected the energy around her arms, and swung. More debris rained down, but the awkward angle and balancing act made it difficult to hit the same spot. She'd enlarged the crater, but only a sliver the length of a table knife opened to the outside air.

She couldn't see what was happening on the roof, but she could certainly hear. Her crew was under fire.

She shifted her weight. One corner of the cot buckled, dropping her unceremoniously onto her back amid the chunks of debris. Another bang and rattle from the door.

"They're very close to getting the door open," Unity said.

Unity's somber tone made her look hard at the door. "If they get in, that gas will kill them."

She couldn't let that happen. The Sovereign would pin their deaths on her, turning her from a traitor into a murderer. And she'd be right.

If Aurora left the guards to their fate, she would be responsible as surely as if she'd gassed them herself.

"Kire, change of plans." She pushed off the floor and set her shoulders. "Fall back and wait for my signal."

"But—"

"Just do it. Unity, get ready to release the door. I'm going out the front."

One Hundred

The *Starhawke* shuddered, snapping Micah's gaze to the bridgescreen. Two ships with Fleet insignia were firing on them, the shudders matching the impacts with the shields.

"Unity, where's Magee?" A quick check of his comband's chronometer told him it had been more than three minutes since Magee had left her room. It shouldn't have taken her that long to make her way through the Embassy.

"At the security station inside. One of the guards questioned her orders and attempted to reach Sly'Kull. We blocked the comm and impersonated Sly'Kull, but we had to tell the guard we would be coming down shortly."

Not good news. They needed Magee outside before anyone at the Embassy caught wind of what was happening at the detention center and Sol Station. "Can you give me audio on her?"

"—answer to you," Magee's voice said into his earpiece, her tone sharp with annoyance. "Sly'Kull wants me outside, so I'm going."

"And I'm under a standing order not to let you leave this building unless you're accompanied by Delegate Sly'Kull," a deep and equally annoyed male voice replied. "I don't care what he said over comms. Until he gets here—"

"He told me to wait outside." Magee sounded royally ticked off. "Those are *my* orders. Which he just confirmed over *your* comm. I'm going. If you want to cover your ass, come with me."

"Good idea. I will."

More shudders, hard enough to rock Micah in his chair.

"Remind me to have a talk with my weapons department," Micah's dad bit out from the navigation console after the next jolt.

Micah glanced at the bridgescreen. His stomach lurched as his dad threaded the *Starhawke* through a gap between two stationary freighters where they really shouldn't fit. If his dad miscalculated...

"Magee is exiting the building with two guards," Unity informed him. "Another is headed for Sly'Kull's room."

He forced his gaze away from the bridgescreen.

"The front door's opening," Knox said. "I've got eyes on her."

An aerial projection appeared to Micah's right, coming from the Yruf scout ship hovering above Knox's position. It showed a starkly lit cement pathway leading out from a white angular building. A dark-haired woman stalked along the walkway, armed guards on either side, both about Micah's size. Her steps and spine were stiff as a board, her face drawn into a scowl.

The Embassy's exterior lights abruptly snapped off, the projection switching to infrared. Three figures moved quickly into frame, converging on Magee and the guards. The infrared turned the two towering Yruf into velociraptors launching themselves at prey, and Knox–

A hard blast struck the ship, knocking Micah against the arm of his chair with a grunt.

"If you've got any tricks, old man," Micah's dad called out, "now's the time to use them."

"Watch and learn, kid," Gryphon replied.

One Hundred One

Jonarel snarled, the cords of his neck stretched tight as he used brute force to haul the damaged cutter up into the cabin of the shuttle. It resisted, the broken section catching on the mechanism designed to fold it neatly against the deck.

Anger burned through him like acid. He channeled it into his muscles, straining against the cutter's dead weight. Curse words in his native language spewed from his lips, sweat dripping into his eyes as he heaved and shoved, working the damaged section up centimeter by centimeter.

A little higher. A few more millimeters.

A nearly silent whisper-click broke through the pounding in his temples, the hull plates sliding smoothly into place, choking off the updraft and silencing the siren's screech.

He set the cutter on the deck with a groan, swiping the sweat out of his eyes with the back of his hand. "Hull sealed."

Kire glanced back from the cockpit. "You okay?"

He waved the question away, stalking past Celia, who had tucked herself into the curve of the outer hull by the hatch in readiness, like a relquir waiting to drop on unsuspecting prey. "Where's Aurora?"

Kire shook his head. "Hasn't broken through yet." He lifted his chin toward the pockmarked section of the roof six meters below.

Weapons fire continued to strafe the shuttle. So far the damage was minimal — except to the exposed cutter. The facility's weapons were not designed to break through a Kraed shuttlecraft's shields.

But he could see movement in the guard towers, figures setting up what looked like anti-aircraft weapons.

"Kire, change of plans." Aurora's voice came over the shuttle speakers. "Fall back and wait for my signal."

Kire's startled gaze met Jonarel's. "But—" he protested before Jonarel could.

"Just do it. Unity, get ready to release the door. I'm going out the front."

One Hundred Two

Lelindia clutched the armrests on the captain's chair as the blasts from the yachts shook the *Starhawke*. With multiple yachts firing at them while Brendan worked to break clear of the remaining traffic, hits were inevitable.

"Remind me to have a talk with my weapons department," Brendan bit out, heading for a miniscule gap between two freighters. She fought the urge to squeeze her eyes shut, watching transfixed as he deftly slid them through.

The cross-traffic thinned on the other side, which made the six frigates loom large, their bulk creating a movable barrier between the *Starhawke* and open space. Her stomach twisted. Nova-class frigates were a step below the Discovery-class cruisers like the *Argo* when it came to weapons and shielding, but still formidable. And significantly larger than the *Starhawke*.

"Engaging hull camouflage."

The eight Fleet yachts reacted immediately. Like a hunting pack, their firing pattern was precisely coordinated to leave no gap large enough for the *Starhawke* to avoid being struck. Each hit gave away their position.

"That is not a standard Fleet maneuver," Brendan grumbled as the *Starhawke* dipped and rolled, the shields flaring with each new hit.

"The station's shielding just activated," her dad warned. "We can't head back that way."

Not without breaking apart when they struck the shield. On the plus side, she didn't have to worry about Siginal getting into the fight anymore. The *Rowkclarek* was on the other side of that shield.

Unfortunately, with the shield at their backs, the *Starhawke's* tiny bubble of open space had shrunk considerably.

"Frigates are firing!"

Brendan evaded, but two of the frigates had timed their shots perfectly. Avoiding one drove them closer to the second. The *Starhawke* rocked hard, warnings popping up on Lelindia's chair console.

Brendan pushed them toward a gap to starboard, swearing a second later when one of the yachts cut across their path, narrowly avoiding a collision. The *Starhawke* tipped to port, the yachts swarming like flies, their shields scraping against the *Starhawke's* when they got too close. "Camouflage off," he barked. "Better to get shot than rammed."

A blast from one of the frigates questioned that assertion.

"If you've got any tricks, old man," Brendan said, "now's the time to use them."

"Watch and learn, kid," her dad replied. "Take us closer to this frigate." A red outline shaded one of the frigates on the bridgescreen. "Get ready to engage the camouflage."

"Dad—"

He didn't turn, but his voice was measured, in control. "I studied the frigate schematics when we came up with this plan, firefly. I'm targeting weapons control areas only. Nowhere staffed with personnel. Trust me. They'll be okay."

She did trust him. But unlike the other battles the crew had fought, these weren't the Sovereign's Teeli minions going after them. These were Fleet personnel who were trying to stop a perceived threat. If any of them got hurt or killed, it would be her fault.

As soon as Brendan changed course to engage, the shields flared and the ship shook, a torrent of blasts striking them from the yachts and three of the frigates. The targeted frigate loomed large on the bridgescreen.

The *Starhawke*'s weapons lanced out.

Lelindia bit her lip, holding her breath as the blasts struck the frigate's hull.

The *Starhawke*'s weapons discharged again, striking the frigate a second time. The larger ship's guns ceased firing.

The yachts did not.

Brendan skimmed along the frigate's hull, heading for open space. "Hull cam—"

Her breath left in a rush as three yachts appeared in the forward cameras, racing toward them on a collision course, cannons blazing.

One Hundred Three

Pointing the shuttle away from the detention center and abandoning Aurora and her crew to their fight took every scrap of willpower Cade possessed.

But the terrifying sounds coming from the main cabin of his shuttle forced his hand.

"He's convulsing," Williams bit out as the med platform rattled. "Reynolds, strap him down."

Don't think, just fly. Don't think, just fly. He repeated the mantra as the shuttle shot toward space. Unfortunately, he felt like he'd left half his body trapped in the detention center.

"*Starhawke*, we've got a medical emergency," Justin said into the comm. "The Admiral has been gassed with an unknown toxin. We need Lelindia's help."

"Understood," Marina replied, but in Cade's hyperaware state, she didn't sound normal. "We're still working on getting away from the station. Can you rendezvous with us?"

Justin shared an uneasy look with Cade. "When you say getting away, do you mean—"

"That we're under fire from a mass of Fleet ships? Yes."

The rattling in the main cabin was replaced by an even more ominous sound... the unbroken monotone hum of the heart monitor.

"He's flatlined." Williams didn't sound panicked. Yet. But the edge in his voice didn't bode well.

"He's coding?" Marina's voice rose an octave.

"Yes," Justin replied.

"Can they—" Cade's voice died as he caught sight of the flight space around Sol Station.

Fourteen Fleet vessels had the *Starhawke* penned in against the space station. The larger frigates held the perimeter while the smaller yachts moved in the interior, their coordinated firing patterns lighting up the *Starhawke*'s shields, revealing the camouflaged ship's location. The camouflage abruptly dropped as a yacht almost slammed into the *Starhawke's* port side.

"Why'd they drop the camouflage?" Justin asked him.

"Had to, to prevent a collision with the yachts." As it was, Brendan was doing impressive maneuvers to avoid most of the Fleet fire in the relatively tight space. But finding an opening between the frigates that the ship could slip through while also dodging the circling yachts was a serious challenge, even for an incredible pilot like Brendan.

And trying to dock the shuttle with the *Starhawke* while it was making those maneuvers? It would get them all killed.

The flatline tone from the cabin underscored his thoughts.

Justin correctly interpreted Cade's extended silence. "We can't dock with them, can we?"

Cade met his gaze, hating the answer he had to give. "No."

One Hundred Four

The accumulated dust suspended in the gas combined with the litter of debris on the ground turned Aurora's cell into a murky swamp. She picked her way toward the door, tightening her shield around her. "Ready, Unity?"

"Releasing door now."

She kicked hard, her shoe connecting with the center of the door, sending it crashing outward. It struck the two guards who had been huddled in front of it, knocking them to the ground.

She lunged through the opening, grasping the door edge and slamming it shut behind her, trapping the gas inside.

One of the guards grabbed for Aurora's leg, her hands sliding ineffectually off Aurora's shield. The second didn't try to move, just brought up her weapon and fired. The bullet created a brilliant white flare and changed trajectory, slamming into the cinderblock wall. Aurora registered the shock on their faces as she kicked the gun out of the guard's hand and darted past.

Thanks to Unity, the overhead lights were out, the only illumination in the cavernous space coming from the red-tinted emergency lighting that outlined the stairways and the perimeter baseboards. But it was still enough to see by, which the other inmates proved, shouting insults at her as she ran to the top of the stairs.

Their bursts of anger, fear, and confusion smacked her from all directions like paintballs.

Two guards waited on the stairs, weapons aimed at her chest.

"Stop!"

When Aurora didn't slow, both guards fired.

The discharges deflected harmlessly off her shield. She knocked the weapon from the first's hand, sending it clattering to the floor below. A quick dodge and jump brought her shoulder into the sternum of the second guard, who sprawled beside the railing as Aurora leapt the stairs two at a time, landing on the ground in a half-crouch.

"Is the main door locked?" she asked Unity as she sprinted toward it.

"Yes," Unity replied. "We're keeping nine heavily armed guards on the other side."

She slowed, mentally recalibrating. So much for the easy part. "Okay." She summoned energy to her hands. "Let them through."

"Lock disengaging."

One Hundred Five

The flash of the *Starhawke's* weapons firing sent Micah's heart rate into overdrive. Everyone had agreed during the planning sessions that they wouldn't fire on the Fleet ships unless absolutely necessary.

Apparently they'd crossed over into absolutely necessary.

A quick check of Unity's projection of the Teeli Embassy showed a mass of writhing motion. He could pick out the two Yruf based on their size and alien facial structure, but he couldn't tell which of the muscular figures was Knox. He couldn't see Magee at all. "Unity, what's happening?"

One of the figures slid bonelessly to the ground. "One of the guards is sedated."

Micah caught sight of a smaller figure – Magee – slumped against the chest of one of the muscular figures. "Does Knox have Magee?"

"Yes."

The second guard staggered, one of the Yruf supporting him as he sank to the ground next to this companion.

"Both guards are out," Knox confirmed. "I've got Isabeau. We're heading back to the transport."

"Sly'Kull just put the Embassy on alert," Unity warned them. "We've blocked comms, but he's shouting orders. All available guards are running to intercept you."

Knox lifted Magee into his arms. "Then we better hurry."

One Hundred Six

Jonarel's hands trembled from the adrenaline coursing through his veins. His focus locked on the building below like he could peel the roof away through a sheer act of will.

Fleet Security swarmed the guard towers like ants — the only location they could access with Unity in control of the electronic door locks — weapons ready as they searched the sky for a target. They had stopped shooting after Kelly arrowed the shuttle in a straight line toward the horizon. She'd circled back, the shuttle hovering silently above the roofline without drawing attention.

"Unity, we need a visual on Aurora," Kire barked.

An image appeared in front of the shuttle's viewport, a dim and grainy black-and-white security camera view. Jonarel spotted Aurora running through the central room of her wedge, headed for a closed door. Four guards staggered to their feet on the upper level and stairway, only one with a visible weapon.

"Where are the rest of the gua—"

He got his answer as the door Aurora was running toward abruptly swung open. Guards in riot gear crowded into the narrow space with shields and weapons up and ready. They hesitated for a millisecond before firing, clearly not expecting to find Aurora barreling toward them. Light flashed in a series of miniature lightning bolts as their shots struck her shield, blotting out the camera feed and making it impossible to see what was happening.

But he saw the aftermath. Weapons and riot shields flew into the air as Aurora knocked the guards away from the door.

He growled, urging her on.

More flashes, more guards knocked aside, and then Aurora disappeared through the doorway. The feed switched to a view of the corridor, where three more guards hit the wall and crumpled to the ground as Aurora raced past.

Kire cleared his throat. "The guards aren't moving."

Jonarel did not take time to think about it. Aurora had reached the exterior door that led to the exercise yard. He darted a glance at the FS officers in the guard towers. Their attention swung in Aurora's direction as she erupted like a starburst through the door, charging out of the building at a dead sprint.

Kelly had the shuttle in motion before the door swung shut, swooping down into the exercise yard like a bird of prey.

Aurora ran straight for the gate in the chain link fence that stood between her and the open space of the yard.

But before she could reach it, the ground ahead of her turned into a rolling boil of dirt, grass, and spraying cement as the FS officers opened up on her.

One Hundred Seven

Bring him to us.

Ifel's words were crystal clear in Cade's head, as though she were standing behind him in the shuttle.

His mind took a second, absorbing the futility of trying to help the *Starhawke* escape the Fleet blockade. The horrifying hum of the Admiral's flatlined heart monitor kicked him back into gear.

He changed course. "Unity, give me coordinates for the Yruf ship."

The information appeared on his display. He blinked. The Yruf were ridiculously close. He could reach them in minutes, but... "How can we dock? They're in sight of the station." Unlike with the *Starhawke*, he couldn't land on the Yruf ship without visual guidance, which would reveal the ship's presence to the station's personnel.

"With all traffic on lockdown," Unity replied, "there is no one flying in the system. We have repositioned so your bay is pointed away from the station and the planet. No one will see you or us."

"Smart," Justin murmured. "The camouflaged ship becomes the visual screen."

Cade didn't care how they managed it, as long as they could save the Admiral.

We can Ifel assured him.

Cade coaxed every bit of speed he could manage from the shuttle as they raced toward the Yruf ship, his nerves stretched to the breaking point.

They couldn't fail, not now, not when they were so close.

The heart monitor gave a small ping, then another.

"I've got a heartbeat, but it's erratic," Williams confirmed. "Give me—"

Cade struggled to block out the flurry of activity in the main cabin, focusing on reaching the Yruf ship, counting out the seconds.

"He's coding again!"

Drew's voice made him jerk, his display alerting him he was off course. He corrected, cursing himself. *Just fly, just fly, just—*

The familiar green and gold lights appeared in the inky blackness, the glow from the bay reaching out to the shuttle. He took them in with far more speed than was technically safe, the Yruf ship swallowing them as he settled the shuttle on the ground with a thump.

The hatch hissed open before he'd powered down the shuttle's engines. He unlatched his harness, turning in his chair just as Ahle and Cegra leapt through the opening, two other Yruf close behind.

Cade's team, with the exception of Williams, backed away from the Admiral as Ahle took charge. He placed several identical objects on the Admiral's forehead, chest, and abdomen as the other

Yruf guided what looked like a mobile diagnostic unit into place beside the Admiral's still form.

The flatline hum droned on, unmoved by the flurry of activity.

Cade swallowed, the emotions he'd shoved aside shouldering their way back in now that he had nothing to distract him.

He trembled from the effort of not yelling, throwing something, or punching the wall. The universe had no justice. Who was he? Nobody. A pilot. A soldier. An insignificant piece in this deadly game.

Yet here he was, safe and sound on the Yruf ship, while those who really mattered – the Admiral, Aurora, the *Starhawke*...

They were fighting for their lives.

One Hundred Eight

"Any chance you can disable the engines on a few of those yachts?" Brendan called out as the *Starhawke* shook again.

"I'm good, kid," Lelindia's dad replied. "But not that good. I can't risk taking out life support or breaching the hull."

They'd tried two more runs past the frigates. Both times they'd been forced to turn back to prevent a head-on collision with a yacht. They'd disabled the weapons on two of the frigates, but trying to take advantage of that weak point had made the yachts more ruthless in their deadly game. The repeated scrape of shields and near misses had Lelindia quietly freaking out as the frigates tightened the net.

She'd never heard of the Fleet using suicide bombing as a tactic, but the yachts were moving like that option was on the table.

She couldn't let that happen. She was a doctor, sworn to protect life, not destroy it.

Blasts from four of the yachts lit up the shields, triggering alerts. "Forward shields at thirty-eight percent," her dad informed them. "Dorsal shields at thirty-three percent."

Brendan dove to avoid a blast from one of the frigates, but had to change course abruptly as two yachts converged on them.

A shot from another frigate clipped them, sending a jolt through the deck. "We have to do something," Brendan said through gritted teeth.

"And soon," her dad warned, anxiety thickening his voice. "The station's warming up their cannons."

The worried look Brendan shot her dad made Lelindia's stomach curdle.

"Tehar, can we handle a direct hit from the station?" she asked.

The Nirunoc met her gaze. The shadows in her golden eyes drove a spike of fear through Lelindia's chest. "With shields depleted? Uncertain."

One Hundred Nine

The sharp pops and crackles of destruction grated across Jonarel's skin as the shuttle's hatch opened. The hood of his battle suit provided some relief against the sensory onslaught, but not enough. He gripped the back of the closest chair, his claws digging into the fabric, anchoring him.

Pandemonium rained onto the detention center, the coordinated lines of fire from the FS officers chewing up the dirt and grass and sparking off the shuttle's shields. The smell of scorched earth and vegetation made his lip curl.

"Do you see her?" Celia shouted from her position on the opposite side of the hatch. Her eyes were half-closed as she squinted against the bright flashes of strobing light.

Despite the pain, he had never been more grateful for his enhanced senses. His eyes automatically filtered the light bursts so he could see into the dark spaces between. He spotted Aurora running toward the chain link fence, her shield flashing a pearlescent white every time a discharge struck it. "Yes!"

A brighter burst and a screech of metal blew the gate she had been running toward off its hinges.

The moment she was in the open, the assault became a torrent, so much firepower from the guard towers striking her shield it crashed like thunder and lit the yard bright as midday.

Her steps slowed, her hands over her head, palms up in a defensive posture that tore a growl from his chest. On her next step she stumbled on the uneven ground, falling to one knee.

She was still ten meters from the shuttle, the weapons fire battering her. And she was not getting to her feet.

"We need to hurry!" Kire shouted from the cockpit. "Unity says the anti-aircraft weapons are almost in position to fire."

The shields would hold against a few shots, but even Kraed defenses were not invulnerable.

Grabbing two rifles from the weapons locker, he loaded them with non-lethal rounds and tossed one to Celia. "I will fetch her. Cover me."

She eyed him for a moment, then turned toward the cockpit. "Unity, tell Aurora we're coming. We'll be laying down suppressive fire on the towers. Non-lethal," she added.

"Got it," Unity replied.

"I'll nudge us as close to her as I can," Kelly called out.

Jonarel glanced at the cockpit. Kire had turned in his seat, watching them, worry shadowing his eyes.

Jonarel tapped two fingers against his battle suit as a reminder of the protection it provided.

Kire got the message, giving him a decisive nod. "Retracting the shield covering the hatch."

One Hundred Ten

Micah's heart pounded against his ribcage as the *Starhawke* shuddered for what felt like the thousandth time.

He refused to look at the bridgescreen. Instead his gaze locked on the infrared projection showing Knox and the two Yruf hurrying through the vegetation, the Yruf bent so low to the ground they were almost running on all fours.

The four heat signatures tracking them from behind were steadily gaining ground.

"Forward shields at thirty-eight percent," Gryphon called out. "Dorsal shields at thirty-three percent."

He squeezed his eyes closed. This was NOT going according to plan. "Unity, please tell me Aurora's on the shuttle."

Unity's hesitation nearly shoved Micah's heart out of his chest. "She's encountered problems."

"Problems?" he hissed, his eyes snapping open. "What kinds of problems?"

"She's under fire."

His throat closed completely. Unbidden, the image of Aurora standing in the middle of Stoneycroft, shield glowing, surrounded by flames, seared into his mind's eye.

"Jonarel and Celia are making their way to her."

"What about the Admiral?" he choked out.

"He's onboard the Yruf ship."

One thing had gone right.

"Ahle's working to clear a toxin and restart his heart."

Holy hell. "Can you help Aurora?"

Unity sounded pained, apologetic. "The moon has risen."

The *Starhawke* jolted, shaking him. He clung to his chair.

"But..." Unity added.

Micah's gaze snapped back to the Embassy projection. The angle abruptly shifted, streaking toward the four guards chasing Knox's group. It swooped over them, all four sailing backward, hitting the ground like they'd been struck by a concussion wave.

"Yes!" He leapt to his feet, punching his fist in the air. And instantly regretted it as he was flung to the deck.

One Hundred Eleven

The controlled bursts of Aurora's energy field that had stunned but not seriously injured the guards she'd encountered had required a lot of concentration. Maintaining her shield when she was outnumbered nine to one had made it even harder. But that was a drop in the bucket compared to what she encountered after she blasted the gate to the exercise yard off its hinges.

"—Aurora. Jonarel and Celia... you... suppression... non-lethal."

She barely made out Unity's voice over the ringing in her ears and the cacophony besieging her. A moon's worth of pressure buried her beneath her shield, making it impossible to get her feet under her. She couldn't lower her hands, either. How many FS officers were firing from the guard towers? Twenty? Forty? It felt like a hundred. She couldn't see anything, her eyes squeezed closed against the harsh glare as shots struck her shield in rapid succession.

At least Unity's control of the facility's locks had kept the guards from reaching the yard. But even that reprieve wouldn't last forever.

Her focus snapped abruptly forward, latching onto a sharp switch in Jonarel and Celia's emotional fields. Up to now she'd sensed their fury and anxiety. Now she was getting fatalistic determination.

Panic clawed up her throat as she sensed them moving fractionally closer. Her eyes opened to slits, searching for the shuttle she knew was there but couldn't see.

And then she did, two forms silhouetted by the shuttle's cabin light. "No!" she shouted, but the word was instantly buried under the avalanche of firepower.

They couldn't survive this. She was barely hanging on.

What had Unity tried to tell her? Something about suppression? Didn't matter. She could feel them creeping closer. She had to reach them first.

A rush of adrenaline surged through her body. She staggered toward them on her knees, driving her shield up and out, struggling to encircle them. The added pressure from the exertion shoved her into a low kneel, her arms trembling over her head.

Be strong, be strong, be strong, be—

And then an arm of iron pressed against her back, and another slid behind her knees, lifting her against a muscled chest but keeping her hands free.

"I have you," Jonarel's voice rumbled in her ear. "Focus on your shield."

As if she needed the reminder. Teeth grinding, she drew on every scrap of energy she had, fortifying the shield surrounding the three of them. Each inhale took a conscious force of will, each second lasted an eternity.

And then they passed under the shuttle's protective canopy. Her muscles went limp a split second before a blast rocked the shuttle hard enough to jostle her in Jonarel's arms. His growl rumbled against her cheek, but he remained upright, carefully depositing her in one of the cabin chairs and fastening her in.

She pried her eyes open, catching Celia's splotchy dark outline trading places with Kire's slender form in the cockpit.

Jonarel sank down next to her, and Kire dropped into the chair on her other side. Then the shuttle was in motion. A powerful blast made the shuttle jerk and shudder. Her body flopped like a ragdoll in the hands of a toddler.

Jonarel slipped his arm around her shoulders, holding her steady. She appreciated the assist. She felt as weak and disoriented as a newborn.

Kire tapped his comband. "We've got her."

"Thank the stars," Marina replied.

Her voice sounded funny, but Aurora was too tired to analyze it. Her eyelids closed and her head dropped onto Jonarel's sturdy shoulder.

"Roe? You okay?"

She managed a murmured, "Mm-hmm," but that was all she had left in the tank.

"Justin?" Kire said softly. "Tell Cade we've got her…"

That was the last thing she heard before she lost consciousness.

One Hundred Twelve

"Cade?"

Cade's neck creaked as he ripped his focus from the Admiral and met Justin's gaze. "What?" The word came out harsh, biting, but he couldn't control it. He was too raw.

Justin absorbed the verbal jab without flinching. "Kire reported in. They've got Aurora. She's okay. They'll be here soon."

Justin's words slid over him like oil on ice, not penetrating. "They got her out? She's okay?"

"Yeah."

He couldn't believe it. Accept it. Not until he saw her. Touched her. Held—

A gasp of air filled the hushed atmosphere of the shuttle.

Cade's head snapped around. Was that the Admiral? Was he—

His angle on the med platform was mostly obscured with the Yruf crowded around it, but the deep inhalation had come from that direction.

He remained still as a statue, as did the rest of his team, their gazes on the Admiral.

The gasp repeated, strained and labored, but undeniably there. It was the most wonderful sound Cade had ever heard.

Inhale. Exhale. Inhale. Exhale.

He could hear them both now, the rhythm growing more consistent but still scraping through the Admiral's throat in a painful rasp.

U-2 dropped from the alcove above Cade's and Justin's seats, hovering between them. "Ahle has identified the chemical composition of the toxin and is working to neutralize it," they said in a low tone.

"Is he—" Cade cleared his throat. "Is the Admiral going to live?"

Unity bobbed. "It will take time, as the toxin was lethal and we are still learning about your physiology. But yes, he is out of immediate danger. With Lelindia's help, we believe he will make a full recovery."

Cade exhaled, sinking back into his chair. "You saved his life." Stating the obvious seemed to be all he could manage at this point.

"We still have much to learn about healing blunt trauma." Unity's voice darkened to a tone Cade hadn't heard them use before. "But the war that destroyed our planet gave our doctors more than their share of experience dealing with the effects of lethal toxins."

One Hundred Thirteen

Lelindia gasped as the *Starhawke* bucked. Alarms blared, alerting anyone who wasn't paying attention that they'd been hit by a blast from the station.

"Dad!"

Lelindia's father lay partially slumped over the tactical console. He pushed himself up, shaking his head as if to clear it. "I'm okay." His energy field engaged, but his gaze darted to the display. "The aft shields are gone."

Gone.

She shot a frantic look at Brendan. "Brendan—"

His attention was on his console, his shoulders hunched as he continued to dodge the fire from the Fleet ships. "It's a matter of numbers, firefly." His voice was tight with strain. "If we're getting out of here, we have to disable the yachts."

She swallowed hard, her gaze meeting her dad's. The same realization shone in his eyes. It was either them or the Fleet personnel standing in their way.

Her hand dropped to her belly. Raehn's lifeforce pulsed within her. Was this how her daughter's story would begin? With Lelindia ordering the deaths of innocent people to save the people she loved?

Sahzade! She called out in desperation, needing Aurora's wisdom and experience now more than ever.

But all she got back was silence.

Terror gripped her, tossing her into her worst nightmare. Her family – her *child* – was in mortal danger, and the only way to save them was by sacrificing people she didn't know.

She was a doctor. The Nedale of the Suulh. Defender of life itself.

Her hand splayed over her swollen stomach. She was also a mother, guardian of her unborn child.

Her daughter, or her soul?

"I can't." The words escaped her lips on a wisp of air. But the breeze grew stronger, building into a mighty storm that swept through her, clearing away all doubt. "I can't," she said firmly. "We can't. There must be another way."

Her dad met her gaze, pride and sadness blending in his soft smile.

Which told her the inescapable truth. There was no other way.

"The station's cannon is almost recharged," he said. Just stating a fact.

A moan behind her made her turn.

Micah stumbled onto the bridge, his hand on his head as he wove drunkenly. "Ifel," he muttered. "Unity."

Libra shot out of the chair beside Lelindia like a pearlescent bullet, catching Micah under his arm as her energy field engulfed him. She guided him to the chair she'd vacated.

He sank down with a groan.

Lelindia wrapped her hand over his forehead, her energy field diving beneath his skin, healing the concussion that shone red and angry to her Nedale senses.

His sigh of relief switched abruptly to a sharp inhalation as he straightened. "Head for the frigates!" he shouted, pointing at the image on the bridgescreen.

Brendan, bless him, didn't hesitate. The *Starhawke* swung toward the two frigates they'd fired at previously.

"The station's firing!" her dad cried, gripping the edge of his console.

She braced, too, her energy field and Libra's flaring out to touch every person on the bridge – a last ditch effort to protect them.

A streak of movement on the bridgescreen and a supernova of light made her gasp. A moment later the streak resolved into the sturdy shape of *Gladiator*, gliding beside them.

The *Starhawke* barreled toward a tiny gap between the two frigates, *Gladiator* acting as a moving shield, helping to deflect the incoming fire from the other ships. Four yachts raced toward the *Starhawke* on a collision course.

"Don't change course." Micah's body poised like a swimmer about to dive beneath the surface.

Brendan obeyed the order, the yachts growing frighteningly large in the camera feeds.

Lelindia's entire body vibrated, her energy field bracing for catastrophe.

But rather than ramming the *Starhawke*, at the last moment the Fleet ships veered off, leaving a clear path to the starscape.

"Engage the camouflage!" Micah shouted.

"Camouflage engaged," Brendan confirmed right before the *Starhawke* punched through the gap into open space.

The remaining frigates and yachts fired in synchronized bursts, searching for their lost target, but now that the *Starhawke* was no longer penned in and the yachts couldn't provide physical interference, Brendan avoided the blasts with comparative ease.

Lelindia stared, open-mouthed, as the *Starhawke* changed course. *Gladiator* stayed tucked beside the *Starhawke*, the *Starhawke*'s camouflage concealing both ships from view. "What just happened?"

"We thought you could use a little help," Unity said over the bridge speakers.

"A little help?" She had the urge to leap up and hug the non-biological, but they didn't have a physical presence she could touch. "You saved our lives! That second shot from the station could have killed us."

"We knew *Gladiator* could handle it." Unity sounded as relieved as she felt. "We've made extensive improvements, after all, especially to the sensor deflector. We would have been here sooner, but it took time for us to disengage from the docking clamps and work our way through the station's shield after the lockdown on all departures. Your exit caused quite a stir."

She slumped in her chair, a laugh that had a tinge of hysteria rising in her throat. "I noticed." She stared at the bridgescreen. "What about the yachts? I was sure they were going to ram us. Why did they turn away?"

"We didn't give them a choice," Unity replied, the cheerfulness bleeding out of their voice. "We went against your wishes. You and Aurora didn't want us anywhere the Fleet might notice us."

"You infiltrated their ships," Brendan said, turning from his console to face Micah, the one person on the bridge who clearly wasn't surprised by Unity's explanation. "The Yruf scouts snuck in while all attention was on us and tagged the yachts."

"They had to," Micah said simply. "It was the only way to help us." He turned to Lelindia. "And before you start worrying, know that the Yruf are extracting Unity from the yachts right now. There won't be any trace left when the yachts return to the station. In fact, Unity was able to leave evidence of a variety of system malfunctions to explain the unexpected glitches with the yachts' navigation."

"We'll be extracted from the Embassy and detention center tomorrow night," Unity added. "We've been keeping the cell doors sealed, monitoring the gas. We were working to neutralize it, but the gas broke down on its own shortly after Aurora's departure."

"Gas?" Lelindia spun to face her mother. "What gas?"

Her mom held up a hand, her attention on the comm. "Hang on a moment, Kire," she said into the comm before turning to Lelindia. "Both the Admiral's and Aurora's cells filled with a toxic gas during the extraction. There was nothing we could do to help, so I chose not to tell you."

Fear shot through her. "What happened? Are they okay?"

"I was just getting an update from Kire. Aurora's fine, and the Admiral's stable. But he'll need our help when we rendezvous with the Yruf."

She lifted halfway out of her chair, her energy field tingling under her skin. "What's wrong with him?"

"He coded."

Fury suffused her cells. The Sovereign had tried to kill him.

She should have expected the sadistic psychopath would have a draconian plan for foiling any attempt to extract the Admiral.

She turned to Brendan, her gaze flicking to the shadowy image of *Gladiator* on the bridgescreen, partially concealed by the *Starhawke*'s curves. "Unity, I know *Gladiator* isn't as fast as the *Starhawke*, but work your magic to keep up. Brendan, get us to the rendezvous point ASAP."

One Hundred Fourteen

Jonarel held onto Aurora like a lifeline during the flight to the Yruf ship. It was the only thing keeping him sane as he waited for word from Kire that the *Starhawke* had escaped the Fleet blockade.

His mate was out there fighting for her life — for the life of their child — and he was utterly powerless to save her.

But if Lelindia were in his place, she would put Aurora's wellbeing ahead of her own. She always had. Watching over Aurora until Lelindia could reach them was the one thing he could do for them both.

Aurora remained dead to the world, bonelessly slumped against him. Her steady breathing suggested she was resting, although her non-reactive behavior reminded him more of a coma than sleep.

He should have asked Lelindia about the scope of Aurora's abilities, what to do for her if she overexerted herself. He should have asked his mate — told his mate — so many things before they parted.

At the time, keeping her on the *Starhawke* had seemed like the safest course of action. He had not wanted her anywhere near the detention center, anywhere the Sovereign might reach her. On the *Starhawke*, Tehar could protect her. The battle suit could protect her.

But now that the ship was in danger, he was berating himself with every curse he knew. Why had he agreed to abandon his mate and their unborn child? He should have insisted on staying. He should have shown Celia how to use the cutter. He should have—

Kire's hand darted to his earpiece, then his comband. "Marina, please repeat that."

Jonarel's muscles wound into tight springs.

"We made it out," Marina said over the comband's speaker. "The camouflage is engaged and the Fleet ships aren't following us."

Jonarel's heart stuttered, weightless in his chest for a millisecond before it began leaping around with wild abandon.

"Yes!" Celia cheered from the cockpit.

A broad grin spread across Kire's face. "That's great news, Marina. We should arrive at the Yruf ship shortly. How quickly can you reach the rendezvous point? The Yruf were able to stabilize the Admiral, but the gas did serious damage. He's going to need Suulh healing."

"Hang on a moment, Kire." Marina's voice cut off.

Jonarel sighed in frustration. He had hoped to hear Lelindia's voice. Marina had settled the worst of his fears, but he could not relax until he had confirmed for himself that his mate was unharmed.

"Kire? We're going to get there as quickly as we can. We have *Gladiator* using our camouflage to stay hidden, so that may slow us down a bit. If you fly your shuttle over as soon as we reach the rendezvous point—"

"Probably not the best idea," Kelly interjected from the cockpit. "We took a lot of damage. We're almost to the Yruf ship, but we're limping along. I'd rather not take the shuttle even for a short hop until I've given her a solid onceover."

"What about the other shuttle?" Kire asked Marina. "They're already on the Yruf ship."

"The Admiral's still being treated on it. I don't know if they'll have him moved to their med bay by then. But Micah says he can ask Ifel to send her transport to pick us up."

"That would be great," Kire said.

"I will be on that transport," Jonarel growled.

Kire glanced at Jonarel, his lips twitching. "Did you get that?" he asked Marina.

Amusement tinged her voice, too. "Yes. And I have someone who has a message for him."

His mate's melodic voice came over the speaker, making his fingers curl and his skin tingle. "Jonarel? I'll see you soon."

"Yes, you will, my checana."

Kire's face contorted like he was holding back a laugh as he closed the channel.

Jonarel did not care one bit. His mate was alive and well, and soon she would be in his arms.

A yellow glow surrounded the shuttle, drawing his attention outside the viewports. The Yruf ship had enveloped them, swallowing the starfield.

Celia was out of her chair as soon as Kelly settled the shuttle onto the deck. She crouched next to Aurora. "How is she?"

He stroked a hand down Aurora's disheveled braid. "Still unconscious."

Celia's mouth pinched. "She wore herself—"

A thump from the shuttle's ramp made them all turn. Cade bounded onto the shuttle, a scowl on his face when he caught sight of Aurora in Jonarel's arms.

A few months ago, that look would have sent Jonarel into fits. Now he saw it for what it was – the deep concern and self-blame of a man who had been unable to protect his mate from harm. He understood better than anyone what Cade was feeling right now.

With that in mind, he motioned to Cade and slowly eased away from Aurora. Cade slid into his place, his hands cradling Aurora with exquisite reverence and tenderness.

Cade met his gaze, a sheen of moisture coating his eyes. "Thank you for bringing her back to me," he whispered, his voice husky.

Jonarel inclined his head. "Always."

Cade rested his cheek on top of Aurora's head, closing his eyes with a sigh.

A pang of longing wound through Jonarel's chest. He needed to find Ifel, get to her transport.

As if his thoughts had summoned her, Jonarel caught Ifel's whisper-like approach up the ramp. Her graceful form filled the hatch opening, blocking out the golden glow from the bay. Her gaze settled on Aurora and Cade for a long moment, like she was studying a rare flower in bloom. Then she turned to him. "I understand you wish to go to the *Starhawke*," U-1 translated, detaching from the ceiling alcove and floating next to Jonarel's shoulder.

He canted his head back to meet Ifel's gaze. "Yes. To see my checana." Physically looking up to someone was an unusual experience for him, but he did not mind with Ifel. She had earned his respect, and now she had his gratitude as well.

"Kelly and I will go, too," Kire said. "Shuttle repairs can wait. For now, we need to take over bridge duty so Aurora's and Lelindia's families can come here. Celia, what about you?"

Celia leaned her shoulder against the shuttle's bulkhead. "I'll stay here with Cade, if that's okay."

She was attempting to look relaxed, but Jonarel knew her well enough by now to see her underlying agitation. The cause was a mystery, though.

Ifel's tongue flicked. "Then come with me. Our ships are returning, and we will reach the rendezvous point quickly."

The walk through the Yruf ship to the bay that held Ifel's personal transport would have fascinated Jonarel at any other time.

But even the shifting bulkheads and strange lift could not distract him from thoughts of his checana. By the time he was settled into the sleek black vessel beside Kire, his claws itched. Unsheathing and retracting them did nothing to allay the discomfort.

Kire leaned toward him. "You know she's okay, right?" he murmured.

He stared straight ahead. "I know."

"But?"

"But... she is my checana."

Kire tapped him playfully on the arm. "I'm sure she's eager to see you, too."

Lelindia proved him right. When Jonarel stepped out of Ifel's transport into the *Starhawke*'s shuttle bay, he caught Lelindia's alluring scent from across the room. The moment their gazes locked, he was in motion, closing the distance like a predator chasing down prey. Except she was hunting him, too. She raced toward him, launching into his arms. He hauled her against him, her hands locking around his neck, pulling his mouth down until it captured hers.

Her sighing moan blotted out everything except the taste of her on his tongue, the silky texture of her hair and skin beneath his palm, and the thundering of the blood in his ears. "Checana," he breathed, pulling back just long enough to see the yearning in her eyes before claiming her mouth again.

The kiss might have lasted an eternity if someone had not cleared their throat. Loudly.

Lelindia jerked back, her cheeks turning a fetching shade of pink. "Sorry, Dad," she murmured, untangling her fingers from Jonarel's hair.

Jonarel set her on her feet, their battle suits allowing her to slide easily down his body, but he kept one hand on the small of her back. He needed that physical connection, now more than ever.

Gryphon chuckled. "Nothing to be sorry about, sweetheart. But the Admiral needs you and your mother."

"Right." Lelindia lifted her chin, but the longing didn't leave her warm brown eyes. Her focus remained on Jonarel like she was drinking him in. *Later* she mouthed silently.

On that point, he had no doubt.

One Hundred Fifteen

Lee-Lee and Jonarel's enthusiastic greeting brought a smile to Micah's lips, and Birdie, standing beside him, gave a little snort. If they hadn't all just been through hell, he would have been tempted to let fly with a wolf whistle.

But his attention quickly shifted to Ifel's transport. Kire and Kelly exited at a much more sedate pace than Jonarel's bounding sprint, U-1 floating behind them. Micah held his breath, watching the opening, but no one else appeared.

The sharp bite of disappointment dug into him.

He'd been so sure Celia would be with them. Every other member of the crew was here with the exception of Aurora. Why had Celia chosen to stay behind?

And how much of a lovesick idiot was he that he actually believed she'd be eager to see him? That she'd want to make sure he was okay?

"Expecting someone?" Birdie leaned in, her shoulder brushing his.

He flinched. Birdie could read him almost as well as Aurora and his dad. He had no illusions that she hadn't picked up on his interest in Celia. But he tried to shrug it off. "Not exactly."

"Mm-hmm." She wasn't buying what he was selling.

Which made it official. He was the biggest idiot in the galaxy. Yeah, he'd made huge strides in becoming Celia's first male friend, but when it came to the something more he craved — the something more Aurora had specifically warned him he could never have — he and Celia were living in different star systems. No, different galaxies. He had a better chance of surviving a spacewalk without a spacesuit than he did of getting Celia to express romantic feelings toward him.

Stellar light, he was in big trouble.

His dad's hand rested lightly on his shoulder.

He didn't look back at him, working to keep his emotions from showing on his face. Not that anyone other than his parents and Birdie were focused on him. Lee-Lee and Jonarel were hard to ignore until Gryphon cleared his throat.

The pair broke apart with obvious reluctance.

Kire stepped forward. "Kelly and I will take over here. I'm sure you all want to check on Aurora and the Admiral."

"Yes," Micah's mom replied, slipping her hand into Micah's and tugging. She hadn't moved more than a meter from his side since he'd stumbled onto the bridge and she'd engulfed him in her energy field.

"Birdie? You and Kai coming?" Micah asked.

Birdie exchanged a look with her dad. "I want to see the Yruf ship, but that can wait. We'd be in the way right now. We'll stay here.

Tell Aurora I'm eager to see her," she added as Micah's mom gave a firm tug.

He let her pull him toward Ifel's transport. Lee-Lee had healed his head trauma with amazing efficiency, but he remembered the look of pure terror on his mom's face when she'd practically flown to his side to catch him. If keeping him close now made her feel better, he wasn't about to argue.

She let go long enough for Unity to harness them in, then she wrapped his hand in both of hers and rested her head against his shoulder.

His dad, seated beside them, watched them with a pained smile.

Which yanked him out of his self-absorption. His dad had just successfully piloted them through a no-win scenario, but rather than being able to relax, the poor guy was dealing with the unsettling emotions pouring off him and his mom.

Forget about Celia. Focus on Aurora, he told himself. *She needs you.*

Which actually helped distract him for the short flight to the Yruf ship. Ifel and U-2 greeted them when they exited the transport, giving Micah's and Lee-Lee's parents their first look at the Yruf leader. Micah's dad was clearly entranced, but Micah's mom barely made it past introductions, her focus in the direction he assumed they'd find Aurora.

Lee-Lee's family and Jonarel went with Ifel to the med bay, while U-2 guided Micah's family through the maze of shifting bulkheads until they reached the bay where both the *Starhawke*'s shuttles sat.

Unity glided toward the one with the lowered ramp. Micah spotted Celia standing at the top of the ramp, still dressed in the form-fitting battle suit Jonarel had provided to the extraction team. The sight of the material defining every toned muscle in her lithe body did nothing to help his state of mind.

Her attention locked onto him like a targeting system, and his pulse leapt.

But as they walked closer, he couldn't tell whether she was happy to see him or annoyed. "Cade's with Aurora," she informed them, tipping her head toward the main cabin.

His mom practically dragged him up the ramp, passing Celia with barely a glance. But she stopped like she'd hit a wall when she saw Aurora and Cade.

The tight bands of her fingers loosened around his, her sigh of relief filling the cabin.

Cade's eyes opened, his gaze sweeping over the three of them with an assessing look, as if to confirm they were okay. "Welcome aboard," he whispered.

Celia slipped into the shuttle, standing behind Micah close enough that the slightest movement would bring them into contact. He resisted the urge to turn around.

His mom released his hand, kneeling beside Aurora. "Has she woken?" she asked Cade.

"No. I figured it was better to let her sleep until you got here."

His mom smiled, the first genuine smile he'd seen on her face since Aurora was arrested. "Thank you. But I think it's time for Sleeping Beauty to wake up."

One Hundred Sixteen

"Aurora."

Cade's voice settled over Aurora like a warm blanket. She pressed her cheek into his chest, savoring the delicious sensation of his arms wrapped around her. She wasn't ready to wake up. She wanted to stay in this blissful half-conscious state, snuggled in the arms of the man she loved.

Cade responded with a happy sigh, shifting her closer.

But her contentment turned to confusion as aches reported in from every part of her body. Her muscles complained like she'd run back-to-back marathons while carrying a shuttlecraft over her head. She frowned. Why was she so sore? The last thing she remembered was—

Her eyes snapped open. She raised her head so quickly that she clipped Cade's chin.

He grunted, loosening his hold on her.

Her vision blurred and her forehead throbbed. Maybe sudden movement wasn't a great idea.

The Admiral. The gas. Was he alive? Where was he? For that matter, where was she?

"It's okay, Aurora."

Her mom's voice.

She blinked rapidly, focusing on the blurred outlines of the four figures crouched beside her. Her mom, her dad, Micah, and Celia.

Her mom reached for her hand, her energy field sweeping over her, warm and loving. She drank it in like water on parched earth. Micah clasped her other hand. Her body jerked like she'd touched a livewire.

"Sorry." He lifted his hand.

She grabbed it, keeping him from pulling away. His touch, combined with her mom's energy work, was attempting to jump start the drained battery of her own energy field. Unsuccessfully, it seemed.

At least the thumping behind her eyes steadily switched from a pounding tympany to a tapping snare drum, turning down the volume on her aches and pains.

Her eyes struggled to focus, taking in the details around her. She was still on the *Starhawke*'s shuttle. U-2 hovered behind Micah, and Cade sat in the seat Jonarel had occupied when she'd passed out.

"How are you feeling?" he asked, his eyes clouded with worry.

Instead of answering him, she lifted her face toward his, her lips brushing against the velvety smoothness of his mouth and the slight rasp of stubble on his chin. "You're here."

The worry melted into something else entirely, making her heart beat erratically. His mouth came down on hers in a tender kiss. "I'm here. And so are you."

A drop of moisture squeezed out of the side of her eye. Then another, and another.

She didn't want to cry. Didn't want to come unglued. But she didn't have the strength to stop the growing stream. It overflowed, pouring down her cheeks.

"Hey." He brushed the tears away with his thumb. "It's okay. Everyone got out."

Everyone. That meant the Admiral was alive.

She bathed in the sea-green of his eyes, her emotions intertwining with his in their special dance. But her internal GPS began cataloguing every emotional resonance she recognized.

Lee-Lee and her parents were with the Admiral, as was Jonarel, Knox, Cade's team, and Ifel. Kire and Kelly were much farther away, maybe not even on the same ship. "Where are we?" She peered around the cabin, noting the golden glow. "On the Yruf ship?"

"Yes," her dad answered. "Ifel had her transport waiting to fetch us from the *Starhawke* as soon as we reached the rendezvous point."

"Are Kire and Kelly on the *Starhawke* with Iolana and Kai?"

Micah grinned. "I see that internal GPS is working fine."

"Yeah." She stretched her neck carefully side to side, wincing as her muscles seized. "But the rest of me could use some TLC."

"Are you up to walking to the med bay?" Celia asked. "That's where Lelindia and Marina are."

She glanced at Cade. "I might need a little support."

A spark of mischief lit his eyes. "No problem." He stood, sweeping her into his arms in one deft movement.

She groaned as the cabin spun, her connection to her mom and Micah cutting off. She looped her arms around his neck and dropped her head on his shoulder. "I said support, not carry," she muttered. But oh, did this feel good.

His arms tightened around her. "I'd say you're very supported."

So would she. The way his voice rumbled through her entire body was delightful. Ordinarily she'd be horrified at the thought of being carried into a room, but considering the day – hell, the month – she'd had, her pride could take a hike.

One Hundred Seventeen

Carrying Aurora to the med bay made Cade feel like king of the world. Not that he would ever tell her that. He loved her ability to take care of herself — her independence, her self-sufficiency. But once in a while it was nice to be needed.

As the lift closed in around them, he tightened his grip. But the deck didn't rise with its usual speed, gliding up much more sedately. Unity looking out for them, no doubt.

He took advantage of the delay to nuzzle her hair, rewarded with her contented sigh. He could feel the warmth of her body through her clothing, the moisture from her breath tickling his neck, the solid weight of her in his arms. He noted every tactile sensation, giving gratitude for the gifts that they were. He and Aurora had spent so much time apart recently — not completely cut off from each other, yet never touching. Not like now.

He followed U-2 down the corridor into a part of the ship he'd never seen. But even though the layout was alien, he recognized the med bay as soon as he stepped through the doorway. It didn't hurt that his team, Knox, and Jonarel were gathered around Lelindia, Marina, and Gryphon, whose energy fields surrounded the Admiral, lying still in a pod-like bed.

Knox turned toward them. "Aurora!" He crossed the room in long strides.

Aurora lifted her head and gave him a weak smile. "Hey, Knox. Fancy meeting you here."

Knox smiled back, but frown lines grooved between his brows. "Are you hurt?"

Aurora flicked one hand. "Just drained. And a little dizzy. Nothing Lelindia can't fix." Her gaze moved past Knox's shoulder. "How's your dad?"

He glanced back, heaving a sigh. "Much better, now. I'm trying not to think about what would have happened if the Yruf hadn't been able to neutralize the toxin you were exposed to. And if Lelindia couldn't do what... well, what she can do."

"Is he awake?"

"Lelindia's got him in her version of an induced coma while they work on him. She said it helps his body accept the healing better."

Cade nodded. "She did the same thing after he was injured in the engine room explosion. He'll wake up on his own."

"That's what she told me."

"What about Isabeau?" Aurora asked Knox.

He cleared his throat. "She's sedated for now, resting in one of Ifel's holding areas. We can talk more later." His pointed look made it clear he wanted her focusing on her own issues right now.

Cade wholeheartedly agreed.

Ahle approached them, his diamond-pupiled gaze on Aurora. He greeted her parents with the Yruf head tilt, then gestured to one of the empty pods.

"Do you want to lie down?" Micah translated for her.

"I'd rather stand." She turned her head, meeting Cade's gaze, a ripple of self-consciousness passing through her field. "That is, if you don't mind me leaning on you a while longer."

His throat constricted with a rush of emotion. "You can lean on me forever."

That brought a fresh flow of tears coursing down her cheeks. Her eyes blazed with the raw strength of the emotions sweeping over her. They struck him so forcefully he almost dropped her. Instead, he gaped at her, overwhelmed by what he was sensing from her as the words left her lips.

"I think I'll take you up on that offer."

One Hundred Eighteen

Lelindia registered Aurora's arrival in the med bay with her Nedale senses, the heightened awareness letting her know her energy sister was nearby. The burst of joy that Aurora's presence triggered lit her up inside, but it also pulled her attention in opposing directions. The Admiral still needed her, but she could sense something was seriously out of whack in Aurora's energy field. Had she come in contact with the same toxin and been unable to clear it?

She'd been horrified by the extent of the damage the toxic gas had caused to the Admiral's cells in such a relatively short time. But she'd recognized the pattern of destruction immediately. She'd seen a liquid version of it injected subcutaneously on Persei Primus.

The gas form wasn't nearly as fast acting, which was the only reason the Admiral was still alive. Thanks to her mom's help, her dad's assist, and an extra boost from little Raehn, the healing was going much quicker than if she were alone.

She took a peek in Aurora's direction and blinked. Blinked again. Cade was carrying Aurora in his arms.

Anxiety smacked into her as her Nedale senses leapt into action, analyzing what she was seeing. Aurora hadn't been kidding when she'd told Knox she was drained. Lelindia had never seen her in this condition before. To her senses, Aurora's physical resonance looked almost... Human. Very little of her Suulh energy shone through.

Aurora turned in her direction, meeting her gaze with a weak smile. *Hi* she mouthed, tucking her head in the crook of Cade's neck and shoulder.

What exactly had happened at the detention center?

Hi she mouthed back, scanning Aurora for any signs of trauma, but coming up empty. She glanced at the Admiral, then back at Aurora. *Two minutes* she projected to Aurora.

Okay Aurora projected back. She whispered something to Cade and he started walking in Lelindia's direction, Libra, Micah, and Brendan on their heels.

Good. Whatever had happened, she wanted all the help she could get to correct it.

But first she needed to finish healing the Admiral. His cells were responding well. She'd restored their structural integrity and fluid functionality, although his lungs and throat still looked inflamed to her senses. That was to be expected after what he'd been through. In many ways, this was far worse than the damage from the explosion she'd healed last year. That had all been blunt trauma and his body's natural reactions to it.

But there was nothing natural about the toxin he'd been exposed to. If Ahle hadn't had the knowledge and skill to stop the rampant destruction the toxin unleashed, the Admiral's body likely would have broken down into its organic elements before she reached him.

She'd focused on giving his immune system a roadmap to follow, which it was doing with dogged determination. She'd also suppressed the Admiral's pain receptors so he could rest easily until he woke up. She'd give him another healing later, after his system had a chance to find its internal balance. And after she'd figured out what was wrong with Aurora.

When she released her energy field and looked up, she discovered Aurora was back on her feet, although Cade's arms were wrapped around her from behind, pretty much holding her up as she leaned against him. "How's he doing?" Aurora asked.

Lelindia stood and stretched the kinks out of her back. "He's going to be uncomfortable when he wakes up, but thanks to Ahle's quick work and the healing energy of three Nedales, he should be well on his way to a full recovery in a few days."

A wriggle put an exclamation point on her comment. She gave a startled laugh, resting her hands on her belly. "Did you enjoy that energy work, little one?"

Another wriggle.

"I'll take that as a yes. Then why don't we help out your Aunty Aurora?"

Two wriggles.

"Okay, then." She turned to Jonarel, who'd stood silently beside her during the entire healing session. "She's a born healer, this one."

His golden gaze warmed, so full of meaning. Of promise. Of hope. "Just like her mother."

One Hundred Nineteen

Aurora could have stood in the circle of Cade's arms all day.

Well, not literally. She'd been on her feet for a couple minutes and her knees were already starting to protest the effort of keeping her vertical. But having her body aligned with his, all those wonderful points of contact, the tender strength of his touch – it was like standing inside love.

And completely impractical for a healing session.

She eyed Lelindia as she came around the med pod. "Nice outfit." It matched the ones Jonarel and Celia were wearing, which gave her a pretty good idea of the intended function.

Lelindia's wry grin confirmed it. "Thanks. It's a battle suit. Jonarel made them. He was rather... insistent."

Frankly, she was amazed Jonarel had agreed to be separated from Lelindia at all. Lelindia must have been insistent as well.

"So, do you want to tell me what happened?" Lelindia folded her arms, looking at Aurora the same way she had when Aurora was a child who regularly bent or broke their parents' rules.

She shrugged, her muscles protesting the movement. "It took a bit more effort to get out of the detention center than I'd expected."

Lelindia nodded.

Aurora got the sense a mountain of questions waited behind that easy acceptance, but Lelindia didn't seem inclined to follow up.

"Do you want to lie down?" Lelindia asked, gesturing to the empty med pod Ahle had indicated earlier.

"Nope." She'd already shown more vulnerability in the last couple hours than she was comfortable with. Lying down for a healing session with everyone watching – especially Knox and Cade's unit – was not something she could handle right now.

Lelindia's emotional field flashed with understanding. "Then Micah, can you please take Cade's place behind Aurora?"

Cade gave her a quick hug. "I'll be right here," he whispered before carefully transferring her to Micah's care, remaining in her peripheral vision.

The moment Micah touched her, she got the sizzle pop sensation of energy potential she'd felt before, but without the satisfaction of her energy field engaging. Funny, really, in a morbidly fascinating way. She'd always wondered what it would feel like to be completely human. If this experience was any indication, she wouldn't like it.

"Does this feel different to you?" Micah murmured, wrapping his arms around her.

"Yeah."

He grunted, clearly catching the underlying exasperation in her tone. "Don't worry. Lee-Lee will fix it." He put pressure on her waist, encouraging her to give him more of her weight.

She complied because she didn't have much choice.

Knox had tactfully turned to engage Justin, Drew, and Gonzo in conversation, while Celia had pulled Reynolds aside. That left only Williams watching the proceedings, his emotional field filled with the same curiosity Lelindia showed whenever she faced an unusual medical problem.

Lelindia rested one hand on Aurora's shoulder and the other on her elbow, while Marina moved to Aurora's other side, mirroring Lelindia. "Libra, if you'll take Aurora's hand next to my mom, and dad, if you'll do the same next to me, you and Libra can complete the circle."

Aurora met Lelindia's gaze. "This feels weird."

Lelindia grinned. "That's because you're an impatient patient."

She opened her mouth to protest, then reconsidered. "You're right."

"Of course I am. Now relax. With the power this group can bring, we should have you juiced up in no time."

Lelindia's energy field engaged first, the beautiful emerald green making her look like a woodland sprite, especially with Jonarel hovering behind her. Marina's followed, then Gryphon's, and lastly her mom's. The green, gold, and pearlescent white wove together on the opposite side of the circle between her mom and Gryphon, then began flowing back toward Aurora.

The moment the combined energies touched her, her energy field ignited like a struck match, flaring out in all directions in an explosion of bright white. She gasped, the sudden burst of power filling her energy vacuum — a flashflood charging down a dry riverbed.

Peripherally, she sensed the reactions of everyone in the med bay as her energy hit them without warning, wild and unfettered. But she couldn't stop it, couldn't contain it. It overwhelmed her, submerging her, drowning her in its depths. She couldn't breathe, couldn't think, couldn't—

A blissful coolness slid over her, gentle as an autumn breeze but solid as an oak. The cool touch tamed the raging chaos, steadily drawing it back, wrapping it in loving tendrils and lifting her out of the whirlpool.

Her chest expanded, sweet air filling her lungs. The sensation of intense power remained, stronger than anything she'd ever experienced before, but the support of Lelindia's field restored her equilibrium, putting her back in control.

And firmly on her own feet.

"Whoa," Micah murmured. "That was a rush."

She glanced over her shoulder.

Her brother looked like he'd just stepped off the biggest, baddest roller coaster ever built. His hands were still gripping her waist, but he was almost an arm's length away, as though he'd been blown back. Or maybe she'd stepped forward. Hard to say.

"You okay?" she asked him.

"Yeah. Just... wow."

"I know." She turned to Lelindia. "Not what I'd expected."

"Me, either." Lelindia shook her head, a puzzled frown shadowing her face. "I'm not sure what happened. I felt this intense jolt, but–" She blinked, her hand and gaze dropping to her belly. "I think it was her."

"Her? What do you mean?"

Her frown deepened. "It shouldn't be possible..." She looked up, her face a picture of stunned wonder. "But she's grown. In the last few seconds, she's noticeably grown. I can see the physical changes in her development." She placed Aurora's hand over the swell of her belly. "I think she's the one who supercharged you."

One Hundred Twenty

Jonarel's stomach clenched. Their daughter... "Is she unwell?"

Lelindia turned, her hand and Aurora's still on the curve of her belly. A curve that was more pronounced than it had been moments ago. "No. If anything, I'd say she's more robust."

His hand covered theirs, needing to reassure himself. "Are you certain?"

The bemused look he had come to know so well flitted across her face. "Mom, care to weigh in on this?"

Marina looked Lelindia over with a critical eye. "I agree with her. She's fine. In fact, she looks like she's planning to make her appearance sooner than we expected."

His airways tightened. "How soon?"

Marina shrugged. "Tough to know for sure, but I'd say two months, more or less."

Two months. Their daughter could be with them in two months. Joy and terror warred in his chest. Where would they be when that happened? With his family on Drakar? With the Suulh on Azaana? Hiding out in Fleet space? Or tracking down the Sovereign in Teeli space?

He had not realized he had instinctively drawn Lelindia to him until she snuggled into the crook of his arm with a sigh. "One thing's for certain," she said. "She's going to keep us on our toes."

"That's a given," Aurora agreed. "And now that I'm back on mine, I want a status report on the *Starhawke*. How is she? Any problems?"

Aurora's and Lelindia's parents shared long looks.

Aurora's spine stiffened. "What happened?"

"We hit a few speedbumps," Aurora's dad replied, "but with Unity's help, we handled it."

Aurora's eyes narrowed. "And the ship?"

"The shields will need recharging," Gryphon answered. "And probably repairs. We didn't have time to run any diagnostics yet."

Aurora's gaze moved in a slow sweep around the group, finally zeroing in on Lelindia. "What exactly were you hit with?"

Jonarel's fingers curled around Lelindia, locking her against him. He did not want to hear his mate describe the dangers she had faced without him there to protect her. But as the *Starhawke's* engineer, he needed to know every detail.

"Eight yachts, six frigates, and one shot from the station," Lelindia said like she was reciting a ship manifest.

The air evacuated Jonarel's lungs, the deck beneath his boots tilting.

"*What!?*" Aurora voiced what he could not. "What happened to engaging the hull camouflage?"

"The Fleet ships were ready for it," her dad answered with a calm that raised the hair on the back of Jonarel's neck. "We tried several times, but the Fleet ships' flight and firing patterns were coordinated, planned. They made it impossible for us to stay hidden long enough to break through. We had multiple near collisions that would have destroyed one or more of the yachts and crippled the *Starhawke.* I had to switch off the camouflage."

"So how did you escape?"

"Unity," Micah answered. "They brought in *Gladiator* as a moving shield, and also took control of several of the Fleet ships to redirect them out of the way."

Aurora's mouth hinged open. "But—"

"They've already been extracted," Micah assured her. "As far as the Fleet's concerned, the ships suffered a series of uncommon but completely explainable malfunctions."

"Huh." Aurora's gaze met Jonarel's. "What about your dad? I'm guessing he freaked out when the *Starhawke* came under fire."

"I do not know." Not for certain. But his imagination filled in the blanks quite easily. In the heat of the moment, the potential of a war with the Fleet would not have concerned his father as much as the imminent threat to Tehar, Lelindia, and Raehn.

"I can answer that." Libra raised her hand. "Since it was my job to keep in contact with Signal to make sure he stayed put."

"And did he?"

"Yes, under extremely vocal protest. I also suspect Rowk engaged in a bit of mechanical intervention that kept the ship's engines from coming online."

One Hundred Twenty-One

"Ready to discuss Isabeau's condition?" Aurora asked Knox as he rejoined their group.

After overseeing Magee's extraction, Micah had an investment in Knox's answer.

Knox gave a fractional nod. "One of the Yruf doctors looked her over. Physically, she seems fine. But mentally and emotionally, I don't know if she—" He halted, his composure cracking. He took a moment before continuing. "Since her vitriol is focused on you and my dad, I wanted you with me when we wake her. And Lelindia. Seeing you should get a reaction from her, and Lelindia can assess her physical state. Those two pieces of information should give us some idea what we're up against."

Knox's professional detachment wasn't holding up under the strain. Magee's condition had etched deep canyons of pain across his face. "Would you be willing to give me your professional evaluation of her condition?" he asked Micah's dad.

"Of course, although I think it would be better if she didn't see me, at least until after this first meeting." His dad glanced at Cade. "Can Ifel or Unity set up a way for me to observe their interactions?"

Cade turned to Unity. "Any problem with Brendan using the display in my cabin?"

"Nope," Unity replied, "although we have other cabins prepared as well. We assumed some of you would want to stay onboard until the Admiral is well enough to be transported to the *Starhawke*."

Knox's shoulders lost some of their tension. "I definitely would."

"So would I," Lelindia added, "and Jonarel's staying with me."

A hint of a smile touched Jonarel's face at Lee-Lee's definitive tone.

Micah looked at Aurora. "Sis? You staying?"

She bit her lip, clearly torn. Her gaze focused on one of the med bay's bulkheads like she had X-ray vision that could pierce through the solid material and show her the *Starhawke*.

"If you're worried about the *Starhawke*," Justin said, "we're happy to help." His gaze swung between Cade and Aurora. "That is if you're okay with us taking the shuttle over. Williams is the only one needed here. The rest of us," he gestured to Drew, Gonzo, and Reynolds, "can help Kire and Kelly with the diagnostics and repairs."

"Fine by me," Cade said.

"Me, too," Aurora agreed, although Micah caught her wistful sigh. "Thanks, Justin. What about everyone else?"

Marina and Gryphon exchanged a look. "We're not ready to leave the Admiral," Marina said.

"Or Lelindia," Gryphon added.

"Mom? Micah? I'm assuming you're staying with me and Dad?" She probably already knew the answer. Their emotions would be pretty damn easy for her to read right now.

Micah nodded anyway. "We're with you." He wasn't remotely ready to be separated from her so soon after her rescue. And based on how his mom had clung to him on the flight over, she was in the same boat. They'd both feel better knowing exactly where Aurora was.

"I'm staying, too."

He glanced at Celia in surprise. She'd moved right beside him, her shoulder almost brushing his arm. "I'd like to be in the room when you wake Magee," she added, her gaze on Knox. "She knows me, and I can help with her evaluation."

Celia's neutral delivery belied her underlying point. That point hit Micah like a spear to his solar plexus.

Celia had personal experience as a captive who'd been tortured. And like Magee, she'd been at the mercy of those manipulating her.

His hand was halfway to her shoulder before he caught himself and dropped it. She'd been reserved ever since he'd arrived. If he touched her now, even in a show of solidarity, she might nail him to the deck.

"That's a good idea," Knox agreed. "You might be exactly who she needs to help her through this," he said, echoing Micah's thoughts. "Micah, you should join us, too."

"Me?" He hadn't expected that. "But I'm not..." A Fleet officer. A trained psychologist. A trauma survivor. Take your pick. "How could I help?"

"You're Aurora's brother. We need to find out if Isabeau has a negative reaction to you, either as a threat or a target. If that's not the case, and you were never assigned a role in her alternate reality, I'm hoping you might serve as a bridge to draw her back into this world."

One Hundred Twenty-Two

Aurora focused on two things as she followed Unity down the undulating corridor to Magee's holding compartment. Putting one foot in front of the other and breathing in and out.

The energy supercharge hadn't just infused her cells with power. It had also woken up her mind like the galaxy's strongest espresso shot. While she'd been locked away at the detention center, her overactive sense of responsibility had been forced into hibernation. Not anymore. All the concerns that had been dormant now converged in a jabbering horde, each one demanding her attention.

The *Starhawke.* Her crew. Cade. Her parents. Micah. Cade's team. The Yruf. The Suulh. Feylahn. The Admiral. Knox. Magee. Raehn.

The list kept growing like a vine, spreading out new tendrils. And every single one was at risk of obliteration by the scorching firestorm racing toward them.

So she kept her feet moving on the black and gold patterned deck, concentrated on breathing in and out on a four count, and let her subconscious figure out the next move forward.

"This is it." Unity floated next to what looked like a solid bulkhead.

The scaled surface rippled, shifting apart like water diverging around a boulder, the bright light inside spilling out.

Aurora stepped inside, taking in the compact sanitation station to her right and the waist-high platform ahead of her where Isabeau Magee lay, her chest rising and falling rhythmically.

Lelindia approached the platform first, and Aurora followed, Unity beside her. Knox, Micah, and Celia hung back, staying as far away from Magee as the room permitted.

Lelindia's gaze traveled up and down Magee's body with the precision of a scanner. Anger painted broad strokes through her emotional field, the muscles around her mouth and eyes tightening millimeter by millimeter. "They hurt her." The accusation had fangs and claws. "And left her with the scars."

"I know." She'd heard the same testimony as the rest of them, had been expecting what Lelindia was seeing. But staring at the truth was different than hearing it secondhand. "How do you want to handle this?"

"I want—" Lelindia's emotions flared with a protectiveness that would have given Jonarel a run for his money. Her hands fisted at her sides. Were her mothering instincts kicking into high gear? Or had the battle at Sol Station and the Admiral's near death pushed her to her limits? She certainly seemed to be struggling to find her usual bedside manner.

"You want..." Aurora prodded when Lelindia continued to glower at Magee. Or rather what had been done to Magee.

Lelindia put a visible effort into reigning in her temper, taking a deep breath and letting it out slowly. Her emotions stabilized. Somewhat. "I want to heal her before I wake her. She'll have to deal with her mental and emotional scars, but I don't want her to keep carrying the physical ones."

Knox cleared his throat. Aurora caught him swiping a drop of moisture from his eye. She studiously ignored reading his emotions, respecting his privacy. His relationship with Isabeau was his business.

"Micah, can you please join us?" Lelindia asked.

He moved beside Aurora, resting his hand on top of hers at Magee's hip and placing his other hand on Magee's knee. Aurora placed her hand on Magee's shoulder as Lelindia moved to Magee's other side. But when Aurora engaged her energy field, it flashed like lightning, making both Lelindia and Micah jump, before it settled into the pearlescent glow she was used to.

Yeah, clearly Magee wasn't the only one with some personal trauma to work through.

Lelindia eyed her. "We good?"

She didn't detect any concern or hesitation from her energy sister, which made her feel a little better. She nodded. "Ready."

Lelindia's field engaged, flowing steadily to surround Magee, Aurora, and Micah. Aurora sent her field gliding through Lelindia's, the two intertwining in perfect harmony and visual beauty. The familiar sensation, the connection with her energy sister and brother, settled her rampant thought train, grounding her in the here and now.

They were alive. They were safe.

Time to get to work.

One Hundred Twenty-Three

Lelindia fought tears of anguish and rage as she catalogued the evidence of past trauma on Magee's body. More crimes the Sovereign needed to be held accountable for.

But the healing session acted as a balm, Aurora's stalwart presence warming her like sunshine after weeks of unending rain. And the boost – both from whatever had happened during the recharging session and Micah's influence – made relatively quick work of erasing the physical evidence of Magee's torment.

Restoring her mind would be a much more challenging mountain to climb.

When she was satisfied that she'd cleared away all traces of the Sovereign's malevolence, she turned to Knox. "Are you ready for me to wake her?"

Knox stepped closer. "How will that work?"

"Like flipping a switch. I'll neutralize the compound the Yruf use to keep her under. She should wake up immediately."

"With no idea where she is," Celia added, moving beside Lelindia.

"And surrounded by people she may hate." Knox ran his fingers over his beard as he scrutinized Magee. He turned to Aurora. "Any recommendations?"

"Besides keeping you, Micah, and Lelindia behind my shield at all times?"

Knox gave her a rueful smile. "You didn't include Celia."

Aurora lifted one brow. "Celia took down Signal in their sparring match. I have no doubt she can handle Isabeau."

Celia's lips quirked at that.

Knox nodded, meeting Lelindia's gaze. "Then I guess we wake her."

Aurora made a shooing motion to Knox and Micah to get behind her while Celia stayed beside Lelindia.

Lelindia rested her hands on either side of Magee's head. "Here we go."

It really was like flipping a switch. By the time she'd pulled her hands back and stepped behind Aurora's shield, Magee's eyelids fluttered.

But when they opened, Magee didn't turn her head or look around. She just stared at the ceiling, not moving, as the minutes ticked by.

No one else moved either, until Knox finally spoke. "Isabeau?"

Magee's face scrunched up, but she still didn't move.

What's she feeling? Lelindia projected to Aurora.

Not much Aurora projected back. *Mild confusion.* She nudged Knox with her elbow, nodding to Magee.

He took a step closer as Aurora adjusted her shield. "Isabeau? It's Knox."

Magee's face scrunched tighter, then she blinked and turned her head. Her eyes still looked distant and unfocused. "Knox?" It sounded like a name she'd heard before but couldn't quite place.

"Yes, Knox." He swallowed. "Do you remember me?"

The vagueness in her eyes began to dissipate. "Of course I remember Knox. He's..." She paused, her lips pursing. "He's..." she tried again. Halted. "He's... important to me," she finally finished.

Knox's chest rose and fell in fits and starts. "Do you know why I'm important to you?"

Magee sat up slowly, almost like a sleepwalker. She stared at Knox without seeing him. She seemed completely oblivious to everyone else's presence, even though Aurora was only a hand's breadth from Knox. "He's my... We... No." She shook her head. "Knox wouldn't do that. He wouldn't. Never."

Knox took a step forward, Aurora's shield moving with him. "I wouldn't do what?"

Magee bent her knees and wrapped her arms around them, hugging herself as she began to rock. "Knox wouldn't lie to me."

The strangled sound Knox made tightened Lelindia's chest.

"No, I wouldn't. I would never lie to you, Isabeau."

"Never lie," Magee repeated. "Never lie, never lie, never lie." Her rocking got more violent, almost tipping her off the platform.

Knox bumped into Aurora's shield when he tried to move within reach of Magee. He shot Aurora a dark look. "Let me through."

For a second, Lelindia thought Aurora would refuse. Her gaze darted to Celia, standing at the ready behind Magee. But at Celia's nod, Aurora passed the shield around Knox, reforming it behind him.

Knox's eyes narrowed at the exchange, but his attention returned to Magee. "Isabeau? I'm here." He stepped next to the platform, positioning himself so if Magee did tip over, she'd fall against him. "I'm right here."

The rocking slowed. "Knox isn't here. No one's here. It's just me. I'm all alone."

"You're not alone." Knox's voice thickened. "Not anymore. We rescued you. I'm here."

"Here?"

The desperate, disbelieving hope in that whispered word cratered Knox. He looked like Magee held his still beating heart in her hands. He reached for her, but Celia caught his arm before he touched her. Celia shook her head, miming that Magee needed to be the one to make first contact.

His forearm flexed in Celia's grip, but he nodded in understanding. When Celia released him, he leaned over so he was eye level with Magee, his hands braced on the edge of the platform. "Isabeau. Look at me."

The rocking stopped.

"Please. Look at me. I'm right here beside you. You're safe now."

"Safe?" High-pitched, breathy. A child's voice. "Safe?" Deep, bitter. A prisoner's voice.

But when Magee lifted her head, her gaze locked onto Knox like she was seeing him for the first time. Her spine straightened in shock. "Knox?"

"Yes." His knuckles turned white as he gripped the table, fighting to obey Celia's order. "It's me."

"Knox." His name was a sigh, a whimper, a groan. Magee lifted a trembling hand toward his face. He leaned closer, but she was the one who made the connection. When her fingers touched his cheek, stroked along his beard, a sob racked her, her entire body shaking. She threw her arms around his neck, pressing her cheek to his.

And let loose with a vicious banshee cry when she caught sight of Aurora.

One Hundred Twenty-Four

Magee's terror scraped icy fingers across Aurora's back while her hatred slashed with razor-sharp blades at her face.

She braced against the onslaught, not trying to fight it or subdue it. The Sovereign and Kreestol had done this.

Magee hissed, jerking back so hard she dragged Knox half on top of her on the platform. "You!"

The torpedo of rage hit Aurora squarely, knocking the air from her lungs. But the panicked fear underneath it was far more painful. She remained perfectly still. The breadth of the chasm between what she'd sensed as Magee touched Knox, and what was slamming into her now made her entire body ache. "Lt. Magee."

Magee bared her teeth in defiance, but she curled into Knox, hiding as much of herself as possible from Aurora's gaze.

Knox's emotional field raged, chaotic, a plethora of emotions colliding and exploding like meteors hitting atmosphere. His gaze darted between Aurora and Celia, silently asking them what to do next. But his body remained frozen, a physical shield for Magee to cower behind.

Unfortunately, Aurora didn't have a good answer for him.

Celia's gaze shifted to Micah. She gave a small nod.

Micah seemed to know exactly what that meant. He moved to stand shoulder to shoulder with Aurora. "Hi, Isabeau."

Whatever Aurora had expected him to say or do, his *I know we just met but we're going to be great friends* tone caught her completely by surprise.

It tripped up Magee, too. Confusion flitted through her emotional field, her death grip on Knox's neck loosening a fraction.

"I'm Micah. It's nice to finally meet you."

Magee's tongue flicked out, moistening her bottom lip, which was quivering from adrenaline and fear

"How are you feeling?"

Aurora almost turned and stared at her brother. His tone and emotional field were relaxed and upbeat, as if he was chatting with a good friend who'd been laid up after a surfing accident, not a traumatized Fleet officer he'd never met before.

Magee's brow furrowed, her body shifting on the platform as she surreptitiously tested her muscles. "I feel... good." Surprise wound through her field, though whether from the realization of her improved physical condition or the fact she was answering questions posed by a total stranger, Aurora couldn't tell.

"That's great!" Micah pumped enthusiasm into the room like liquid sunshine. "Are you hungry? Thirsty? Can I get you anything?"

More confusion. "I..." Her gaze darted to Aurora, then back to Micah. "I'm... thirsty."

He grinned. "No problem. I'm going to walk right over there," he pointed at the sanitation station, "and get you a drink. Wait here."

Magee pressed closer to Knox, who was still in an awkward hunch over the platform. Her focus locked on Aurora as Micah stepped away.

Aurora didn't so much as twitch. Whatever Micah was doing, it was working. Magee's fear and rage were still pulsing dully, but Micah had successfully created a projection of happiness and calm. It acted as a buffer between Magee and Aurora that was making it difficult for Magee to focus on her programmed emotional reactions.

"Here you go." Micah stepped right through Aurora's shield — the only person who could pull off that trick — and held out a metal cup to Magee.

She eyed the cup with suspicion.

"It's water." Micah lowered it so she could see the clear liquid inside.

"I'll take some," Knox said, reaching for the cup. His voice didn't quite pull off Micah's level of cheer, but it successfully masked the emotions still ricocheting through his field.

He took a large swallow, then offered the cup to Magee. "It's good, Isabeau," he said softly.

She looked between Micah and Knox, then her gaze settled on Aurora. She accepted the cup and took a defiant drink, practically daring Aurora to stop her.

It almost made Aurora smile. Almost. It was the first glimmer of the real Magee she'd seen coming through.

Magee drained the cup, then held it out to Micah.

"More?"

"Yes. Thank you."

"You've got it. Be right back."

Micah walked through Aurora's shield again like it wasn't even there, so she released it. At this point, the only one behind it besides Aurora was Lelindia, and Aurora stood between her and Magee.

Knox moved into a more comfortable position, resting one hip on the edge of the platform with his body angled toward Magee, who continued to glare at Aurora over his shoulder. But her heart wasn't in it, not like it had been. Knox's nearness and Micah's cheerful optimism were acting as a powerful antidote to the Sovereign's toxic influence.

Magee's gaze drifted to Aurora's left, her brows rising sharply. "Dr. Forrest?"

"Hello, Lt. Magee." Lelindia inclined her head, her hands clasped loosely in front of her.

Magee's head dipped. She was looking at Lelindia like she'd sprouted antennae. "What are you doing here?"

Lelindia's closed-mouth smile was the picture of serenity. "Just making sure you're well."

"Oh." Magee considered that for a moment. "Am I? Well?"

Lelindia's smile stayed in place, although the muscles around her mouth tightened. "You're in excellent health."

Celia slipped silently from behind Magee, moving to stand next to Lelindia.

Magee's brows climbed higher. "Lt. Cardiff? You're here, too?" Magee shook her head like she was flinging off water, then turned to Knox. "Are we on the *Argo?*"

"No."

Micah jumped in before Magee could ask a follow-up. "Here you go." He gave her a jaunty grin and held out the full cup.

She accepted it, taking a drink as her focus returned to Aurora. The suspicion and anger swirled up like an undertow in her field, but without the solid anchor she'd had before. She gripped the cup like a miniature shield. "Are we on the *Starhawke?*" Her voice wavered but she held Aurora's gaze.

"No," Aurora answered softly, doing her best to project an air of kindness and compassion. "We're not."

Magee's gaze swept the room before shooting back to Aurora. "Then where are we?"

Magee kept saying *we*, not *I*. That was a good sign. Her subconscious was starting to accept she was part of their group. Unfortunately, answering her question could sabotage every bit of trust they'd built.

One Hundred Twenty-Five

"We're on a ship." Micah poured as much eagerness into his voice and emotional projection as possible. Magee was responding to his efforts far better than he'd hoped, probably because she'd been programmed by the Teeli and the Sovereign to be highly suggestable.

Magee dragged her attention away from Aurora. "Which ship?"

"It's called *Unity*." Hopefully Unity and the Yruf would forgive the presumption. He honestly didn't know if the ship had any other name or designation.

"*Unity*? I've never heard of it." Magee's gaze flicked over the interlocking scales of the bulkheads. "This isn't a Fleet design. Is it Kraed?"

"No, it's an... independent," he said with absolute sincerity, walking the tightrope that would keep him from lying to her.

She peered at him. "Is it yours?"

He laughed, and her lips curved in an unconscious response. "Nope. I'm a marine biology professor. This space trekking thing is new to me."

"Then who owns it?"

"The captain's name is Ifel."

Magee accepted that with a slow nod, her gaze drifting back to Aurora like a moon in orbit around a planet. "Why are you here?"

You. Aurora was the one person Magee hadn't called by name. It was a distancing tactic, a way to keep her separate, to label her as *other.* And she'd asked it like an accusation.

Aurora had noticed it, too. He could see it by the rigid set of her shoulders and the look in her eyes as she considered how to answer Magee's question.

"I asked for Aurora's help," Knox said. "Aurora's, Lelindia's, and Celia's." Apparently Knox had caught the distinction, too.

Magee blinked. "But she's—" She gestured angrily with the cup, water sloshing onto the deck. "She—" She leaned into Knox, bringing her mouth next to his ear. "She hurt me," she hissed in a stage whisper.

Knox glanced at Aurora, then Celia. They both shook their heads.

Micah agreed. Magee wasn't ready to hear the truth. She needed to come to it on her own.

Pulling back, he rested his hands on Magee's shoulders. "Isabeau, do you trust me?"

Magee's jaw worked, her gaze darting to Aurora. "I..." She swallowed, confusion and uncertainty creating lines on her face.

Knox looked like Magee was twisting a knife in his belly. His voice grew strained. "Isabeau, do you believe I would never do anything to hurt you?"

That got a small nod. "Yes."

"Do you believe that I would never lie to you?"

Another nod.

Knox's breath eased out on a sigh. "Then I need you to believe me now. This is a safe space. No one here will hurt you. I promise."

Magee chewed on her lip, her hands clamped around the cup she still held.

"He's right," Micah said softly.

Her gaze skipped to him.

"I'm a marine biologist, remember? Space isn't my thing. I wouldn't be here if I didn't believe this was a safe space. I guarantee that no one will hurt us here." He'd never projected so much positive energy in his life, doing everything he could to help Magee get past this first hurdle.

Magee dipped her head, bringing her mouth to Knox's ear.

This time, Micah couldn't hear what she whispered, but he heard the choked sound Knox made in response, somewhere between a groan and a sob.

Knox shifted on the platform, taking Magee into his arms and tucking her head under his chin. His hands shook and his eyes squeezed shut as he held her close, tenderly stroking her hair. When he finally spoke, Micah could barely make out the husky words.

"I promise, Isabeau. I will never leave you."

One Hundred Twenty-Six

Watching Aurora on the display in his cabin should have been easy for Cade. After all, she was no longer stuck in a detention cell on Earth. They were on the same ship, only decks apart.

But her nearness also amplified her emotions, amplified the pain, anger, and helplessness she experienced when Magee reacted to her.

"Don't." Brendan's hand clamped onto Cade's wrist.

He glanced down in surprise. He hadn't even realized he'd turned toward the door.

"She can handle it." Brendan's compassion washed over him, but his grip stayed locked. "I know it's hard, but you can't go down there right now."

He knew the truth of Brendan's words, could already feel Aurora's emotions smoothing out as she reined in her response.

He looked at Libra, who huffed and folded her arms, glaring first at Brendan and then at the image on the display.

"I know." Cade blew out a breath.

Brendan released his wrist.

"It's just that she's already gone through so much..."

"Yes. She's a leader. Like you. Comes with the territory."

He shot Brendan a wry smile. "You sound like Aurora."

Brendan smiled in return. "Gee, I wonder why?"

They watched the interplay between Aurora and Magee in silence after that, Brendan making notes on his tablet, Libra scowling and shifting restlessly, and Cade not hearing a single word. All his focus was on Aurora – the emotions she was wrestling with, the way she stood like a soldier on the front line braced for enemy fire, the inherent nobility of her expression.

She was still dressed in the exercise uniform she'd worn at the detention center, although she'd taken a moment to smooth out and rebraid her hair. Lelindia stood near enough that their arms almost touched. Clearly he wasn't the only one who wanted Aurora close.

Carrying her to the med bay had been pure bliss, only their clothing separating them. He craved more tactile connection, skin to skin, but that would have to wait. He wasn't even sure when they'd be returning to the *Starhawke*. The Admiral hadn't woken yet. Unity had promised to alert them when he did.

And then they'd have to face the consequences of their decisions. They were fugitives, every one of them. That didn't matter much to him since his job – protecting the Admiral and the Union – hadn't changed. Same for his team. It was like going deep undercover.

His gaze strayed to Brendan and Libra. They were different. So was Micah. For them, life had been upended and spun in a centrifuge. Brendan seemed to be taking it in stride, but Cade worried about Micah. Extended space travel would be tough on him. And

Libra wasn't a pilot like Brendan or a healer like Marina. He suspected her lack of a clear role was at least partly responsible for her bad mood. Well, that and the Sovereign's attempt to capture and cage her entire family. She had some strong opinions about that as well.

"I'm glad Knox is staying with her," Brendan said, startling Cade out of his thoughts.

He glanced at the display. Everyone except Knox and Magee had left the room. Magee was in Knox's lap, her fingers stroking his beard. Then the image cut out.

"We'll alert you if anything changes," U-2 said, hovering closer. "Ifel has requested that you all join her in the reception hall."

"Reception hall?" Brendan asked.

"Cade refers to it as Ifel's throne room, but the more accurate translation of its function is reception hall."

Brendan's brows rose. "Can't wait to see it."

The glade outside Cade's cabin was conspicuously empty of Yruf, as it had been when he, Brendan, and Libra had come up on the lift. So were the corridors they traversed. He suspected it was the Yruf's way of giving Brendan and Libra time to adjust and deal with their current circumstances rather than a lack of trust. Seeing the Yruf en masse could be overwhelming.

By the time Unity led them to the expansive space of the reception hall, Aurora, Lelindia, Celia, and Micah were already there with Ifel. Jonarel had joined the group as well.

Aurora didn't stand on ceremony. As soon as Cade drew within reach she wrapped her arm around his waist and pulled him against her side so they were hip to hip.

Worked for him. He slid his arm around her shoulders and rested his cheek against the silky smoothness of her hair. It smelled of the generic shampoo bar she'd been given at the detention center, rather than the scent she preferred, but he didn't care. "I've missed you," he murmured.

"Ditto." She tipped her head back, rose onto her tiptoes, and brushed her lips over his. "More than you know."

"Oh, I know."

Heat flared in her eyes, and something far more potent. "I guess you do."

"Aurora?"

They both turned.

Micah was watching them with amusement and a hint of longing. "Ifel wants to discuss what we're going to do now that we've thoroughly burned all our bridges."

Aurora lifted one brow. "She used that phrase?"

"No." Micah grinned at her. "I extrapolated."

Aurora's smile didn't quite reach her eyes. "I see. Well, I had some time at the detention center to think about this." She turned to her dad. "What are the ramifications to your financial situation from all this?"

"Do you mean am I now a pauper because we broke you out of jail?"

Aurora's lips tightened. "Yes."

"No, I'm not."

Aurora exhaled, her shoulders relaxing beneath Cade's fingers.

"While I can't access any Far Horizons resources without risking detection, I have a separate personal fund that I inherited when my parents died. After I met your mother and realized the Teeli could potentially throw our lives into chaos at any moment, I thought it wise to stash that money in accounts that weren't traceable to me or your mother, in case we needed to go into hiding."

Celia snorted. "I'm impressed, Brendan. You were actually prepared for this."

Brendan shrugged. "As mate to the Sahzade, it was the one thing I could do to protect her." His gaze swept over Micah and Aurora. "And our family."

"How much are we talking about?" Aurora asked.

Brendan's lip curved up. "Enough that you can take money off your list of things you're worrying about."

Aurora acknowledged the point with a nod, then turned to Micah. "What about you? I know you originally wanted to help fight the Sovereign, but now I've hijacked your entire life."

"Not entirely. Birdie and Kai are with us, now."

"Right." Aurora rubbed her temple. "How are they handling this?"

"They're fine." Micah shrugged. "Happy to be on the *Starhawke*. Birdie's eager to see you again."

"So that's two more," Aurora murmured. "Which brings our total to twenty-two. My crew, your team," she glanced up at Cade, "my family, Lelindia's parents, the Admiral, Knox, Isabeau, Birdie, and Kai."

"Twenty-three," Lelindia amended. "You forgot the Little Nedale."

A complicated knot of emotions collected in Aurora's emotional field as her gaze dropped to where Lelindia's hands lay against her rounded stomach. "Twenty-three," Aurora agreed on an exhale.

He settled her more securely in his arms, offering his strength and support.

To his surprise, she leaned into him. "Feeding everyone is easy. With all the Suulh onboard, we'll be lucky to keep up with the growth rate of the plants in the greenhouse. But we won't be able to go to Drakar for repairs. Is that going to be a problem?" she asked Jonarel.

"Unclear. We can replicate much of what we need onboard. Installation will be the challenge." He turned to Cade. "How is Bella at spacewalking?"

"She'd rather be inside the ship next to the engines, but if there's a problem that needs solving, she'll be right there with you."

"I can help, too," Aurora offered. "Just tell me what you need. Spacewalking never bothered me."

"That's because, unlike the rest of us, you have a built-in spacesuit," Cade teased.

She shot him a look over her shoulder. "And so would anyone out there with me."

"Then sign me up."

Micah cleared his throat. "Ifel says Unity can help, too. The Yruf are used to repairing their ships in transit."

Aurora nodded. "That's good to know." Her gaze moved to Ifel. "Are you planning to stay with us?"

"Of course we are!" U-2 chirped from above them, sounding more than a little indignant. Then in a more solemn tone, translating for Ifel, "Your goals are our goals. Your lives are intertwined with ours. Together, we will end the Sovereign's reign and free your people and ours."

"Which brings us to the bigger issue. Every Fleet ship will be gunning for us. And every civilian vessel will report us. How long can we keep the hull camouflage engaged before we start draining power from engines and life support?"

Jonarel shifted his weight. "Ordinarily it would not be a concern for several weeks. But the diagnostic reports I have received from Tehar and Bella indicate the *Starhawke's* shields took significant damage escaping Sol Station. We cannot maintain the camouflage while simultaneously restoring the shields. We also will need to recharge near a star."

"Could we go to Azaana?" Lelindia suggested. "Their star is almost identical to Sol and we wouldn't need the hull camouflage there."

Aurora was already shaking her head. "The Fleet will be looking for us to head for Kraed space. Even if that weren't an issue, the Sovereign will make a move, probably a big one, in response to our escape. We need to be in Fleet space, not five days plus away. We also need to hook into the ICS. We can't do that in Kraed space. I'm counting on Kire and the Admiral being able to get us in without triggering any alerts."

"The Yruf ship could act as our camouflage," Micah said. "Their ship could hide us just like the *Starhawke* hid *Gladiator*. Better, in fact, because they can separate."

"That's true." Aurora smiled at her brother. "That would help during repairs, but it won't solve the recharging problem. If they're surrounding us to camouflage us, they'll also be blocking the solar energy we need."

"So we're looking for a system in Fleet space where we can hook into the ICS undetected," Cade said, "and also not be seen by passing Fleet or civilian ships while our shields recharge?"

"Correct."

A plan steadily took shape. "What we need is advice from someone who's used to hiding from the Fleet and the Feds, who's used to sneaking around Fleet space, going undetected. Someone who's worked as a smuggler."

Aurora met his gaze, a gleam in her eyes. "We just happen to know a smuggler."

"Yes, we do. And she owes you a favor."

"I guess she does." Aurora turned to Jonarel. "How quickly can you activate those tracers on Nat's comband and shuttle?"

One Hundred Twenty-Seven

Natasha Orlov stared at the news feed playing on the display on *Phoenix*'s compact bridge, shock fusing her body with the pilot's chair. The newscaster's voice overlaid two images she recognized instantly, but her brain refused to fit the pieces together.

"...broke out of the detention center in the late evening and escaped in two shuttles that FS believe belong to the *Starhawke*."

Admiral Schreiber and Aurora Hawke had been arrested? For *treason*? It had happened weeks ago, but she hadn't known, not until Marlin dragged her up here, demanding she watch the news vid he'd found.

If it hadn't been for him, she'd still be in the dark. She never watched news vids. They always featured people she didn't know.

Except this time, she did.

"Five people were killed during the escape, including four FS officers and the facility's Executive Officer."

Killed? She didn't believe it. Not for a second. Aurora and the Admiral wouldn't kill anyone, even to escape prison. They'd held onto their honor code while being tormented by Tnaryt's sadistic rule. No way would they kill fellow Fleet officers.

"Admiral William Schreiber and Captain Aurora Hawke are considered extremely dangerous."

Their photos reappeared on the screen, Aurora's hair in the neat braid she preferred, the Admiral's bald head gleaming dully. The unflattering lighting in the images – most likely their prison intake photos – gave them both an air of menace that fit the newscaster's narrative but clashed with Nat's memories of them.

Dangerous? Sure, but only if you were trying to hurt people they cared about. And news flash – they cared about everyone, even strangers who kidnapped them. Like her.

"Captain Hawke's ship, the *Starhawke,* was being held at ESS-1, commonly known as Sol Station. The crew destroyed the docking clamps keeping the ship moored then fired on the Fleet ships blockading the station to make their escape."

An image of the *Starhawke* appeared on the screen, though the term "image" was generous. The ship's hull composition made its lines indistinct and wavy in the image, just faint brush strokes over a starfield. The only reason she recognized it was because she'd seen the ship up close and personal.

"The whereabouts of the *Starhawke,* Admiral Schreiber, Captain Hawke, and her crew are currently unknown. If you see them, do not approach the ship or the fugitives. Move to a safe distance and contact the FS emergency line immediately." The instructions appeared in bold letters at the bottom of the display.

The screen blanked out.

Nat let her head fall against the headrest, her mind spinning like a tornado. The Admiral was head of the Galactic Fleet, and Aurora was the youngest officer promoted to Commander. She'd looked it up while she'd been onboard Aurora's ship, needing to know as much as she could about the people who'd rescued her. And they'd been exactly what her instincts had told her they were — dedicated, honest, and honorable career Fleet officers.

Who were now wanted for treason.

"What do you think?" Marlin asked from the co-pilot's seat, his fingers laced over the slight paunch of his stomach.

Marlin had been with her on Tnaryt's ship, had suffered the same horrors at Tnaryt's hands and been rescued by Aurora's crew when they saved Nat. In fact, if it hadn't been for Aurora's crew, Marlin would have died in the galley of Tnaryt's ship, burned to a crisp when the ship broke apart falling out of orbit.

She shuddered at the memory. She hadn't allowed herself to think about it for months, and with good reason. Any thoughts that brought her mind around to the Sovereign—

"Nat?"

She beat back the creeping gloom. "I think it's crazy. The Admiral and Aurora aren't traitors to the Fleet."

Marlin's round face brightened. "Good. We agree. So what are we going to do about it?"

"Do?"

Marlin scratched the hairline of his receding curly grey-brown hair. "Well, they saved our lives. We'd be dead if it weren't for them. Now they're in trouble, and you and I have two ships and a tough-as-nails mercenary crew on our side. Shouldn't we help them?"

What a change. The scared-of-his-own-shadow cook she'd partnered with to salvage the *Phoenix* had turned into a veteran, battle-tested fighter who spent most of his time hanging out with Kenji, a burly mercenary twice his size. The man Marlin had been would have cowered at the thought of getting involved with people accused of treason. This version of Marlin wanted to wade into the thick of it.

"How can we help them? We can't even find—"

The *Phoenix's* proximity alarm blared. Nat snapped her chair upright as red warning lights bathed the bridge.

A ship materialized outside the viewport, blocking the starfield. A ship that hadn't been visible a second earlier.

Nat's hands reached for the nav console on pure instinct. Heavy footsteps thundered up the stairs to her right.

"Natasha!" Isin burst onto the bridge, skidding to a halt beside her chair. "Alec, weapons!" he ordered.

"Belay that order, Alec," she barked as Alec's projection appeared on her other side. "I know them."

Had, in fact, just seen an image of this very ship on her screen.

"It's the *Starhawke*."

One Hundred Twenty-Eight

Aurora had debated how best to reveal their presence. The tracers had confirmed that both Nat and her shuttle were onboard the gold and red ship orbiting the small moon below them, but Aurora had been reluctant to drop the hull camouflage until she confirmed the ship was friendly.

And with good reason. The first time she'd met Nat, she'd been a prisoner on Tnaryt's ship. With the way Nat played fast and loose with rules and laws, it was always possible she was a prisoner on this one, too.

Her dad had given her the answer, showing Kire how to hack into Nat's comband using the tracer as the link so they could listen in to whatever was going on around Nat.

Turns out Nat had been talking with Marlin about her.

"Hail them," Aurora told Kire.

A moment later an image appeared on the *Starhawke's* bridgescreen, giving her a glimpse of the bridge of the other ship.

A man who visually screamed intimidation sat in the center captain's chair, his muscles straining the fabric of his black shirt and his dark-eyed gaze promising dire consequences to anyone who opposed him. The jagged scar etching the right side of his face strengthened the impression. However, the emotions she sensed from him were protective, not aggressive. And he was leaning ever so slightly in Nat's direction.

Interesting.

By comparison, Nat and Marlin, seated in the two forward chairs, looked like a couple kids. They'd lost the haggard edges and hollowed cheekbones they'd had the last time she'd seen them. Big improvement. The change in Marlin's emotional field was even more remarkable – calm, upbeat, eager. If she wasn't looking right at him, she wouldn't have recognized his resonance.

"Sorry for the sudden appearance, Nat. I hope we didn't startle you too much." She knew exactly how much she'd startled them. The man in the captain's chair had been out for blood until Nat had said the name *Starhawke*. The fact that he'd recognized it proved he knew at least some of Nat's history.

"Excellent timing, as always." Nat propped her chin on her hand. "We were just talking about you." The gleam in her pale aqua eyes as her gaze flicked to the comband on her arm indicated she'd figured out Aurora had been listening in.

"So, you've heard the news."

Nat nodded.

"We're being hunted by the Fleet and, thanks to the newscasts, probably most Union citizens. We need help, but it's not compulsory. You don't have to get dragged into this. If you want us to go, we'll go."

Nat's mouth curved in a crooked smile. "As I recall, *I'm* the one who dragged *you* into this."

Aurora snorted. Nat's sense of humor had expanded since they'd last seen each other. "You're not afraid to converse with accused traitors to the Union who broke out of the Fleet brig?"

Nat considered the question for a moment, then turned to the man behind her. "Are we, Isin?" she asked in an overly solicitous voice.

He gave her a withering look. "No, Natasha, we are not."

"Didn't think so." She swiveled back, her gaze shifting to Aurora's left. "Hi, Cade."

Cade nodded. "Nat."

"Staying out of trouble?"

"Not for a moment."

Nat's smile widened. "Glad to hear it." She met Aurora's gaze, excitement building in her emotional field like a rising tide. "So, Aurora, tell me, what can my crew and I do for you?"

Nat's excitement was infectious. An answering smile tugged on Aurora's lips. This just might work.

"I need a favor."

Captain's Log

Art Imitating Life

This was the hardest book I've ever written by far. It took a year to work my way through the rough draft and reach the end. There were so many questions I didn't know the answers to, so many roadblocks I kept running up against, so many moments when I wanted to throw my head back and howl in frustration. I often felt like Aurora and I were living parallel lives, both stuck in a box we weren't sure how we'd get out of.

Which ironically helped enormously in the writing. I could channel all those uncertainties, irritations, and moments of hopelessness into Aurora, who was going through a similar emotional roller coaster. When neither of us could talk to anyone else, we could always talk to each other.

The Witness Stand

The core concept for this book has been in my notes for years. The vague line item read something like *Aurora tries to convince the Galactic Council the Teeli pose a threat. The Council claims she is the threat and tries to arrest her. She becomes a fugitive.*

At the time, I had no idea how I was going to get to that point. It just felt inevitable that the Sovereign's habit of framing others for her crimes would eventually ensnare Aurora. I also hadn't planned for the Admiral to be the one caught first. That popped up unexpectedly at the end of book five while Aurora was cooling her heels in Teeli space.

The first draft of this story followed the what ifs posed by the crew in the opening chapters. I'd assumed the evidence against the Admiral would come from his secret trip to Gallows Edge and resulting interactions with Tnaryt. I wrote more than ten scenes for witnesses who never took the stand in the book you just read. I also had Aurora's crew present in the courtroom for the Admiral's trial. In that version, Aurora wasn't going to be arrested until near the end of the story.

But as I dug deeper into the draft and got advice from friends who actually know something about legal proceedings — thank you Jake and Dale (there's a reason I don't write legal thrillers) — the evidence tracked differently than expected, taking me into a new direction. It also made Aurora's prequel story a critical piece of her history.

I integrated a few details from the excised scenes into the final narrative, but most of that original draft is sitting in my clip file. I'm hanging onto the scenes since a lot of interesting facts came out in the writing, as well as a few new characters who might turn up later as the series progresses. It's one of the great joys of writing about Aurora and her crew — I never know exactly where they'll lead me next!

Isabeau & Knox

Tormenting Magee wasn't in my master plan for this series. In fact, when she was introduced in book one, she was barely a blip on my radar. I knew she'd be present in Admiral Schreiber's life but her role was more like an NPC than a main character.

That all changed in HONOR. When Cade walked into the Admiral's office and discovered an oily stranger sitting at Magee's desk, it turned Magee into a pivotal piece on the board. Placing her in the sadistic hands of the Sovereign in LEGACY hurt my soul, but I consoled myself with the knowledge that one day, she'd be rescued. Reaching that point in this book lifted my spirits enormously.

Writing the scenes between her and Knox at the end made me cry. I'd always known Knox cared about her, but I'd assumed it was in a kid sister kind of way. Then I put them together, and Knox let me know just how wrong I'd been.

What awaits them in the future? Your guess is as good as mine. But I can't wait to find out!

Thank you for reading. Enjoy the journey!
Audrey

Audrey Sharpe grew up believing in the Force and dreaming of becoming captain of the Enterprise. She's still working out the logistics of moving objects with her mind, but writing science fiction provides a pretty good alternative. When she's not off exploring the galaxy with Aurora and her crew, she lives in the Sonoran Desert, where she has an excellent view of the stars.

For more information about Audrey and the Starhawke Universe, visit her website and join the crew!

AUDREYSHARPE.COM

www.ingramcontent.com/pod-product-compliance
Lightning Source LLC
Chambersburg PA
CBHW022358110726
47903CB00004B/1039